"Stop!"

Skye looked around and was surprised to see that she recognized the road they were on. Now was as good a time as any to start making some new memories.

"What?" Jake asked in alarm as he slammed on the brakes.

"We used to park here, remember?" She undid her seat belt and slid over to him. "We used to stop here on the way home."

She grinned nervously at him. Yes, she wanted to get home to Grace, but she'd been in a bed—by herself—for the past four months. It was time to fix that starting right *now*.

Jake was stiff in her arms. "We did," he said through gritted teeth.

"Are you going to kiss me, Jake Holt?" she whispered against his lips.

He turned his head. "The doctor said— He said we shouldn't stress you out too much. Physically."

Skye sighed in disappointment. "Not even if I want to be stressed? Just a little? Not even a kiss?"

Jake didn't reply for a moment. Then he sort of chuckled and said, "When we used to stop here, I don't remember it ever being *just* a kiss."

* * *

His Lost and Found Family
is part of the Texas Cattleman's Club: After the Storm series—As a Texas town rebuilds, love heals all wounds…

HIS LOST AND FOUND FAMILY

BY
SARAH M. ANDERSON

MILLS & BOON

Published in Great Britain 2015
by Mills & Boon, an imprint of Harlequin (UK) Limited,
Eton House, 18-24 Paradise Road, Richmond, Surrey, TW9 1SR

© 2015 Harlequin Books S.A.

Special thanks and acknowledgement are given to Sarah M. Anderson for her contribution to the TEXAS CATTLEMAN'S CLUB: AFTER THE STORM series.

ISBN: 978-0-263-25248-4

51-0215

Harlequin (UK) Limited's policy is to use papers that are natural, renewable and recyclable products and made from wood grown in sustainable forests. The logging and manufacturing processes conform to the legal environmental regulations of the country of origin.

Printed and bound in Spain
by CPI, Barcelona

Award-winning author **Sarah M. Anderson** may live east of the Mississippi River, but her heart lies out west on the Great Plains. With a lifelong love of horses and two history teachers for parents, she had plenty of encouragement to learn everything she could about the tribes of the Great Plains.

When she started writing, it wasn't long before her characters found themselves out in South Dakota among the Lakota Sioux. She loves to put people from two different worlds into new situations and to see how their backgrounds and cultures take them someplace they never thought they'd go.

Sarah's book *A Man of Privilege* won the 2012 RT Reviewers' Choice Award for Best Mills & Boon® Desire™. Her book *Straddling the Line* was named Best Mills & Boon® Desire™ of 2013 by CataRomance, and *Mystic Cowboy* was a 2014 Booksellers' Best Award finalist in the Single Title category.

When not helping out at her son's school or walking her rescue dogs, Sarah spends her days having conversations with imaginary cowboys and American Indians, all of which is surprisingly well-tolerated by her wonderful husband. Readers can find out more about Sarah's love of cowboys and Indians at sarahmanderson.com.

To my agent, Jill Marsal, who saved this book and quite possibly my career by keeping calm and carrying on, even when I couldn't. You've made me a better writer, and it's a joy to work with you!

One

Jake Holt could not believe his eyes. What on God's green earth had happened to Royal, Texas?

Yeah, he'd been gone for four years after cutting off all contact with his family and his hometown. He expected some things to have changed. But this? He drove down what had been the main commercial drag. Fast-food restaurants and big-box stores all looked like someone had run over them with a freight train. He passed the hospital, where it looked as if a whole wing was missing.

Jesus. It looked as if a bomb had gone off here. Or...

Or a tornado had blown the town to bits.

The thought made him nervous. Jake cast a withering glance at the papers in the benign-looking envelope on the passenger seat. Divorce papers. Skye had sent him divorce papers. He probably shouldn't be surprised—he hadn't spoken to her in almost ten months. He'd been out of the country, setting up an IT at a new oil site in Bahrain. He'd been busy and she'd made her feelings clear.

Part of him knew the marriage was over. They wanted different things. He wanted to be free of their families and their never-ending feud over land. He wanted to wash his hands of Royal, Texas, for good. He'd wanted to get his business, Texas Sky Technologies, off the ground, which required a lot of hard work. He'd wanted to be a success and give her everything she wanted.

Except he couldn't. Skye wanted the impossible. She hadn't been able to let go of the crazy notions she'd had about coming back home and resolving the family feud and somehow bringing the Taylors and Holts together. He didn't know why. Maybe so they could join hands and sing in perfect harmony and share a soda together.

No matter what her reasons, it wasn't going to happen. The Taylors and the Holts had been arguing, suing and occasionally shooting over the same piece of land for at least a hundred years and nothing Jake did or said was going to change that. Hell, he couldn't even get his own family to accept that he'd fallen in love with Skye Taylor. How was he supposed to convince her parents to accept him as a son-in-law?

Easier just to pick up and start over somewhere new.

Or it had been, until it all fell apart.

Still, Jake could not believe that she'd actually had him served with divorce papers. Skye had been his world for so long. They'd sacrificed everything to be together once.

The papers were dated eight months ago. Jake wasn't about to sign the damn things and mail them off. Not until he made good and sure that Skye was done with him.

Which was why he was back in his least favorite place in the entire world—Royal, Texas. If Skye could tell him to his face that it was over, then it was over. Twenty years of his life spent loving her—done.

God, he hated this town.

He'd come home after all these years on the assumption

that Skye was here. But now? Now he hoped she *wasn't* here. It looked as if the tornado that had blown through town had left a wake of complete and total destruction in its path.

Despite the long months apart, and the evil divorce papers, he prayed she wasn't here, that wherever she was, she was safe. That she hadn't been in the path of that twister.

He didn't even know when the twister had hit. He was jumping to conclusions, but the whole prodigal-son-returns-home thing had him on edge. He needed information before he did anything else. And the best place to get information in this town was the Royal Diner.

As he headed into the heart of the town, the damage got worse and worse. Trees were gone, nothing but twisted stumps left. The car lot where he'd bought his first truck was vacant, save a pile of rubble where the building used to stand. Plenty of places had tarps over their roofs and boarded-up windows. The walk-up ice-cream shop where he used to take Skye for a cone was off its foundation entirely, sitting four feet away on the sidewalk where he'd dared to hold Skye's hand in public.

He'd turned his back on this town four years ago. Said he didn't care if he never saw Royal—or the people in it—ever again. But now that he was here, it was almost too much.

Just when he thought he couldn't take it, he came upon a block that was mostly okay looking. Jake was thrilled to see the Royal Diner was still standing. People were sitting inside, drinking coffee.

He felt himself breathe. It wasn't all gone. The diner was still here.

He pulled up in front and sat, thinking. He didn't want to care about Royal, Texas, because he'd told himself for years that he *didn't* care.

But seeing the town so wounded, and not knowing

who'd lived and who'd died—it tore him up in a way he wasn't prepared for. He was worried about his family, for God's sake. He was worried about Skye. Just because it was over didn't mean he hoped something awful had happened to her.

Someone walked past his car and did a double take. Jake didn't recognize the man, but then, he didn't recognize the town anymore. Things had changed.

He needed to know how *much* they'd changed. Forewarned was forearmed and he needed to know what had happened before he sucked it up and went home.

So, gritting his teeth, Jake got out of the car and walked into the diner.

What had been a pleasant midday hum died the moment the door shut behind him. He recognized Amanda working behind the counter, although he was surprised to see she was pregnant.

"Jake? Jake *Holt*?" She froze in what seemed to be true shock—or horror. "Is it really you?"

"Hi," Jake said, putting on a smile as the silence closed around him. He could feel the shock rolling off of every single person in the restaurant. Even the cook leaned out of the kitchen to look at him.

He'd been in tight spots before, dealing with angry international businessmen who didn't speak much English and had their own ways of doing things. But this? This was the tightest spot he'd ever been in.

"What?" someone demanded from one of the booths in the back of the diner. "Did someone say Jake *Holt*?"

Then, to Jake's surprise, his brother, Keaton, stood up.

"Jake?" Keaton looked at him as if Jake were a zombie who'd stumbled into the diner fresh from the graveyard. "What the hell?"

Jake looked around the room, but he found no moral support. Everyone appeared to be thinking the same thing.

Even Amanda, who'd always been a sweetheart back in school.

This was not how he'd wanted it to go. He'd wanted to locate Skye and hash it out for once and for all in *private* with no one—or at least not their families—the wiser. He wanted things to go back to the way they used to be, back when it was him and Skye against the world. And if he had to confront his family, then he'd wanted it to happen in the privacy of the Holt home, without an audience.

Which is what he had right now—one hell of an audience. The diner was mostly full with the lunch crowd. Plenty of witnesses with waggling tongues who would probably be more than happy to spread the news of the less-than-happy family reunion from here to San Antonio.

Damn.

"Hello, Keaton." Jake tried to sound as if he were glad to see his brother, but he didn't pull it off.

The diner was so quiet he could have heard a pin drop. He wasn't sure anyone was even breathing.

Keaton's jaw was clenched—and so were his fists. Yeah, this wasn't a happy family reunion by any stretch of the imagination. "Where have you been?" To his credit, at least it didn't come out as a snarl.

"Bahrain," Jake replied, trying to keep his tone casual. After all, he was basically announcing this to the whole town. "I had a big job there. It just wrapped up."

A light murmur rippled through the onlookers. Jake couldn't tell if that was a good thing or a bad thing.

"I heard about the storm," he went on. Might as well put some lipstick on this pig. "I came home as soon as I could to see if I could help."

More murmuring. At least this time, it sounded like a positive reaction.

Keaton gave him a look of white-hot death, but then he seemed to realize that they had an audience. "Do you have time to have a cup of coffee?" He motioned back to the booth.

"Sure." Just a casual cup of joe with the man who'd forced Jake to choose between the Holt land and the woman he loved. No big deal.

He walked past his brother and slid into the opposite side of the booth. Keaton stood there, glaring down at him for a moment before he took his seat.

The diner was still unnaturally quiet—so quiet, Jake could hear Amanda's footsteps coming toward. "Coffee?"

He tried to be polite. "Sure. I take it you're not Amanda Altman anymore, huh?"

"Been married to Nathan Battle for over a year," she said with an awkward grin.

Jake nodded, hoping the gesture concealed his surprise. He'd thought they'd broken up a long time ago. "That's great. Congratulations."

"It's good you're back, Jake," Amanda said. She paused and then, after a worried glance at Keaton, added, "Things may have changed, but it's still good to come home."

He forced a polite smile. "Not sure how long I'll be here," he said. "But I'll do my best to help out."

Amanda gave him a look before the cook rang the bell and yelled, "Order up!"

And then it was him and Keaton. His brother had changed, but then, hadn't everything? Fine lines had settled in around his eyes and his mouth. They might have been the lines that went with smiling. Maybe Keaton had been happy after Jake had slipped off into the night with Skye four years ago. Maybe he'd gotten married, had some kids. Had a nice life. Jake could be a big enough man to hope for that.

There were no smiles now.

Jake took a sip of his coffee and felt something inside him unclench. He'd had coffee the world over, but there was something about the coffee at the diner that tasted like...

Like home.

He was not going to be glad to be back, no matter what Amanda said. And he was not staying long, either. The look on Keaton's face made it plenty clear he wasn't welcome. Some things never changed.

Slowly, the noise level in the diner began to return to normal conversation levels. Still, Keaton said nothing. And Jake wasn't about to fill the void. He had *nothing* to say to his brother.

Nothing polite, anyway.

Finally, Keaton cracked. "Bahrain?"

Jake nodded. "I run a successful information technology company that specializes in creating the IT infrastructure on oil drilling sites. We do jobs around the world. The Bahrain job was a major win—I beat out some NASDAQ companies for the right to that job."

Of course, none of that information was exactly secret. If Keaton—or anyone else here in Royal—had really wanted to, they could have searched for Texas Sky Technologies online.

Keaton's jaw worked. "Texas Sky, right?"

Jake stared at him. "You looked me up?" Had his brother...missed him?

"Yeah, I really had no choice," Keaton replied with a snort. "Imagine my surprise when the people who answer your phones insisted that you didn't have a brother. Like I didn't even exist."

Okay, so Jake maybe hadn't talked about his family in warm, glowing terms with his employees, but that didn't explain why his receptionist hadn't forwarded the messages.

One other thing was clear from the way Keaton had said he didn't have a choice—the man hadn't missed Jake. "Did you ever consider it's not the rest of the world, Keaton? Maybe you just bring that out in everyone." He started to slide out of the booth. Sparring with his brother was not getting him any closer to finding Skye. He did not have time for this.

Keaton put up an arm to block Jake's exit. "How long were you there for?"

Jake was stuck. He'd come in here to get information about Skye and he still had nothing. So he gritted his teeth and settled back in. This was for Skye. "Almost ten months. It was a yearlong contract, but once you factor in the vacation time, it was just short of ten months."

"So you have no idea, then?"

"No idea about what?" Which pretty much answered the question, but that was all Jake was going to give the man.

"About Skye."

And just like that, the power balance in the booth shifted.

Jake took in the angry look on Keaton's face and did what he had to. He blurred the truth. "Bahrain isn't exactly a woman's paradise. She wasn't up to joining me on this job."

"I imagine not."

Jake didn't like his brother's sarcastic tone, and fought the urge to lunge over the table and grab Keaton by the collar. He wasn't the same hotheaded kid. He was a businessman—a darned successful one at that. He could negotiate with businessmen from China to South Africa to Bahrain.

He would not let Keaton win. Not now, not ever.

So he let that nugget sit while he sipped his coffee. "Something you'd like to get off your chest, Keaton?" he finally asked.

"Did you at least have the decency to marry her?"

He. Would. Not. Kill. Keaton.

Not yet, anyway.

"Actually," Jake said in his coolest voice, "I don't see what that has to do with you in the least. What goes on between me and Skye is our business. Not yours." He would absolutely not tell his brother a single iota of information more than he had to—and his questionable marital status was at the top of that list.

"You should have married her." Keaton made a show of sipping his coffee.

Jake didn't want to have his brother all up in his business like this. This was not how the plan was supposed to go. He was supposed to swing into Royal, find Skye, confront her if she was here and swing right back out again. Whatever problems he and Skye had were between the two of them. Keaton was not a part this. No one in their families was.

So much for that plan.

"Again, not your concern."

"You're so sure of that, huh?" Keaton shook his head in obvious pity.

Jake bristled. Why was Keaton insisting that he should have married Skye? The man had spent years trying to push Skye and Jake apart—not enter them into holy matrimony. "Positive."

"Positive," he said, his tone deadly serious. "Oh, yeah, you're *positive*! You always did think you knew everything, didn't you?"

That was it. Jake didn't have to sit here and take this. Keaton was always doing this—lording it over Jake. Jake hadn't missed his brother at all in four years. Not once. And this was why.

"Been good seeing you, Keaton. Give my best to Mom and Dad." He tried to slide out of the booth but Keaton grabbed his shirt. Immediately, the conversation in the diner dropped to an audible whisper.

"I need to congratulate you, Jake." The sarcasm had slipped back into Keaton's tone and he had a mean glint in his eye. "You're a father."

Jake's stomach dropped. It couldn't be true. He and Skye had always been careful, always discussed waiting to start their family until they were a little better situated. No, he wasn't a father because it just wasn't possible. Instead, this was Keaton trying to screw with him, as always. He probably didn't even know where Skye was. "Funny, Keaton. Real funny." He shook free of his brother's grip and bolted out of the booth. He tried to smile at Amanda as he all but bulldozed his way out of the diner.

As he walked, his mind raced through the options. He was going to kill his brother. Keaton had always been a jerk about Jake and Skye, but this? This took the cake. Jake was not a father. Skye hadn't been pregnant when they'd called it a day.

Had she?

He thought back to the last time he'd lain in bed with her in his arms. They'd gone out to dinner—a fancy thing, because he was making more money now. Business was good. He was trying to show her that he could take care of her, give her the very best in life. But dinner had been tense. They hadn't spoken much. They'd had sex when they'd gone home, but it'd been...

It'd been missing the spark that had held them together for so long. The evening was supposed to be about showing Skye that they still had something worth saving. But apparently in the end, it'd shown them—her—that what they'd had was already gone.

A few days later, their world had erupted. Skye had insisted that, if Jake loved her, he'd go home to Royal with her and start a family. And Jake had insisted that, if Skye loved him, she never even would have asked him to come back to this pit of a town.

The fight had been—well, he tried not to think about the things he'd said. And he tried extra hard not to think about the things she'd said. He'd gone to a hotel the next morning and left for Bahrain the next week.

He could not be a *father*. He just couldn't be. And if he was—that was a huge *if*—then Skye had even less business serving him with divorce papers. But he'd had no other contact with her. Not so much as a peep.

So Jake did the only reasonable thing. He ignored his brother—who had followed him out of the diner, calling his name—and kept walking. He wasn't about to sit there and let his brother mock him. There were other ways to find Skye. Ways that did not involve additional humiliation at the hands of Keaton.

He made it to his Porsche Turbo and got the door open before Keaton caught up to him. "Wait," he repeated, shoving the door closed.

"Go to hell. You want to mock me? Fine. But I don't have to sit there and take it. For the record, I didn't come back to Royal for *you*. I didn't come back for Mom and Dad. I came back for Skye and Skye alone. We'll deal with our relationship just like we've always dealt with things— on our own. You and the Taylors and this whole town can go to hell. I'll even buy you a handbasket."

Keaton leaned against the car door so that Jake would have to go through him to open it. Which was an option that was on the table, as far as Jake was concerned. "You pigheaded fool," he started.

"That's how you want to play this? Fine." Jake's hands curled into fists. "You're nothing but a traitor. I wouldn't trust anything you said even if you had it notarized. I tried that once, remember? I trusted you with my deepest secret and what did you do? You ran to Mom and Dad as fast as your chicken legs could carry you. You tried to break me and Skye up more times than I can count because being a Holt was more important than being with her. You are nothing to me, Keaton. We are not brothers. I am not a Holt. Not anymore."

If Keaton was insulted by this tirade, he didn't show it. Instead, he just kept on leaning against the door, looking at Jake as if he pitied him.

Jake had dreamed of calling his brother out. *Dreamed* of it. But saying those words to his face didn't leave Jake with a sense of lightness or of closure. He only felt worse. And he'd long since vowed not to feel bad about his family. Those days were over. "Get out of my way, Keaton. Or I will get you out of my way. Last warning."

"Her name is Grace."

Grace. He wanted to tell Keaton to go to hell again, but his voice suddenly didn't work, so he settled for glaring.

"She was eleven weeks premature," Keaton went on. "She was in the neonatal intensive care unit for almost three months."

Images Jake had seen in movies of tiny little babies hooked up to wires and tubes suddenly overwhelmed him. He struggled to ask, "The—the hospital? Wasn't that hit during the storm?"

"She wasn't in the hospital during the storm." But damn the man, he didn't elaborate.

They stood there for a moment. Jake realized he was breathing in great gulps, but he couldn't help it.

"Aren't you even going to ask?" Keaton demanded. He sounded frustrated.

"Ask what?"

"*Anything*, man. You've had absolutely no contact with Skye in the last four months—maybe even the whole time you were being a big shot in Bahrain. You obviously have no idea what's going on."

"Maybe I do," Jake snipped, trying to keep his temper under control. He would not give Keaton the satisfaction of getting to him. He would *not*. "Maybe I've been texting with Skye this whole time. How would you know?"

"Because," Keaton replied, anger and exasperation edging his voice, "Skye's only come out of the medically induced coma the doctor's had her in a couple of weeks ago. You can't talk to a woman who's been unconscious—*oof*!"

Whatever else Keaton was going to say was crushed out of him as Jake grabbed him by the shirt and slammed him back against the car. "She *what*?"

"She's been out the last four months, Mr. Big Shot," Keaton said as he tried to push back against Jake's grip. It didn't work. "And Grace is yours. She's a Holt. All the tests came back that she was 99.9 percent positive for being a Holt, which means that her father is either me, Dad or you. And neither Dad nor I have so much as looked at Skye in four years. So it's you. She's your baby girl."

The weight of these words made Jake's knees weak. He had to step back and lean on the car's hood to keep his balance.

His baby. His and Skye's. Who'd been in a coma for months. While he'd been working in Bahrain.

Oh, God. What had he *done*?

"Where?" That was all he could get out.

"Skye's still at the hospital. She's awake, but she doesn't remember much of anything that might have happened in the last few years. Couldn't tell us anything about where you *might* be or why."

"And...the baby? Grace?" The name felt strange on his tongue. His baby. Everything about that felt strange.

"Funny thing about her," Keaton said, after a dramatic pause that made Jake want to tear his brother apart. "She's been handed over to the closest living relatives. Which is me and Lark. You remember Skye's older sister?"

"You and...Lark?" The way Keaton had said her name—in the same sentence as his own—there hadn't been any sneer then. None of the mocking tone he'd always used when he talked about the Taylors.

"Yes. Me and Lark. We have her until Skye can take over. Or until your sorry ass showed up."

"You're taking care of Grace? *With* Lark? I thought—I thought you hated the Taylors. You hated them *so* much."

That's why he'd left. He might not care for Skye's family, but he'd loved Skye since he was seven and she was six. She'd always been more to him than a Taylor. She had been his *everything*.

Keaton looked him in the eye. "Things have changed, Jake. Welcome home."

"How are you feeling today?" The man in the white coat smiled at her.

"Better. Less…fuzzy," Skye replied. Which was the truth. She was sitting up in bed, her eyes open. Her brain was almost working. She felt as close to normal as she had since…since…

Damn. *Almost* working—but not quite.

"Do you remember my name?"

Skye thought. "You're my doctor? Dr. Wake…" She scrunched up her face as the man gave her a hopeful smile. "Dr. Wakefield? Is that right?"

"Excellent!" He nodded and made a note on the tablet he was carrying. "That's very good, Skye. Do you remember her name? She's my research assistant," he said, handing the tablet to the woman in nurse's scrubs standing next to him.

The name was there, but it kept slipping through Skye's mind like a strand of wet spaghetti. Just when she thought she had it, it slipped right past her again. "Julie? Juliet? Jules? Something like that." She leaned back against the bed. The effort of trying to remember was draining. But she didn't want to close her eyes. She was *so* tired of sleeping.

"Very good," Dr. Wakefield. "You got it on the first try—Julie Kingston. What year is it?"

"2013, right?"

Julie and Dr. Wakefield shared a look, which she didn't like. She wanted Jake. She wanted out of this hospital. She wanted him right now.

"When is Jake going to get here?" she asked. Because she'd been awake for almost two weeks and he hadn't shown up yet. She didn't understand why, but she was sure that if Jake wasn't here, there had to be a good reason.

"Skye," Julie said, "can you remember where Jake is?"

"He was…" He'd been somewhere. Somewhere else. But why? Something pulled at her memory, but it wasn't even a slippery noodle she couldn't keep a grip on. It was more like a thin line of smoke that vanished as soon as she tried to touch it. "I don't know." She hated this feeling, of not knowing what was going on. "His company is just starting to take off. Maybe he got that job in New York? But I thought he'd be back by now…"

"That's all right," Dr. Wakefield said in a comforting tone. "Do you remember Grace?"

Skye frowned. They were *always* asking her about Grace. Did she remember Grace? No. Did she remember everyone—the doctors, her sister—asking about Grace? Yes. "She's my daughter."

The words made her want to cry. Her baby—the baby she'd wanted for *so* long—and Skye had no recollection of her at all. She didn't know if her own child was chubby or had hair or looked like Jake or *anything* about her. Just that Grace was her daughter.

"Is the baby okay? Am I well enough to hold her now?"

Dr. Wakefield pressed along her head. There was one area along the side that was still tender. "We have a physical therapy protocol for patients in a coma to keep their muscles from atrophying, but you've lost a lot of strength.

You should be able to hold Grace as long as you're sitting, with pillows to help bolster your arms." He gave her an apologetic smile. "It'll be some time before you can carry her. I'm sorry about that, Skye."

"That's all right," she said. "As long as I can hold her." She couldn't help it—her eyes started to drift shut. "When can I go home?"

"Soon," Dr. Wakefield said. He sounded as if he meant it. "We'll start the process of releasing you to your next of kin."

"That's Jake," she said, yawning. "Can you call him for me? I want him."

"Of course," Julie said in a soothing voice. "I'm sure it won't be long—*oh*!"

At this, Skye's eyes opened and there he was.

Jake.

He looked so, so good. But…there was something off about him, too. Somehow, he looked older than she remembered—more fine lines around his eyes, thinner in the face.

"Skye?" He stood there, his mouth open. If she didn't know any better, she'd say he was in shock. "Oh, my God—are you all right?"

"Jake!" she cried in pure joy. "Oh, thank heavens—I was beginning to think you'd forgotten about me. Where have you been? I've missed you so much." She held up her arms, which took some effort. But he was worth it. God, she was *so* glad to see him.

He turned to the doctor. "Is she all right? I don't want to hurt her."

Julie gave Jake a warm smile. "Go on, you won't hurt her. Just be gentle."

"All right." He walked to the side of the bed and sat in the chair, staring at her as if he'd never seen her before. He took one of her hands in his. "It's good to see you."

"We'll leave you two alone," the doctor said. *Dr. Wakefield*, she mentally corrected. So she wouldn't forget. "Mr. Holt, when you're finished visiting, my research assistant Julie here or one of the nurses can give you the list of things Skye will need to transition to a home environment. She'll be ready to be released in a day or two."

"Sure," Jake said. He didn't sound quite right. Why was he acting so…oh, what was the word? So—so aloof.

Then they were alone.

"I am glad to see you," he told her, rubbing his thumb over his knuckles.

"I'm glad to see *you*. I dreamed of you all the time."

"That's…good." He swallowed nervously as he stared at where their hands were joined. "What, exactly, did you dream?"

"It—well—I don't know if I have the words. I lose words sometimes. Like *aloof*." His eyebrows jumped up as he looked at her quizzically. "Just as an example," she added, feeling silly. Jake wasn't necessarily being aloof. She was pretty sure this was the first time she'd seen him, after all.

Then she realized what the problem was. "I must look awful," she said with a grimace. "If I'd known you were going to get here today, I'd have done…something." Point of fact, she couldn't actually remember the last time she'd showered and there was a section of her hair that had been shaved off.

"No, no—you look fine," Jake said. He gave her an off-kilter smile. "Feels like it's been a long time."

"I'm sorry," she said as she held out her other hand to him and, after what felt like two beats too many, he took it in his. "I've been asleep for so long…"

"Don't be sorry. It was an accident," he said firmly. "The important thing now is that you're awake. How are you? Is there anything I can do for you?"

"I haven't seen Grace. Is she okay?"

"Yes," Jake said. "You'll get to see her soon. But tell me more about how you are. What did you dream?"

"Really, just a bunch of images, you know? Things we did." She grinned at him. "Where we did them."

"Oh." His cheeks shot a deep red. "Those were good things. And good places."

She leaned toward him. He did look different from how she'd seen him in her dreams. Had he always been this thin? She couldn't be sure.

Well, that didn't matter. She was awake and he was here. Soon, they'd get Grace. That was all that counted right now. It wasn't that she wanted to spend more time in bed—there'd been enough of that—but if she remembered right, they could do just fine without a bed. "When you talk to the doctor, ask how long before I can do certain *things*, okay?" She waggled her eyebrows at him.

"Sure." He squeezed her hands and gave her another tight smile. Then, finally, he leaned over and did what she'd been waiting for—he kissed her.

Except it was a small kiss, a mere brushing of his lips against hers. Not a passionate, soul-consuming kiss. Not the kiss she'd dreamed about.

Why not?

"I'm going to go check on Grace," Jake said when the too-short kiss was over. "Your sister has her."

"Yes, Lark. Because you weren't here?" She shook her head, which was not the best idea she'd ever had. Her head began to hurt. "I missed something, didn't I? You had a job in New York, right?"

"New York?" He looked at her as if she'd sprouted a second head. Or maybe a third one. Oh, what she wouldn't give for a haircut—a good one—right about now. She wanted him to look at her with the love he'd always had in his eyes. "I did have a job there."

Oh, good—she'd gotten that part right. Suddenly, she was tired—the excitement of Jake's arrival had worn off, apparently. She yawned and tried to hide it behind her hand, but she didn't do a very good job. "Sorry," she mumbled. "I'm just so tired of being asleep."

Finally, Jake looked at her with the tenderness she recognized. "Well, I'm here now. I'll talk to the doctor and do what I need to in order to get you set up." He leaned over and kissed her on the forehead. "You rest up. Grace needs you to get better."

"Okay," she agreed, having trouble keeping her eyes open. "But you'll come back for me, right?"

There was another one of those long pauses as he stared at her. "I will *always* come back for you, Skye." He squeezed her hand. "Now get some rest. I'll see you soon. I promise."

"Good," she told him as she squeezed back. Then his warmth was away from her.

Jake was here, she thought as she drifted. He was going to get Grace. And he'd come back for her.

Everything was going to be perfect.

Two

"What's wrong with her?"

Both the doctor and his research assistant looked at Jake with raised eyebrows. Okay, maybe that had been a little gruff—but seriously?

She was different. Or rather, she was the same as she'd once been—but not the same woman she'd been the last time he'd seen her. Skye hadn't looked at him with that kind of adoration in a long time. And when was the last time she'd wanted sex? When was the last time she'd *wanted* him?

Jake had only taken one job in New York. And that had been two years ago. It'd been a small job, but it'd led to bigger and better things.

Two years ago. That'd been the last time things had been good between them. After Jake had started getting those bigger and better jobs, things had begun to fall apart.

"Skye had a traumatic brain injury," the doctor explained. "I'm her surgeon. Dr. Lucas Wakefield," he added, sticking out his hand.

Jake shook it. "But what does that mean?"

"It means that, as near as we can tell, Skye was driving into Royal when the tornado hit. We suspect her car was picked up and tossed around."

"And?" Jake demanded. Julie's eyebrows went up again, but Jake was past caring.

Skye had driven into a damn tornado. Why? That wasn't like her. She was more careful than that. She knew how Texas weather could be. She would have taken shelter or gotten off the road or something.

"Think of it as a concussion—only the most extreme kind. We kept her under for a few months to allow her brain to heal and it took her some time to wake up after we cut back on the drugs we were using to induce the coma. Her memory is…compromised."

"And what does *that* mean?" Jake demanded. What was it going to take to get a straight answer out of the man?

"She's got what the layperson might call amnesia," Dr. Wakefield explained. "She doesn't seem to have the last two years, although her long-term memory is mostly intact. Anything that happened right before the accident is probably gone for good."

For the second time that day, Jake had to lean on something to keep his legs underneath him. "Will she—will she get those two years back?" Would she remember how things had broken between them? Would she remember the fight? The divorce papers?

When he'd seen her just now, she hadn't had her ring on. She hadn't had her earrings in, either—the big diamond studs he'd bought her just as things had started to go south on them. He wondered where they were—lost in the storm or left behind on purpose?

"Hard to say. The brain is an amazing organ. For now, we recommend keeping any shocks to the system to a bare minimum. Obviously, she knows about your daughter."

Grace. *His* daughter, Grace.

"But," Dr. Wakefield went on as if Jake weren't on the verge of collapse, "if there were…other surprises, I'd keep those close to the vest."

"You want me to, what—lie to her?"

Julie said, "Not lie, no. Think of it as glossing over. She's going to be confused for some time. Too much too soon would be a severe shock to her system. We don't want her to have a setback."

Jake shook his head, hoping to get the world to stop spinning. None of this was right. None of it.

Skye didn't remember how they'd broken up. Why they'd broken up.

And he couldn't tell her.

God, what a mess.

Julie handed him a packet. "She'll have to do physical therapy to regain her muscle strength. This is a preliminary list of stretches and exercises you'll need to help her with at home during her recovery to rebuild her strength to a point where PT will be helpful to her. In a week or two, you'll need to bring her into the office so she can work with a therapist."

He stared at the sheet. The top one had a photo of a woman in a spandex unitard laying on the floor and another woman in hospital scrubs stretching her leg so that it pointed straight up. "Me?"

"Are you two married?" Julie eyed him. Closely. "If so, you're her next of kin. We had planned to release her to Lark Taylor, but if you're here, you'll be the one in charge of her care."

"We are married," he said, feeling the full impact of those words. He'd sworn vows to her, vows to be there for her in sickness and in health, until death parted them. She'd wanted to break those vows, but because she'd been in a coma and he'd been in a different hemisphere, they hadn't managed to do that just yet.

Then something else dawned on him. "I suppose you're going to tell me that I can't take her back to Houston?"

"That wouldn't be wise," Dr. Wakefield said, giving Jake a suspicious look. "I'd like to continue to monitor her recovery. I have colleagues in Houston that I could refer you to, but I'd prefer to remain her primary. Consistency of care can't be overestimated at this point."

He was going to have to take care of her. He was going to have to look at her and know he'd lost her and not tell her that. He couldn't tell her about the slow way the spark had died or how she'd had him served with papers.

Instead, he was going to have to take care of a woman who thought she still loved him because she couldn't remember how she'd stopped loving him.

And to do that, he was going to have to stay in the pit that was Royal, Texas.

How could this get any worse?

Jake had broken the cardinal rule. No matter how bad things were, never, *ever* ask how they could possibly be worse.

Because a man never knew when a dog was going to try and break through the door to get to him.

Jake stood on the front porch of a nondescript house in a nice part of town. He was pretty sure this was the address Keaton had given him. On the other side of the door, the dog was howling and scratching like a crazed beast. Jake debated getting back in the car. If the dog got out, Jake would prefer to have a layer of metal between the two of them.

Seconds ticked by more slowly than molasses in January. His fingers started twitching toward the doorbell to ring it again. They knew he was coming, right?

The dog still going nuts, Jake was just about to start pounding on the door when he heard the lock being turned. "Nicki!" Keaton shouted. "Knock it off! Back up!"

The barking ceased almost immediately, then the door cracked open and the first thing Jake heard was the wailing of a baby. An unhappy baby.

"About time," Keaton grumbled, opening the door and standing aside. "You woke her up. Next time, just knock. That doesn't seem to set Nicki off nearly as badly as the doorbell does."

"Sorry." And truthfully—with all that screaming? Jake actually *was* sorry.

Keaton got the door closed behind him. Jake's eyes took a moment to adjust to the dim lighting. The blinds were down and in addition to the screaming he heard the sounds of…classical music?

"This way," Keaton said, stepping around Jake. "Watch out for Nicki."

Jake eyed the dog that was now sitting next to the door. The dog's hackles were up and it was growling, but at least it hadn't attacked. "Nice doggie," Jake said as he stepped around the animal. Man, he hoped that thing was well trained. "Good girl."

"Yeah, we just got her a few weeks ago. Australian shepherd. Nicki goes with me out to the ranch—I'm training her to keep tabs on the cattle. She's really good at it." As Keaton spoke, he walked confidently though the house. He led Jake—and Nicki—past large framed landscapes of Texas in all the seasons—bluebells in one, the bright summer sky in another. They walked past shelves that seemed to overflow with books, all of which looked uniformly well-read. This was not the pristine, almost sterile kind of house that Skye had grown up in. This was a home that seemed lived in. But it didn't seem particularly feminine.

"This your place?" he asked, trying to keep his tone casual.

"It's Lark's. We're building a place of our own." Keaton didn't offer any more details.

Jake had a lot of questions from that one statement, but before he could figure out how to ask them, they entered a room that had probably once been a tidy great room. Except now there were baby blankets draped everywhere, mats with mirrored things attached spread over the floor and more stuffed animals than Jake could count. There were bookshelves in here, too, but the books had been cleared off the lower ones and bins full of toys and things that Jake didn't recognize now filled the space. Plus, there was an absolutely huge television along one wall that seemed out of place in the worst sort of way.

In the middle of it all, on a couch that was piled high with cloths and diapers, sat Skye's sister, Lark, with a small, squalling baby in her arms. Lark was wearing medical scrubs. Maybe she was a nurse?

At the sight of them, Lark got a mean look about her—a look Jake recognized from days long gone. It was a look he'd seen more often on Vera Taylor's face than on Skye's, but the hatred was unmistakable.

"Babe," Keaton said, crouching down in front of her. He rubbed his hands over her thighs. "You remember Jake, my—my brother?"

"No," Lark said. But it didn't sound as if she was answering Keaton's question.

"Lark," Jake said, trying to be polite about it.

The baby cried even more. Jake wouldn't have thought that was possible, but it was. This morning, he hadn't been a father. Now he was faced with a wailing infant.

Skye wasn't supposed to have any shocks to her system. He wished someone had given the same orders for him because he wasn't sure how much more he could take.

"Where have you *been*?" Lark snapped. Her eyes filled with tears, and Jake noticed the dark circles underneath.

"Babe…" Keaton said, touching her face. It was a tender gesture.

Jake wasn't sure what part of this scene made the least amount of sense. Keaton had always said Lark Taylor was a stuck-up bookworm who thought she was better than everyone else—and Jake had never argued that point much. Lark hadn't liked Jake. The feeling had been mutual.

"I was in Bahrain. I came back for Skye and for our daughter." The words were coming easier now. But he stared at the little baby still crying in Lark's arms and the room began to feel smaller.

"Oh," Lark said. "So glad to see that you've decided to acknowledge her. Where have you been since she was born? Do you even know how old she is? Do you know *anything* about her?"

Before Jake could reply, Keaton spoke. "Lark," he said in a soft voice, trying to draw her attention back to him. "We talked about this."

"But you know him, Keaton. You *know* he's going to take Grace and disappear. Just like he always does."

Yeah, that stung. "I promise, I'm not going to walk off with that baby."

"Because you keep your promises, right?" Lark shot back at him. The baby was really letting loose now. "I wouldn't trust you farther than I can throw you."

Okay, that stung more. Jake nervously eyed the baby—his daughter—and fought the urge to cover his ears. Unfamiliar panic began to build in his chest. "I don't know where you think I'm going to go with an infant, not when Skye's doctor insists she needs to stay local. Despite what you assume about me and Skye, I do *not* disappear. I had a job in Bahrain, but it's over now. I'm *going* to take care of my family."

Keaton and Lark exchanged a look. Jake couldn't take his eyes off the baby. She was small and bald and an interesting shade of red—although he hoped that was from all the screaming and not her natural color. "How old is she?"

"Three months." Lark began rocking and patting the baby on the back. She wasn't looking at Jake, but that was okay. At least she was telling him what he needed to know. "She was eleven weeks premature—that's their best guess. She was in the NICU for two months. And since Skye was still under when Grace was ready to leave the hospital, she was turned over to her next of kin." She looked at Keaton. The anger she'd directed at Jake was gone from her eyes; now he saw something else there. "That's us."

Jake recognized the emotion. Lark looked at Keaton the way Skye used to look at him. It'd been a while, though.

He sat in a nearby recliner and dropped his head into his hands, trying to keep his emotions in check. When had Skye stopped looking at him like that? And why hadn't he noticed when she did?

"Since she was so early," Lark went on, "she's got a bunch of health risks that full-term babies don't have to worry about. She shouldn't be outside in this weather and she shouldn't be around strangers. If she got sick, she could wind up back in the hospital. Or worse. She's a full-time job right now."

Jake knew that shaking his head wasn't going to help a damn thing but he did it anyway. He had jobs waiting now—Bahrain had been very good for him. He couldn't take an infant with health risks out of the country. Hell, he couldn't even take Skye to Houston.

Trapped. He was trapped in this town.

"Keaton said he told you about the blood tests," Lark said into the silence.

"He did."

"He said you didn't know about Grace."

"I thought…" He didn't know what to do. His entire world—everything he *thought* he knew—had been turned inside out in the space of about four hours.

He didn't trust his brother and he didn't trust the Taylors—with the exception of Skye.

He thought that his brother would never trust a Taylor either. Yet here Jake sat, in Lark Taylor's house, watching her and Keaton cuddle and soothe a fussy baby. Together.

"What did you think?" For the first time since Jake had walked into this house, he heard the attitude in Keaton's voice.

He didn't want to tell them this. But his back was against a wall—a wall covered in four-inch spikes. As much as he hated it, he needed both Lark and Keaton right now. He had a bunch of questions and they had the closest thing to answers.

"Skye and I…" He absolutely could *not* tell them about the divorce papers. "I had that big job in Bahrain coming up. It was a yearlong contract and she decided she didn't want to spend that much time in a foreign country. Bahrain may be richer than sin, but it's not exactly a progressive state."

All of that was true enough. She hadn't wanted to go to Bahrain and she hadn't wanted to stay home alone. She'd wanted him to stay with her. And he'd picked the job over her. That had been the proverbial straw that had broken the camel's back.

"Is that it?" Keaton said with a snort.

"Yes." And since Skye might never remember the fight, there was no one to contradict Jake's lie.

Lark looked victorious, but strangely, it didn't make her seem any happier. "Were you married? Skye said you were but she didn't have her ring on and who knows, with that memory of hers." She looked at Jake's hand.

Jake spun the plain gold band around his finger. It'd

been the only ring they'd been able to afford when they slipped off into the night together four years ago.

"Yes. We got married three days after we left."

Silence followed this statement. He and Skye had driven to Houston and found a preacher who would marry them. He'd been wearing his old boots and a pair of jeans, but Skye had been in a simple white skirt and a bright blue top. She'd been so beautiful that day…

"So what are you going to do now?" Keaton finally asked. "Because Lark is right. We're not going to stand aside and let you disappear off into the night with this baby. We're not going to let you do anything that would put her at risk."

Jake gritted his teeth. He had no choice but to stay here. He looked at the baby girl. She was still crying—but at least now the decibel level wouldn't shatter glass. Jake tried to smile at the baby, but the terror the tiny baby—his *daughter*, for crying out loud!—was sparking in his chest was making breathing difficult.

He'd never held a baby before. He didn't have the first idea how to do any of the basics—bottles and diapers and everything else. He and Skye had wanted to wait.

That wasn't true. Skye had wanted a baby from the very beginning. But Jake had looked at the reality of being a young couple barely scraping by and he'd convinced her that they needed to wait until their financial situation was more secure.

That was another thing she'd thrown back in his face during the fight, another ultimatum she'd issued. Have a baby or it's over.

He'd said after the Bahrain job. He was going to make a fortune in Bahrain. Another year, and they'd be set.

"Skye is going to be released to my care, maybe to-morrow."

"Are you going to be able to take care of her?"

Jake would have normally taken umbrage at his brother's attitude, but right now? Yeah, it was a danged good question.

"I don't know."

Near silence descended upon the room. "We could keep her," Lark finally said, looking at the baby.

"What?"

"We could keep Grace—just until Skye gets settled. Keaton and I know her schedule. We know how to take care of her. She shouldn't be out in this weather, anyway, not until she's stronger. That way, you can focus on getting Skye back into shape. You can bring Skye over here to visit the baby, but she won't have to get up in the middle of the night."

Could he do that? This was his daughter. A daughter he'd only known about for...five hours, but still—his flesh and blood.

He didn't want to be a monster about this. This wasn't him abandoning the baby. This was him getting Skye to the point where she could take over, right?

Plus, if he left Grace here, that would prove that he wasn't going to skip town again. "Would that be okay? I don't want to impose, but the sooner we can get Skye back to full strength, the better."

Lark sighed as she looked at Grace. "Keaton and I already have it all worked out and, really, she's an angel."

"I'll need to get a house of my own. The whole point of you keeping the baby here is to give Skye room to recover at her own pace." To put it less tactfully, he didn't want to sleep under the same roof as Keaton and Lark—even if they were being really good to Grace.

"You're actually going to stay?" Keaton sounded doubtful.

Jake let the comment slide. "Skye's doctors are here and I'm not going to do a damn thing that might set her back. I know you don't believe this, but I didn't know about the tornado until this morning. Hell, I don't even know if Mom and Dad came through all right." If he'd known...

"Mom and Dad are okay," Keaton said in a quiet voice. "Some property damage. The ranch house is being rebuilt, but they were in Florida and Alabama, checking out some retirement properties, so they weren't in the line of the storm. We've had them over a few times."

"Good. I'm glad." Strangely, he was. He'd spent the last four years pointedly not caring about what his family was doing. They'd wanted him to put the family above Skye. Nothing was more important to him than Skye.

"They adore Grace," Lark said in a way that made it pretty clear that this absolved most of their sins in her eyes.

"And they've come to see that Lark is nothing like her parents," Keaton went on. "I think they're realizing that not all Taylors are lying, cheating dogs."

Bitterness rose up in the back of Jake's throat. Oh, sure—now his parents were going to open their arms and welcome a Taylor into the family. But not for Jake and Skye when he had needed them to.

"What about your parents?" he asked Lark.

She dropped her eyes. "They're...okay. Fine."

"Whit Daltry's got some houses for rent in Pine Valley," Keaton said, changing the subject. "I think a couple of them are furnished—not too far from here. I'll call him."

"Thanks. That'd be great." He was not buying a house. He was not staying in Royal long. Just long enough to get Skye back on her feet and figure out where they stood.

Just then, the baby made a little hiccup-sigh noise that pulled at his heartstrings.

Lark shifted Grace off of her shoulder. Keaton picked the baby up so smoothly that Jake was jealous. "Grace, honey—this is your daddy," Keaton said as he rubbed her on her back. Then, to Jake, he added, "You ready?"

Not really—but Jake wasn't going to admit that to Keaton. He tried to cradle his arms in the right way. Then Keaton laid the baby out in them.

The world seemed to tilt off its axis as Jake looked down into his daughter's eyes. They were a pale blue—just like her mother's. Up close now, he could see that Grace had wispy hairs on her head that were so white and fine they were almost see-through.

She didn't start bawling, which he took as a good sign. Instead, she waved her tiny hands around, so of course he had to offer her one of his fingers. When she latched on to it, he felt lost and yet *not* lost at the same time.

He was responsible for this little girl from this moment until the day he drew his last breath. The weight of it hit him so hard that, if he hadn't already been sitting, his knees would have buckled.

This was his daughter. He and Skye had created this little person.

God, he wished she were here with him. That they could have done this together. That things between them had been different. That he'd been different.

But he couldn't change the past, not when his present—and his future—was gripping his little finger with surprising strength.

"Hi, Grace," he whispered. He shook his hand a little, raising her fist with his pinkie finger. "It's so good to meet you."

The baby smiled, which made Jake feel ten feet tall. "Hey, she's smiling at—"

Then a horrible noise—and an even more horrible smell—cut him off.

Keaton began to laugh. The dog whined and put its paws over its nose.

"Sorry," Lark said, rising quickly. "She's about due for another bottle, too."

"Time for your first lesson—diapers," Keaton said as he clapped Jake on the back. "Welcome to fatherhood."

Three

"Grace is with Lark, right?" Skye asked. She knew Jake had answered that question at least three times already, but she wanted to see her daughter.

"Are you asking because you don't remember the answer or because you don't trust me?" Jake grinned at her from the driver's seat. It was an easy grin that warmed her from the inside out—but there was something underneath it that had an edge.

She was going home. With Jake. The past few days had been the longest of her waking life. Skye had been ready and willing to leave that hospital far behind and get back to making new memories with Jake.

"I just…I just want to see her again. I remember you already said yes," she hurried to add. "I feel like I've missed so much." She laughed. "Probably because I have."

The process of being released from the hospital had taken most of the day. Late winter twilight settled over the landscape as Jake drove toward their new home. "And… we're not going back to our apartment, right?"

"That's right," he said gently. "The doctor wants you to stay close to the hospital. I rented a house. It's close to Lark and the baby and not too far from the hospital."

"I wish I remembered Grace," she said, an impotent frustration bubbling up. "Why is Lark keeping her?"

"Because Lark is a nurse and you need to recover," he answered smoothly. "We'll go over and visit, I promise. And I always keep my promises, don't I?"

"Yes…" She tried to make sense of that hidden edge to his words It was almost as if he was mad at her. But did that make any sense?

No, it didn't. He was probably just upset that she'd been hurt so badly. Jake had never been the best at expressing his feelings. She knew there were holes in her memory and she didn't know if those holes would ever get filled.

But she was still here and she was getting better. She'd just have to make some new memories with Jake. And with Grace.

She looked around and was surprised to see that she recognized the road they were on. "Stop!" she cried, feeling hopeful. Now was as good a time as any to start making some of those new memories.

"What?" Jake asked in alarm as he slammed on the brakes. His right arm flew across her chest to keep her from lurching forward.

"We used to park here, remember?" She undid her seat belt and slid over to him. "We used to stop here on the way home."

She grinned nervously at him. Yes, she wanted to get home, but she'd been in a bed—by herself—for the last four months. Four months without Jake. It was time to fix that starting right *now*.

Jake did not bend much in her arms. She ran her fingers

through his hair and pulled him down to her. "We did stop here, didn't we? I didn't get that wrong, did I?"

"We did," he said through gritted teeth.

"Are you going to kiss me, Jake Holt?" she whispered against his lips.

He turned his head. "The doctor said—he said we shouldn't stress you out too much. Physically."

Skye sighed in disappointment. "Not even if I want to be stressed? Just a little? Not even a kiss?"

Jake didn't reply for a moment. Then he sort of chuckled and said, "When we used to stop here, I don't remember it ever being *just* a kiss."

Skye leaned into him, feeling his warmth. The hospital had been cold. But Jake had always run hot. She'd loved curling up against him in the middle of winter, letting his body warm hers until things started to get downright steamy.

"I've missed you so much," she told him. It felt like an important thing to say. She was pretty sure she'd said it before, but she wanted to say it again.

He didn't respond. Not the way she'd hoped. Instead, he said, "Sorry, traffic. Can you buckle up? I don't want another car accident. I just got you out of that hospital." He said it in a jokey kind of way, as if she was supposed to laugh along with him. But she didn't.

"All right. But later I'm going to kiss you. I don't care what the doctors said."

"Later," he agreed. He waited until she was buckled up and then he drove on.

"How long will we be in Royal?" she asked. "I know how much you hate it here. I wish you didn't have to stay just because of me."

He tensed. "Aren't you glad to be back home?"

"I guess..." He shot her a worried look. "What?"

"I thought you'd be glad to be here, that's all. You'd talked about coming home—remember?"

"Oh, I know. I wish our families would see the light of day and put the feud to rest." She sighed. She was missing something again. It was as if there were a fog over her mind that was so thick that it hid things from her. But when she tried to grab it or push it aside, it slipped through her fingers. It was both there and *not* there. Just like her memory, apparently. "But I'd rather be with you than deal with my parents. Have you seen them? I don't think I have. I've seen Lark. And I want to say that… Didn't Lark come in and talk to me? While I was sick? She's with Keaton now, right?"

"Yeah, that's right." He gave her a tight smile.

"Good. I'm glad. I knew the Taylors and the Holts could get along if they just…just…oh, shoot. I lost another word."

"It's okay," Jake said quickly. "I understand what you mean. Hey—here we are."

Jake turned past a big sign that announced they were in Pine Valley. They drove past spacious homes set far back from the road.

"Is this where we're going to stay? This is nice," Skye said, glancing out the window.

"I wanted to get the best for you," he told her. "This is a furnished house, but if there's something you want from the apartment back in Houston…" His voice trailed off. "Or I can buy you new things, too. Money is no object."

"Since when?" she demanded. "I mean, we were just getting comfortable. I don't think we should drain the bank accounts dry."

"Oh. Um, well—hmm. The last job," he said, stumbling over the words. "I, uh, I did a great job and I got a huge bonus."

"You did? Oh, Jake—that's wonderful!" But then confusion set in again. "Is that why you weren't with me? In the accident? Because of the job?"

"Yeah. This is it." He pulled into a long drive. "This house has a small gym in it. That's why I picked it. That way you can use a couple of machines to help you regain your strength."

"Oh, good thinking." Because the one thing she did not have right now was a lot of strength. She hated feeling weak, but she wouldn't be that way for long.

Jake parked and Skye undid her belt again. She got the door open as he went around the front of the car, but when she slid out of the seat, her legs almost didn't hold. "Whoa," she gasped, clinging to the door for support. She'd gotten out of the bed on her own, but the rest of the trip had been in a wheelchair. She hadn't realized how weak she actually was.

"Easy, now," Jake said. "I've got you."

The next thing she knew, he swept Skye up into his strong arms as if she weighed nothing at all.

She giggled as he carried her up the steps to the front door. "It's like we're married," she said, resting her head against his shoulder.

"Yeah," he said. He sounded unconvincing. "Just like that. I carried you over the threshold of that hotel the night we got married, didn't I?"

"Mmm." Without loosening her grip, she twirled one finger through the short hairs on the back of his neck. "That was a good night, wasn't it? You were so handsome."

Jake set her down long enough to get the door open. Then, after the barest moment of hesitation, he picked her up again. "And you were beautiful," he said, sounding very serious about it. "You still are."

She laughed again. God, she'd missed this man. "I really need a shower before I'm going to start buying that line from you." Which was not a half-bad idea. "Or a bath? What does this place have? I think I'd need a bench in a shower."

"Your choice. There's a whirlpool tub that'll be good for soaking and a separate shower. I think it has a bench in it." He carried her over the threshold. "Welcome home, Skye."

"Oh, wow." Dusky light streamed in from floor-to-ceiling windows, illuminating a massive, well-appointed great room with leather furnishings and a comfortable-looking couch. Along one wall was a stone hearth. Skye craned her neck and saw that the great room opened onto a kitchen. She couldn't see much of it, but she caught glimpses of gleaming stainless steel and granite counter-tops. "Jake, this place is gorgeous! Are you sure we can afford it?"

"It was a big bonus," he told her. He carried her over to the comfortable couch and gently set her down. He tried to stand, but she wasn't going to let him go.

She held tight and pulled him down. He didn't fall into her the way he normally did, but he didn't pull away. "I missed you. This," she told him as she brushed her lips against his. "Feels like it's been forever."

"Yeah," he agreed. He pressed his lips to hers and sighed. Skye knew that noise. He always did that when he was ready and willing to take things to the next level. The first time he'd sighed against her mouth like that, she'd pulled away and demanded to know what was wrong, what she'd messed up. And instead of telling her she wasn't a good kisser, he'd only pulled her in closer and kissed her hard.

So she opened her mouth and traced her tongue over his lips and waited for him to take the next step.

He didn't.

He stood up and damn it all, she wasn't strong enough to hold on to him. "Um, yeah. Don't want to overdo it on your first night home."

She frowned at him. "You won't break me, you know."

"I know, I know. Hey, are you hungry? I could order some food. I drove past the Tower Pizza—it's still standing. I'll get you a green pepper and mushroom."

"Oh. Okay." Something still felt…off. She groped around in her mind, trying to get the fog that had covered everything to shift or just go the heck away, but it didn't. "But you don't like mushrooms. You don't have to eat them just for my sake."

He paused halfway to the kitchen. "I'll get two pizzas. I know you don't like pepperoni. Then we can have some for lunch tomorrow. Sound good?"

She snickered at him. "Two pizzas? That must have been some bonus."

A shadow crossed over his face. But he said, "It was. I'll be right back. Then we'll see about getting you into the shower."

Skye liked the sound of that. She looked down at her loose-fitting yoga pants and unisex T-shirt emblazoned with the hospital's logo on it. This was not a good look—in fact, she probably resembled an escaped mental patient more than anything else.

She just wanted to put this whole brain-injury thing behind them and get back to their lives. And Grace—she needed to get Grace, although the concept of a small human that was her daughter wasn't something she had a firm grasp on just yet. Grace Holt was still…an abstract idea.

They'd get to Grace. Lark had the baby so Skye felt okay just focusing on Jake right now.

It really did feel like longer than a few months since she'd been with him. But her dreams had been wild and varied and had always had a glimmer of something that might have been a memory at the core of them—like parking at that spot and making out.

That settled it. Shower first, real clothing second, seducing Jake third.

She was going to remember this.

Jake stood in the kitchen, forcing himself to breathe evenly.

Jesus, she was going to kill him. He was halfway amazed he wasn't already dead yet.

What the hell was going on? That doctor hadn't been lying when he'd said that Skye had lost the past two years. It was as if the whole seven hundred and thirty days hadn't happened. The Skye that was sitting out there on that couch was the Skye he'd run away with—bold and forward and unable to keep her hands off of him. She was the Skye he'd been unable to stay away from, come hell or high water.

Gone was the quiet, distant woman who didn't care how much he hated this town, didn't want to share a pizza with him—didn't want *him*. The Skye on the couch had no clue that other Skye had taken over the past two years of her life.

She didn't remember falling out of love with him.

She still thought she loved him.

And she seemed hell-bound to prove it.

What was he supposed to do here? The jerk move would be to just start sleeping with her. But the doctor seemed to think she'd start to recover some of her memories and once she did—once she remembered the divorce papers he'd shoved into his glove box—she'd accuse him of taking advantage of her while she was confused.

But she was throwing herself at him and damn it, his stupid body had apparently decided that, yeah, maybe they could *all* forget about the past two years and go back to how it'd been. Jake had fought himself to keep from kissing her back in the car.

And that kiss on the couch? God, she'd been warm and soft and inviting. He wanted to keep going, to remember those good times—like their wedding night—with her.

He was stuck between a rock and a very hard place.

Finally, he managed to will his body to stand down. He dialed Tower and ordered the pizzas, but they'd be almost forty-five minutes.

Fine. He could get Skye into the bathroom and close the door and…go run on the treadmill that was supposedly in the basement of this house to cool down.

He could not sleep with her. He *would* not, even though they were still technically married. Because it was just that—a technicality. The divorce papers that had been waiting for him had made her position on the matter of their marriage plenty clear. She might not love him like she once had, but he couldn't use her—even if she wanted to be used. When she remembered, she'd wind up hating him. And since they had a daughter to consider, he didn't want that, either.

When he was sure he could keep himself under control, he went back into the great room. "The pizza will be here in about—" He checked his watch. He'd been standing in the kitchen for a while. "Forty minutes. Do you want to have a bath first?"

"That would be great," she agreed with a glint in her eyes. He didn't like that glint. It spelled only one thing—trouble.

"Let's try walking this time," he said. He was supposed to make sure she exercised, right? And that would probably take a lot of energy. If he could make sure she was tired out—as the doctor recommended—then maybe she would stop throwing herself at him.

She scowled at him, as if she'd been counting on him carrying her everywhere. Well, too bad. He didn't need to feel her weight in his arms, her body pressed against his. Nope. Didn't need it at all. Not even a little.

Yeah, right.

He took hold of her hands and got her up on her feet. "You go first," he told her. "I'll be right behind you."

More scowling. "Can't you put your arm around me?"

"No." When she glared, he added, "The doctor said you had to use your muscles."

The disgruntled look faded into something that was worry instead. "If I fall…"

"I'll catch you," he told her. And he meant it.

He put his hands on her shoulders and turned her toward the stairs. The bathroom in the master suite was where he was headed—but it was at the far end of the house. What normally would have been a thirty-second trip took close to three minutes. He kept his hand on her back the whole time, so she'd know he was right there.

"Down the hall," he told her. "Keep going."

"This place…is a lot…bigger than our apartment," she puffed.

"You're almost there, Skye. You can do it." He said it because it seemed like the thing to say to someone who was working really hard. He could see sweat bead up on the back of Skye's neck as she took slow steps, her hands brushing against the wall for added support.

"Are we…there yet?" she panted.

"Into the bedroom," he instructed, guiding her with his hand.

"Thought you'd…never ask. Oh! Pretty!"

The bedroom was done in royal blues and warm golds, giving the whole thing a celestial feeling. A king-size bed was tucked into a wide bay window. To the left, there was another fireplace with a flat-screen television mounted over the mantle. On the right was their destination—the bathroom.

Skye had almost come to a complete stop. "Bath or shower?"

"Bath," came the weak reply.

Jake had her sit on the toilet while he got the water going. He took some towels from under the sink and laid them where she could reach them. "Okay," he said as he checked to make sure that the shampoo and soap were within easy reach. "You bathe and I'll be back to check on you in—what's wrong?"

He asked because Skye had sighed heavily and her lip was quivering. He knew what that meant—she was trying not to cry. "I don't know if I can get in by myself," she said in a low whisper. "I'm sorry."

"Don't be, babe." Although he was pretty sorry, too. This was going to be torture, pure and simple. Because he saw immediately what he was going to have to do—strip those clothes off of her and get her into the tub.

And if she was hard to resist when she was dry and clothed, how was he going to keep his hands to himself when she was naked and wet?

He pulled the oversize T-shirt off of her and was nearly knocked off his feet. She wasn't wearing a bra. She'd never really needed one—so he shouldn't have been surprised. Still, to be suddenly confronted with her breasts was doing very little to help his resolve.

"I need you. To stand," he forced himself to say. "So I can get you out of those pants. And into the tub."

She looked up at him and managed a beautiful blush. But she held out her hands for him to pull her up. When he got her on her feet, she looped her arms around his neck and let him carry most of her weight.

"It'll…it'll get better, right?"

"Absolutely," he agreed, trying to figure out how to get the pants off without touching her bottom. "You're already so much better than you were yesterday. Think about how good you're going to feel tomorrow."

Finally, he gave up. The pants were loose, but not so

loose that they'd just fall right off her hips. He had to skim his hands down over her skin. And down. And down.

He found himself eye to eye with the V where her legs met. There'd been a time—say, about two or three years ago—when he'd have taken every single advantage of this position and lavished attention on her body.

But he didn't now. He *couldn't*. He absolutely could not take advantage of a woman who wasn't entirely in her right mind. So he forced himself to stand.

She gave him a weak smile. "Takes you back, doesn't it?"

"It was a *great* honeymoon. Don't think we left the hotel room for three days," he told her as he half supported, half lifted her into the tub. "Easy," he cautioned as her foot slipped. "I've got you."

It'd been such a freeing thing—running away from home, getting married and not caring a lick whether their parents approved or not. Jake had a new job and Skye had just graduated from college. They weren't little kids who were in "like" anymore. They'd become grown-ups who could do what they wanted, when they wanted. And what they'd wanted to do was each other.

So they had. For three straight days. That was their honeymoon.

It'd taken Jake eight months to pay off the cost of the hotel on their credit cards. And it'd been worth it.

Finally, Skye was settled into the tub. The water barely lapped over her nipples as she sank lower. "Mmm, this feels good," she murmured and that was enough to make breathing much more difficult for Jake.

He needed to get out of this bathroom and he needed to do it right now. But before he could say *I'll be back*, she asked, "Did you say this had jets?"

"Yeah." Which was fine. Figuring out the controls on the whirlpool was something to focus on besides her nude body. He got the jets going. "Okay, I'll check on you in a few minutes to see if you need help getting out."

"But I…" He heard a small splash. "Jake, I'm tired. I don't think I can wash my hair."

God was punishing him. That had to be it. This was some sort of cosmic joke—divorce papers from the woman who suddenly loved him again.

He dropped his head. "Okay, but when the doorbell rings, it's the pizza and I'll have to go." Maybe he'd get lucky and the pizza would come much faster than advertised.

The tub had one of those fancy faucets that looked like an old-fashioned telephone, which was great and also really awful because he had no excuse not to help her. He could do this. He could take care of her while she was in the tub, and he wouldn't touch anything but her hair. He was a man of principle, damn it. He was not the horny teenager he'd once been. So what if he hadn't been with a woman since the last time with Skye? So what if that was ten months ago? He was master of his domain and his domain was currently closed for business.

So it was time to suck it up and keep his hands to himself. Or just confined to her hair. That was it. He wasn't even going to look at her breasts again. Nope.

He had to lean across the tub—and across her—to turn the tap back on. The water was still warm, but he let it run until it was the right temperature. Then—repeating *Not looking* to himself over and over—he moved the faucet over her head in slow, even strokes.

"Lean your head back," he told her and even he didn't miss how deep his voice had suddenly gotten. But he kept his eyes locked on her fine white hair.

It was nearly translucent when it was wet. He squeezed the shampoo into his hand and started on the side that hadn't been shaved. Slowly, he worked the shampoo into her hair.

The results were…not pretty. "Did you do this in the hospital?"

"I don't… No? I don't think so. Lark… Hmm. I think Lark did a dry shampoo? Is that a real thing?"

"Sure," he said. He rinsed her off. "I'm going to do that again, okay?"

"Okay, babe," she said. "It feels wonderful. Thank you so much."

She was leaning back, her eyes closed as he lathered and repeated a third time, just to be sure he didn't miss anything. Then he put in some conditioner. It helped to have a concrete task that required his attention. He absolutely did not want to hit the side where she'd cracked her head. The hospital had shaved the hair down, probably months ago. Right now, on one side she had the long, platinum white hair she'd worn since forever and on the other, a patch of hair that was only an inch and a half long. "This is a good look for you," he told her as he rinsed her again. "Almost punk. Very edgy."

"You like?" She sounded sleepy.

Good. Between the difficult trip up here and the warm, soothing bath, maybe she'd just crash out in bed and he could go sleep on the couch. He was not sleeping in the bed with her and that was final.

"It's different," he told her. "Okay, your hair is done. I'll just go wait for the pizza and…"

She opened her eyes and looked up at him and he knew he was so, *so* screwed. "But, babe…"

Maybe this was karma. He'd done something in a former life and now this life was balancing the scales or however that worked. He must have been a terrible person in that former life because this? This was going to drive him mad.

She hadn't had a real bath in months. She was tired and exhausted.

He had to wash her.

Deep breaths. Think of…oil drills. Computer interfaces. Cloud computing. Yes. Nothing sexy about that.

"Lean forward," he told her. She managed to pull herself up and hug her knees to her chest, resting her head so she could watch him.

"This isn't quite how the honeymoon went, is it?"

"Nope," he replied, all of his attention focused on the soap and the washcloth and…and the oppressive heat he'd lived through in Bahrain. Hot and dry and miserable. And he'd been alone. It'd been hell on earth.

His thoughts firmly centered on the furnace that was Bahrain, he began to wash her back.

Small circles. Back and forth. Getting months in a hospital off of her. Eyes only where they needed to be. Gently. Not too hard.

Other things were hard, though. To the point of pain.

He used the faucet to rinse off her back and shoulders. Then, because he didn't want to seem like a jerk, he said, "Need me to do your arms?"

She held one out and he repeated the process. *Eyes on the elbow*, he told himself as he worked on her body. He finished that arm, then did the other.

"Legs?"

Legs were harder. She leaned back and let her arms float in the water, which meant her breasts were right at the water line again. Plus, when she lifted one leg and set it on the side of the tub, it left him with a view he had trouble *not* admiring.

He resorted to mentally running through that old kid's song—*Hip bone connected to the thigh bone, thigh bone connected to the knee bone*—just because it gave his brain something to do.

Skye hummed. It was a sound of pleasure—relaxation and happiness and maybe a touch of eroticism as he massaged her skin. "God, I'm so glad you're here." She managed to wiggle her toes at him and damned if it didn't get his blood pumping fast.

Okay, he thought, adjusting his pants. *Faster*.

"Jake…" she said, soft and pretty.

The doorbell rang.

Thank God. "Pizza," he said. "I've got to pay the guy."

"I don't want to go back downstairs," she called out behind him. "It's too far away."

"I'll bring it up here. We'll watch TV and call it a date." The words were out before he realized they were leaving his mouth.

What the hell? He was not going to pretend it was a date. They didn't date, not anymore. They were in the process of splitting up and calling it a day. Hell, he shouldn't even be looking at her naked anymore, much less touching her. She was vulnerable. Her memory was compromised. He could not let an injured woman make bedroom eyes at him and he especially could not let the bedroom-eyes thing work.

As he hurried down the long hall toward the steps, he made a deal with himself. If she remembered the way things had fallen apart—and still wanted to try again—well, he'd try again. They had a daughter, after all.

But she had to remember. And as the doctor himself had ordered, she had to remember on her own.

Which meant he was acting as her caregiver here. Not a husband.

Although they were still married.

God, what a problem.

He paid for the pizzas and found a roll of paper towels in the kitchen. Fine. Perfect. Their first year married, when he'd been building his business from scratch and Skye had been taking whatever graphic design job she could get, this actually had been their idea of a hot date. A rented DVD—a cheap one—and a pizza. It hadn't mattered that it was a cheap date. All that had mattered back then was that they were together.

As he headed back upstairs, he hoped like hell she was out of the tub and wearing…something. He didn't know what. Even those clothes she'd come home in would be better than nude. He was going to be strong, he really was. But he'd appreciate it if he didn't have to have his resolve tested on a second-by-second basis.

He hurried back to the bedroom and was crushed to see that the bed did not contain a fully clothed, dry Skye. "Skye?"

"I need help, please," she called out from the bathroom. "I'm…I'm afraid I'll slip and hit my head."

Dammit. He set the pizzas down on top of a dresser that was at the foot of the bed and, girding his loins as much as humanly possible, went back into the bathroom.

She was still naked.

Of course she was.

Four

Jake stood in the doorway, staring down at her.

Skye shivered. The water was cooling off, but she was pretty sure that wasn't the reason why she was trembling.

No, it was the way he looked at her—with such *desperate* hunger that shivers raced over her body.

She just needed to hold him, to feel close to him again. She'd been alone in a bed for months. *Months*. She needed his warmth. She needed him.

She saw him swallow. "Let's get you out of there," he finally said.

She held out her hands and he pulled her to her feet. Water sluiced down her body, heightening her awareness. After the bathing massage he'd given her, every square inch of her skin felt alive and awake. It was a wonderful feeling, to know she was still alive.

"One foot at a time," he calmly instructed her as he took hold of her arms. "Easy does it."

She got out of the tub and stood still as he wrapped a

big, fluffy towel around her. Then, he looked around and found a bathrobe hanging on the back of the door. "We'll use this. I'll try and get some clothes for you tomorrow. I can have someone go to the apartment and get your things, too." He sort of smiled at her. "I think this is the first time I've ever dressed you. Feels weird."

She laughed. "Definitely not normal," she agreed.

Once he had the robe belted around her waist—it was comically huge on her—he rubbed her hair dry. Well, really, half of her hair. He didn't get near the sore spot.

"Dinner is served," he said with a flourish when he was done.

Skye walked—slowly—out of the bathroom. She felt a million times better—clean and shiny and new.

"Here we go," Jake said, helping her sit on the bed. He got the pizza, set the boxes in front of her and then sat on the other side.

Once they both had a slice, he asked, "Do you want to watch something?" He pointed to the big TV on the wall behind him.

"No, let's talk. I missed so much. How was the job?"

He looked down. "The job. It was good. A little more complicated than I anticipated, though."

"Is that why you got such a nice bonus?" Because this was a very nice house. Huge, yes—but that tub had been divine and the bedroom was gorgeous. They were certainly more comfortable than they'd been when they'd first gotten married. This place would have been out of their reach.

"Yeah," he said, studying his pizza. "Is yours good?"

"The best," she said, taking another bite. It wasn't glamorous or all that seductive but the pizza was quite possibly the best thing she'd ever eaten. "So, what's the plan?"

"The plan?"

"I mean, we're here, Lark has Grace. I wish she could

be here with us, but I know it's not fair to ask you to take care of both of us."

"Um…yeah. The plan. Well, I'm still hammering out the details. Whit Daltry—he's the man I rented this house from—said we could go month-to-month. Your doctors want you to stay local, and I imagine that Grace's do, too. It might be a little while before I can get you back into the apartment."

Something about his answer wasn't right. But, try as she might, she couldn't identify what, exactly, was wrong about it. She didn't have much of an appetite left. "I guess I'm not used to real food," she told him, feeling sheepish and not knowing why. She'd only managed one piece, but he'd eaten almost half of his pizza.

"That's fine. I'll run it down to the fridge." He closed the box lids. "Let me get you tucked in. Tomorrow, we have to do some exercises and you're going to need your rest tonight." He cleared his throat. "I'll, uh, I'll sleep on the couch."

She stared at him. That definitely wasn't right. "What?"

"That way I won't bother you with my tossing and turning," he explained, as if this were a good enough reason for him to *not* sleep in the same bed with her. "And I have to do some work. I don't want to wake you up when I come in later."

"You're going to *work*? But I'm home now. I thought…"

"Skye," he said in a serious voice. "The doctor wants you to rest up. We'll have your exercises tomorrow, but otherwise you shouldn't be overexerting yourself. You need to rest."

"But I'm tired of resting," she snapped. "I'm tired of being in bed alone. I'm here and you're here. I want *you*." When he didn't say anything, she added, "Don't you want me, too?"

"Of course I do. You're all I've ever wanted," he said,

but it wasn't a declaration of love. It wasn't even a declaration of desire. It sounded like...an argument. One he'd had before. Had they fought? "But I'm not going to risk endangering your health for a little lust."

His words cut into her and she wasn't sure why. Lust? What about love? "Can't I at least *hold* you? I've dreamed of sleeping in your arms, Jake. I'm so tired of being in a bed alone." For some reason, she was on the verge of crying. She started blinking. "Please don't leave me alone."

He was glaring at her, as if she were stabbing him in the back instead of asking for her husband to join her in the bedroom. "Is that what you really want?"

"Yes," she said as she wiped at her eyes. "I just want you. We don't have to fool around. You're right. I want to get better, faster. I just don't want to be alone tonight."

He got off the bed and picked up the pizza boxes. "Fine. But I need to log on and check a few things. After that, I'll come to bed." Then he left the room.

It should have felt like a victory, but it didn't. Why didn't he want to be with her? Why was this a fight?

Why had he rebuffed her advances at every single turn?

She dropped her head into her hands, which was not a smart thing to do. Her sore spot throbbed and, darn it all, she *was* exhausted.

Maybe Jake was right. After all, she wasn't operating at one hundred percent. She was barely even able to walk on her own. She probably didn't realize how bad off she still was. And he had said that the doctor had warned that she shouldn't over—overex—overexer—oh, hell. She couldn't even come up with the word. She shouldn't overdo it.

She felt ridiculous. Jake was right. She needed her rest and here she was, pitching a fit about sex.

Skye managed to get the robe off and get underneath the covers. From now on, she'd listen better when he told her something. Of course he only had her best interests at heart.

She yawned, sinking down into the soft bed. The sheets were flannel, so much softer than the scratchy things she'd laid on in the hospital. As much as she wanted to be awake, she couldn't push back against the exhaustion.

Tomorrow, she'd apologize for being petulant. That'd smooth everything over.

But for now, she'd just look forward to waking up in Jake's arms.

Finally, he couldn't stall any longer. Jake had contacted his office assistant and read her the riot act about not forwarding calls from Keaton about this whole mess. He'd replied to emails, one from an oil company in Saudi Arabia about a three-month job and one from a company that was trying to get approval to run a pipeline from Alaska to Louisiana. That was a yearlong gig, but it was in North America. It'd be easier to travel and still see Grace.

He'd even gone down to the little home gym and run at a punishing speed on the treadmill, hoping to burn off the excess energy that Skye seemed to have inspired in him.

Now he was sweaty and hopefully not appealing in any sense. He had on the ratty pair of sweatshorts he slept in and an old T-shirt he'd gotten for free in college. Nothing "hot" there.

It was close to eleven when he silently slipped into the bedroom. It was dark and Skye didn't move on her side of the bed. Good.

He managed to avoid stubbing his toe on the dresser as he worked his way to the bed. But the bed shifted when he sat down and he saw how the covers had gotten tangled up around Skye.

Dang it, it was cold enough in the room that he was going to freeze to death without at least a corner of the blanket. He managed to wrestle a part of it away from her. He thought for a second that he'd managed to do so without disturbing Skye, but then she rolled over and curled up against him.

Oh, *hell*. She wasn't wearing anything. Not even the robe.

He didn't know where to put his hand. Wrapping his arm around her waist would put him too close to her bottom. But bending his arm at the elbow caused physical pain. He settled for stretching his arm out as far as possible along the bed.

"Hmm?" she hummed sleepily.

"It's okay," he told her, praying she wouldn't wake up anymore. "I'm here now."

"Mmm. Love you," she mumbled in reply. And then he felt her body relax into a deeper sleep.

It was hard *not* to feel it, frankly. She had one knee bent so that it overlapped his thigh and her small breasts were pressed against his chest—not to mention the tight hold she had on his waist. He was trapped under her body. It was not the place he wanted to be.

Jake lay there, repeatedly running through the very good reasons why he was gripping the bedsheets with enough force to tear them into strips. She was mentally compromised. She didn't remember that she wanted a divorce. She had forgotten that she didn't love him anymore.

But as the minutes ticked by into hours and the sleep deprivation began to mess with him, he wondered if she would get those two terrible years back at all. Maybe the drifting apart, the fights—the big fight—would all be gone for good.

Maybe…maybe she would love him again. They could just go back to where they'd been before it all fell apart on them. He knew they couldn't really do that—they had a daughter now. No matter what form the future took, Grace would have to be a top priority. But…

What if Skye fell in love with him all over again?

God, his head was a mess—and he wasn't even the one who'd smacked it in a car wreck, for crying out loud. Would it even *be* possible to go back—hit the do-over button and begin again?

As she slept in his arms, he thought and thought and *thought*. Could she still love him?

Could he still love her?

Well, he knew the answer to that question. Of course he still loved her. Even as their marriage had unraveled, he'd loved her. He always had. He'd never stopped.

He just… Hell. He just hadn't done a great job of living with her.

Not that he was doing a great job of living with her right now, either. Of course she didn't remember him going to live in a hotel for a week before he flew over to Bahrain. He'd made sure the rent was covered for the year he was gone on the off chance they would decide to give it another try. He earned twenty times what Skye did with her graphic design business, after all. He wasn't looking to punish her. He just hadn't known if they could be together anymore.

Ten stinking months had passed and he was no closer to that answer. In fact, given the way she was sleeping on him, he'd say he was even further from a definitive answer than he'd been this morning.

If he could do it all over again, would he?

He lifted his arm and settled it around her bare waist.

He would. Heaven help him, he would.

Man, he was so screwed.

When Jake emerged into consciousness the next day, a couple of things hit him all at once. The combination was better than any coffee jolt. He went from zero to one hundred in three blinks of the eye.

Skye was rubbing his chest in long, even strokes.

Her hips were slowly tilting forward and back against his hip.

And he had a raging hard-on.

When he jolted into awareness, she murmured, "Good morning." Then her hand began to slip lower.

"Um, hey," he said, grabbing her hand before she could grab anything else. "Morning. You want some coffee? I'll go make coffee." He tried to peel her off of him, but for a petite woman, she was surprisingly good at anchoring him to the bed.

"I don't want coffee," she all but purred as she tested the grip he had on her hand. "I want you."

"How did you sleep?" he blurted out, desperate to avoid telling her *no* and equally desperate to avoid telling her *yes*. Blood began to pound in his ears, although he wasn't sure how much of it was panic and how much of it was lust.

"Wonderfully." And this time, she did purr as her hips flexed again. "I love waking up with you."

She had, once. Morning sex was the bonus of being married. So was afternoon sex. And evening sex.

His body surged up—and up—at the memories. No. No! He was not going to give in. He was stronger than this.

"We should—we should probably, uh, do the physical therapy exercises first thing," he sputtered. Anything to avoid upsetting her—or taking advantage of her. "Doctor's orders."

In the grand scheme of things, it wasn't much of a lie. The doctor had, in fact, told Jake to make sure she did her exercises and stretches. Just not at—he turned his head and found a clock—8:43 in the morning. Crap. Maybe the doctor had. He must still be trying to adjust to central time after all those months in Bahrain.

"Can't it wait?" she asked as she kissed his shoulder. Then she skimmed her teeth over his skin.

"Nope." He yelped in surprise as desire hammered at a few very specific areas of his anatomy.

"Doesn't sex with my husband count as physical therapy?" At least she didn't sound upset—not yet, anyway. She was still trying her level best to seduce him.

And she was doing a pretty damn good job at the moment. Every fiber of his being wanted to roll into her and feel her move underneath him. He knew what she liked—it'd be easy to pin her hands over her head and drive in hard until their bodies surrendered to each other.

And, his traitorous mind unhelpfully pointed out, it'd erase the lackluster memory of their last lackluster sex.

The time when he'd accidentally gotten her pregnant. Damn.

"Skye, baby," he pleaded as she nibbled her way up his shoulder and toward his neck. "Please. I don't have any condoms and you haven't been exactly on the pill recently. If I got you pregnant right now, that doctor of yours would probably have me arrested."

That worked. She stopped nibbling and tilting and trying to get her hand free of his grip. "Oh." The disappointment was obvious.

In his relief that he'd found an argument that she would buy, he made a fatal mistake. He loosened his grip on her hand.

She knew it, too. Before he could respond, she'd wiggled her hand out of his and slid it down his shorts. Then she wrapped her fingers around his erection. "Other ways to have fun," she said, sliding her hand up and then down his length.

"Skye!"

"Don't be so shocked," she scolded him. "We used to fool around like this all the time, remember?"

Man, how could he forget? No man forgot the first time someone else's hand brought him to climax. It just didn't happen.

He wasn't going to make it. He was going to lose it and ravish her and hate himself the moment they were done because—

Suddenly, from somewhere far away, a bell rang.

The doorbell.

Jake didn't know whether to laugh or cry. And he didn't stop to think about it. He pried her hand off of him and all but threw himself out of the bed. "I'll get it. And start that coffee. And then we'll do the prescribed exercises."

He didn't know if she was upset or disappointed or what. He didn't stick around long enough to gauge her reaction. Instead—and he was not proud of this—he bolted from the room and raced down the stairs. As he flung the door open, he realized he'd been saved by the bell. The thought made him laugh.

"Morning?" Whit Daltry gave Jake a confused look when he opened the door. "Everything okay?"

"What?" Jake realized he must be quite the sight—bed head and yesterday's workout clothes and laughing his fool head off. "Oh, yeah. Everything's fine. Skye just told a joke, that's all."

Then Whit turned and Jake realized the man wasn't alone. "Jake, this is my fiancée, Megan."

"Ma'am," Jake said, shaking her hand as well.

"It's so nice to finally meet you," Megan said. She opened her mouth to say something else, but then took in his appearance and seemed to think better of it. "We're sorry to wake you," she said tactfully. "But we wanted to see if there was anything we could do for you and Skye."

Yeah, Jake could guess what she was thinking. Megan had probably heard a whole truckload of gossip by now. Four years' worth. He cleared his throat and willed his anatomy to stand down, for God's sake. "Come in. Skye's not up yet—we were just about to do her PT."

"We won't keep you from your therapy…" Whit began.

"No—it's fine. Come in. I insist!" Because if he could get Whit and Megan to hang out for a while, then Skye wouldn't be able to pick up where she'd left off. He wracked his brain for something that would convince the two of them to stay. "It's—uh—it's a beautiful home. And Skye really loves how you decorated the bedroom."

"Thanks," Whit said as he continued to stare at Jake as if he had boiled lobsters crawling out of his ears. "We usually rent this to oil executives who are in town for more than a few days."

Jake backed up a step, hoping to get Whit and Megan to follow him in. They didn't. "Well, it's just wonderful. Megan!" he said a little too loudly as another bolt of inspiration struck him. Megan jolted in surprise and stepped to the side, so that she was half hidden behind Whit. Aw, crap—Jake wasn't making the best of impressions here, but desperate times called for desperate measures. "Skye's going to need some clothes and necessities. I'm going to try and hire someone to bring the rest of our stuff from Houston. But that's going to take a few days. Where's a good place to pick up a couple of outfits?"

"I can get her a few things. Do you know her size?"

"Uh…" He didn't want to go check because that meant he'd have to go back into the bedroom where Skye was probably still naked. "Small, probably. Most of her things were lost in the storm."

Megan and Whit shared a look. *Hell.* Jake could just imagine what the gossip was. No, actually—wait. He couldn't. And he didn't want to. He and Skye had probably been the hot topic of gossips on and off ever since they'd slipped away the night after the very public fight with their parents. People would believe whatever they wanted to.

Whit nodded. "Big city, Houston. Nothing like Royal. We're just up the road, so if you need anything, you give us a call," he added. "We've sure been worried about Skye for these past few months."

"I'll pick her up a couple of outfits," Megan added, backing away slowly. "Lounge pants and the like. Good for doing therapy in."

Crap, they were leaving. "Are you sure you can't stay?"

"We really must be going," Megan said. "But it's been nice to meet you. I'll drop off a few things for Skye."

"Jake," Whit said with a nod of his head.

"Thanks," Jake said, resigned to the fact that this distraction had been temporary. Maybe when Megan brought by the clothes, she and Skye would start chatting. Yeah, that'd be good—some quality girl time to divert her attention from sex.

He shut the door and then, just because he needed to have some sense knocked into him, he banged his head against the wood a few times.

"Who was it?"

At the sound of Skye's voice, Jake whirled around. She'd made it halfway down the steps and was leaning heavily on the railing.

She was wearing the T-shirt and pants she'd come home in, but she looked a million times better than she had yesterday. There was a brightness about her that made him want to stare. Aside from the haircut, she was the woman he'd loved *so* much.

"Whit Daltry and his fiancée, Megan," Jake explained, trying to find somewhere else to look and not doing an awesome job of it.

"What did they want?" She took another cautious step downward.

"To see how you were doing. Megan offered to pick you

up some clothes." He considered his options. The good news was that she was dressed and out of the bed.

How much longer was he going to be able to keep this up?

"Well, you're almost down here. Might as well see how you take the rest of those steps and then I'll get the coffee."

He climbed up the last few steps and took her arm—if he had a grip on her, she couldn't grab him. Then they made it down the rest of the way.

"Whew," Skye said. "That's hard work." She tried to give him a jokey smile, but she couldn't quite pull it off.

"This is why we have to do the exercises first," he explained as he led her to the couch. Once he had her sitting down—and the recliner reclining—he said, "It's going to take a while before you're back up to full strength. If you overexert yourself, it's going to knock you down."

"Overexert! That's the word I couldn't remember." She grinned up at him, but then her face darkened. "I'm sorry, Jake. I should have listened to you. I know I can't do everything all at once."

That was all it took to make him feel like a jerk. "It's okay, babe. I can see how you want to make up for lost time."

A smile lit up her face. "I just don't want to miss another second with you."

His heart about stopped. He wanted to tell her the truth. He needed to—this wasn't just a matter of self-preservation, but of honor. He felt wrong letting her go on under the delusion that they were still a happy couple.

"Skye..."

"Yes?" She looked up at him with her big blue eyes. She'd always been his blue-eyed Skye. Always.

And the doctor had said not to tell her the truth. It would upset her and that would be a setback. And the more setbacks she had, the longer Jake would be trapped in this godforsaken town.

"I'm—I'm really impressed you made it downstairs on your own."

"Thanks, hon." But the trip had clearly taken a lot out of her. She leaned back in the recliner and closed her eyes. She looked younger right then, more like the woman he'd run away with and less the like woman he'd left behind. "I believe someone's been trying to make me coffee since I woke up?"

"Right," he said, thankful for the concrete task. "Then we'll do the exercises."

"Can't wait," he heard her groan as he headed to the kitchen to figure out the coffeemaker.

He laughed.

It was a good feeling.

Five

Jake brought her coffee and a bowl of cereal. "After we do your exercises, I'll run out to the store and get some of the things you like," he said when she scowled at the boring bowl of flakes. "We can't survive on delivery pizza, after all."

"I would kill for a croissant," she admitted.

She ate her cereal. Suddenly, she was not looking forward to the exercises. Her mind still thought she was in shape—but Jake was right. The trip downstairs had taken a lot out of her. Stupid legs and their stupid muscles.

Still, the coffee was good and the cereal was…filling.

Jake took her dishes and then came back into the room. He helped her stand and then he was lowering her to the ground. "On your back," he said.

She did as he said, but she waggled her eyebrows at him. "I thought you'd never ask."

He grinned at her, but it seemed…forced somehow. "Okay," he said, looking at a pile of papers on the coffee table. "Let's start with leg lifts. Doesn't that sound awesome?"

She gave him a look. "Not unless you're suddenly defining *awesome* in a new and unpleasant way."

Jake watched her lying there for a moment. "Aren't you going to start?"

"Start what? There are a bunch of different leg lifts. Straight leg? Bent leg?" Heck, even all this talking was wearing her down. "I can't see the picture, you know."

"Oh. Sorry." He held the paper in front of her face. Ah. Bent leg lifts. "It says to keep your feet flat on the floor and extend your leg until it's straight for ten reps, then do the other side."

"Wonderful," she grunted in an entirely unsexy way as she tried to get her legs to bend. "A little help here?"

Jake paused again, and then helped her bend her legs. "Right first," he said. "I'll count."

Skye managed to do a whole three leg lifts before she ran out of steam. "Can I quit now?"

He wrinkled his nose at her. "Seven more. Move that leg, Skye."

"You're going to have to help me," she informed him. Her leg was already shaking from the effort. "I can't do this."

"Yes, you can." Then, after another moment's hesitation, he put his hands on her calf. "Slow and steady wins the race."

Despite the sweat that was beginning to bead on her forehead, she grinned. This was not one of their sexier touches, but even just his hand on her leg was enough to make her more...energetic.

They managed to make it through the rest of the set until Jake finally guided her foot back to the floor. By this time she was panting. "I'm gonna need a reward after this," she told him.

He froze. "I can get you some ice cream. You probably shouldn't have wine just yet."

"That's not the reward I was thinking of," she grumbled as he helped her do the next set of lifts.

"I'm just trying to get you better," he quickly defended.

"Hmph," she replied, but then the lifts got harder and harder and it took all of her concentration to make it through the last few. "Are we done now?"

"You're cute," he said in an offhand way as he flipped to another page. "Here—this one is in the same position."

"Oh, joy."

"Pelvic tilts." He held the picture in front of her. "Set of ten reps. It says…" She saw him swallow. "Lift your bottom off the ground and squeeze your muscles. Hold for five seconds. This one's for your abs and glutes."

"And *then* we're done?"

"Nope. Then we get to do stomach exercises." He had the nerve to sound happy about this.

"Better be a damn good reward." She tried lifting her bottom up, but she couldn't hold it for a count of five.

Jake sighed wearily and then slid his hand underneath to help hold her up. "Focus on squeezing your muscles."

"I hate you right now. You know that, right?"

He didn't reply.

After the pelvic tilts, he helped her roll over and then helped her lift her leg straight toward the ceiling. If she'd thought the stupid leg lifts were hard before, these lifts left her so drained that she couldn't even complain about them.

Then, halfway through the second set, a muscle cramp hit her with the force of a sledgehammer to the butt. "Ow. Ow ow ow *ow*! Cramp!"

"Where?" he demanded, sounding as panicked as she felt.

"Here. *Here*! OW!" She managed to get her hand up to point to the cheek in question.

Then he put his hands on her bottom and began to rub. "Does this help? Because if it doesn't, I'll stop."

"More!" she shouted.

So he kept going. He kneaded her muscle until the cramp had passed. "Better?" he asked.

Well, she was. But she wasn't in the mood to tell him that just yet. "Just a little longer," she said. Now that the sharpness of the cramp had faded, she had to admit the massage was nice. More than nice. "I don't know how much more I can do." That was the truth, too. She didn't want to cramp up anymore.

Then Jake's hands left her body. The loss of his touch and heat made her want to whimper. "Let's see... We're supposed to do two more on the floor, but they're stretches. Damn."

"What?"

"Nothing," he hurried to say. "I just have to stretch your legs. Roll back over."

Skye managed to do that. Then Jake picked up her leg. "Keep the other one straight," he said, studying the picture. "And keep this foot flexed."

Skye did as he told her to as he lifted her leg so it was perpendicular to her body. The tension was tight in the back of her legs. "Feeling that?" he asked

"Oh, yeah." He was standing between her legs, his hands on her body. What she wouldn't give to not be wearing these ugly clothes. And she hated that she was too weak to do much of anything but let him stretch her muscles.

They did the one leg, then the other. Another cramp hit her, this time in the calf. "Ow!"

"Here?" he said, going right for the sore muscle.

"Ah, that's it." She sighed in relief as he worked the tension out of her body.

"I'll call Lark later, ask what we can do to avoid the cramps," he said, not looking at Skye as he massaged her body.

She managed to get her hands up and get hold of his shirt. "Thank you, babe," she murmured, trying to pull him down into her. She might not be able to do anything that was terribly energetic right now, but she could still properly kiss him.

"What are you doing?" he asked, looking alarmed.

"Kissing you," she replied. "I want something to make all that worthwhile."

For a moment, she wasn't sure he was going to let her kiss him—but she didn't understand why. Why was he pushing back against sex so hard?

"Just a kiss," he murmured, looking at her lips. "One kiss. As your reward." Then he put his arms on either side of her head and leaned down into her.

Oh, how she had dreamed of this—feeling his weight surround her.

"I…I missed you, Skye." He said it as if he couldn't believe it. "I missed this."

"Me, too, babe."

He lowered his lips to hers. At first, it seemed as if he was just going to give her a chaste little peck. *Oh, no*, she thought as she ran her fingers into his hair. Now that she finally had him, she wasn't about to settle for a half kiss. It was all or nothing.

"Skye," he groaned into her as she ran her tongue over his lips. "Oh, babe."

And then? *Then* he kissed her. He kissed her *hard*, taking everything she offered. If he'd kissed her like this before the exercises, she would have had more to give him. As it was, she was barely able to loop her legs over his, damn it.

Not that he needed any help. He thrust against her, with only the ugly pants standing between them. *"Oh,"* she moaned into his mouth. "Oh, *Jake*."

She shouldn't have done that because he stopped thrusting against her and kissing her. "Sorry," he mumbled as he pushed himself off of her. "Didn't mean to let it go that long."

She stared at him in confusion as he stood. "You didn't?" She managed to prop herself up into a sitting position— she wasn't going to let him get away from her, not this time—but when she tried to stand, her legs went all gelatin on her. "Oops!"

So she couldn't chase him down. But failing to stand on her own worked as a way to lure him back, too. He was by her side in an instant, lifting her up and setting her back onto the couch. "Easy, babe," he said. His voice was gentle, but his face? It was dark and pissed-looking. "You're overdoing it again. You need to recover before you try anything else. I'll get you something to drink."

"I'm not done with you yet," she called after him. She wanted another kiss—and a whole lot more. She wanted to be sweaty and naked beneath him, their bodies joined together in every way she could physically manage and a few she probably couldn't.

He paused in the doorway to the kitchen and turned back to look at her. "Are you sure?"

"Of course I'm sure. You can't kiss me like that and expect me not to want to seduce you."

He gave her a tight little smile that didn't look happy. "I won't," he promised her. "I won't."

I. Can. Not. Sleep. With. Skye.

And he was going to keep repeating that particular statement until he got it through his thick skull.

But dammit…when she'd been mouthing off to him during PT and then so desperate for a kiss—well, maybe he wasn't as strong a man as he liked to think.

Because right now, she was acting exactly like the woman he'd loved his whole life. Sassy and sultry and ready to challenge him at the drop of a hat.

He knew darned well and good that, if she could, she'd chase him down and refuse to settle for just a kiss.

What was he going to do? He hadn't even been alone in the house with her for twenty-four hours yet and her recovery was going to take weeks—months, even. Months of fending off her advances—of trying to find a way to do so without upsetting her. How long before she remembered that she'd wanted a divorce? How long would he have to play the part of the doting husband? How damn long would he have to lie in bed with her and not make love to her?

Plus, there were also the logistics of the situation. Yeah, he could afford to pass on the next job—but how long could he do that before his company's reputation took a hit? That was no small thing. Yes, he was a millionaire—but he worked for his fortune. He couldn't retire, not yet.

And then there was the fact that he was, at this very moment, living in Royal, Texas. He'd vowed never to come back here and yet, here he was.

He'd run into Keaton within fifteen minutes of crossing city limits. How much longer could he possibly avoid his parents—or worse, Skye's parents? He did not want to deal with Gloria and David Holt, even if Keaton and Lark said they were nicer humans now. And Jake especially did not want to deal with Vera and Tyrone Taylor.

But…he was stuck. Hell, at this point, he didn't even feel all that good about leaving Skye alone so he could run to the store and grab some real food. What if she got it in her head to try the stairs on her own and, after this round of exercises, failed to make it?

Horrible images of her lying broken on the stairs, her head bleeding from where she'd hit it on the railing or wall, crowded into his mind.

Damn it all. He needed help and he couldn't ask Lark and Keaton to ride to his rescue again. They had his daughter. That was more than he should even have to ask of them. But he needed *someone*.

His stomach lurching, he picked up his phone and dialed the old number from memory. Funny how easily it came back to him after all this time.

"Hello?"

Mom. For a second, he almost hung up. The last time they'd spoken, on that horrible night when everything had come to a head, she'd been more concerned with backing up his father than understanding how much Skye meant to him. He'd vowed never to speak to his parents again. But Lark and Keaton had said they'd changed.

"Hi, Mom. It's me—" He didn't get anything else out.

His mother made a little strangled noise and said, "Jake? Jake, honey, is that you?"

"Yeah." He swallowed. He was doing this for Skye and for Grace. Not for himself. "It's me."

"Keaton said you were here, but I was afraid to get my hopes up—oh, honey." She made a noise that sounded like a sniff.

Oh, God—don't cry. He couldn't deal with that right now. "Yeah. I'm back in town. Looks like I'm going to be staying for a little while."

There was a weird click on the other end of the line. "Jake." He started at the gruff sound of David Holt's voice. Lord, Jake was barely prepared to talk to his mother, but his father, too? This was rapidly going from bad to worse. "Where are you at?"

Still, he'd made this call. He had to plow through, no matter how much he wanted to hang up. "Skye's with me. I got us a place in Pine Valley."

"Have you seen Grace?" his mother asked.

"Yeah. Yesterday. I don't know if Skye is strong enough to go see her today, but I'm hoping to take her tomorrow."

"Did you two get married?" his father demanded.

Jake gritted his teeth. "Yes. Three days after we left." He waited for—well, he didn't know what. The parents he knew would start reading him the riot act about throwing his lot in with a lying, cheating Taylor.

"Good," his father said. "You should have."

"Well, I did." He tried not to snarl it, but he wasn't sure he succeeded.

His mother made a tired noise. "How's Skye today? Is she all right?"

"Fine. We just did her exercises and she's resting."

"We've prayed so hard for her—for both of you," his mother said.

"You *did*?" That didn't mesh with the way he remembered his parents issuing that final ultimatum that he stop running around with Skye and start acting like a real Holt—more like Keaton.

"Oh, honey, I know things ended badly—" his father made a *harrumphing* noise "—but we're just so glad you're okay and Skye is getting better. Is there anything we can do to help?"

Jake actually pulled the phone away from his ear and stared at it. Maybe these weren't his parents. Maybe they'd been replaced by space aliens or something.

Keaton and Lark had said that Gloria and David Holt had changed. But never in his wildest dreams had Jake figured they would have changed *this* much. "You're not mad at me? At Skye?"

There was a pause on the other end of the line. Jake realized he was holding his breath. "What good's it going to do?" his mother finally said. "It would just drive you and Skye away again—and this time you'll take Grace with you."

"She's a sweetie," his father added, sounding thoughtful.

"Now," his mother went on in a businesslike tone, "you tell us what you need."

He didn't know what else to say at this point. *I'm not sorry I left? I'm not happy about being back?* Yeah, that didn't seem like the way to go.

"Well, groceries, I guess. Skye's still pretty weak. I'm afraid to leave her alone, but there's not much to eat in this house."

"Of course. I was going to run errands this afternoon anyway. I'll pick up some of your favorite things and, oh! I'll bring a dish," Gloria said, which made Jake smile. That, at least, hadn't changed. "Jake," she added, and he heard her voice waver. Was she crying? "Honey, we're glad you're back."

"We sure are," David said. He didn't sound happy, but then, Jake's dad wasn't the most expressive of guys.

The fact that he was even admitting out loud that he was happy Jake was here was...well, it was something. What, Jake wasn't sure, but it was *something*.

"Yeah, okay," Jake said. He gave them the address and added, "See you soon." He hung up.

He stared at his phone, feeling a weird time/space disconnect. He almost dialed the Taylor number, but then he remembered the look on Lark's face when he'd asked if her parents had been by to see the baby.

One set of parents at a time. And right now, his parents were the safest bet. Jake could deal with the Taylors later. Plus, if his parents were in the house, Skye couldn't try to seduce him again. So that counted for...something.

He sighed. No matter how he dressed it up, he was not looking forward to this. "Babe?" he said, going back into the living room.

"Hmm?" She blinked at him sleepily. "Were you on the phone?"

"Yeah. I called my parents." Or, at the very least, he'd called people who sounded like his parents.

Her eyes opened wider. "And?"

He didn't want to upset her, so he stuck to the facts. "They're going to pick up some groceries so I won't have to leave you alone."

"They…are?" She looked confused, which Jake supposed wasn't weird—he was still pretty confused by the whole conversation himself.

"Yeah. Mom's bringing a dish. They seemed excited to see us." He made sure to emphasize the "us" so that Skye would know she was included in that.

"But I—I look terrible!" Her brow wrinkled. "Oh, man—I'm still wearing the same clothes as yesterday."

He grinned. Of all the things to worry about, that was really pretty low on the list. "You look fine. And remember how I said Megan was going to pick up a few things for you?"

She sat back in the chair and he could tell she was thinking—hard. "Oh. Okay. I remember that."

"Good, babe. You just rest, okay? I'm going to go take a quick shower." He wasn't exactly vain, but yeah—first time he saw his parents in four years? He wanted to be dressed a little better than his workout gear.

She sank back into the chair and let her eyes drift closed again. "Maybe tomorrow we can shower together."

He froze. What was he supposed to say to that? He'd barely kept it together when she'd been in the tub and he'd been fully dressed. How was he going to keep his hands off of her if they were *both* wet and naked?

Six

Skye was working up the energy to kiss Jake again. She'd been sitting on the couch for a while, watching game shows and dozing, and she was pretty sure she'd recovered from the stretching enough that she could get to her feet and walk over to where Jake was sitting at the table, working on his computer.

She didn't like that. Something in her mind wanted to complain about the amount of time he worked—but that also felt foolish. After all, he'd only logged a couple of hours last night. And he'd only been sitting over there for about thirty minutes this morning, after he'd showered and shaved and come back downstairs looking more handsome in a pair of jeans and a light blue button-up shirt than she remembered.

So it wasn't as if he was ignoring her or anything. He *had* to work—she was only starting to think about what the hospital bills were going to look like and she had no idea where she was with any of her clients. She could only hope they'd found other graphic designers to finish their projects.

But that kiss earlier...*wow*. That was the kind of kiss a woman dreamed about. For a blindingly clear moment, she hadn't felt weak or tired or confused. She'd been the woman she'd been before the accident—claimed by a single kiss from Jake Holt.

She needed more. One was not enough. It never had been.

She managed to get the footrest down on the recliner and her bottom scooted to the edge of the seat when the doorbell rang again. She shot the door a dirty look. Who were all these people and why were they constantly foiling her plans to seduce her husband?

"I've got it," he said as he shot her a wry smile. "Don't get up."

It'd taken too much effort to get the footrest down. She wasn't going to put it back up. Instead, she sat, listening.

"Oh, hi—that's great. Come on in." Jake led a curvaceous, beautiful redhead into the room.

Jealousy gripped Skye, which was ridiculous because she didn't even know who this woman was. But she was beautiful and Skye couldn't help but envy her curves. Skye looked down at her small breasts and not-there hips that were hidden under baggy, unisex clothes, and remembered her own half-and-half haircut. Ugh. No wonder Jake wasn't interested.

"Skye, this is Megan Maguire—she's engaged to Whit Daltry, the man we're renting the house from."

She was not in the mood for visitors. She just wasn't. "Hi."

"It's so good to meet you, Skye," Megan gushed. "We're all just so glad you're awake! You were quite the story."

Jake cleared his throat and shot what looked like a meaningful gaze at Megan. But then he looked back at

Skye. "Megan stopped by this morning—remember? I told you that she was going to pick up some new clothes for you."

"Jake said you were a small—I hope that's right," Megan said with a wide grin.

Skye cringed. Her mother had always picked out clothes for her—dressing Skye as though she were a mini-Vera Taylor in frilly dresses and white pants that wrinkled and stained if Skye looked at them wrong.

In Houston, Skye had favored simple clothes—blue jeans and yoga pants, with light cotton tops. She'd had a couple of sexy dresses for when she and Jake were able to afford a night out.

Megan held up a big shopping bag. Yes, Skye did remember Jake saying something about Megan bringing clothes for...oh! Because his parents were coming over and if she remembered anything, it was that she was always trying to win over Gloria and David Holt—or, at the very least, Gloria.

Things had changed and she had a second chance to make a first impression. Skye forced herself to smile. God only knew what was in that bag, but it couldn't be worse than what she had on now. "Yeah, I'm a small." She eyed Megan's figure and wondered what kind of clothes this woman had picked out—certainly not the sort of thing that would fit Skye's flat chest.

She shouldn't be jealous. She knew this was an overreaction. Jake had always reassured her that he loved her body just the way it was.

Megan looked her over. "I grabbed a few other necessities. Would you like me to brush your hair out?"

Skye touched the side of her head. "Would you? It's still kind of hard to lift my arms at this point."

"Sure can." Megan beamed.

"There's a bathroom down here," Jake said, looking

relieved. "I've got some work to do. Megan, thanks so much," he added.

He helped Skye to her feet and then led her to the bathroom. Done in creams and reds, it was lovely, much like the rest of the house. "I'll leave you ladies to it," he said as he escaped.

"All right," Megan said gleefully before turning to Skye. "First order of business—we've got to get you out of those hideous clothes. No offense."

"None taken. Thanks for doing this for me. I don't even know you."

"I manage the Royal Safe Haven animal shelter," Megan explained as she unpacked the bag she'd been carrying. It contained a brush, hair bands, deodorant and a small makeup palette with a pink lipstick, a nearly matching pink blush and three shades of eye shadow. "I thought you might want to feel pretty after being in a hospital for so long," she explained.

Skye gaped at the goodies. Never had pink lipstick looked *so* good. "How did you know?"

"You've been in that bed for a long time and I've got eyes," Megan told her as she laid out three pairs of yoga pants—black, gray and navy—and some really cute tops. "That Jake Holt is a fine specimen. I just figured that any woman would want to look her best for him." She held up a six-pack of bikini briefs. "Will these work?"

Skye nodded. They were the right size and in bright patterns. Sure, cotton underwear wasn't silk and lace, but she could envision how parading around in nothing but a tiny pair of panties would be sure to get Jake's attention. "Perfect."

"Which top do you want right now?"

"That one," Skye said, pointing to the one that was a robin's-egg blue with a white trim.

"I thought so."

Megan helped Skye get her T-shirt off and the new top over her head without commenting on Skye's underwhelming assets. Then she got the brush. "Any spot I should avoid?"

Skye showed her where the hair was shorter. "It's still a little sore," she explained.

"Very punk," Megan said approvingly. "Although if you wanted to experiment, a pixie cut would look fabulous on you."

"I've never had it short," Skye said as Megan brushed her hair. "I don't even know what that would look like."

"No worries, then. How about a low ponytail pulled to the side?"

"You're good at this," Skye told her as Megan began to create order out of the chaos that was her head.

"Dog grooming," Megan laughed as she twisted in the hair band. "Okay, let me see your face."

In short order, Skye had shadow on her lids, a little blush on her cheeks and a touch of color on her lips. "He always was a fine specimen," Skye said as Megan applied the finishing touches. She didn't know why she was opening up to this woman, but she felt as if she needed to explain. "We've been together since I was six and he was seven."

Megan whistled. "That long?"

"He's always been the one," Skye told her. "Always."

"Then you'll look your best for him." Megan helped Skye stand.

Skye looked at her reflection. The side ponytail managed to hide the shorter hair. The makeup was subtle, but the color on her cheeks and the shade of the shirt made her eyes pop. "Wow, I look *normal*."

"Is that good?"

Skye snorted. "Compared to where I was? This is *fabulous*." Sure, she wasn't dressed for a hot night out on the town, but just to be wearing a top that fit her was such a vast improvement. "You think Jake will like it?"

"I think he'll have a hard time keeping his hands off of you," Megan said with a wink.

"Mission accomplished!" Skye replied. She pivoted. She still had on the baggy pants, but the top was fitted with darts at the waist. She looked like a woman again. "It's wonderful. I can't thank you enough, Megan."

"Don't mention it," Megan said. "We all had to pull together after that storm. You have Jake give me a call if you need something else."

"I will." Skye hugged Megan. This—this was something she'd wanted. She and Jake had been on their own for so long, with no one else who'd come to their aid when they needed it. Skye had wanted to return to Royal because she'd missed the community—even something as simple as a neighbor who was good at dog grooming. "Come visit again," she told Megan. "And when I'm stronger, we'll have to go out for coffee or something."

Megan gave her a sly smile. "Oh, I have a feeling I'll be seeing you again before too much longer. I'll leave you to that fine specimen of yours."

After Megan left the bathroom, Skye managed to get the baggy pants off and, leaning heavily on the counter, put a cute pair of pink and white panties and the new gray yoga pants on. It was only when she was pulling everything up that she noticed her stomach—and the long red scar that cut across the lower part.

That's right, she thought, tracing the scar with her fingertips. *I had a baby. Grace.*

Longing filled her. She'd wanted a child so badly, but they'd been waiting until their finances were a little more stable.

And somehow…she'd had Grace. She didn't remember

even being pregnant. She hated that. She should remember being pregnant. But it just wasn't there.

She found herself staring at her hand. She didn't have her ring on—she didn't have her earrings in, either. Maybe Lark had them? If they hadn't been lost in the wreck? She couldn't remember.

Suddenly, she wanted that ring and those earrings back. Jake had gotten them for her…had that been last year? Yes, that seemed about right. He'd gotten her very expensive diamonds because—because—damn it. Because he could afford them, he'd said. To make up for the small wedding ring. Was that right?

Skye wanted to thump the side of her own head to try and jar some of the memories loose from the holes they were all stuck in.

She wouldn't have lost the earrings in the tornado, would she? She studied her earlobes. The diamonds had had screw backs, she remembered. It'd taken her almost ten minutes to get them in properly when Jake had given them to her on…on their anniversary. Yes, that felt right. And she'd just left them in. It was too hard to take out every night. She'd gotten used to them being there, as if they were a part of her. Just like the ring was.

The screws wouldn't have come unscrewed, would they? Those were serious earrings. And her lobes hadn't been torn through, she saw. So the earrings were…where?

She wanted them back. Jake had bought them for her.

She would not panic. She just had to remember to ask her sister if the hospital had given her the ring and earrings. Those were things Jake had given her. She hoped she hadn't lost them.

After a final check of her reflection, she decided she'd ask Jake to take her to see her daughter soon.

But the first order of business was to show Jake the new and improved her.

* * *

Jake tried to focus on his work. He had several emails from his contacts in Bahrain that required his full attention. The system he'd helped install had experienced a few hiccups since his departure and he really, *really* didn't want to have to fly back over to the Middle East at this point.

Ah, good. The North American job he'd bid on wanted to schedule a video interview to discuss what Texas Sky Technologies could do for their project and they were flexible on the start date. If Jake wanted to take two weeks of the vacation time at the beginning of the contract, he could.

That was good. He'd sent back some times he hoped he'd be available for the interview and then considered the best way to go about making sure he was.

Maybe if the visit with his parents went well, they could come by again. Or Jake could take Skye to Lark's and let her play with the baby. There had to be a way to make it work.

That was a lot of ifs and he knew it.

He kept glancing back toward the small hall that led to the bathroom. How long had they been in there? Jake was afraid Megan would let something slip that would confuse Skye. And that would be bad.

It wasn't helping that his parents would be over soon. He was nervous. The last time he'd seen either of them was... that last night. Jake and Skye had been having a romantic dinner at Claire's, the nicest restaurant in this town. It'd been the anniversary of their first time together. For a couple as inseparable as Jake and Skye had been, there really wasn't a first-date anniversary or first-meeting anniversary. They'd always just been together. So they'd taken to celebrating their first time. Romantic dinner, candles, wine—the whole nine yards. Jake had been out of college for a year and Skye had just graduated. They'd been

adults and had decided they could go public with their relationship.

In retrospect, it wasn't the smartest thing they'd ever
done. The blowup had been epic. He and Skye had left the
next night and he, at least, had never looked back.

That was all in the past now, he reminded himself. And
he couldn't change the past.

"She'll be out in a minute," Megan said, sailing into
the room. "I got her all fixed up." She handed Jake the re-
ceipt for the clothes.

"That's great." But even as he said it, he realized that
might not be a good thing. He was already having enough
trouble keeping his hands off of Skye in those hideous
clothes. How hard would it be to steer clear of her when
she looked good?

He dug out his wallet and handed Megan two fifties.
"Really appreciate it."

"I'm happy to help. I tried not to say anything that might
confuse her," she added. "I don't know if you realize it, but
the whole town has been rooting for her to pull through.
She's come to symbolize Royal. We're all just thrilled that
she's on the road to recovery." Megan looked at her watch.
"Oh, I've got to go—a transfer of kittens is coming in. You
call me if you need anything else, okay?"

"Thanks," Jake said, showing her out. And he did appreciate it. But he still would feel weird about having to call
someone for help—someone who wasn't Skye, that was.

Man, he was not used to this depending-on-other-people
thing.

"Jake?" From behind, Skye's voice reached out and caressed him. "What do you think?"

He knew even before he turned around that he was
in trouble. He could hear it in her voice—she knew she
looked good.

I. Can. Not. Sleep. With. Skye, he repeated as he pivoted.

Even knowing that she was going to look better didn't prepare him for what he saw. Megan had gotten her hair smooth and in a neat little ponytail. He couldn't even see the shorter hairs. The clothes were close-cut and flattered her slender figure. And...

And she was wearing makeup. Of course she was. Megan would have come prepared, damn it.

"Well?" She managed to do a little turn to show him how the tight pants cupped her bottom. His hands started to itch. Would it be so wrong to help himself to her body, instead of helping her through a rep?

Yes. Yes, it would. He ground his teeth together and forced his hands to stay at his sides as she finished her turn.

"You look amazing," he told her—and he was not glossing over the truth this time.

"I feel *so* much better," she told him. "I need to write Megan a thank-you note." Her brow wrinkled. "Can you remind me to do that?"

"Sure." Then, helpless, he watched her take hesitant strides to where he was standing. She wobbled a little, but she kept her balance and didn't collapse into his arms.

She was going to kiss him and, because he wasn't looking at the Skye who'd served him with divorce papers—hadn't been talking to that Skye for the last day—he was going to let her. He was powerless to resist this Skye.

Her arms slid around his neck. Yes, she leaned into him a little more than she might normally, but she seemed so far from the woman he'd had to carry into the house yesterday that he couldn't mentally reconcile all the different versions of Skye in his mind.

As she pulled his head down to hers, all he could think was that this was *his* blue-eyed Skye. *His.*

He sagged back against the door as he surrendered to her kiss. The weight of her body against his took what control he had and smashed it to small, unrecognizable bits. He knew—*knew*—there were valid reasons why he shouldn't be kissing her, shouldn't be encouraging her to kiss him some more, but for the life of him, he couldn't remember what those reasons were.

Not when she nipped at his lower lip. Not when she opened her mouth for him. And not when she rubbed against him, her body setting his on fire.

He couldn't help it. His hands slid down her back until he was palming her bottom. Small and firm—just like she was—just enough to hold. Perfect for him. Perfect.

"Jake," she whispered as he directed his kisses lower— down her neck, toward her exposed collarbone. "Don't stop. Don't—"

The bell rang. Again.

This was getting to be a pattern.

They both jumped. "What is with that damned doorbell?" Skye demanded. Then she looked at him and smiled. "Lipstick. Pink is not entirely your shade."

The doorbell rang again. Jake scrubbed the back of his hand over his face and steadied Skye on her feet before he answered the door.

And there, on the stoop, stood his mother. She seemed smaller than he remembered, the lines on her face a little deeper.

"Jacob Holt! Oh, my baby...I can't believe you're here!"

Next to him, Skye gasped as Gloria Holt rushed into the house and swallowed Jake up in a massive mama-bear hug.

"Uh—hi, Mom," he said, struggling to breathe through the grip she had him in.

"And Skye!" Gloria released Jake and turned to Skye, who looked like a deer caught in the headlights.

The next thing either of them knew, Gloria had wrapped her arms around Skye. "My word, it's just so good to see you up and about. We've been worried sick about you, sweetie."

"You...have?" Skye asked.

"Easy, Mom," Jake said, trying to pry his mother off of his wife.

"Son," David Holt said, as he came through the door next, his arms full of paper grocery sacks. Which meant there wouldn't be any awkward hugging from the older man. At least, not yet.

"Dad," Jake said. "Let me help you out."

"I got it," his dad said gruffly. Yeah, some things hadn't changed. "Skye, it's good to see you up and around."

Skye gave David a worried smile. "It is?"

"Oh, dear, you don't remember, do you?" Gloria clucked. "You look so much better than you did in that hospital."

"You came to see me in the hospital?"

"Why, of course we did! I made it in two or three times a week to spend time with Grace and I'd come sit with you and read to you." Gloria looked wistful. "I've been praying for you to come back to us."

"You *have*?" This time, Skye was less worried and more confused.

"Mom," Jake said with a warning in his voice. "We're taking it slow and easy here." Because this crash course in Holt reintroductions wasn't going down easy. Skye was beginning to look panicked. Since his dad wouldn't let him help with the groceries, Jake stepped back to wrap his arm protectively around her waist.

"Oh—yes. Of course. I'm sorry, sweetie."

"You read to me?"

"I'll just put these away," David said, neatly sidestepping a conversation that might contain emotions. *What a surprise*, thought Jake.

"I sure did." Gloria watched her husband until he was

safely in the kitchen. "I know David isn't the best with expressing his feelings—"

Jake choked. Yeah, that was one way to put it.

"But," Gloria went on, "when they found you pregnant and they managed to save you and Grace—well, you gave us a granddaughter. We're family now, honey."

Then Gloria swallowed them both up in another monster hug. Jake was afraid she was crying.

"Anyway," Gloria said, stepping back and dabbing at her eyes, "when Jake called this morning, I jumped at the chance pick up some groceries. Honey, you just look wonderful. I'm so glad you're both here together."

"Mom," Jake said again, glaring at her. "Slow. Easy." *Stop talking before you screw something up*, he mentally added.

Because the last thing he needed was his parents to inadvertently set Skye off.

"Of course, dear," she said, patting his arm. "I brought a casserole—chicken enchiladas. Your favorite, Jake!"

"That sounds…good," Skye said, sounding a little better.

"I'll get the last bags," David Holt said as he passed by them. "Your mother bought enough to last you weeks."

Gloria was still standing there, beaming at the two of them. Well. Aside from his mother's habit of talking enough for both her and her husband, this actually wasn't bad. His parents were acting how Keaton had said they would—warm and welcoming to a Taylor daughter.

But Jake needed to get his mom to stop talking. Now.

"Let me get Skye back to the couch," he said to Gloria. "Then I'll come help put away the groceries."

"Oh, I can—" Jake cut her off with a look that he hoped like hell said, *Go into the kitchen, please*. "Ah. Yes. Groceries. Then we'll have lunch!" She headed into the other room.

Jake walked Skye over to the couch.

"They seem nice?" she said.

And he couldn't help it. He loved this woman. He wanted…he wanted so much with this Skye. But what would happen when she got those two years back? "I think they're really trying," he said with a quick kiss. "Lunch?"

She leaned back with a dreamy smile on her face. "Lunch sounds good," she called after him as he hurried to the kitchen before his mother could do something else that put everything at risk.

"How is she?" Gloria asked in a quiet voice as she opened the cabinet doors to find a place to put a box of spaghetti. "She looks a lot better."

"She is better—but the doctor said that we can't overload her with information right now. She's lost about two years and I'm not supposed to tell her what she's forgotten. She's supposed to remember it on her own."

His mother paused, another box of pasta in her hand. "What did happen in those two years, Jake? Heavens, those four years?"

Great. Wonderful. Just when he thought things couldn't get any worse. Time to go with the supershort version. "We got married. I started a company. We lived in Houston, but I traveled for work. Skye had a freelance graphic design business."

His mother nodded her head thoughtfully. "Is that where you've been for the last four months? On a job?"

Jake shut his eyes and breathed deeply, trying to find the calm. He would not get into a fight with his mother. A fight would upset Skye and, after all, his parents were trying to help. He could cook for Skye now. That was a good thing.

"I was in Bahrain," he told her. "In the Middle East, working on IT for an oil-production facility." Then, because his mother was obviously not buying this as a good-enough reason for the radio silence while Skye had been hospitalized, he added, "I was contractually bound to stay there and finish the job. Skye knew that. She didn't want to go to Bahrain. We had agreed, but she's forgotten all about Bahrain and I *really* don't think reminding her of it is the best thing for her mental well-being right now so please, for the love of God, go easy on her. As far as she remembers, the fight at Claire's is still kind of fresh in her mind."

His mother just regarded him with that all-knowing look that had always spelled trouble back when he was a kid sneaking out past his bedtime to meet Skye. But she didn't nag, thank heavens. Instead, she said, "All right, dear. I'll keep it light. Can I talk about Grace?"

"Yes, but I haven't taken Skye to see her yet. I was going to let her get a day of rest under her belt first. It's fine if you talk about Grace, but don't ask about the pregnancy. Skye doesn't remember any of it and I don't want to stress her out."

Just then, David Holt came back in with another armful of groceries and the covered dish Gloria had been using for church socials since probably before Jake had been born. David glanced at the two of them and said, "Everything okay in here?"

"Fine," Jake said. And that? That was a lie. Not a gloss, not a half-truth. A flat-out lie.

Nothing was fine now. He was living with a woman who didn't remember falling out of love with him. He was standing in a kitchen in Royal, Texas, talking to his parents. Less than two miles away, his brother was probably singing Jake's daughter to sleep.

Jake had no idea what was going to happen next month, next week, tomorrow—hell, at the rate he was going, the next ten minutes were going to be chock-full of surprises. At this point, even Bigfoot ringing his doorbell wouldn't be *that* astounding.

"Sweetie," Gloria said, sounding…nice about it? "I know this has probably been a lot."

"Yeah," he agreed, wondering if he was actually on the verge of apologizing to his parents. His parents, for God's sake. "I'm sorry. I'm just worried sick about Skye and trying to figure out how to take care of her and Grace and not lose my business in the process."

"Are you all talking about me or what?" Skye called out from the living room.

"Sorry," Jake called back. He saw that his dad had carried in a variety pack of tea. "Thirsty? We have tea now."

"Please," Skye called back. "You know how I like it."

Jake went to find the kettle, but somehow, his mother beat him to it. "Go on," she said, shooing him out of the kitchen. "You two have a lot to catch up on. I'll get lunch ready and we'll all eat together."

Great. He wasn't looking forward to it, but on the other hand, the longer his parents stayed here, the less opportunity there'd be to find Skye so…*tempting.* "That sounds good."

Jake went to sit next to Skye. "How is it in there?" she asked in a worried voice. "Are they mad at us?"

"No, babe," he said, taking her hand in his. "I think…" He sighed. "I think they've changed. Grace helped."

"So they're not upset? Really? Oh, Jake—that's great!" She leaned her head against his shoulder. "I always hoped we'd be able to come back, you know."

He was going to get an ulcer at this point. He did, in fact, know that. Skye hadn't said much about it their first two years together, but after that?

Yeah, she'd started voicing that hope. She wanted to be able to come home, see if maybe their families would be able to accept that she and Jake were married. And Jake had had no interest in even testing the waters. He wouldn't say it was *the* issue that drove a wedge between them, but it was still a spike that got hammered into that wedge.

"I know," he told her, mostly because he couldn't think of a better evasion. He wanted to go through the list of reasons why he didn't want to stay here—but he didn't want to upset her, especially not after dressing down his mother for the exact same reason. "We'll…we'll visit. When you're better and Grace is stronger, we'll—"

"But Jake," she said and he knew he was doing a lousy job of tap-dancing around the truth of the matter. "I thought we might, you know, be able to move back here. To come home. This would be a great place to raise Grace…" Her brow wrinkled. "When can I see her?"

"Let's get through the night," he told her. "This is your first day home, after all—I don't want you to overdo it. If you feel up to it tomorrow, I'll call Lark and we'll go over."

These were all perfectly reasonable responses. So why did he feel so bad about saying them?

Hell, he didn't know. He didn't know anything anymore.

He knew even less when Gloria came out carrying a plate loaded with her famous chicken enchilada casserole and a napkin for Skye. Jake got his own plate and they all sat around and ate and chatted as if the past two years hadn't happened—not to mention the last decade.

His mother was warm and effusive—she managed to keep the conversation light, as promised—and his father let his mother do the talking. There was something comforting about it. No one accused him of betraying the Holt family name to consort with a no-good Taylor. No one tried to convince him to drop Skye for "a nice girl." It was almost…normal. It was how it should have been all those years ago.

Which was great, but also another obstacle he was going to have to deal with sooner or later. Because this was exactly the sort of family interaction Skye had wanted more and more, and if she thought this was the new normal, she was going to demand it long after she recovered.

And Jake...

He wanted his wife back. The wife she was being right now—not the quiet, resentful woman she'd morphed into over the past couple of years.

Would he even consider moving back to this town? To just acting as if the past had blown away in a tornado—like they were doing right now?

"I'll get these things," Gloria said, gathering up the plates after they'd finished the meal.

"I'll help," Jake offered.

For a moment, he thought his mother was going to refuse his help, but then she and his father exchanged a look. David gave her a little nod and she said, "Why, that'd be nice. Will you two be okay?"

"Sure," harrumphed David as he dug out his phone. "I can show Skye pictures of Grace, if that's okay."

"That should be fine..." Jake said nervously as he followed Gloria into the kitchen.

"You have pictures?" Skye gasped.

Suddenly, this seemed like a bad idea. He knew he couldn't filter Skye's world for forever, but...well, his father had always been a man of few words. Surely he wouldn't set Skye off, would he?

Gloria already had the dishes in the dishwasher by the time he got in there with his own. Jake wasn't sure what he was supposed to say—were they still keeping it light? "Thanks again for getting groceries. How much were they?"

Gloria waved him off. "Don't worry about it."

"Mom, I'm going to pay you back. That was at least a hundred bucks' worth of groceries. I didn't expect for you to foot the bill." Already, his irritation was growing. He should have stayed in the living room.

She leaned against the counter, a stern look on her face and her arms crossed over her ample chest. He knew he wasn't going to win this argument. "It's a small price to pay to make up for how we treated you two," she said in a matter-of-fact kind of way.

"What?"

"We shouldn't have forced you to choose. I guess that, deep down, I knew that if you'd stayed on the ranch with us, you'd have come to hate us for driving Skye away. We wasted a lot of time trying to keep you two apart and it never did us a lick of good."

Jake stood there, gaping at her. "Really?"

From the living room came the sound of a happy Skye going, "Awwww! Look at her tiny hands!"

Jake tried to regain his footing. "Why are you apologizing now?"

"Why do you think? You're here. Keaton said you weren't planning on disappearing again, but this has troubled my conscience for the last four years—your father's, too, although he's still too stubborn to admit it. We've missed you terribly."

"Mom, I don't know what to say." He scrubbed a hand through his hair. "I—I didn't think you missed us at all." Actually, after that last fight? He'd been operating under the assumption that not only did his parents not miss him, but they were actively glad Jake was gone.

"And her feet!" came the gushing squeal from the living room.

"Oh, now." His mother brushed aside his comment with a wave of her hand. "Of course we did. Your father took your leaving real hard. He did a lot of soul searching about the land dispute and realized it wasn't worth losing his son over."

"Really?" Because that was not the impression Jake

had gotten when his father had said, *Either you're with us or against us.*

His mother looked at him as if she were really seeing him as an adult for the first time. "Of course, that was before the tornado knocked down town hall."

"What? What does that have to do with anything?"

She gave him a small smile, but there was no joy in it. "As they cleared away the rubble, they found the original land deed that shows the Taylors moved the fences."

What had he thought earlier today, about not even knowing what the next ten minutes had in store for him? Because he'd pretty much nailed it. "So—what, Tyrone Taylor just gave the land back?"

"Oh, no. I believe he's claiming the deed was forged— that sort of thing. There's probably going to be a lawsuit. Keaton is handling that. But you being gone and then your father being proved right—well, it's taken the fight out of him. Especially now."

In the background, Skye cried out, "She's so *small*! Oh…"

"Why now?"

"Why, Grace, of course. And I expect that Lark and Keaton will start a family before too much longer. To see Lark with Grace…" Gloria sighed in contentment. "The land will go to our family no matter what."

"So…now what?"

"That's what I was going to ask you," she said. "Will you two stay?"

What would it take for a bolt of lightning to strike out of the blue and fry him where he stood? Because being electrocuted had to be more fun than this conversation. "Mom, we have a life in Houston."

"I know, I know. But I'd sure love to have my grand-baby close by while we're still here. Keaton told you we're thinking of retiring to Alabama?"

"Yeah, he mentioned something about that." It hadn't made any sense at the time, but now—knowing that the feud was all but over and that his father wasn't going to fight Tyrone Taylor anymore? It made a lot more sense now.

"If you stayed, you two could move into the ranch house. It'd be a great place to raise a family."

If. That was one hell of an *if.* Jake hadn't wanted to stay because he wanted nothing to go with his family or the feud.

But if the feud was close to being resolved and half of his relatives were going to be living in Alabama, of all places...

It was still a huge *if.* "I just need to focus on Skye and Grace right now. But," he added when his mother busted out her disappointed face, "I'll think about it."

She beamed at him. "Thank you, dear."

"Jake?" Skye called out. "You've got to come see these!"

Jake was grateful for the out. He and Gloria headed back to the living room, where David was sitting next to Skye and holding his phone so she could see it. "Babe, look," Skye said. Her eyes were welling up with tears. "That's our girl."

The photo was of an impossibly small baby—so swaddled that Jake could barely see her face—lying in Gloria's arms. David was crouched down next to her, the silliest grin Jake had ever seen on the man's face. "Wow," he said. Had he ever seen his parents look so happy? Not when it involved a Taylor, that was for sure.

"Jake said if I was feeling up to it, we'd go see her tomorrow. Lark's got her." Skye sounded enthusiastic as she said it, but there was no missing the yawn she tried to hide behind her hand.

"Take pictures," Gloria ordered. "We'll send you these."

"Oh, good. I want to do baby announcements and everything. I've missed so much…" She looked up at Jake. "I feel like I've missed years."

He didn't want her to get those years back, which was selfish and shortsighted, but it was what it was. He wanted her to stay like this. He didn't want her to remember that he hadn't been enough to keep her happy, that she'd wanted something more.

"Well," Gloria announced, "you need your rest. But you call us if you need anything, you hear?"

"Thanks, Mom." He walked them out to their car. "It's…it's been good to see you again."

And the funny thing was, he wasn't sure if that was a lie or not. He just didn't know anymore.

He wasn't that surprised when his mom hugged him, but when his dad hugged him? Yeah, that wasn't what he'd expected. "Son," David said, "I'm—well, I'm glad you're home."

Which was probably as close to an actual apology as Jake would ever get out of the old man. "Me, too, Dad."

He was stunned to see the old man's eyes watering when David abruptly let him go a second later. "We'll be seeing you," he said gruffly and all but ran to the car.

Gloria shot Jake an I-told-you-so smile and waved before she got in the passenger side.

Once they were gone, Jake stood there and tried to process everything. The storm, the baby, the feud, his family, Skye's family—and Skye. Always, he came back to Skye.

She'd remember, wouldn't she? And when she did…he might very well lose her again.

He didn't want to lose her again. He'd already lost her once—nearly twice, in that accident. Could he do what it would take to keep her? Even if it meant dealing with everything, all at once again?

Was this how Skye felt? That suddenly there was so

much new information to process and none of it made a lick of sense?

He couldn't stand out here all day—that much was for sure. What if Skye got it into her head to come look for him? She wasn't steady enough yet.

When he got back into the house, he saw that Skye had her eyes closed. She opened them when he shut the door. "I don't remember your parents being that nice, but they wore me out. I think I need a nap."

"Good plan." If she slept, he could finish up his email.

"Will you snuggle with me?" She held up her arms—not in the way that said she wanted him to help her stand, but in the way that made it clear that she wanted him to pick her up like he had last night. "Please?"

The answer should be *no*. A firm *no*. He had things to do and he was having enough trouble keeping his hands off of her to begin with.

"Please, Jake. You're right—I'm too tired to do anything right now. Including walk."

How could he say no to her? He couldn't. He *couldn't*. And he was tired, too. His head couldn't process anything on the little sleep he'd gotten last night.

So he swept her into his arms and carried her upstairs. She rested her head against his shoulder and yawned. "We'll try to see Grace tomorrow, right?"

"Right," he agreed as he carried Skye into the bedroom and set her down on the bed. Then he kicked off his shoes and slid in next to her, pulling the covers up over both of them.

He wrapped his body around hers, and buried his nose in her hair. He shouldn't be in bed with her, shouldn't be holding her tight. He absolutely should *not* be thinking about ways he could make this work.

He didn't know how to make it work, though. What about his business? What about the jobs he'd bid on?

And their families. If he fought for her again, he'd have to deal with his family and hers. Maybe his family had changed. Maybe, instead of the death sentence that coming back to Royal had always felt like, it'd be…tolerable.

Could he do tolerable? Could he do it for her? For them?

Her body relaxed into sleep in his arms and he found himself thinking of their wedding. Of finally having escaped from the oppressive feud, of no longer giving a damn what their families thought. Just Jake and Skye, together—forever.

This was forever, wasn't it?

He could not lose her again. He didn't know who he was without Skye. The ten months in Bahrain had been so far beyond hell on earth—he'd been little more than a zombie. He'd left half of himself behind when he'd left her. Plus, she was now the mother of his child.

Maybe he was too tired to be making decisions. Maybe he should get up, go back downstairs and get some work done. Maybe he should still try to keep his distance from her…

Or maybe he should fight for her. For them. He should show her that, no matter what happened in the past, whether she remembered it or not, he would always be here for her.

And then, maybe when she remembered how they fell apart, it'd be tempered by the new memories of how they'd put themselves back together.

He could love her again. He could give her what she wanted. He could *be* what she wanted. Because if he didn't at least try, she would be gone. Again.

He pulled her in close and kissed her on the forehead.

He *wouldn't* let that happen.

He just wouldn't.

Seven

Skye was floating through yet another dream—this time, Jake was lying next to her in bed, his arms around her, his warmth surrounding her.

She was so tired of this dream. It was a nice dream, but she wanted it to be real. She wanted the real Jake, not just the ghost of him that drifted through her sleep. "I want you to be real," she sighed in frustration.

"I am," he replied, kissing her on the neck. "I'm right here, my blue-eyed Skye."

As his lips moved over hers, his hands skimmed over her back and down to her bottom, where he squeezed. Languid heat began to build in her body—which wasn't something she remembered happening with Dream Jake. Dream Jake had always slipped between her fingers, leaving her frustrated and alone.

When he nipped at her earlobe, she felt more than just a foggy touch. She felt his teeth.

She was awake. This was really happening. She hoped. Oh, how she hoped. "Jake?"

He cupped her face in his hands and kissed her again—on the forehead this time. "I want you so much, but I want you to want me, too."

She blinked the last bits of sleep from her eyes. What was he talking about? She'd done nothing but want him since he'd walked into the hospital two days ago. "Of course I want you. The accident didn't change that. Nothing could."

"You're sure?" He looked so serious about it. "Because I'm not going to let you go."

How could he even say something like that—about letting her go? She had the feeling that he was talking about something else—but she couldn't grasp what it was.

Or maybe he was just talking about the coma she'd been in. Yes, that made more sense. "You were all I thought about."

Guilt—which was not a sensual emotion—washed over his face. "Skye…" But instead of explaining why he looked guilty, he pulled her into a fierce hug. "I will always come back for you," he whispered into her hair. "Always. You are mine."

Something in the embrace turned from emotional to erotic. His body started to rock against her and she clung to him, praying that no one would stop by or call or do anything to interrupt them. This time was theirs and she didn't want to miss another moment with him.

"My blue-eyed Skye," he murmured against her lips before he kissed her.

"Oh, Jake," she groaned. "I love you."

He growled as she nipped at his lower lip. He pulled away and grabbed the hem of her shirt. It came off easily without even touching most of her hair. Skye made a grab for Jake's buttons, but he captured her hands in his. "You first," he said. "I want to see you so bad."

He slid the lounge pants over her hips, leaving her in nothing but the cotton panties. He looked her over, naked hunger in his eyes. "You are *so* beautiful," he said again and she knew he telling the truth. "The most beautiful woman I've ever seen."

He leaned into her, his hands skimming over her arms, her shoulders and down her back. His touch was light and warm, but she shivered, anyway. "Jake…"

He worked the panties off her hips. "I want to kiss you over every square inch of your body until you can't even breathe," he murmured against her neck.

"Oh, my," she said, angling her head back so he could have better access. Her legs were aching from propping herself up against him, but she didn't want to pull away. Not yet. Not when she finally had him back in her arms. "I think that can be arranged."

This time, when she went for his shirt buttons, he didn't try to stop her. Her fingers seemed to have forgotten the basic mechanics of undressing a man, because they fumbled with the first button. "I can do this," she told him in frustration as she failed to get yet another button on the first try. She didn't want to get hung up on this step— what if there was another interruption? She couldn't bear it. She just *couldn't*.

He tilted her head up. "Don't mind me," he said with a serious look in his eye. "I'm just watching you be naked. Trust me, the view from here?" He whistled.

She grinned at him as some of her nervousness faded. He was always doing that, finding a way to put her at ease. No matter what, he was still her Jake. Finally, she got the danged buttons undone and slid the shirt off his arms.

"Oh," she breathed as the hard planes of his chest were laid bare for her to see. She stroked her fingers over the fine hairs that covered his chest and arms, then leaned up and pressed a kiss to his chest.

Jake sucked in a hot breath. "Oh, I missed you, too."

But when she went for his belt buckle, he grabbed her hands again. "Don't," he gritted out, "don't want it over too soon."

Skye giggled again. "I remember…" she said as Jake crawled between her legs. "I remember this."

"Yeah?" he asked as he dropped his mouth to her breast. "Tell me what you remember, babe."

"I remember…" There were images floating around her head, all muddled up with the heated desire he was unleashing upon her body. Her brain might not be operating at full capacity, but her body seemed to have a better recall. Muscle memory, she wanted to call it. Because her muscles remembered. "I remember the first time you touched my breasts. And I was—oh, Jake!" she gasped as he scraped his teeth over her nipple.

"Go on," he murmured against her skin as he shifted to the other breast. "Tell me what you remember."

"I was nervous because—because I was so small and you were unhooking my bra and…and…" They'd been teenagers, nervous and fumbling in the front seat of his truck—wanting *so* much and afraid of it, too. Afraid that the further she went with Jake, the less they'd be friends. Afraid that he'd get her padded bra off of her and see how little she really had and it wouldn't be enough for him. But the need to be with him then—just like now—had been too strong to ignore. He'd gotten her bra unhooked and looked at her small breasts and said—

"And I said you were perfect," he finished for her. "Perfect for me." Then he rolled her nipple between his tongue and teeth. "Because you are, Skye. You are the only woman for me."

"Jake," she moaned. She did remember this—how he'd

always lavished attention on her breasts, made her feel special instead of lacking.

But things were different now, too. Her nipples were tight and hot under his kisses, but it didn't feel exactly the way she remembered it. Was that because she was remembering wrong, or because her body had changed?

"I *love* your body," he said, his mouth trailing down her belly.

He was almost to the C-section scar—a thin, angry red line that stood out like a flashing light on her pale skin. "Even—that?"

He found the scar and kissed the length of it. "Even this. This gave us our daughter. Your body is amazing. This isn't a scar, babe. It's a tattoo of strength and I don't ever want you to be ashamed of it."

Her throat closed up at his sweet words. "Oh, Jake…"

But that was as far as she got before he moved lower. Jake ran his hands up and down her legs as he sat back and adjusted her hips. He leaned down and pressed a kiss to her inner thigh, then he put his mouth against her sex and began to stroke her with his tongue. "Oh, Jake!"

He sat back on his heels, but didn't stop touching her. Instead of his mouth, his fingers began to rub over her. The heat was anything but languid now. Skye began to writhe.

Skye was filled with warmth and lightness. This was the man she loved—the man who could strip her down and lay her out and make her want him. She couldn't remember being as happy as she was right now.

Then he slipped a finger inside of her.

Skye's hips twisted as she responded to his touch. It was more than she was used to—but not enough. She needed even more. "Jake," she groaned, desperate for something to hold on to.

Then his mouth was on her again and there was nothing slow or funny about what he was doing to her body. She ran her fingers through his hair and held on as he worked her up to the point where she couldn't hold back. The orgasm hit her with so much force that she came all the way off the bed as she cried out, "Jake!"

"Oh, babe," he moaned from between her legs. "I've missed you so much. *So* much."

She fell back onto the bed, panting. "How could I forget?" Then she managed to lift her left foot and nudge at the huge erection that was straining behind his jeans. "Might need a refresher on *that*," she tried to say in a joking tone.

"Woman," he growled again as he shoved himself away from her. He yanked his jeans off, along with his boxers.

"Don't stop," she moaned. "Babe, don't stop."

But he looked at her, his eyes wide.

And he stopped.

What the hell was he doing?

Jake stared at her. His blood was pounding in his ears—and a few other places—and he could still taste her sweetness on his tongue. He'd—he'd decided to fight for her. That realization emerged from the haze that was his brain.

But…should he really be having sex with her? At least, right now? Shouldn't he give it another week—another day—so she could recover? Shouldn't he be putting her needs above his own?

"Jake?" She was staring at him with those huge blue eyes of hers. *Perfect.* She was just perfect. Always had been. And he'd always had so much trouble saying no to her.

She lifted herself up and hesitantly wrapped her fingers around him. He shuddered at her touch, but he was powerless to put the brakes on, powerless to do anything but love her. Slowly—so slowly it was driving all reason out of his mind—she stroked him. And this time, there was no doorbell to save him from her. From himself. "It's okay. I've waited too long for this."

If only she knew how long she'd been waiting.

"But what if—?" What if he got her pregnant *again*?

"Then I'll remember. Oh, babe, I want you so much." She stroked up, down, up again and it obliterated any reasonable thought. He hadn't had sex in over ten months. Ten months without this woman under him—beside him—on top of him. It felt like a lifetime. He couldn't stand it anymore. Not when she was here, loving on him like this.

He gently pushed her back onto the bed and lowered his mouth to her breasts again. She'd always been a little insecure about how small she was, so he made sure that she knew how much he loved her just as she was.

Soon enough, she was shifting underneath him, lifting her hips up so that she could be closer to him. "Jake," she begged. "Jake, *please*."

He fell into her. He couldn't stay away from her—he'd never been able to. His father had punished him each time Jake and Skye had been caught together. Jake had gone to college a year before she had. He'd gone to Bahrain without her. But he'd come back for her. He would *always* come back for her.

He didn't want to crush her slim body, so he propped himself up on his hands and fit himself against her.

"Jake," she hissed as he teased her with his tip. *"Jake."*

He couldn't hold himself back, not with her tantalizing warmth surrounding him. He thrust into her, gently at first, but then her fingernails found his back, spurring him on. *"Mine,"* he said as he surrendered to her. "My blue-eyed Skye."

"Oh, yes," she gasped out as her body tightened around his. He buried himself in her over and over again. Nothing between them. Not now, not ever.

He sat back on his heels and pulled her hips down into his, thrusting hard. "Skye," he ground out.

Then she cried out his name and it pushed him over the edge. With the last bit of self-control he had, he pulled out as he came. Condoms. He was going to have to get some condoms immediately.

He collapsed onto the bed next to her and drew her into his arms. They were both breathing hard. "I love you, Skye," he said low and close to her ear. "Nothing—not even comas—can change that. I've loved you since I was seven and I will love you to the day I draw in my last breath."

"I don't ever want us to be apart, Jake." Her breath hitched her chest up. "Even when I was asleep, I missed you so much. Don't ever leave me again."

He froze. Was she remembering something—or was she still operating under the assumption that he'd just been in New York for a job for a while?

He *hated* this. There were many things that had gone wrong between them, but lying hadn't been one of them. They were always honest with each other. Even if he was only glossing over the truth, it still sat wrong in his craw.

He knew he needed to tell her about the past two years—he couldn't keep secrets, not from her. He *knew* that it would be better if she heard it from him before she remembered it on her own.

But he couldn't. Not just yet. After all, on her first full day home from the hospital, she'd not only had to deal with surprise visits from neighbors, but from his family as well—well-meaning as they were. Then he'd ravished her, essentially.

She had to be exhausted and the last thing she needed was another emotional shock. They'd have time to discuss everything that had happened right before her accident later. After they'd settled into the house and she'd gotten some of her strength back and they'd had a chance to spend a little time with Grace.

He had time to show her what she meant to him before the past caught up with them. A week, maybe. Skye would be much better by then.

He hoped. God, he hoped.

Eight

"Can we go now?" Skye asked for the fourteenth time that morning.

"Noon," Jake repeated. And then, because he was having trouble keeping his hands off of her, he leaned over as she held her leg lifts and kissed her. "Just a little bit longer."

Skye was not mollified by this announcement. She'd woken up in a good mood, but once Jake had gotten her back on the floor do to the exercises, that mood had turned into impatience. "I just want to see her," Skye said as she struggled her way through the exercises. "I just want to hold her."

"I know," he repeated, trying to keep her calm. "Lark said to come over at noon. We still have three hours. Let's stretch."

He couldn't believe it, but as he stood over her and lifted her leg toward the ceiling, he found himself flirting with her. Yesterday, he'd been desperate to not flirt with her. But today? It was the best weapon he had in keeping her distracted. "Maybe we should try this in bed," he joked.

That got him a funny look. "And how do you suggest we pull *that* off?"

"I have my ways." She laughed, which he took as a good sign. "Here, roll over." He began to give her a massage.

"Mmm, good," she murmured as he worked at a knot in her shoulder. "I hadn't realized how tight I was."

Jake laughed. This was the Skye he'd run off with— the one who could make a suggestive joke and tell him what she wanted.

When she rolled back over again, he couldn't help himself. He lowered himself to her and kissed her. "As a reward," he murmured against her neck.

"You make me wish I was doing PT three times a day," she said as she grinned up at him.

She started to deepen the kiss—and Jake was tempted to let it go on—but they had to leave the house today. So he sat back and pulled her into a sitting position. "Shower?"

Her eyebrows jumped. "Together?"

"If that's what you want." He kept asking her variations on that—did she want to watch this? Do that? Eat that?

But what he was really asking was if she wanted him. He wasn't going to sit around and watch them fall apart again. When she remembered—it was just a matter of time—then he wanted her to have some new, better memories to counterbalance the bad ones. Memories in which he'd taken care of her—in which he'd still loved her, still fought for her.

She would remember that he'd left. He wanted her to remember that he'd come back for her and for Grace.

He helped her into the bathroom. She was getting stronger, he could tell—despite the hard workout, she was able to get undressed on her own. Jake stripped out of his own clothes and helped her to sit on the bench after he got the water to the right temperature. The shower was roomy and the showerhead could be removed from the wall so he was able to rinse her hair. "I'll try to put it back like it was," he offered.

She leaned back, her head resting on his stomach. "Try?"

"*Try*." Then he had her lean forward so that he could wash her back again.

"You know," she said in a casual way, "I kind of thought you were avoiding me when you gave me that bath."

Jake froze, but then thought that might trigger something in her mind, so he went on lathering up her body. "Why would you think that?"

She managed to pivot and look up at him. "I thought… it just seemed like you didn't want me. I was afraid maybe I'd done something I couldn't remember that, you know, wasn't so good."

"I did want you. I *do*," he hurried to say. "Honestly, I was afraid of hurting you." Which, again, was not the whole truth. But there was some truth to it. "All I want is for you to get better, faster. I don't want to do anything that might mess that up."

She beamed at him. "Okay, good." She took the soap. "Now it's my turn."

"What do you—*oh*." Skye ran the soap over his body and, damn it all, he went hard in an instant at her touch. "Skye—you don't have to do this."

"Who said anything about having to?" she demanded as she stroked him. "I want to. You're taking care of me. Let me take care of you."

"I don't—want you—to overdo—it," he ground out as she worked on him. So she'd lost two years. She remembered what he liked—the strong, sure strokes. Then she rinsed him off and ran her tongue over his tip. "Like this?" she murmured, her voice vibrating up through him.

"Just like that," he managed to say. He leaned forward and braced his hands on the wall of the shower as she licked his tip and stroked his length and did everything she could to drive him wild with lust.

"Skye," he warned her as he tried to pull back. "Wait—let me—"

"No," she said as she held fast to him. "You, Jake Holt, are *mine*."

She claimed him then—took everything he had to give as the orgasm almost brought him to his knees.

Hell, it actually did—he sank down in front of her and clutched her to his chest as he waited for his pulse to return to normal. "My perfect Skye," he got out.

"Was it okay?"

He looked at her. "Okay? No." Her face started to crumble, so he quickly said, "Great? *Yes*."

He was hers. She'd said so herself.

He gave her a wicked grin. "Your turn."

Before she knew what was happening, Jake had parted her legs, grabbed her by the thighs and pulled her so that she was barely sitting on the bench. "Perfect," he murmured again as his mouth closed in on her.

The warm water cascaded down over them as he worked his tongue over her and his fingers into her. Maybe yesterday he had been worried about hurting her—holding back just a little, just in case.

He did no such thing today. Her body, already relaxed from the shower, gave itself over to his touches as they came harder, faster—

"Jake!"

"Come for me, babe," he said against her sex. "Come for me."

So she did. Her body lit up as the desire overwhelmed her. *Alive*. She was alive and getting stronger here with Jake. It was all she'd ever wanted.

After one of the longer—and better—showers in recent memory, Skye finally got into a clean set of clothes and Jake mostly got her hair brushed back over into a side ponytail. Skye didn't even attempt eyeliner or mascara—her arms were already tired and she wanted to save her strength for holding Grace—but she managed to put on a little makeup without Jake's help. Gloria had asked for pictures, after all. Skye wanted to look as normal as possible.

"Ready?" Jake asked, a big smile on his face.

She nodded. It felt good to know that she'd put that smile there, that he'd returned the favor. She didn't remember them having a bench in the bathroom in their apartment, but if they moved back here to Royal permanently, they'd have to make sure they had a bench in their new home.

She wanted to tell Jake that—but something held her back. Jake had made his position quite clear—he was never coming back to Royal. She remembered *that*. But hadn't that been because of his family? Well, her family, too.

They'd had a lovely lunch with his parents—people so warm and friendly that she almost couldn't believe they were the same two who had forced Jake to choose between the Holt ranch and Skye. And now, after a careful trip down the stairs and out to the car, they were going to go see Keaton and Lark and…

Grace.

Skye's heart tried to skip a beat at just the thought of the tiny baby in all the pictures David had showed her.

"Nervous?" Jake asked her as he backed out of the driveway. "Or just excited?"

"Both," she admitted. "I hope I don't drop her!"

"I don't think that'll happen," he assured her. "We'll get you set up on Lark's couch and you can just hold the baby."

"I hope I can feed her," Skye said. "I want to help take care of her."

Jake shot her a silly look. "You may want to avoid dia-

per duty for a while longer. I'm just saying, I may be emo-
tionally scarred for life from *that*."

Skye laughed at him. "Jake," she said, feeling light and
free. "I don't know if I've ever been this happy."

All the silliness bled out of his face. "We were happy,"
he told her. "When it was just the two of us."

"Oh, I know—I don't mean that we weren't. I love living with you. It's just, well, you know—our families are
getting along and we have a baby now. I secretly hoped
that this would happen."

At least, she'd thought it was secret. But Jake said heavily, "Yeah, I know."

"You do?" She didn't remember telling him that. In
fact, she'd thought she'd done a very good job hiding that
from him because she knew that he'd never wanted to
come back here.

"I mean," he quickly corrected, "I suspected as much."
All serious now, he looked over at her. "Do you still want
to come back here?"

At least, that's what he said. But deep inside one of the
holes in Skye's memory, she heard a different question.

Why do you still want to go back there?

She tried to grab hold of that other question, that other
memory—but she couldn't. "I don't know," she admitted. "You're right—we've been so happy on our own. But
there's things I missed—having a friendly neighbor fix my
hair or lunch with your folks, or my sister babysitting so
we can…shower together." She gave him what she hoped
was a coy smile, but the stony look on his face rebuffed her
advance. "It's not something I want to fight about, Jake."

His jaw worked, as if he was trying to say something
and also not trying to say something at the same time,
which left her greatly confused. What was in that damn
hole in her memory? What couldn't she grasp? "Jake?"

"You know," he said through clenched teeth, which undermined the casual tone of his voice, "you've only been home for a few days. We're going to be here for a month, maybe—your doctor wants you to stay close. So let's not worry about this right now. Let's just focus on you getting better and seeing Grace, okay?"

She looked down at her hands. All the light, happy feelings from the shower earlier were gone now. "Did I do something wrong?"

"Of course not," he said. "I don't know about you, but this has been a pretty awesome day. Especially the shower part."

"I don't mean that. I mean…am I forgetting something I did? Did we have a fight?" He didn't answer, but she could tell he was gripping the steering wheel with enough force to break it off the column. "Is that…?" She swallowed, her throat suddenly closing up on her. "Is that why you weren't with me when I hit that storm?"

Jake didn't reply, but then, he was pulling into another driveway. He put the car in park and leaned over. "You were pregnant," he told her as he cupped her face in his hand. "You didn't want to travel to the job with me. I think you'd decided to come see Lark while I was gone."

Suddenly she had tears in her eyes. "Did we fight?"

His mouth opened, but instead of answering her question, he leaned over and kissed her. She let him because she couldn't remember what she couldn't remember, but Jake's love surpassed it all. "Whatever happened in the past isn't as important as what happens in the future, Skye."

"But—"

Just then, the door to the house opened up and there stood her sister with a small bundle in her arms. "Skye?"

"Oh!" What were they doing, sitting here and having… well, a conversation, although a highly strange one, when their daughter was just over there? "We should go."

"Yup," he agreed, getting out and coming over to her side of the car.

She wanted to walk on her own two feet. She didn't want to be too weak even to walk to her own daughter. But her left leg tried to buckle on the fourth step and Jake had to put his arm around her waist and half carry her to the door.

But the frustration at not being able to use her body in a normal, typical way disappeared in an instant as Skye looked down at the baby in Lark's arms. "Oh, Grace," she said, choking up. "My little bit of Grace."

The baby—with bright blue eyes and almost no hair—was looking around, as if everything were new and surprising. "Come inside," Lark said. "I don't want her to get too cold, but we were waiting for you—weren't we, Grace?"

Skye and Jake followed Lark as she led the way into a large room filled with every kind of baby toy imaginable. "I don't—*we* don't have any of this stuff," Skye said. She'd been so focused on just getting her strength back up to the point where she could carry Grace that she hadn't even considered all the things a baby required.

"Don't worry about that," Lark said with a suspicious grin. "Come over and sit down. She's due for a bottle in about half an hour. I'll show you how to prop your legs up so you can talk to her."

Lark and Jake traded places. "You look great," Lark said as she helped Skye down onto one side of a couch that had tall sides. "I mean, you look really great."

"Thanks. Um…what was her name?"

"Megan," Jake said without looking up. "Megan Maguire. Engaged to Whit Daltry. How's Daddy's little girl today, huh?" he cooed to Grace.

"Megan bought me some clothes and makeup and brushed my hair so it hid the short spots. I feel almost normal, you know?"

"It's wonderful," Lark said. "Here." She extended the footrest and adjusted the height so that Skye was tilted back a bit. "Now, bend your knees up—yes, like that. Let me just lay down this blanket—perfect." She turned to Jake. "Ready?"

"Yup."

Skye's chest clenched at the huge grin on Jake's face as he looked down at their daughter. He loved Grace. Oh, that made her so happy she was on the verge of crying again.

Jake slid down on the couch next to her. "Say hi to Mommy, sweetie," he said as he laid Grace in Skye's arms.

She couldn't help it. The happiest tears of her life cascaded down her cheeks. "Hi, Grace," she said, her voice shaking with emotion.

"She's beautiful," Jake said. "Just like her mother."

"I wanted her for so long," Skye said. "*So* long. You have no idea."

"I do, babe. I do." Jake slid his arm around her shoulder and held her close. Grace opened her eyes wide as she looked up at both of them and made a cooing noise.

"She likes you more than she likes me," Jake told her. "The first time I held her, she gave me a 'present.'"

"I'm still laughing about that one," Lark said. She sat down in an easy chair that was close enough to the couch that she could sweep in and snag Grace if Skye lost her grip.

Not that Skye had any plans to do that. She held Grace tightly, feeling the little muscles moving underneath the blanket. "How is she?" she asked Lark. "I mean, what's she like?"

"She sleeps a lot," Lark replied. She wore a satisfied grin on her face. Skye wasn't sure she'd ever seen her sister look so happy. "That's typical of preemies. And her lungs are still developing. It's risky for her to be around a bunch of new people. We don't want her to get sick."

Grace made a little grunting noise in the back of her throat and both Skye and Jake startled. "What's wrong?" they said at the same time. But even as she asked it, Skye thought the noises seemed familiar. Had she heard them before?

Lark laughed. "Nothing—she's fine, I promise. That's just a noise a lot of preemies make. She's almost caught up to her gestational age—how developed she would have been if she'd been full term. She likes to make that noise when I put her on the ground."

"What?" Jake said. Skye could tell that he didn't exactly like that idea.

"Tummy time," Lark said, motioning toward the floor. "She needs to spend a few minutes on her tummy every few hours. It'll help her build her neck strength and keep the back of her head from getting flat."

"Oh." Skye saw a square mat decorated with black and white swirls and red ladybugs. "Okay. That's good to know. I guess we'll get something like that—right, Jake?"

"Absolutely," he said.

Grace made a different sounding grunt. "Oh, here—she wants to look around," Lark said. "Are your legs stable?"

"I...guess?"

Lark leaned over and shifted Grace from Skye's arms so that the baby was almost sitting upright between Skye's thighs. Lark then undid the swaddled blankets a little so that Grace's impossibly tiny hands were free. "I'll go work on lunch," she said. "Holler if you need me. Jake, you're okay?"

"Fine," Jake said, giving Grace one of his fingers to hold on to. "I've got her."

Lark left them alone. "She's perfect," Skye told Jake. "I mean—just look at her little hands!" She offered a finger and Grace grabbed it in her other hand. "Hi, sweetie," she said again.

Grace was apparently testing out her facial muscles because she kept opening her eyes up wide and wrinkling her forehead up and stretching out her mouth. She was, hands down, the cutest baby Skye had ever seen.

"You did such an amazing job, Skye," Jake said in a quiet whisper.

"But I haven't done *anything* yet. I haven't even fed her."

"You *made* her, babe. You're amazing," he said and she heard the waver in his voice. "I'm so in awe of you. Thank you for giving me a daughter."

"Oh, Jake." The tears started up again. She leaned her head against his shoulder and held hands with her daughter and decided that *this* was the happiest she'd ever been. In this perfect little moment of being a family for the first time.

Skye had no idea how much time had passed before Grace's little noises took on a different tone and she started to cry. "Lark?" Skye called out in alarm. "What's the matter?"

Lark came in carrying a bottle. "She's right on schedule. Jake, why don't you help me change her and then Skye can feed her. Sound good?"

"I'm getting the short end of this deal," he said goodnaturedly. "Let's go, Grace." He picked her up and disappeared to where Skye had to assume there was a changing table.

Her daughter. Her perfect little daughter. Oh, how Skye wished she could even remember being pregnant, but it just wasn't there. Her pregnancy wasn't even a fog that slipped through her fingers—it was just the blankness of nothingness.

Why couldn't she remember it? There was something that didn't add up about the whole thing—the baby was just now catching up to her gestational age. She was as old as she'd have been if Skye hadn't been in the accident.

And Jake had said that Skye didn't want to travel with him while she was pregnant...but if that was true, why was she driving back to Royal by herself? It was about a ten-hour drive. Why would she have made that trip alone?

She didn't know. She just didn't know, damn it all. And not knowing was *so* frustrating.

"Here we are, all clean for Mommy," Jake said as he rounded back into the room. Then he looked up at her. "What's wrong? Are you okay?"

"I'm—fine. Just trying to think," she replied with an apologetic smile.

He gave her a long look. "Are you up to feeding her?"

Lark came in behind him. "Let me get a pillow for your arm." Lark got Skye all tucked in. Jake put Grace back in her arms and all of her frustrated worries disappeared again.

She knew that she'd wanted this—a child. A family. And not just Grace and Jake, but the bigger family—Lark and Keaton and the Holts, too.

Except there was still something missing.

"Have you talked to Mom and Dad? Did they say if they were going to come by?" Skye asked Lark as Grace drank her milk.

"Ah...well—see, they've been busy. Recovering from the storm." Lark must have seen the look of alarm on Skye's face. "Just a lot of property damage. They were fine and the house was okay. Dad's just busy. Well, you know how they are."

Skye dropped her gaze back to Grace. Were her parents too busy to see her? To see Grace? David and Gloria had taken all those pictures on their phones—it was clear that they'd spent a great deal of time with Grace. "Lark—that reminds me, Gloria said to take pictures."

So Jake came back and sat beside Skye and Lark took several photos and then emailed one to the Holts and to

Keaton. "He's out on at the ranch with the dog," Lark explained.

Skye decided she wasn't going to worry anymore. Jake had said what mattered now was what happened next—Skye getting stronger, Grace getting stronger. All of them getting under the same roof. That's what she had to focus on, not what her faulty mind couldn't reconstruct.

So she studied her daughter as she ate and then watched as Jake burped the baby and ate the lunch her sister made.

Jake and Lark had clearly been making plans while they were getting Grace changed, because Jake said, "I've got to do a work thing on Friday night, Skye. I'll bring you over here and you can play with Grace."

"Okay," she quickly agreed. "I can handle lying on the floor," she added in a joking tone.

"Perfect," Lark said, looking mischievous. "It's a date."

Nine

Friday night didn't come fast enough. Jake had taken Skye over to Lark's once a day for the afternoon feeding and playtime, which was nice, but it always felt as if the visits were too short. Skye was looking forward to spending the evening with Grace.

Finally, the appointed time arrived and Jake drove her over. Skye was surprised when Keaton answered the door. A part of her wanted to recoil the way she'd always done when they were kids. Keaton hadn't ever liked her very much.

But he gave her a warm smile and said, "Skye, good to see you up."

"Thanks," she said. New feelings crowded out the old shame at being caught by Keaton. "How's Grace today?"

"Fussy," he admitted. "Rough night last night."

Skye's heart began to beat out a worried tempo. "Is she okay?"

"Fine," he hurried to assure her. "Babies cry. Come on in."

Skye was aware that today, she was able to make her way back to Lark's overstuffed living room without Jake having to hold her up. As much as she hated the exercises, they were working. She still used Jake as backup when she went up and down stairs, but she could now do short distances by herself.

Lark was standing in the living room, wearing a skirt and a jacket. She'd fixed her hair and was even wearing makeup. Instantly, every single one of Skye's warning bells went off. Lark had never been one to get all dressed up unless she had a good reason—and Skye was positive that a girls' night in with a three-month-old was not a good reason.

"Hi!" Lark said in a too-perky voice. "You should change. Here," she said, thrusting a garment bag into Skye's hands.

"I'm almost afraid to ask." Skye opened the bag up and tried to make sense of the light-colored fabric inside. "Is this…a cream-colored linen pantsuit?"

"Indeed it is," Lark said, trying not to giggle. "Just what all the mothers of babies are wearing this season. It's something Mom gave me a while back."

"At least it's not a pageant dress," Jake said.

"I have to wear this? *Really?*"

"Um…"

"Lark," Skye said severely. "Why on God's green earth would I need to wear a pantsuit to play with my baby?"

"You better tell her," Jake said, taking her hand and stroking her palm, as if that would calm her down.

"I have a surprise for you. Jake's going to stay with Keaton and Grace and we're going out. Our mother would have a heart attack if she saw you out in public in yoga pants. Now," she said, holding up her hand and cutting Skye off before she could protest, "go get changed. We've got to get moving."

Skye changed, a sinking pit of anxiety in her stomach. At least she'd put on makeup after her shower with Jake today. And—she looked in the mirror—yes, her hair was passable.

But she'd been looking forward to spending time with Grace all day long. If she wasn't going to get to do that now, why hadn't Jake brought her over earlier?

And what had Lark meant about their mother? Maybe, Skye began to hope, she was going to go see her parents. The five days without so much as a peep from them had not gone unnoticed. Gloria and David had stopped by one more time and Skye had been over to Lark's every day.

But she hadn't seen her parents yet. And she didn't know why.

That must be what was going to change—yes, it seemed right, especially if Jake and Keaton were going to stay here. Okay, this made sense, Skye decided. She and Lark were probably going out to dinner with Vera and Tyrone Taylor.

She hadn't seen her parents in…in…well, since the night before she and Jake had run away, obviously. She hoped they weren't still mad at her. How could they be? The Holts had forgiven Skye and Jake. Surely the Taylors had, too?

When she was dressed, she emerged from the bathroom, feeling awkward in the scratchy linen. This was not her normal attire. The yoga pants were. Back in Houston, on the mornings when Jake had to work early and she just had some freelance work to do, Skye would lounge around in her yoga pants. She'd always paused to think about what her mother would say if she saw Skye in such attire. Vera would have thrown an epic fit that her beautiful, model-perfect daughter would dare play down her features. All the more reason for Skye to own several pairs of yoga pants.

Lark was waiting for her. "Ready?"

"I guess so?" Skye said as she kissed Grace on the top of her little head. Then she kissed Jake, although that felt weird, with both Keaton and Lark watching them. "Wish me luck."

He grinned at her. "You'll have fun," he promised. She gave him a look. It might be good to see her parents again, but that didn't necessarily mean it was going to be "fun." Vera and Tyrone Taylor were many things, but that wasn't one of them.

They headed out. Skye's legs felt pretty decent, actually. That was a good sign for tonight. Skye settled into Lark's car. The silence was almost too much for her. There was so much she'd missed—and not just from being asleep for four months. She'd missed more than four years of her sister's life. "Was Mom unbearable while I was away?"

"Oh, God," Lark said with a weary sigh. "I mean, I was always jealous that you were so beautiful and the favorite but…" She shrugged. "I didn't realize how much Mom and Dad focused on you until you weren't there. Then, suddenly, they were criticizing my every move. My every outfit," she corrected.

Skye winced. "I didn't mean to abandon you to them. Not entirely. I was pretty mad at you, wasn't I?"

"Furious," Lark agreed. But she didn't sound angry about it, or even that bitter. "I was…well, I was not kind about you and Jake. I was trying so hard to be the perfect Taylor daughter—so that Mom and Dad would care about me like they cared about you."

Skye snorted. "I don't know if I'd describe trying to force me into beauty pageants as 'caring.'" Lark gave her a look. "But I understand what you're saying."

"You were the favorite," Lark repeated. "I could do nothing right. And I couldn't believe that you would just *throw* that away."

"But I had to," Skye said. "I love Jake. I had to be with him."

"I know. I guess that was the other reason I said what I said to you. You were going off to be happy and I...I wasn't brave enough to go get what I wanted. I was afraid."

"Lark..." Skye reached over and put her hand on her sister's shoulder.

"It's okay," Lark said, shooting her a smile. "You just knew what you wanted earlier than I did."

"You and Keaton, huh?"

"Me and Keaton. I should have listened to you all those years ago when you tried to tell me there was something about a Holt."

The two of them laughed. "I told you so," Skye said.

"You were right. Can I tell you something?"

"Sure. Anything." Skye relaxed a little bit. She couldn't fix whatever might be wrong between her and Jake right now, but being like this with Lark was a gift in and of itself. It was good to have her sister back again.

"Keaton and I are trying to have a baby."

"What? But...you're not even married yet!" She thought. She was pretty sure. She looked at Lark's hand, which just had a diamond ring on it. Not a wedding band.

Of course, she didn't have her wedding band on, either, and that didn't mean she and Jake weren't married.

"I know," Lark said with a nervous grin. "I don't know if I've ever been so happy as when it was him and me and Grace. I felt like—like that was who I was supposed to be. I can be a better mother than our mother is." She gave Skye a warm glance. "Does that shock you?"

"No, no..."

"And I know it sounds silly, but maybe another grandbaby would help heal the rift between our families, you know? You've seen how much Grace has won over Keaton's folks."

"It doesn't sound silly at all," Skye admitted. "I always

thought the same thing." She sighed. "But there's so much I lost. I have this feeling I'm missing something—something *huge*—and I don't know what it is."

"Are you sure it's not a baby? Because I found her," Lark said with a laugh.

"Ha ha. Very funny. Are you going to tell me where we're going?"

"Soon," Lark replied. "I know the doctor said you might get your memory back, you might not. But you were happy, weren't you?"

"We are happy," Skye agreed. She looked out the window. The surroundings looked…familiar. "Where are we?"

"It won't take long," Lark said with obvious glee in her voice.

Skye doubted that statement. "This isn't going to be some sort of party, is it?"

"No," Lark said way too quickly. "Why do you ask?"

"Lark," Skye groaned.

"Oh, look! We're here!" Lark said as she turned into the Texas Cattleman's Club.

Skye managed not to say something snarky and juvenile as she groaned. Again. "Is there anything I can do to convince you to take me home? Bribery, maybe?" Because Skye didn't have "polite and social" in her tonight. She just *didn't*. Plus, she did not want to be wearing this damn cream-colored linen suit. It was half a size too small and itched.

"I want to show you the new childcare center they added last year," Lark said in a too-bright tone. "When Grace gets stronger, you can bring her here."

"And I had to wear a linen pantsuit for that, huh?"

"Come on." Lark all but dragged her out of the car and into the TCC. Skye hadn't really been in here. She'd come for dinners with her parents, but the TCC was an old boy's club in every possible sense of the word. Her father was a longtime member.

Lark led Skye into what was unmistakably a childcare center. Toy stations and rainbow colors decorated a room with pint-size tables and chairs. "Wow, when did *this* happen?"

"Last year. After they started admitting women," Lark said.

"Wait—they admit women now? How long was I gone?"

Lark smirked. "Pretty long. Come on." She led Skye down a long hall. "Check this out," she said in that too-bright tone again. She opened the door and basically shoved Skye through it.

"Surprise!" a crowd of women all shouted together. And it was quite a crowd. Gloria Holt was there, along with Julie Kingston and a few other people Skye recognized from the hospital.

"It's your baby shower," Gloria said, grinning from ear to ear as she led Skye to a chair at the front of the room. "Well, baby shower and welcome-home party."

Skye took in all the people. She saw Megan Maguire. "Goodness, you look wonderful, Skye! Did Jake fix your hair?"

Skye's cheeks colored. "He's getting better."

Megan grinned. "He gets any better, and I'm going to hire him to groom dogs!"

Julie Kingston came up to them. Skye almost didn't recognize her, since she was wearing a nice outfit instead of scrubs. "Hi, Julie," Skye said, putting on a nice smile.

"Hey, you remember my name! That's great," Julie said. "How are you doing?"

"Better. I've been able to spend some time with Grace—Lark's still taking care of her," Skye said. "But it turns out that I'm currently perfectly suited to lie on the floor and play with a baby."

Julie nodded knowingly. "I'm so glad you've got Lark. She's a great nurse." Lark blushed under the weight of the compliment.

"We'll have to get together soon, maybe for coffee?" That'd be good, Skye decided. She could slowly ease back into the Royal, Texas, social circle one coffee date at a time.

Julie paused. "Oh. Well, I'm actually not sure how much longer I'm going to be here."

"What?" Lark asked, sounding truly shocked. "But you're terrific at your job and…I really like working with you. I'd hate to lose your friendship."

Julie gave Lark a weak smile. "I know, Lark. But…well, things change. We'd still be friends, though—just because I'm somewhere else doesn't mean we can't keep in touch. I just don't know how I'm going to break it to Lucas." When Skye blinked at her, she added, "Dr. Wakefield."

"Well," Lark said, "if there's anything I can do to help, just let me know."

"Thanks, I will. Now if you'll excuse me." Julie went over to the punch bowl and seemed to study it.

"Skye," Lark said, leading a slender woman with brown hair over to where Skye sat, "this is Stella Daniels, our acting mayor. She's done an amazing job getting this town back on its feet."

"It's such a pleasure to meet you, Skye," Stella said, giving her a politician's handshake. "We can't tell you how glad we are that you're on the road to recovery. I couldn't help but feel that your fate and the town's fate were intertwined. If you can come back from that storm, so can Royal!"

A handful of other women applauded.

"Thank you," Skye said, feeling more than a little awkward. She tried to grin, but the noise in the room was

much louder than she was used to and everyone was looking at her.

"Let's open the presents," Gloria announced. She was
clearly having the time of her life, showing pictures of
Grace to anyone who'd stand still long enough to look at
them. "Then we have cake and punch!"

"Um…" Skye said. Presents? She realized that this must
be how Lark had always felt—the focus of attention, but
unsure of what to do or say.

And where was her mother? Surely Vera Taylor would
come to her own daughter's baby shower.

Wouldn't she?

Skye took a breath, hoping the throbbing in her head
would ease. Maybe her mother was just…running late or
something. And in the meantime, Skye was here with all
these wonderful women who'd gone to so much trouble to
throw her a party. She could do this. And once she did it,
she could go home. So she dug deep for her old-fashioned
manners. "Thank you so much, everyone," she said. "This
is such a thoughtful gesture. We can't thank you enough
for everything you've done for us."

The guests beamed, so she figured that was the right
thing to say. Lark started piling beautifully wrapped presents onto her lap and Gloria sat next to her, dutifully recording every gift and giver in order.

And once Skye got going, it was actually fun. She
hadn't done a single thing to get ready for Grace. The cute
little onesies, the adorable blankets—even the diaper cake
was new and precious. Skye let herself get swept up in the
excitement, *oohing* and *aahing* over every darling outfit.

This was what she'd wanted. The little swimmer diapers? She wanted to take Grace to a pool this summer
and splash in the water with her. The adorable sun hats
and sunglasses? Perfect for playing in the yard. And the
stroller? Walking would be good for both of them. She

could see it now—Grace bundled up in the cute dresses, strapped into the stroller with her hat on, Jake and Skye taking turns pushing her as they walked.

There was so much she wanted to do with her baby— things that she had forgotten, along with everything else. But for the first time, it began to feel like it was possible.

A couple of times, the door opened and an older man would stick his head in, see the mass of women and baby things, and back out of the room pretty quickly. "Some of the older members haven't adjusted to women being allowed into the club," Stella explained.

"When's that going to change?" Megan wanted to know.

"Well," Stella said, standing. "This is as good a time as any to announce that I've just been asked to be a member of the TCC." The group burst into applause. "I'll be inducted along with Colby Richardson. He's already a member of the Dallas branch but this makes his Royal membership official." She positively beamed. "Aaron— that's Aaron Nichols, my fiancé," she explained to Skye. "Aaron and I will be staying in Royal. He's going to open a branch office of his company."

"How wonderful, Stella!" Gloria said. "Does that mean you'll stay on as mayor?"

Stella grinned. "At least until the next election!"

Everyone laughed in a good-natured way. But then Paige Richardson said, "Actually, I think Colby will be returning to Dallas soon."

Megan gasped. "Oh, Paige—really?"

Paige dropped her gaze. "He's been such a big help," she admitted. "But…he's got a business to run…"

Skye was confused. Was Paige talking about her husband leaving town? No, wait—had there been two Richardson boys? They'd been older than she was. She couldn't remember.

Then Gloria cut the cake and Lark passed out slices and

the group fell back into easy conversation. As exhausted as she was, Skye was glad she'd come. Yes, she was tired and yes, she couldn't wait to burn this pantsuit, but this was a community of people who were there when you needed them. She and Jake had left this behind and had been on their own for years, which had been exhilarating but also…scary. There'd been no one to fall back on when the going got rough.

This was better. Warm, comfortable. Maybe she and Jake would stay. This was the kind of place to raise a family—and raise them right. No more Taylor/Holt feuding.

The moment the thought crossed her mind, the door opened again.

"What is this?" a voice boomed and Tyrone Taylor walked into the room, his wife trailing behind him.

The room fell silent. "Ladies, this is the Texas Cattleman's Club, not a…"

Then he saw Skye, a plate of cake balanced on her knee and baby things in a pile next to her. "Oh," Tyrone said, all the wind taken right out of his sails. "There's my girl," he added in an even louder voice.

"Mom! Dad! I didn't think…" Lark went to greet her parents. She seemed to realize that the whole room was listening.

"Yes," Vera said, giving Lark air kisses on her cheeks. "We just finished dinner and…thought we'd drop by." She leaned back and appraised Lark's outfit, then sighed wearily. "I suppose that's better than those horrid scrubs you wear…" she said with a dismissive flick of her wrist.

Then she headed for Skye. "Did you have a lovely party, dear?" She stroked Skye's hair. "Where is your ring? I assumed you'd married that Holt boy."

"I did. We *are* married," Skye said, her cheeks getting hot. That Holt boy? "His name is Jake."

"Mom, Skye lost the ring in the storm," Lark said quickly.

"And he hasn't gotten you another one?" Vera *tsked* several times. "I see you at least had the good sense to wear that pantsuit." The room was quieter than church on Sunday. "Next week, we'll go shopping for some proper things," Vera went on. She leaned down, her voice dropping to an almost whisper. "I'm sure we can find something that suits your figure *somewhere*."

"That's quite enough of that, Vera," Gloria said, bustling up. "Cake?" she asked, thrusting out a plate of cake with pink frosting.

"Heavens, no. Don't you know what that will do to a figure? Well," Vera simpered, giving Gloria a cutting look, "I guess you would."

The silence was so sharp it could have cut glass.

"Ah," Tyrone said. "We'll let you get back to your little party. You take care, sweetie." He winked at Skye.

Humiliation burned her cheeks. *Too little, too late*, she thought. "Yeah, okay. Thanks for stopping in," she forced herself to say as if the plan all along had been for her parents to show up and belittle the entire baby shower.

After they showed themselves out, the women stood around in awkward silence. There were no more gifts to open, and no one seemed to be in the mood for seconds of cake.

"Well," Lark announced, "I think I need to get Skye home."

That was enough to get Julie and the nurses talking about how Skye needed to be sure not to overdo it in these first days home. Soon enough, Skye was back in Lark's car, a plate of cake for Jake in her lap. Gloria had promised to load up all the baby things, wash everything and deliver it all tomorrow afternoon, along with the typed list of gifts. Skye gathered that was part of making sure she didn't overdo it.

When they were safely in the car, Skye asked, "Were Mom and Dad always that bad?"

Lark sighed. "No, not to you. To me, yeah."

"God, and I never caught on." Skye felt stupid.

Lark shook her head. "Mom can be very subtle when she wants. When we were growing up, I think you looked so much like she used to that at first she liked you better, but then..." She shrugged. "Sometimes it feels like she's competing with you. She doesn't do that with me. But I guess it's because she thinks I'm such a lost cause it's no competition to begin with."

Skye gaped at her sister. "Really? That—that makes a *lot* of sense, actually." It would explain that victorious grin at seeing Skye in this stupid pantsuit. "I thought—when you made me put this thing on—I thought we were going out to dinner with them."

"They...they had plans, Skye. But they were able to stop by."

"You're making excuses for them," she told Lark. "Don't do that. They were horrible tonight and we both know it. What I want to know is, did they come see me when I was in the hospital? Gloria said she read to me."

"She did. But Mom and Dad...they came once. I think it upset Dad to see you like that, so they stayed away."

They hadn't come. They hadn't sat by her bedside and talked to her or read her books or done a single thing that might have made her feel better. "What about Grace? Gloria and David had all these pictures of her. Did Mom and Dad see her? Did they hold her?"

"They..." Lark sighed. "Okay, I don't want to upset you, but when we had Grace tested and the results showed she was Jake's daughter, they...they didn't seem to want to have anything to do with her."

"With me," Skye added. She supposed this wasn't a shock, none of it. Vera had never been the warm, loving kind of woman who held fun baby showers and went out of her way to get groceries. And Tyrone refused to have anything to do with the Holts.

Still, Skye was their daughter. And Grace? Their only granddaughter—at least for now.

Maybe her family never would accept her, not as long as she was married to Jake.

Which reminded her. "Lark, do you have any of my jewelry?"

"Oh! Yes," Lark said, clearly relieved to have something else to talk about besides their parents. "Well, sort of. You had earrings in, but the side that hit the car—that stone is gone. So I have a diamond of yours."

"Not a ring?" She'd never taken it off, not once since they'd married. "Not my wedding ring?"

"No," Lark said apologetically. "I'm sorry. Either the wind took it or..." There she paused, so unexpectedly that Skye's head popped up and she stared at her sister. "Well," Lark said hastily, "there really isn't an *either/or*, is there? It was lost in the tornado."

There it was again, that feeling that there was *something* that Skye should know and simply didn't. "What aren't you telling me?"

"Nothing," Lark answered quickly. "We're home. Do you want to come in and say good night to Grace?"

Skye sighed. "Yes," she said, but she wasn't happy that Lark was holding out on her.

Just like she thought Jake was sometimes holding out on her, too. They both acted as if something had happened that Skye couldn't recall and she shouldn't be allowed to know what it was. It was infuriating.

But—was she really mad at Lark and Jake? Or was she just mad? After all, her parents had treated her like crap tonight. Wasn't she still mad at them? They were having dinner—alone—in the same building where the baby shower was. How were those "plans" more important than seeing their daughter?

Okay, fine. Skye was just mad. She was probably tired, too—it'd been a long day.

She'd go inside and kiss her daughter and have her husband take her home.

But tomorrow, she wanted some answers.

Ten

"How are things going with Skye?" Keaton was standing in the doorway of the living room, a towel slung over his shoulder.

Jake looked up at his brother from where he lay on the floor, next to Grace. The baby was on her tummy, making those weird grunting noises. Jake had been giving her pep talks on lifting her head up, but so far, no progress.

"Fine," he said. He was still having trouble reconciling the Keaton before him with the Keaton who'd tried to undermine him for years. "I hope she's having fun at that baby shower."

"She remember anything?"

That's what Keaton said. What he meant was, had Skye remembered not telling Jake she was pregnant—or why?

Jake would not fly off the handle at his brother. The man had changed, after all—caring for Jake's daughter, building a house for Skye's sister—definitely not anything

Jake would have ever figured him for. Maybe things could be different now. Better, even.

But Jake still didn't know how to trust his own brother. So he said, "Not much. I'm hoping that no one says or does anything at the shower to upset her tonight. We've been focused on her physical rehab for now."

Keaton snickered. "I bet you have."

"Watch it," Jake snapped.

Keaton held his hands up in surrender. "Easy, man, easy. Whatever you're doing, it's working. She looks a hell of a lot better than she did in that hospital."

That was good. Truth be told, they were having a lot of sex—the kind of sex they'd had in the first year or so of their marriage. And it did seem to be making Skye very happy. Jake wasn't complaining, either. "She wants Grace to come home with us," Jake admitted.

"Yeah?" Keaton thought about this for a while. "Home, where? You going to take them both back to Houston?"

All in all, it was probably the most diplomatic way of asking the same question Keaton had asked when Jake had first met his daughter—*you going to slip off into the night with your baby?*

And truthfully? Jake wanted to. Yeah, his parents were being great and yeah, Keaton hadn't stabbed him in the back or anything, but that didn't mean that Jake didn't see the ghosts of events past everywhere he looked.

He wanted to go back to being in charge of his own life again.

"I'm not sure. I actually have a meeting about the next job Monday afternoon—an internet video interview. I planned on bringing Skye over here so she could play with Grace."

"Another year in Bahrain or wherever?" There was no missing the judgment in Keaton's voice.

"North America. Three weeks on, one week off. In

my line of work, that's a really cushy schedule." He could probably do one week a month in Royal. It wouldn't be as if he lived here, after all. It would just be…a vacation house where his wife and child lived. And Skye would be happier if she stayed here, he knew. Even she remembered wanting to come home. She just didn't remember telling him about it.

Jake held up his finger and grinned as Grace did her level best to clamp down on it. "You're already pretty strong, aren't you?"

Grace sighed.

God, this little girl pulled at him in ways he'd never imagined possible. She'd only been a part of his life for a week and already he was having trouble remembering what it'd been like before.

Three weeks on, one week off—was that something he could really do? Go three weeks without seeing Grace?

Hell, could he go that long without *Skye*? Yeah, he'd spent ten months away from her, but that had been when things were bad between them. Right now, that seemed like such a distant memory as to have been another life. Right now, she was the woman he'd always loved. The woman he always wanted to love.

He didn't know. He just didn't know.

Keaton was staring at him. Jake got the feeling his big brother wanted to say something—several somethings— and none of them would be complimentary.

So Jake decided to change the subject.

"Mom said the tornado turned up the original land deed in town hall?" The Holt family had long claimed the Taylors had stolen part of the Holts' land—and the Taylors had always claimed the Holts were on their property. Neither side had proof. The land deeds had long been lost.

Keaton nodded. He went to a drawer and pulled out a piece of paper that had been folded over and over. "The original is with our lawyers," he said as he unfolded the copy. The deed took up almost half of the dining-room table.

Jake picked up Grace. Even if Lark had said it was okay to leave the baby on the ground, he still didn't like it. It just felt wrong. Plus, Keaton's dog was right over there. Jake didn't want to leave Grace where the dog could get her.

Keaton was unfolding a second sheet of paper—a map. "This is the current fence line," he said, pointing to an ugly red line down the middle. "And according to the deed, this," he said, pointing to a blue line almost three inches away, "is the original property line."

"What's the scale?" Jake said, rubbing Grace's back.

"One inch equals one thousand feet."

Jake whistled, which caused Grace to start. "Sorry, sweetie," he said. "That's close to a half mile."

"Actually, you figure in how long the fence runs, it comes out to almost two thousand acres."

"*Damn*. Dang," Jake quickly corrected. There was a child in the room.

"I could use the land," Keaton told him. "The ranch's finances are still struggling from the tornado. More land means more cattle and better grazing. There are several small lakes and a spring on what they claim is their land that would make a big difference in how many cattle I can support. Hell, the value of the land alone is close to two million."

"What's it going to take, then?" Jake asked. "To get the Taylors to admit they're in the wrong?"

"Don't know," Keaton said. "If we only had some independent proof—so that Tyrone can't claim I forged it…" He shook his head. "I tried, you know. I went out there to make peace, for Lark. Told him I wanted to marry his daughter and maybe we could just let bygones be bygones."

"How'd that work out for you?"

"Oh, you know—the usual. He accused me of forging the documents. And they've basically disowned Lark."

Independent proof. That's what Jake needed. Irrefutable evidence that Skye's great-great-great-grandfather or whoever had moved the line and misappropriated Holt land.

How the hell was Jake supposed to get that?

Keaton sighed. "It's not all bad. Tyrone's stuck. He can't sell the land without a bill of sale and we will sue him if he 'finds' one. And if he can't get rid of the land, it'll be handed down to Lark and Skye, just like our land will go to us. We just have to wait him out."

"Great. Another generation of waiting. Yippee."

Keaton snorted as he pointed to a black square that almost sat on the red line. "I'm not waiting. I'm building Lark a house. Mom and Dad offered to let us have the ranch house when they retire to Gulf Shores, but…I wanted her to have someplace that was her own. It's going to have a gourmet kitchen and a library for all of her books and plenty of room. She says maybe we'll have three or four kids." Keaton laughed. "Can you imagine? Me and Lark with four kids all running around."

Actually, Jake was having a lot of trouble imagining that. "Which side of the fence are you building?" he asked, eyeing the map.

"The Holt side—but," Keaton said with a mean grin, "man, it's snugged up against that fence line. You could walk out of the house and cross over into what Tyrone claims is 'his' land. You know, you could take over the ranch house after Mom and Dad move out. We'd be neighbors."

Jake could. He could go back home and erase all the bad memories of the past, the same way he was trying to do with Skye now. He could put his family in his childhood home and just…

Pretend nothing had happened? Wasn't he already doing

that? He was hanging out with Keaton, as if the man had never betrayed him. He was taking care of Skye, as if the past two years had been nothing but a lousy dream after too many burritos.

Could he do that forever?

What about when she remembered? Would she still want him? And would she go on pretending that the divorce papers had been a figment of his imagination—or not?

When they'd first run off, they'd gotten a one-bedroom apartment and set up their computers on a rickety table they'd bought at a thrift store. They'd lived cheaply and worked from home, him on building his IT business, her on her graphic design business. They'd spent most of the day—and the night—together. If the mood hit them, Jake would pull her out of her chair and take her to bed. And when the bed was too far away, he'd take her to the couch.

It'd just been them against the world for about eight months. Him and Skye, like it was supposed to be.

Then his business had started to take off. He'd won a couple of bids, got some good references and begun taking more jobs. He'd been home less and less, although Skye still worked from home. They'd moved into a better place after one lucrative job, gotten nicer things. They'd left the rickety table behind.

There'd been a time when that…hadn't worked as well. They'd had better stuff—nicer cars, better clothes and a much nicer place—but Jake had been working insane hours. He hadn't been home as much. He'd missed her, but he hadn't been able to back off from the job. Texas Sky Consulting had been taking off and a secure financial future that was completely independent of either of their families was no small thing.

When international clients had started inquiring about Jake's services, he'd asked Skye to come with him. They'd jetted around the world together and on those trips, they'd gotten a taste of the closeness that had marked their first year together. Yeah, Jake still worked, but Skye was included in dinners and parties. And since neither of them spoke anything besides English and a little Spanish, they stuck together even more.

But then…then they'd gone back home. He'd gone back to work. And left Skye alone.

To see the love in her eyes dim a little more every day.

As Jake patted Grace's back, he remembered how he'd felt during those times. There was a wall between them, things left unsaid. He hadn't liked it then and he didn't like it now.

The fact of the matter was, he'd put his business before Skye. He'd convinced himself he was doing it for her—providing for their future together—but was that really reason enough to work seventy-hour weeks? To go days without touching her?

Weeks without touching her?

"Mom has offered," he told Keaton. "I'm thinking about it. It'd make Skye happy to stay here."

"Yeah? Would it make you happy?"

Jake gritted his teeth. *Not yet it wouldn't*, he thought—but he kept that to himself. Luckily, Grace started to fuss. "Is it bedtime?" Jake asked, looking at the clock.

"Yup. Let me get her bottle. You want to do this on your own?"

"Yeah," Jake said. He got why Skye was always saying she wanted to care for the baby herself. There was something sweet about being the one to feed and burp—and yes, even change the diapers.

As he fed and rocked Grace until she fell asleep, Jake realized that he didn't know much, but he knew that he loved Skye and that he loved Grace.

He'd almost lost his family once.

He'd do anything to hold on to them.

* * *

"Oh," Skye whispered when she saw Jake rocking Grace to sleep. "Hi."

Jake smiled up at her—the picture of a doting father. Skye was filled with love. She'd wanted this—something told her she'd known this was what would happen. A baby would solve so many of the things that had driven her and Jake away from Royal in the first place.

And Grace had. Skye was close to Lark again. By all appearances, Jake and Keaton had spent an evening together without killing each other. And Gloria was going to wash all the baby things and bring them over to help Skye get the house ready for when Grace could come home.

Grace just hadn't worked her charm on Tyrone and Vera Taylor.

Jake held up his hand, as if to say, *Just a minute.* He carefully got up and laid the baby down in her crib.

Skye joined him, leaning against his shoulder as they watched their daughter sleep. Grace was perfect—getting stronger every day, too. Just like Skye.

Jake leaned down and kissed her lightly. "Ready to go home?"

"Do we have to?" Skye knew the answer to that, but still, she wanted to stay with Grace.

"We'll come back tomorrow," he promised her. Then he kissed her again. "I'll make it worth your while."

She grinned and took his arm. After the semi-disastrous baby shower, she wouldn't mind falling asleep in Jake's arms. "Good night, my little bit of Grace." She leaned down and tenderly ran her hand over her little girl's head. "Sleep well."

Lark was waiting for them downstairs. "I have to work tomorrow, so it'll just be Keaton," she told them. "Oh, and Skye—here's your diamond."

"What?" Jake said. "What diamond?"

"My one earring," Skye said, handing him the little bag with one earring and a post in it. "Lark said they didn't find the other diamond or my wedding ring."

The blood drained out of Jake's face. "Oh. Well. I'll… hang on to this for you, okay?"

They said their goodbyes to Keaton and Lark and then Jake took her home. "I wish I had my ring," she told him in the car. Exhausted, she slumped against the window, watching the brownness that was Texas in February slide past. "You should have seen the look my mother gave me tonight. It made me almost feel like we weren't married anymore."

He made a choking noise. "We are, babe. We are still married."

Still.

What a strange word.

She looked at him. His wedding ring glinted in the light of the dash. Still. *Still.*

Something wasn't right.

She closed her eyes and tried to think—but no, she was too danged tired to come up with the echo of something Jake might have said once—*why do you* still *want to go back there?*

Why aren't I enough for you?

Skye jolted straight up in her seat. What the heck was that? She looked at Jake.

"What? What?" he repeated. "Are you okay?" He looked over at her. "You can't let your mom get to you, babe. I never really understood why you wanted to come back here, to be closer to that."

"I just…" She sighed. She didn't remember discussing this with him, but on the other hand, the conversation had a familiar feel to it. "I wanted things to be different. Better."

Jake was silent after that, which left Skye feeling kind of hopeless and she wasn't even sure why. After all, things were better. Lark and Keaton, Gloria and David—those relationships were one-hundred-percent better now than when Jake and Skye had slipped off into the night four years ago.

She was too tired to think—and definitely too tired to be reading something into Jake's nonresponse. They were almost home anyway.

He pulled into the drive and shut the car off, but he didn't get out right away.

"Jake?" Had she crossed some line she didn't remember she shouldn't cross?

"It's nothing," he said. "I bet you're beat. Let's get you to bed."

Even though Skye's legs were getting stronger, Jake scooped her out of her seat and carried her into the house. She let him. She rested her head on his shoulder as he carried her up the stairs. Then he went back down to lock up while she used the bathroom. She got into bed and a few minutes later, he climbed in with her.

He pulled her into a tight embrace, but it wasn't an erotic touch. He clung to her as if he were afraid she'd be blown away with the next strong wind that roared through.

"Skye," he said in such a serious voice that a pit of nerves opened up in her stomach.

"What is it?" Because there had to be an *it*—a something that she didn't know but should.

He laced his fingers with hers and held them over her heart. "I wanted things to be better, too."

She let those words sift through her mind. He could be talking about their parents or her accident or Grace being a preemie or any number of things.

But she didn't think he was. She thought he was talking about the two of them.

"Are we…are we okay?"

When he didn't answer immediately, the nerves kicked

straight over to stark panic. She didn't know if she was going to cry or not.

"We are," he said, but he didn't sound convinced. "I have loved you for twenty years, Skye. Nothing—*nothing*—has ever changed that. And nothing ever will. You know that, right?"

"I do," she said, her voice shaking. "You know I love you too, right?"

He lifted up her left hand and kissed her bare ring finger. "I just…I don't want you to forget that, that's all."

"I couldn't, Jake. I couldn't—not you."

He rolled into her, saying, "Don't," as he kissed her. "Don't forget this, my blue-eyed Skye."

"I won't," she promised him as their bodies joined again and again. "I will always remember you, Jake."

Eleven

Why aren't I enough for you? Skye looked around, but she couldn't see where Jake was. His voice just *was*.

You were—when you were here, she said back—or thought back—or however they were talking.

Except they weren't talking. They were shouting. They were fighting. And Jake…Jake walked away? From her?

She jolted awake, her heart pounding as she gasped for air. Was that real? Had that happened? Or had it been a dream? No, not a dream—a nightmare.

It had to be a nightmare because Jake was lying in bed next to her. He'd sworn he loved her and then made love to her, and she was safe in his arms. They were home in Royal and they would go see Grace tomorrow and…

Except for one thing. She could still see the scene. Their apartment in Houston, her standing at the window, Jake packing up a bag and saying, "I already signed the contract." He'd made no move toward Skye—made no attempt to comfort her. "I leave in two weeks."

She pinched her arm, which hurt. She wasn't still dreaming. She was *remembering*.

"So it's settled, then," she'd said to him. God, she remembered how the distance between them had felt impossibly huge.

Skye began to panic.

"You could still come with me." That's what he'd said. Not that he loved her, not that he couldn't live without her.

"You could still stay. We could go home together, start our family." That was what she'd said back. Not that she couldn't bear to lose him, not that he was her everything.

And he'd left. He'd left without another word.

And she'd...

Oh, God. *Oh, God.*

She'd thrown her ring out the window.

Skye began to sob.

One minute, he was asleep. The next, Skye was making horrible choking noises.

"Babe?" he said, trying to keep calm as he pulled her into his arms. "Babe, you're okay. I'm here now. I'm right here."

"Oh, Jake," she wept. "I didn't mean it. I didn't mean it."

No. God, no. Had she been— "It's okay," he soothed as he stroked her hair and her back, trying to calm her down. "What happened?"

"I—the dream."

Jake forced himself to breathe in and out. "What did you dream?"

"We had a fight. And I woke up, but it wasn't a dream, was it? It *wasn't*." It was hard to understand her through the tears.

Jake's hands stilled against her. "What—" He swallowed, trying desperately to keep his cool. "What else did you remember?" The word cut into his mouth as if he were chewing glass.

Because this was it. This was the moment he'd been dreading.

"Bahrain? But I thought you were in New York for that job. But you were going to Bahrain. For, like, a year. A year!"

Damn. She *was* remembering—sort of. Her brain was trying to put the past back in place.

"Babe," he said, rubbing her back. "It's okay, babe."

"You left. You left *me*."

He was not supposed to lie to her. He could gloss over the truth. Julie at the hospital had said so.

But how could he gloss over this? He could convince her it'd all been a bad dream, that he'd been in New York for a short time instead of another country for almost a year.

He could...he could convince her that she was wrong. He could make her think that she couldn't trust her own mind. He could make himself look like a better man—at the expense of her mental health.

No, he couldn't do that. Not to her.

Still, he tried to sidestep the heart of the matter. She was already upset—and that was something the doctors had said he needed to avoid. He didn't want to make it worse.

"I came back," he told her. "I came back for you."

She gasped again. "You—you really *did* leave me?" When he didn't answer, she demanded, "For how long?"

"Skye..."

"For how long, Jacob Holt?"

There was no way to sidestep this. His only choice was to go straight ahead. "For about ten months."

"To New York?"

"To Bahrain."

That, apparently, was too much. Suddenly, Skye was

out of his arms and out of the bed. "You left me for ten months to go to *Bahrain*?"

"Skye…" he said in what he hoped was a calming voice.

"No—don't *Skye* me." She dropped her head in her hands. "Oh, God—I do remember. I remember *everything*." Then she was hurrying to the bathroom before he could get the damned covers off.

"Skye, wait!" he called as the door shut behind her. He made it to the door, but it was locked. Damn. "Skye, listen—things are different now."

"Did you even know about Grace?" came the muffled cry from the bathroom. "Did you even know about her before you showed up here?"

"No. I didn't hear from you for months. You didn't tell me."

"Oh, God…"

"Skye," he pleaded. "I'm trying. I came back for you. I'm taking care of you. I'm renting a house in Royal, Texas, for crying out loud—and you know how much I hate this damn town. I mean, I'm even considering taking the ranch house from my folks so that you and Grace can stay here because I know that's what you want, dammit."

"But I…I threw my ring away. Did I want a divorce? Oh, God—I did, didn't I?" This was followed by more crying.

"Skye—please, babe. Yes, I came home to find divorce papers waiting for me. But that's not what I want and I've spent the last couple of weeks doing everything I can to show you that you—you and Grace—come first in my life."

He rested his head against the door. This was where he'd come to in his life—talking to a bathroom door while naked. "I wanted things to be different, too. Better. I didn't want things to end like they did. You've got to believe me, babe."

"Why didn't you tell me? Why did you let me carry on like we were still in love?"

"Because we *are* still in love," Jake insisted. "I love you. Nothing has changed that, Skye. Not divorce papers, not amnesia—not anything."

There was no response.

He tried the knob again. Still locked. He could break down the door, but somehow he didn't think that was the best way to keep her calm right now.

"I didn't tell you because the doctor told me not to upset you. He said you had to remember it on your own. Well, now you have. I'm not hiding anything from you, Skye. We have a child now. We can make this work. I love you and I love Grace. We have the family you always wanted. Don't throw that away, Skye."

"Even if I want to stay in Royal?"

Jake swallowed. What the hell. He was already living in Royal, after all. "Even if you want to stay in Royal." He heard her sniff. "Skye, come back to bed. Things will seem better in the morning, I promise."

The door opened—but just a crack. "Will you still love me? Tomorrow?"

"I will still love you *always*," he promised, knowing the words were true. "I couldn't stop even if I tried."

She gave him a teary smile. "Okay. We'll talk tomorrow, right?"

"Absolutely. Anything you want. But come to bed now, okay? The doctor would string me up by my toes if he knew I was letting you get this upset."

She nodded and opened the door. Jake walked her to the bed and tucked her in, then slid in next to her.

They lay together in the silence for a long time.

Neither of them slept.

Jake spent the next two days doing everything except throwing himself at Skye's feet and begging for forgiveness. And there were a few times when he considered that to be his best option.

Skye's memory was returning in fits and starts. "Were you in Venezuela for six months?" she asked at one point.

"Yes." This was a kind of hell, having her pass judgment on all his past sins all over again. "You came down for a few weeks, but you didn't like it there, so you came back."

Because that was all he could do right now—be completely honest about the past. It was clear that she was going to recover most, if not all, of those memories and the last thing he wanted to do was undermine her trust in him a second time.

"Right. I hated Venezuela," she replied. "Are you going to take another job like that? Like Bahrain? Where you're gone for months and months at a time?"

"No," he promised her. "I don't want to leave you or Grace for that long. That was the mistake I made last time. I won't make it again."

Every time they had a variation on this conversation, Skye would nod her head and say, "Okay," and that would be it for another hour or so, until she got another piece of the puzzle and wanted to know where it fit.

They went to see Grace. Lark was home the second day and could clearly tell that something was off, but she didn't say anything.

Desperate to avoid having their dirty laundry aired to Lark, Jake focused on Grace with a laser-like intensity. He fixed the bottles and changed the diapers and did everything he could think of to show Skye how devoted he was. When his mother showed up with all the presents that Skye had received at the baby shower, Jake even sat there and acted as interested as he could as they showed him everything. There was only so much enthusiasm he could muster for onesies, but he tried, dammit. He tried for Skye.

They hadn't made love again, but that was okay. Skye

was still sleeping in bed with him and there, under the cover of darkness, she began to talk to him.

"I still feel like I'm missing things," she said. "I don't— I don't have Grace, you know? I don't remember being pregnant. I don't know if it was an easy pregnancy or a hard one or anything."

"It'll come back," he told her. "And if it doesn't, we'll have to have another baby so you can remember it."

She hugged him. "You'd have another baby with me?"

"Of course. We're a family, after all. I'm in this for the long haul, no matter what."

"Oh, Jake—I don't want a divorce," she told him. "I just want you."

"Then I'm yours."

Which was all very good and well.

Except for one thing.

He had a job interview on Monday.

Twelve

Skye's head was still a mess—but she was starting to set things to rights again.

She'd remembered most of how it had gone bad—Jake had kept taking longer and longer jobs away from home, but he didn't want to come back to Royal. Skye remembered feeling trapped and abandoned and those memories were hard.

But they were softened by the Jake she had by her side right now—the man who helped her with her exercises and cooked her meals and played with their daughter. The man who talked about moving out into his parents' ranch home so Grace would have wide open spaces in which to grow up, just down the way from where Keaton and Lark would live. The man who talked of having another baby, once they got Grace home and she was stronger.

Sometimes, it was hard to reconcile the two versions of Jake that were fighting for space in her head.

So, when Monday came and he said he had to do something for work and he was just going drop her off at Lark's, she did her level best not to worry about it. "You're not flying out to Siberia or anything, right?" she half joked.

"Nope. Just a phone call," he assured her as he walked in with her.

Lark wasn't there—it was just Keaton. Skye tried not to feel nervous about that—after all, this was not the same Keaton who'd never liked her or her family. This was the Keaton who loved Lark and made her happy and took care of Grace as if she were his own.

"Ready for some tummy time?" Keaton asked Skye. "I think Miss Grace is ready to play with her mommy."

"I'll be back in a couple of hours, okay?" Jake said as he kissed Grace's head. "You have fun with her," he added as he kissed Skye goodbye.

Keaton laid Grace down on the activity mat and waited patiently for Skye to get down on the ground, too. "You want some lunch?" he asked.

"Sure," she said, although as far as she could tell, Lark had been doing all the meals. She wasn't sure if Keaton could actually cook or not.

"How have you been doing?" Keaton asked from the kitchen.

"Better. I'm starting to remember things," she told him as Grace made her little grunting noise. Skye put her hand on Grace's back and felt the baby's muscles working. "You can do it, sweetie," she told the baby. "Stronger every day. Mommy has tummy time, too, you know."

Grace made a cooing noise.

"Really?" Keaton said, the surprise in his voice obvious. "You're getting stuff back?"

Skye mentally smacked herself in the head. What was she doing, telling that to Keaton? She really didn't want to have this conversation with him. If Lark were here, she might be open with her sister. But she still hadn't figured out how to interact with Keaton outside of talking about the baby. "Yes."

Keaton came to the doorway and looked down at her. "And you and Jake...you're cool?"

"Yes," she said again, trying to turn her attention back to Grace. The baby was stretching her arms out, which made her look like a Super Baby in training.

"Wow. Okay." Keaton scratched his head. "Well, that's..." He looked at her and paused. "That's great. Really glad to hear it."

There it was again, that feeling that people were holding out on her. But it wasn't as if Skye were having this conversation with Lark. This was Keaton, and she was not comfortable with him. "Yes," she said. "It's great."

She swallowed. Keaton knew something but he didn't appear to be in any hurry to tell her. Maybe she could... find something out? Because she was so tired of knowing she was missing something. She was stronger now.

"It's not like he's not going to fly to Siberia or anything," she added, doing a decent impression of calm. "I'm not worried."

Keaton's eyebrows were almost up to his hairline. "Oh, okay. So...yeah. Well, that's good."

She frowned. That was not an informative response. She picked up Grace and laid the little girl on her chest. For a moment, she forgot about trying to figure out what she didn't know because what she *knew*, right now, was that this was her little girl and together they were getting stronger. She could feel Grace's little heartbeat fluttering against hers.

But she wanted to know what she was missing because it seemed important. It was her future, wasn't it? And Jake had said the past didn't matter, not compared to what would happen in the future.

"I know he said…" She paused. "Shoot. I can't remember where he said his next job was?"

Keaton rubbed the back of his neck, looking uncomfortable. "He told you?"

"Yes, of course." She hoped it came out sounding confident. "We don't have secrets."

"Well…" Keaton sighed. "I'm glad you're okay with it. I didn't think that being gone three weeks out of the month was the best thing, but Lark and I are happy to help out when he's gone." He smiled encouragingly.

Was *that* what Jake was doing—interviewing for a job that would take him away for three weeks of the month? "Oh, yeah—that'll be great. We're still working out the details," she said, feeling stupid.

Because they weren't working the details out at all. Jake was still putting work ahead of her—her and Grace.

No, it wasn't ten months in Bahrain or even three months in New York—but only seeing him one week out of the month? How was she supposed to take care of Grace by herself? She couldn't bear to leave Grace here at Keaton and Lark's for much longer. She'd been focused on getting stronger so they could bring Grace home—together.

Skye wanted her family, damn it. She wanted the people she loved most—Jake and Grace and the other babies they'd talked about having together—all under one roof, living side by side, day in and day out.

And what if they did have another baby? What then? Would Skye be doing the pregnancy alone—again? Would she be delivering the baby alone—*again*?

Because *why*? Because Jake was out on yet another damned job, talking about how this job would lead to bigger and better things? Things that would slowly erode at the amount of time he was home until they were going almost a year without laying eyes on each other—*again*?

Skye held Grace tight to avoid looking at Keaton. A buzzer went off in the kitchen and he left the room.

What was she going to do now? Skye's mind raced. She had gotten most of her memory back, but she still didn't remember large chunks of the last ten months.

Jake loved her. He'd said it—shown it—time and time again.

But…

Did he love her enough to actually stay in Royal with her? Was she more important than the job?

She didn't know.

But she sure as hell was going to find out.

"Great," Carl said. "Thanks for your time today, Jake. We've been most impressed with your previous work."

Jake smiled into the web camera and tried not to notice how it distorted his grin into a bucktoothed nightmare. "If you have any other questions about how I can adapt the technology to your specific needs, just let me know."

"Great," Carl said again. He seemed to have a limited vocabulary in this regard. "We'll let you know our decision within the week."

The video call ended. By and large, the interview had gone well. Great, even, as Carl would say.

Would Jake actually take the job?

This was his company. This was what he did. And because he wanted to make sure that the job was done well, he'd always insisted on doing it himself instead of farming it out to employees. When Texas Sky did a job, the technology and production would be as promised or better.

He sat there, staring at the computer screen. In four years, he'd created a company worth millions of dollars by sheer dint of the sweat of his brow. He *was* his company and the prospect of giving up control of it—any of it—was hard for him to swallow.

But then, giving up any time with Skye and Grace was even harder for him to swallow.

He'd made this bed by insisting that he was the only one who could do his work. But did it really have to be that way?

After all, if he was the one who did everything—bid all the jobs, did all the on-site work—how much could his company grow? He'd always be doing one job at a time. Sure, the jobs paid well, but...

But what if he wanted to expand? Take on more jobs? Build his clientele?

He could hire out. He could expand now, not at some undetermined point in the future. He could do most of his work out of the office, not on-site. He could keep his company *and* keep his family.

The enormity of this realization stunned him. All he had to do was...let go.

Let go of it all. The control he insisted on having to run his business. Let go of the grudges that kept him from admitting that maybe his family had changed.

That maybe, just maybe, he'd changed.

What better way to show Skye that he had put her first than to do this for her—for them?

The more he thought about it, the better this idea seemed. There was only one hitch in the whole plan— Skye's family. Jake knew the Holts would be happy if he stayed, and Lark would, as well. But Tyrone and Vera Taylor?

Jake should try to talk to the Taylors. He didn't have any illusion that it would go well, not after Skye's descriptions of their behavior at the baby shower. But if he could somehow smooth things out between Tyrone and Vera Taylor and Skye—well, wasn't that what Skye wanted?

Jake was on the verge of calling Tyrone Taylor when the doorbell rang. *What now?* he thought with a growl.

He threw open the door to find a deliveryman standing on the stoop. "Afternoon," he said. "Need a signature." He held out an overnight envelope addressed to Skye Taylor.

Taylor?

Jake signed and took the envelope. He stared at it after the delivery van had driven off. Why was Skye getting overnight packages from...?

He stared at the return address. From Matthews Private Investigations in Houston? What the hell? What did she want with a PI?

Questions swarmed around him like bees. When had she hired the PI? Why? Was she having him investigated? Or his family? Was she looking for ammo in the Taylor/Holt feud? And how had he gotten this address?

The alarm on his phone chimed—he had to go pick up Skye.

He tucked the envelope under his arm and grabbed his keys.

Only one way to find out—that was to ask her.

He could tell something was wrong from the moment he walked into Lark's house.

Oh, everything looked okay. Skye was in the recliner with a sleeping Grace against her chest. Keaton was on his laptop. Soft classical music filled the air. "Hey," he said to Keaton.

Skye didn't look at him.

"Babe," he whispered as he leaned over to kiss Grace on top of her head.

"Let's go," Skye said. "I want to go home."

"Everything okay?" He looked back at Keaton. The man wasn't acting guilty—but there was definitely something off about Skye.

"Fine," Keaton replied as he stood and came to take

Grace from Skye. "I'll put her down. You guys coming back tomorrow?"

"Yes," Skye said, and again, Jake heard the stiffness in her voice.

He didn't say anything about it until they were in the car. "You okay?" he asked without starting the engine. If he had to go in and beat the hell out of Keaton, he didn't want to leave the car running. "Everything okay with you and Keaton?"

"Oh, sure. You know, same old same old." She crossed her arms. Then, catching sight of the envelope on the dash, she asked, "What's that?"

"Actually," he replied, trying to sound calm—even though he felt nothing like calm at the moment. "I was hoping you could tell me that. It was just delivered—and it's addressed to you. From a private investigator."

He watched her as he told her this. What kind of reaction would she have? Recognition? Confusion? Desperation?

Skye cocked her head to one side and picked the envelope up. She opened it and pulled out a typed letter and an odd-looking piece of paper that had been folded many times and was in a protective plastic envelope.

She read the letter and then looked at him. "Did you do this?" she demanded, thrusting the letter at him.

"No," he said reflexively, even if he didn't know what it was yet. "I'm not the one who hired a private eye." He took the letter and read.

Ms. Taylor,

I have located the original land deed in the Texas General Land Office that shows the property line between the Taylor and Holt lands as set 114 years ago. The deed had been misfiled at some point, possibly intentionally. This deed conclusively proves that the

Taylors relocated the fence line, probably at some point in the 1920s.

I have included a copy of the original deed for your records.

Please advise as to how you'd like me to proceed with the deed. I'm sure both parties involved would like to get a hold of this original. Would you like me to forward it to the Holts or the Taylors?
Regards,
Reggie Matthews, P.I.

Jake sat there, blinking at the letter. This was it—the smoking gun that showed the Taylors had cheated the Holts out of all that land. This was what Keaton needed—independent proof of the Taylors' treachery.

But as monumental as this information was, his eyes were drawn not to the deed but to the header on the letter. Ms. Taylor. Skye had already gone back to her maiden name by the time she'd hired this guy. "You hired a PI to dig up the land deed?"

"I…must have?" Skye didn't sound sure.

"Well, you did." When she flinched, he realized it had come out harsh, but what the ever-loving hell? Here he was, doing everything to win her back and she was—what? "Who were you going to give the deed to, Skye? Your family—or mine?"

Because that was the question. Had she been working to end the feud—or looking for a way back into Tyrone and Vera Taylor's good graces?

Her face was creased in concentration as she stared at the copy in her lap. "I don't…I don't remember hiring him. I don't remember what I wanted him to do."

"You don't? Or are you just conveniently forgetting, *Ms. Taylor*?" She flinched again, but he didn't care. Here he was, ready to give up control of his company for her—

and she was working against the Holts. Even if she didn't remember, she'd been willing to hurt not just him, but his family. "You were going to go back to your parents, weren't you? You always wanted to come home. You said so all the time."

Something in her seemed to snap and her confusion disappeared. "Oh, and I suppose you were going to take that job without even telling me? How did your interview go—the one where you're going to be gone three weeks out of the month?"

Jake froze. "What?"

"You had an interview for a job that's three weeks on and one week off, right? Or did you forget to tell me that?"

"What? How did you— Keaton." Damn it all to hell, that man would always, *always* stab Jake in the back.

"Yes, Keaton. I told him I was getting things back and he asked me how we were going to deal with this job you wanted. Jake, I thought you..." Here her voice broke. "I thought you were going to stay with me. I thought we were going to be a family. Because you loved me."

"I do love you," he shot back. "But—"

She cut him off. "Don't you dare say you're doing this for me, Jacob Holt," she snapped. "Don't hide behind that lie." She began to cry, but these weren't weepy tears of sadness. These were mad streaks of water that seemed to cut into her face. "And here I thought you wanted me—you wanted our *family*. I can't count on you, can I?"

"What are you going to do—have me investigated?" he said. Okay, shouted. "Try to dig up more information you can take back to your father so you can be Daddy's little girl again?"

"Go to hell." She opened the door and got out.

"Skye—wait!" He yelled after her, scrambling to get out of the car. She didn't turn around. An old panic flooded his system. Once, he'd lost her because he hadn't fought for her. That's not how he was going to go down this time. There'd be no words left unspoken, not this time. "Skye, dammit—wait. I'm not going to take the job. I don't even know why we're arguing over it. Things have changed. I've changed. Remember?" He tried to get in front of her, to make her listen, but she was pretty darned fast for a woman in her condition.

Before he could stop her, she wrenched Keaton's front door open and stepped inside. "I don't want to hear it." She turned and gave him a look full of heartache and pain. "You didn't even *tell* me about the interview. You lied to me, Jake. What is it about this damn job—this damn company of yours—that means more to you than I do? Than our baby does?"

"It doesn't," he insisted, closing the distance between them.

"This is why I wanted a divorce, isn't it? This is *exactly* why. We got a second chance and what did you do? You made me think you'd changed. But you haven't. *You haven't.* And it's clear you won't change for me. Not now, not ever."

She slammed the door shut in his face. The lock clicked.

Hell. He rang the doorbell, but no one answered; all he heard was that dog howling. He had no choice here. He grabbed his phone and called Keaton.

"Damn your hide," he snarled when his brother picked up. "Why did you tell Skye about that interview? I'm not even going to take the job!"

In the stunned silence that followed, he was pretty sure he heard crying in the background. God, it just went from bad to worse.

"Damn—Jake, I didn't mean to set her off."

"You never mean it, do you?" He couldn't even talk to his brother. Jake hung up. He was done with that man. *Done* with him. This was why Jake didn't want to come back to Royal—his family would always fail him when he needed them most.

Part of him wanted to go after Skye, try to talk some sense into her. But another part of him knew that would be a bad idea. She was already upset. He wanted her to calm down first. Which left only one thing to do.

Jake punched up Lark's number. "Skye's upset," he began when she answered the phone. "She doesn't want to stay with me right now. She's in your house with Keaton."

Lark gasped. "What happened?"

"She's remembering," Jake said. He knew that Skye would probably tell Lark everything, but he couldn't bear to throw himself under that bus. "I've got to try and fix this, but if you could keep a close eye on her until she calms down…"

"Of course. My shift is almost over, anyway. I can be home in twenty minutes."

"Thanks, Lark. I owe you." He hung up again and stared at his damn phone.

Had he changed? He wanted to think he had. He was a father now, after all. That alone changed a man.

But…

He jammed his hands into his pockets, trying to think. What was it about this damn company? That's what she wanted to know. Why did it mean so much to him?

Because it was his. He'd started it on his own, with no help from his family. He'd been free of them.

Except he hadn't been, not really. Everything he'd done had been a reaction to them, to the way they'd tried to keep him from Skye.

Something poked him in the finger. He pulled out the small baggie with an earring and a half in it. A single diamond was all that was left of the jewelry he'd bought for Skye.

He knew what he had to do. He wasn't going to like this, but it had to be done.

He got in the car and headed toward the Taylor place.

Thirteen

"What are *you* doing here?" was how Tyrone Taylor answered the door.

"I need to talk to you." When the older man didn't move, Jake added, "It's about Skye and Grace."

Tyrone didn't give much—but he gave enough. His eyebrows shot up in barely concealed concern and he didn't slam the door in Jake's face.

The man was a tyrant and a bully, but Jake had to hope that maybe—just maybe—he could convince him to make the right call on behalf of his daughter. Jake wasn't even going to attempt to sway Vera Taylor. Tyrone was his target.

"Are they—are they okay?" Tyrone's voice sounded soft, which was unusual enough.

"Doing good," Jake said. No need to torture the older man. "That's not why I'm here, though. There are some things you need to know. I married your daughter four years ago. And you know what? The one thing she wanted was the one thing I didn't want to give her—that was you. She wanted you to walk her down the aisle. She wanted to know that you and Vera still loved her. And I didn't think you two deserved to know how much she still loved you."

That—that was the heart of the matter. Their families didn't deserve them because they'd always put the damned feud before Jake and Skye.

Which was what Jake had done with his job and Skye.

Well, no more. Those days were over.

Tyrone's face reddened, but again, he didn't slam the door. "She made her choice. You."

"Don't you even want to know your grandchildren?" That was the only leverage that Jake had and both men knew it.

"Now, you listen here, Jake Holt—"

"No, I'm done listening to you." He thrust the copy of the land deed filed in the state office a hundred and fourteen years ago. "A Taylor moved the fences. You've been on Holt land your entire life."

"Your brother forged that document," Tyrone sputtered. "He didn't find it at town hall. He made it up."

"Even if that were true, how do you explain this one? Skye hired a private detective who found this in the Texas General Land Office. They have the original on file."

"Lies," Tyrone spat. "Another fake."

"The original has been rediscovered," Jake said. "On file. For anyone—and their lawyers—to see it." Tyrone almost dropped the folder, as if the reality had burned him. "Here's the deal, Taylor. I'm going to move back here with Skye. Keaton's going to marry Lark. The land will stay in both of our families. You can either dig in your blowhard heels and never see your granddaughter ever again or you can suck it up, admit that your ancestor was a thief and do what's best for your family."

The older man's mouth opened, shut, opened and shut again.

And the truth shall set you free, Jake thought. "I want to make Skye happy. I want to give her the one thing I could never give her before—her family. Even if you and your wife don't deserve it, Skye loves both of you and she wants our daughter to know you both."

Tyrone's mouth continued to open and shut as he turned from a tomato red to an eggplant purple.

"I'm going to throw a little party for her," Jake went on. "A reengagement party."

He could get the diamond from her earring set into a ring mount in a day or two—sooner, if the price was right.

This was what he had to do to show her that she meant more than the job. He had to marry her all over again—this time, with both of their families' approval. "I'd appreciate it if you and *Vera*," he went on, struggling to get the name out without scowling, "could come and be happy for our family. For *your* family."

Tyrone looked at the folder, then at Jake.

Yeah, they were done here. Jake didn't think he could pin the old man down to a yes, not when he'd put Tyrone on the spot. So he just said, "Friday night, at the Holt ranch, if you decide to come." Then he turned and went home.

He had a marriage proposal to arrange.

At several points, Skye found herself on the verge of asking Lark if Jake had said anything to her. Lark's phone was certainly ringing a lot. Plus, when Lark answered it, she'd shoot Skye a nervous smile and immediately leave the room. Something was clearly up.

But the moment Skye would start to find the words, Lark would suddenly notice something *very interesting* that Grace was doing that Lark had to just gush over.

Had Jake taken the job? Had he picked the company over her again?

It was almost too much to bear. Because if the answer was yes, what was she going to do?

Divorce him? She didn't remember what she'd been

thinking when she'd filed the first time. Had she hoped that the papers would be a wake-up call? Or had she been completely serious about it? It didn't even appear that she'd told him about her pregnancy. Maybe she had been serious.

She didn't know. What was worse, she didn't know when she'd know—or if she ever would. Those ten months were nearly blank and there was no one who'd been around to fill in the blanks for her.

Did she want a divorce?

She thought about how Jake had been the one to take her home from the hospital, to take care of her even when he knew she'd filed for divorce.

She knew now that all of that was radically different from how he'd been for a while—maybe as long as a year, even. And the things he'd said to her, while he was waiting for her to remember?

Whatever happened in the past isn't as important as what happens in the future, Skye.

Maybe…maybe she was asking for too much. He'd poured his heart and soul into his company. Obviously, the work made him happy. Who was she to ask him to give that up?

She was his wife. The mother of his child.

God, she just didn't know what to do.

Jake kept calling, talking to Keaton or Lark. They always asked if she'd like to talk to him, but she didn't know what to say. He'd asked questions—good ones—about whether she'd been planning on giving the deed to her father or to his family. And she just didn't have an answer for him. She might never have one.

Lark tried to keep her occupied with Grace. Skye didn't see much of Keaton, but she figured he was probably steering clear of her. It wasn't as lonely as it had been when Jake had left her the last time—she had Lark and Grace—but it was uncomfortably close.

Then Gloria came over Friday afternoon. Skye was so happy to see the older woman that she started to cry again. "Oh, now," Gloria said as she wrapped Skye up in a motherly hug. "Everyone fights, dear. It's not the fight that matters so much as how you make up."

"But *how*? I don't know what I don't know. Oh, God," she sobbed onto Gloria's shoulder.

Gloria sighed. "Jake and my David got on like oil and water, but they're more alike than either of them realize— both set in their ways and too stubborn for their own good. But," she went on, striking a hopeful note, "they just need a little space to regroup."

"Have you talked to him?" Skye demanded tearfully.

"I have," Gloria said. "Don't give up on him, Skye. He hasn't given up on you. Now," she added in a more forceful tone before Skye could question her further, "sitting around moping isn't going to help anything. I think we should have a little outing, don't you? It's warmer today. We could bundle Grace up and go out to the ranch. Won't that be fun?" Then she got up and bustled out of the room, describing all the ways that such an outing would be "fun."

Which was a crock, as far as Skye was concerned. Something was up.

"What's going on?" Skye demanded when Lark and Gloria came back into the room.

"Nothing!" both women said at the same time. There was no missing the look the two of them shared.

"I've got Grace," Gloria said with a smug smile. "You two girls go on."

"What's going on?" Skye demanded again as Lark led her to the bedroom and pointed out a bright blue sweater that Lark had apparently picked out on her own. "I mean, this is lovely, but seriously? The last time you brought me clothing, I had a baby shower."

"Sit," Lark commanded, leading Skye into the bathroom and pointedly avoiding the question. "I've almost figured out how to use a curling iron. This will be nice!"

"The more you and Gloria say that, the less I believe you," Skye mumbled. "Easy on the sore spot!"

Lark ignored her complaints. Instead, she said, "Can I tell you something?" as she wielded the curling iron like it was a weapon.

"Always," Skye said, resigning herself to her lot in life.

"I'm pregnant."

Skye sat up so fast she almost caught her forehead on the curling iron. "You are? Oh, Lark!"

Lark grinned, the happiness radiating off of her. "And Keaton and I already discussed it—if it's a girl, we're going to name her Taylor."

"Taylor Holt? I *love* it." It was a perfect name—the two families finally reunited.

"You do?" Lark beamed. "I'm not that far along, so we aren't going to tell everyone yet, but I wanted you to know."

"Oh, Lark," Skye said, her eyes starting to fill with tears. She managed to get to her feet without hitting the hot iron and wrapped her sister in a big hug. "I want our children to grow up together."

"I know. I want things to be better than it was for us, you know?" She leaned back and fanned her eyes. "Sorry. I'm already getting more emotional."

"Don't apologize. Have you and Keaton talked about getting married any more?"

Lark grinned as she went back to curling Skye's hair. She kept up a steady patter—she and Keaton wanted to get married this summer, before Lark started to show. Then maybe they'd take a honeymoon cruise to Alaska. "Or something, as long as we're together," Lark said as she blushed.

Finally, the torture with the curling iron was done. After Lark had misted her hair with spray, saying, "Even Mom would be proud of *that*," she then insisted that Skye let her put on a little blush and some mascara. "You'll feel better with a little makeup on," Lark added, with that sneaky smile that Skye hadn't trusted for decades.

Skye sighed. Clearly something was up. But she didn't know what.

Finally, Lark's phone buzzed. She looked at the message, pronounced Skye "beautiful" and not-so-casually said, "We should go."

"There's a party downstairs, isn't there?" Skye said.

"Of course not," Lark said way too fast.

"Is there any way out of this? I'm not feeling social right now. I just want Jake."

"Trust me," Lark replied with that smile again.

Lark and Gloria got Grace all bundled up in her baby carrier so wind couldn't get to her. Then everyone was in the car. Skye decided to sit in the back so she could keep an eye on her daughter.

She didn't want to go out to the ranch house. She didn't want people to try to cheer her up.

She just wanted Jake. She wanted things to go back to the way they were.

Well, not really. She wanted the closeness they used to have, back when they'd first run off, but she wanted to spend time with her sister and Gloria and maybe, one day, her own parents. She wanted Grace to grow up with her cousins, to know her aunt and uncle and grandparents. She wanted the community where near strangers would throw her a baby shower and be happy for her recovery.

She wanted it all. And she wanted Jake to want that, too.

The drive out to the Holt homestead was not quiet. Gloria could keep up quite a conversation all by herself, but Lark was right there with her. Skye figured they weren't leaving a silent moment, lest she start asking questions again.

So she sat in the backseat and watched Grace sleep underneath her blankets and half listened as Gloria talked about the lovely retirement community they were looking at in Gulf Shores.

Finally, they pulled up at the ranch house. Skye looked around, but she didn't see any signs of a party. No cars parked everywhere, no people milling about. Good. She didn't want to celebrate anything, anyway.

Lark unfastened Grace's carrier and Gloria said, "I'll help you get her inside. Skye, why don't you just sit tight for a moment?"

She looked at them. "No, that's not suspicious at all."

But the two women just laughed and headed inside.

Skye managed to get out of the car. She stood there, holding on to the door for support, and looked around. Oh, she'd missed these wide-open spaces. Even though the wind was blowing and the grass was brown and dry, this feeling of freedom was something she just couldn't get in Houston.

Houston. All of her things were still there. Heck, as far as she knew, her wedding ring was still on the ground outside their apartment. She would have to find a way to go there and…

Stay? Pack up and come back here?

Would Jake be there for any of that? Or would she be on her own?

She heard the front door shut and turned, expecting to see Lark coming back for her. Except it wasn't Lark.

It was Jake.

"Where have you been?" was the first thing out of her mouth. She immediately winced at how bitchy it sounded.

"Working," he said as he came around the car.

"Oh. Of course." She turned her face back to the land. She didn't want to stay in Houston. This was where Grace belonged. And since Jake obviously wasn't going to be a part of the future…

She didn't get too far along that path because suddenly, Jake was in front of her and he was folding her into his arms and holding her against his chest and she let him, damn it. She let him because she didn't know if she'd ever get to hold him like this again.

"Skye," he said.

She was not going to cry at the goodbye. "Yes?" She was going to *try* not to cry, anyway.

"I didn't take the job."

"You *what*?" She jolted back and stared up at him.

"I didn't take it. I told you I wasn't going to," he added with a small smile. "I realized that you were right. The job—the company—will never love me back. It'll keep taking and taking until I don't have anything left to give and all it'll ever give me back is money. And money can't love me. Not like you do, Skye."

"Oh, Jake," she said as tears began to slip free. "I've never stopped loving you. Not even when you drive me nuts."

He laughed at this and kissed her cheeks where the tears had left a trail. "I didn't tell you about the interview because I hadn't decided if I wanted the job or not and I didn't want to upset you. I guess…I was trying to have things both ways and it didn't work. I'm sorry for that. I've decided to take a step back from doing the jobs myself. I'm going to start hiring guys to be on-site so I can stay here with you. It's a little like promoting myself to management," he added with a grin.

"You're going to stay? With me?" She gasped, unsure if she was dreaming or if this was really real.

"You're the one I want, the one person on this earth I need more than anything else." He stroked her cheeks with his thumbs. "I can't walk away from you, Skye. I never could."

"I shouldn't have gotten upset," she admitted. "It's just that everything feels so new in my head—like a year ago is happening at the same time as right now and I'm not sure I'm doing the best job of keeping the past separate from the future. I know you have to work."

"Don't apologize, Skye," he told her as he held her against his chest.

"But I threw away your ring and filed for divorce and I can't remember if I wanted a divorce or if I just wanted to force you to choose. I didn't try hard enough, Jake. And I want to try harder."

"Babe," he said and then he kissed her, hot and hard, and it was everything she wanted from him.

When the kiss ended, he said, "I have something else to apologize for." But he didn't sound sad about it.

"What?" she asked, almost afraid to hear the answer.

"Come inside," he said in a gentle voice. "I have something I want to show you."

She didn't want to. She wanted to stay out here with him where they could get everything settled—the right way, this time. But he'd asked. And she was showing him that she put their relationship first. "All right."

Smiling, Jake escorted her inside. The moment she stepped into the hall, she heard the low hum that went with a bunch of people trying to all whisper at the same time. "Jake?" she asked.

"It turns out," he said, "that I wanted to do something to show you that our relationship was more important to me than anything else, too."

They turned the corner and walked down into the living room. Easily thirty people were standing around, drinks in hand.

Gloria and David Holt were up front, standing next to Lark and Keaton. Grace was in David's arms, and he looked as happy as Skye had ever seen him. And next to them...

"Dad? Mom?" Skye gasped. Her parents were there, looking only moderately uncomfortable.

"There's my girl," Tyrone Taylor said.

"If I could have your attention," Jake said. Then he got down on one knee and there was a ring in his hand. "Will you marry me all over again, Skye? This is the only diamond they could find after the tornado. We can't go back where we were before, but we can make our love new again."

Skye stared down at the diamond—familiar, yet not. She was so stunned that she couldn't even answer. She looked around, feeling overwhelmed.

Her father stepped forward. "I'd like to walk you down the aisle, Skye. That is, if you still want me to. The Taylors and Holts," he said, managing not to sneer in the direction of Gloria and David, "well, we have more in common than I'd given us credit for. We can find a way to coexist. For the sake of the grandchildren."

Vera Taylor sniffed, but for once in her life, she said nothing.

"That's true enough," David said, not looking at Tyrone.

"And we hope you two decide to stay here in Royal," Gloria added before anyone could start sniping.

"Yes," Lark said. Keaton stood behind her, his arms around her waist. "Stay."

Jake turned to her. His hand reached for hers and he smiled hopefully at her. "It's what you wanted, right?"

"Oh, Jake," Skye said. She wanted to say more—how much she loved him, how much she'd dreamed of this moment—but she didn't have any words left.

So she did the only thing she could to show him how she felt.

She kissed him. Hard.

And as everyone cheered at this yes, Jake kissed her back. "I lost you once. It won't ever happen again, I promise you that," he said in a low voice meant only for her ears. "Let me prove it to you every single day for the rest of our lives."

Skye held him to her, unafraid of what her parents or his parents might say. She could hear people talking—sounds of approval flowed around her. But there was no one but Jake. There never had been and there never would be. "I love you, Jake Holt."

He slid the ring onto her finger. It felt different from the other ring—heavier—but she was different now, too. And different could be better.

"I love you too, my blue-eyed Skye."

Then they went to greet their family.

Together.

* * * * *

TEXAS CATTLEMAN'S CLUB:
AFTER THE STORM
Don't miss a single story!

Shea sat on the edge of the bed as reality came slamming back.

Willing her pulse to steady, she took a deep breath in a desperate attempt to clear her head. Still giddy and a bit light-headed, her hand trembled as she ran her fingers through her hair. It had been close. Too close. His touch left her feeling badly in need of something more.

He hadn't made love to her. She should be monumentally happy. Why, then, did she feel ridiculously disappointed?

She'd almost had sex with Alec Morreston.

Even worse, he hadn't forced her. He hadn't held her down or tied her to the bedposts. He'd kissed her. That was all. Apparently, that had been enough. She knew it. And worse, so did he.

The full impact of that realization flooded her mind. Alec Morreston was here to take away her ranch, her home, everything she held dear. She would do well to remember that. He was, inarguably, a very potent package with obvious experience to back that up.

She had to be strong.

TERMS OF A
TEXAS MARRIAGE

BY
LAUREN CANAN

Published in Great Britain 2015
by Mills & Boon, an imprint of Harlequin (UK) Limited,
Eton House, 18-24 Paradise Road, Richmond, Surrey, TW9 1SR

© 2015 Sarah Cannon

ISBN: 978-0-263-25248-4

51-0215

Harlequin (UK) Limited's policy is to use papers that are natural, renewable and recyclable products and made from wood grown in sustainable forests. The logging and manufacturing processes conform to the legal environmental regulations of the country of origin.

Printed and bound in Spain
by CPI, Barcelona

Lauren Canan, born and raised amid the cattle ranches of Texas, climbed a fence and jumped onto the back of her first horse at age three. She still maintains the punishment was worth the experience. She grew up listening to her dad tell stories of make-believe and was always encouraged to let her imagination soar. The multi-award-winning author and recipient of the 2014 Golden Heart® Award happily spends her days penning her favorite kind of stories: those of two people who, against all odds, meet, fall in love and live happily ever after—which is the way it should be. In her spare time she enjoys playing guitar, piano and dulcimer in acoustic club jams and getting lots of kisses and wags from her four-legged fuzzy babies. Visit Lauren's website at laurencanan.com. She would love to hear from you!

I owe my love of telling stories to my dad. Without his inspiration and encouragement, my journey to become an author would never have begun. This story was possible because of the love and support of my critique siblings, Angi, Jan, Jen and Kathleen, who were always there with a shoulder to cry on when I needed one. To the best literary agent in the world, Jill Marsal, who has the patience of a saint. To my dearest friend, Laurel, whose belief in me never wavered. And to Terry, my own real-life hero. He taught me the true meaning of love and happily ever after.

One

Shea Hardin had to admit the man didn't look like the devil. No horns sprouted up through Alec Morreston's thick, expertly styled, mahogany-brown hair, although a few defiant tendrils fell lazily over his forehead. The wide mouth and well-defined lips, while appearing unrelenting, didn't make it to a complete snarl. The near-perfect white teeth, seen briefly in the forced smile as introductions were made, didn't include fangs. In fact, the sculpted features of his face had the potential to be exceedingly handsome, but the lack of any emotion other than cold indifference reduced that potential to tolerable. Just.

She'd sensed his glance several times since entering the conference room adjacent to her attorney's office. She didn't need to look in his direction to know he watched her, silently, recording his first impressions, probably sizing up her abilities, weighing her strengths, discreetly alert to any hint of weakness.

Feminine instinct told her his assessment wasn't limited to her ability to handle this situation. He was also taking in every curve of her body, noting every breath she took, watching every move she made. It was a frank and candid assessment of her female attributes without any effort to conceal his interest. Intuition told her here was a man who knew what a woman needed and exactly how to provide it. His subtle arrogance was at once insulting and alluring.

She tried to swallow but her mouth had gone dry. Endeavoring not to appear affected by this man, she crossed her legs, shook the hair back from her face and fixed her eyes on the old pendulum wall clock. But in spite of her determination to ignore him, there was no denying the heat radiating throughout her body, inflaming her senses, fueling the unwanted need pooling in her lower belly.

Picking up a pencil, she scribbled furiously on the open notepad. She was reacting like a besotted teenager. How could she possibly feel any attraction whatsoever to this man? His chosen path in life was destroying the past; tearing down the treasured remains of bygone eras, replacing them with cold glass and steel fabrications. And this man wanted her ranch. The awareness of her body's traitorous response both stunned and angered her.

She was not going to be intimidated—or enticed—by him or his attorney. The very reason they sat across from her should be enough to dispel any thoughts that Alec Morreston would ever be someone she'd want to know better.

"If everyone is ready, I suggest we begin," said Ben Rucker, her attorney and longtime family friend. He switched on a small tape recorder sitting on the polished conference table amid the varying papers, notepads and legal documents.

"Today is April twenty-sixth. The purpose of this meeting is to address the issue of tenancy concerning the home and land currently occupied by Shea Hardin. In attendance are Alec Morreston, owner of the property, his attorney, Thomas Long, Shea Hardin and myself, Ben Rucker, legal counsel for Ms. Hardin."

Shea smiled at Ben. His tired but astute gray eyes reflected his concern over the situation. He'd practiced law for almost forty years, and she had complete confidence in his abilities, as her father had before her.

"At the turn of the nineteenth century, five thousand one hundred and twenty acres of land running along the western boundary and into what is now the National Forest and Grassland Reserve in Calico County, Texas, were acquired by William Alec Morreston. Later that year, he transferred the entire parcel to a widow, Mary Josephine Hardin. Since that time, descendants of Mary Hardin have continued to live on the land, today licensed as the Bar H Ranch."

Ben reached for his glasses, placed them on his nose and picked up his copy of the original paperwork.

"Rather than a purchase, this transfer of land was handled in a manner similar to what we today call a lease." He glanced over the top of his glasses. "I believe you each have a copy of the original paperwork?" When everyone nodded, he continued. "You'll note the duration was ninety-nine years with a renewal option.

"The first lease term was renewed by Cyrus Hardin, Shea's great-grandfather. The second term, currently in effect, is due to expire at the end of this month—in five days, to be precise. Ms. Hardin would like to retain possession of the property. Mr. Morreston has indicated a desire to reclaim it for his own use. This can be achieved only if Ms. Hardin has not, or does not meet all of the renewal requirements by the end of the month."

Shea glanced at Alec Morreston and once again encountered the full intensity of his gaze. A powerful energy emanated from him, the full force of it focused directly on her. She swallowed hard and looked away, ignoring the increasing tempo of her pulse.

"We didn't inspect the house and outbuildings," Mr. Long advised without preamble. "But we are satisfied that everything appears in satisfactory condition. We concede all stipulations relating to the condition of the property have been met."

Shea closed her eyes as relief washed over her. Reaching out to Ben, she squeezed his arm and then looked at Mr. Long and Alec Morreston. So grateful they'd been honest in their findings, she even managed to send a stiff smile of thanks in his direction. He hesitantly tipped his head as if to say *you're welcome*, but she couldn't help but notice the raised eyebrow and the hint of a smirk in the hard lines of his face, almost as if he knew something she didn't.

Shea returned her attention to Ben. He wasn't smiling, and didn't appear to share in her feeling of relief. No one switched off the tape recorder. No one stood up. It was as though a silent warning had begun to flash in a quickly ascending elevator, indicating the bottom was about to drop out.

"In addition to the condition of the property," Ben said, still not meeting her glance. "Apparently the ancestors of Ms. Hardin and Mr. Morreston believed it necessary to add what I would describe as a personal clause."

"Personal clause?" Frowning, Shea began to page through her copy of the old, handwritten document.

"On page four, about two-thirds down the page." Ben removed his glasses and put down the paper as if he could recall the words from memory. His voice was quiet, his manner unusually gentle. "It states in addition to the actual upkeep, if the renewal of the lease is awarded to a woman, she must be legally wed by or before the expiration of the lease."

Her head snapped up, staring at Ben's face.

"What?" Her jaw dropped in astonishment. She frowned, not understanding or wanting to believe the implications of what she'd just heard.

"It further states—" Ben again donned the thick glasses and raised his chin, a motion that enabled him to use the lower, bi-focal portion of the lenses. "'If the female lessee has no husband or betrothed, the oldest adult male, unmarried, in the Morreston family will be joined to her in matrimony, legally and spiritually, and they shall live as husband and wife for a period of not less than one year to ensure her protection against any and all perils, assist her with all ranching endeavors and ensure she is given fair and equal consideration.

"'The failure of either party to meet these terms will result in the forfeiture of the property to the other. If a marriage does occur between the principal parties, such marriage can be terminated at the end of one year, and at such time the land will go to the Hardin family for another ninety-nine-year duration.'"

He sat back in his chair and tossed the documents onto the tabletop. "You gotta love the Morreston family chivalry."

Silence momentarily filled the small room.

"For what it's worth, Shea," Ben said, "I'd guess the families were very close, and this was their way of ensuring the safety of any woman who might be single and head of household when the lease expired. As you know, it used to be a man's world and a woman by herself didn't have much of a chance. The one year marriage provision was probably intended to ensure she had full support with the ranch. If either didn't want to stay married after that, they wouldn't be required to do so. Ironically—" his eyes narrowed as he looked at Alec Morreston "—the clause was probably intended to protect any female of the Hardin family from the *crooks* who might try and take advantage of her."

The only reaction from Alec Morreston was a deepening of the tiny lines around his eyes, a silent indication he found amusement in Ben's assessment.

"But…" Leaning forward, she placed her elbows on the table for support and rubbed her fingers against her temple, willing her brain to click back into gear. "You're saying… You're telling me the lease can't be renewed because I'm a single woman?"

"If I may," Thomas Long interjected. "What it means, Ms. Hardin, in the simplest terms, is that in order for you to renew the lease you must currently be married or you must agree to marry Alec within the next five days and remain married for at least one year. If you don't agree, the lease cancels. If Alec does not agree to such a marriage, should you choose that option, the lease will be renewed."

For a few moments, speech was impossible. Her eyes remained fixed on Mr. Long as her mind tried to make some sense out of his words. She was stupefied.

"You've *got* to be kidding. This is a sick joke. It's archaic." Although attempting to remain calm, her resolve was quickly slipping away. "This kind of thing isn't legal." She looked at Ben, who sat quietly, tapping his pencil on the tabletop. "Is it?"

Ben hesitated for a few seconds as if trying to formulate his answer. "As far as I've been able to determine, the owner of the property could place any clause, requirement or restriction in the lease that he wished within the existing laws of the time. If the lessee agreed, it became a binding agreement. As to the question of whether it's binding by today's laws, it may very well not be."

Hope flared within her.

"But the problem is, if we sue to have that clause stricken, the courts could declare the entire contract null and void, in which case Mr. Morreston is under absolutely no obligation to renew the lease. And, if the courts didn't find the clause unlawful, by the time they handed down their decision, the deadline would be past. Either way…" Ben made a small gesture with his hands, his palms turned upward, indicating the hopelessness of the situation.

Shea sat back in her chair and stared out the large picture window. How could such a beautiful spring day suddenly turn so bleak and ugly? She trained her eyes squarely on Alec Morreston.

"You knew about this, didn't you?"

"Yes," he replied, his voice deep and throaty. "Thomas caught it and advised me a couple of months ago. You might want to ask your attorney why he didn't see fit to inform you. Since he was obviously aware of your single marital status, it might have saved all of us a lot of time."

Her glance swung to Ben, who shrugged and shook his head. "I'm sorry, darlin'. I thought Mr. Morreston would view the outlandish clause for what it is. It never occurred to me he'd use it to his advantage to try and reclaim possession of the land."

"I don't believe it," she muttered. "I don't believe any of this. Are you all trying to tell me I've got to take this... *insanity* seriously? That I'm going to lose my home, my ranch, everything my father and his father before that worked for, because I'm not married and won't marry *him*?"

The tone in her voice clearly painted the "him" as something disgusting and vile—which, at that moment, was spot-on. In spite of his sexual charisma, her conscious mind told her Alec Morreston was nothing more than a cold-blooded opportunist. And as far as this...lease...how could anyone in his right mind possibly make up such a stipulation?

"Your loss was taken into consideration, Ms. Hardin." Alec pointedly ignored her outburst. His composed voice resonated through the thick silence that had temporarily blanketed the small room. "I'm willing to provide reimbursement for the structures on the property, including the house, as well as compensate for one year's ranch income. And, of course, the proceeds from the sale of your livestock and equipment will be yours, provided you choose to sell rather than relocate."

Shea glared at him, afraid to speak for fear it would release the torrent of fury welling up inside her. Comparing this man to the devil had been much too kind.

"In addition," Morreston continued, "I'm willing to pro-

vide adequate time for you to find another residence. We
understand the relocation process will take longer than the
standard sixty days."

"Alec is making a most generous offer, Ms. Hardin,"
added Thomas Long, as though he felt compelled to point
that out.

Ignoring the attorney, she focused directly on the source
of this insanity, on the devil incarnate. Sitting casually back
in his chair, he appeared relaxed and completely indifferent
to what amounted to the end of life as she knew it. Her basic
principles, her education, her future dreams, pride in her
family—all of it rested within the boundaries of the ranch.
She couldn't imagine what her life would be without it.

"Why are you doing this?" Her voice was firm and unwavering, but her heart pounded and her stomach tied itself into knots.

"It's nothing personal, Ms. Hardin." He tipped his head
to one side as his eyes roamed over her face. "It's just business."

"Oh, really?" she challenged. "That's what you call it?
Destroying a person's life is 'just business?'" She shook her
head in amazement. "You must think you'll make a small
fortune on this deal."

"That's always a possibility," he admitted, shrugging
his broad shoulders.

"I'm curious. What's it going to be? A dude ranch for
your city friends or cheap housing that will fall apart in
ten years?"

"I don't think Alec's future plans for the land need discussion at this—"

"It's good land in a prime location," Alec answered her,
interrupting his attorney. "And the time for its development
has come." His eyes never left her face, his tone hard and
unemotional.

She couldn't help but speculate if they would have been

having this meeting if her dad were still alive. But common sense told her Morreston wanted the land and would have found other reasons to decline the renewal. This little "personal clause" was convenient and tailor-made to suit his purposes.

"You could omit the clause and renew the lease."

"I could," he admitted openly. "But I won't."

Silently she studied the hard, chiseled features of his face.

"Then there is no more to say, is there?" Standing, she gathered her papers and slipped them into the manila folder. She wouldn't grovel before any man, especially some arrogant stranger from New York, particularly when she knew it would do no good. Her hands were trembling due to shock, but she refused to let these contemptuous strangers see any weakness.

"Ben." She pressed her lips together to cover the trembling. "I assume you'll be in touch about what needs to be done?"

On seeing his nod, she gave a tight smile and walked out of the room. Somehow, she cleared the outside door without slamming it. Only when she reached the sidewalk did her vision blur with unshed tears of anger and frustration. Seven months ago, she'd buried her father. And now, in the space of less than an hour, she'd learned she was losing her home.

She swallowed back the overwhelming sense of panic. The ranch was her haven, her security. It was her past as well as her future. Her father had entrusted it to her care and she'd promised him in his final moments that his efforts—and the efforts of all the Hardins before them— would not be in vain.

She was the last, the only one remaining, who could carry the Hardin legacy into tomorrow. Two hundred years of struggle and sacrifice, of unwavering strength, bravery and determination by her forefathers to fashion a better life from this small piece of earth, and now, the future rested squarely on her shoulders. The weight of it was staggering.

Slipping behind the wheel of her old Chevy pickup, Shea tried recalling elements of the discussion. Even though Ben had conducted the meeting, she knew Alec Morreston had carefully orchestrated and controlled the entire presentation. Right down to her walking out of the room. The deliberate downplay of some factors of the contract, the strong focus on others. He was good. She had to give him that.

But there was one thing she'd bet Morreston hadn't taken into account. Her father had always said she was an obstinate, hardheaded female who never knew when to admit defeat. She had no intention of admitting failure so easily and giving in to that arrogant, money-grubbing son-of-a-bitch.

Maybe she would lose her home. But maybe she wouldn't.

Ben had said she must be married before the contract expired. He hadn't said she must be married to Alec Morreston, as his attorney had implied. Somewhere out there was a man who would agree to marry her for one year as a strictly business arrangement. She was going to find him.

She squared her shoulders with renewed conviction and started the truck. There was a lot to do and a very short time in which to do it.

Alec and Thomas gathered their respective documents and prepared to leave Ben Rucker's office. Ms. Hardin's abrupt exit from the meeting, while anticipated, had ended any further need for discussion.

Alec had to admit, he was impressed with Shea Hardin. She was not at all what he'd expected. In her midtwenties, she presented herself as having the maturity of someone much older. Even though this must have been devastating to her, she hadn't shouted or cried or otherwise made a scene as so many others in her position might have done.

She'd been upset, but that was understandable. Her parting words, quietly spoken to her attorney just before she'd left the room, indicated acceptance of the situation and what was to come.

But had she really given up? His success in business was due in large part to following his gut instincts. Rarely in his thirty-six years had those instincts let him down. Right now they were screaming that Shea Hardin had done anything *but* admit defeat.

From the top of the silky blond hair that fell in tousled disarray around her head to the tight jeans hugging her slim waist, then molding her sexy, feminine curves and long, slender legs, she was trouble with a capital T. If you added the delicate, almost angelic features of her face and the wide-eyed innocence of those amazing blue eyes, you had the makings of one hell of a problem. Shea Hardin would have no difficulty finding and persuading some spineless, misguided male to marry her for a year. She had five days to do it. And if she succeeded, he could kiss this project goodbye.

Alec regretted it had to be this way: that this young woman had to be forced out of her home. He'd experienced an uncomfortable twinge of regret even before her attorney had informed her of the hopelessness of her situation.

With a grimace, he tossed the last manila folder into his briefcase and closed it. Regret hadn't been the only thing he'd felt. He couldn't remember his libido ever reacting with the speed and intensity it had to Shea Hardin. A flash of insight told him sex with her would be hot and intense, mind-blowing in its fervor. Illogical anger flared at the idea of her marrying another man, lying in his bed. He shook his head to dispel the irrational notion. Under the circumstances, he'd be the last person on earth she'd ever let come near her.

As he snapped the locks on his briefcase closed, the idea

ran through his mind that he should find her, apologize for this seizure of the land and…what?

He wasn't backing away from this venture. He couldn't. Too much time and money already had been invested. So, what good would it do to apologize? She would soon be out of a home, and no apology would change that fact.

As they walked out of the building and toward the parking lot, Alec couldn't shake the idea that he shouldn't be leaving just yet. And if he was honest, he didn't know if it was concern about the land issue or a ridiculously illogical reluctance to walk away from Shea Hardin.

"Thomas," he said as they reached the car, "drop me off at the local car-rental agency, then drive back into Dallas, to Dallas-Fort Worth International, and go on to Boston. Meet with Rolston in the morning and finalize the plans for construction of his new hotel. You know what we need. Get the contracts signed, and I'll see you back in New York in a couple of days."

"You're staying here?" Thomas's brows rose in surprise. "You really think that's necessary?"

"Yeah. I have a feeling Ms. Hardin is not going to give in this easily."

"Well, keep me posted." Thomas opened the car door and tossed his suit coat inside. "Alec, don't start feeling bad about this woman's situation. You've offered her a lot of money that you didn't have to and you've given her virtually all the time she needs to relocate. Hell, it's *your* land."

"Yeah, I hear you." Alec nodded his head. "We're on the same page. I should be here only a couple of days. I'll call tonight and check on Scotty. Mom had the zoo scheduled for today. I have a feeling by now she should be about ready to go home."

"Your mother is keeping your son?"

Alec nodded. "Ms. Bishop quit. And after just two weeks, her replacement was already looking a bit frazzled." Alec shrugged. "Mother offered to come and stay with him. I flew her in from St. Petersburg just before we left to come here."

Thomas chuckled. "That boy is four going on twenty-four."

Alec smiled. "Don't I know it."

After arranging for a car, Alec eased the large sedan into the lane of traffic heading north. He should be on his way to Boston or back to New York. Instead, he was stuck in a rural north Texas town full of coyotes and cowboys, boots and brawls, dirt roads and bumper stickers proclaiming the South would rise again. He didn't belong here. He didn't want to be here. But he had to protect his right to this land. If it hadn't been mentioned in the reading of his grandfather's will, he wouldn't have known of its existence. Now that he knew, he wasn't about to let it slip through his hands.

The logical thing to do was to bring in a couple of his staff to keep an eye on things. But before the idea could begin to formulate, Shea Hardin's face drifted into his mind, and he squelched the plan before it had a chance to develop.

"Thanks for coming over, Leona." Shea pushed the screen door farther open, welcoming her neighbor onto the wide enclosed porch at the rear of the house. "I really do need your help."

Three days had passed since the meeting in Ben's office and Shea still hadn't come up with a solid plan to save the ranch.

"Are you all right?" Leona squinted and gave Shea a cursory inspection. "You sounded terrible on the phone. Kinda scared me. I was afraid you'd gotten kicked by that damn stallion again."

"I'm fine." She smiled at the older woman. "At least physically. Come on in and I'll fix us both a glass of tea."

Leona Finch was the closest thing to a mother figure Shea had since her own mom died when she was five. Shea loved Leona dearly. In her midsixties, the sun-browned features of her face bore the wrinkles of a lifetime spent on a working ranch. Her speech was as rough as her skin. But she was sensitive, perceptive and in spite of her limited education, profoundly wise.

"So, if you're not hurt, what's the deal?" Leona walked into the kitchen, pulled out a chair and sat down at the table as Shea filled two glasses with ice.

She poured the freshly brewed tea and added a sprig of mint. Setting the glasses on the table, she took a seat across from Leona.

"I've…I've got a problem," she began. "A big one."

"Well, hell." Leona took a sip of the tea and sat back in the chair. "There ain't a problem that can't be fixed. You tell me what's got you so upset, and then we'll figure out how to put it right."

Shea gave her friend a strained smile. She was glad to have Leona on her side. She needed to hear a few of her unceasingly positive assurances that things would work out.

"I'm not sure exactly where to begin. Three days ago I was called to a meeting in Ben's office. It's so bizarre…" Her voice trailed off as she shook her head. Shea looked into her friend's face.

"It seems I've got to find a husband," she told Leona straight out. "And I have less than two days left to do it."

Two

"You've got to do *what*?" Leona leaned forward and Shea saw her eyes narrow as she searched for any sign of a joke.

Shea took a steadying sip of tea. "If I don't get married by the last day of this month, I'll lose the ranch."

"Says who?" Leona's tone was guarded.

Shea recounted the highlights of the meeting in Ben Rucker's office three days earlier. She still had a hard time believing it herself.

"I have no intention of just walking away from everything I love and everything Dad worked so hard to accomplish." Her finger made circles in the condensation forming on the frosted glass. "I've spent the last three days on the phone trying to track down some of my friends from college. The ones I did manage to locate are married or involved with someone. Between the years I was away at school and then Dad's illness, I've lost touch with most of the people I knew in high school."

There had been two loves in her life. The first had been a high school crush who was now married with two kids. She'd met the other, David Rollins, her second year in college. For a while, they had been inseparable and even had talked about marriage. But eventually they both had realized they wanted different things in life. David's plans hadn't included living on a ranch in north Texas. Shea hadn't been able to see herself living anywhere else. She'd tried desperately to reach David, but without any luck. A few of her friends had heard he was living back East, but no one knew exactly where. Some had offered to make calls to try to reach him, but so far he hadn't called.

She pulled a legal pad from under some *Western Horsemen* magazines that lay on the table. "I've made a list of a few possibilities, but—" she shook her head in frustration as she passed the pad to Leona "—it's been a long time."

Leona took the list and set it aside, her eyes locked on Shea's face. "You're not seriously thinking about asking some man to marry you." It was more a statement than a question.

She shrugged. "What else can I do?"

"Do you have even the slightest idea what you'd be letting yourself in for?"

"It will be a business agreement, strictly platonic."

"Yeah, sure it will," Leona muttered, rubbing her hand over her face. "God Almighty. This is the damnedest situation I've ever heard of."

Leona picked up the list, gave her a weary look and began to scan the names. "Tommy Hall. Are his parents John and Grace?"

"Yeah." Shea nodded.

"He got married two weeks ago. One of our hands was his best man." Leona picked up a pen and crossed off his name.

"Duncan Adams. Drinks," she recalled. "A lot. You don't need that grief. Cecil Taylor? I hear he loses more than he makes on the horses over in Bossier City. Unless you're willing to bankroll his gambling, you can scratch him off the list."

One by one, Leona crossed off each man until, of the fourteen names, only one remained.

"What about Tim Schultz?" Shea asked, trying not to sound desperate.

Leona looked at the last name on the list. "Maybe. Isn't

his father the preacher over at that little church east of town?" She frowned in contemplation. "I've never heard nothing bad about him. Kinda quiet. 'Bout your age, right?"

"Yeah," Shea confirmed. "His family only moved to this area a few years ago, but I had some classes with him in college. He's nice enough, I guess."

"So, how do you plan to approach him with this little plan of yours?" Leona laid the pen and pad on the table. "You gonna just walk up to him and say, 'Howdy. Will you marry me for a year? Oh, and by the way, it's strictly business.' I'd sure like to be a fly on the wall when you throw that little tidbit in his direction."

"I'll explain the circumstances, of course." She hadn't rationalized this part of the plan, but obviously it would be necessary. "I'll have to."

"Girl, use your head. Maybe if you talked to that Morreston fellow again—"

"No." Sitting back in her chair, Shea crossed her arms in front of her. Alec Morreston. The mere mention of his name caused a hot blush to spread over her neck and face. The look of male want in his eyes was still vivid in her mind. She'd never experienced anything like it, but even after three days, she knew she hadn't imagined it. And neither had she imagined his cold insensitivity to the havoc he'd caused in her life. She resolutely shook her head. "I can promise you, it would do no good. He's a developer. He lives in New York, probably in some posh penthouse. He doesn't care about the land. He doesn't care about anything but making more money. Probably never got his hands dirty in his life."

"What if you turned the tables on him?" Leona asked, taking another long drink of her tea.

Shea frowned. "I don't understand."

"Well, Ben told you, according to that contract, if you

weren't married by the end of the month, Morreston had to marry you or agree to renew the lease. Right?"

Shea nodded, suddenly afraid of where this was going.

"So tell him you want to marry him."

Shea could only gape in horror.

"Put the problem back on his plate," Leona reasoned. "Think about it. He's a city fellow. He's not going to agree to marry you and live on this ranch. He thinks he's got you bluffed into doing just exactly what you're doing— refusing to use him as a way out."

Shea stubbornly shook her head. "No way, Leona." The idea was beyond bizarre. "Absolutely no way." She still had forty-eight hours.

"I sure wish your father was still alive," Leona muttered.

"So do I, Leona," Shea whispered as she stood and walked to the phone to call Tim Schultz. "So do I."

Shea sipped from the glass of ice water and tried to remain calm. Tonight, before midnight, she had to be married. Tim had finally returned her call this morning. No doubt sensing the urgency in her tone, he'd agreed to meet her at Barstall's City Diner at one o'clock. He was late.

What was she going to say? All the rehearsing in the world couldn't prepare her for what she had to discuss with him. How would he respond? Would he laugh? Would he just walk out? Or, most important, would he agree to do it?

Before leaving yesterday, Leona once more had encouraged her to call Morreston's bluff. But Shea had held firm in her conviction that nothing on earth would make her so desperate to even contemplate such a thing. Heaven help the poor female coerced into marriage with that man.

Instinctively she knew Alec Morreston would be demanding, in bed as well as out. Even if the situation were different, a brief affair with a man like Morreston would take more from her than she could give. She suspected such a liaison would turn into an emotional roller coaster, and that was the last thing she needed in her life.

But it was a moot point. Morreston was long gone. It had taken him fewer than two hours to invade her world and turn it completely upside down. Then he had left, not even bothering to look back as she desperately tried to pick up the pieces from the devastation he'd caused. No doubt, he assumed she would just relinquish her home and quietly disappear. Well, he was in for a surprise—

"Hello, Ms. Hardin." Shea jumped at the sound of the deep voice directly to her left. Her head snapped around and her eyes immediately grew wide in astonishment. She could feel the blood drain from her face as she stared into the amber eyes of Alec Morreston.

"May I join you?"

Before she could respond, he pulled out the chair opposite her and sat down. As his eyes scanned her face, his lips twitched with unrepressed humor at her stunned look. For a long moment, she couldn't speak.

"What...what are you doing here?" she stammered, finally finding her voice.

"I'm about to have lunch," he said innocently, as though misunderstanding the true meaning of her question.

Shea glared at him.

Alec shrugged. "I decided to take a few days and see some of the area. Thought it might be...beneficial...to the future development of the project." He responded as if choosing his words carefully. "Have you ordered yet?"

"Have I...? No." She shook her head. "No. I'm meeting someone." She looked toward the front entrance, no longer sure she'd be glad to see Tim walk through it.

Alec regarded her silently for a moment. "I see. Well, then I'll certainly move to another table as soon as she—or he?—arrives."

If Shea had been nervous before Morreston's unexpected

arrival, that feeling was mild compared to what she was experiencing now. Suddenly, she could relate to every mouse ever caught in a trap that had looked up to find the cat walking in its direction. How on earth was she ever going to present her problem to Tim with Morreston hanging over her shoulder?

"The roasted chicken sounds good," he commented, scanning the lunch specials. "What do you recommend?"

"You really don't want me to answer that."

He glanced at her face over the top of the menu and feigned surprise. But the deepening of the tiny lines around his eyes told her he found her remark amusing.

Before she could deliberate on this newest chapter of the nightmare, another voice beckoned her.

"Um…excuse me. Shea?" Tim Schultz smiled his apology. "Sorry I'm late."

"Tim!" She smiled nervously. "That's okay."

She looked back to Morreston, hoping against hope he would just silently disappear. Apparently, that was not going to be the case. Politeness demanded she make introductions.

"Tim, this is Alec Morreston…Tim Schultz."

Alec stood as the two men shook hands. Over six feet in height, he easily towered over the younger man by several inches while his broad shoulders and lean waist hinted at a muscular, athletic build that made Tim appear almost adolescent in comparison. His reddish-blond hair and fair complexion seemed pale, almost sickly, as opposed to Morreston's dark features.

"Well, if you'll excuse me," Alec said, a grin tugging at the corners of his well-defined mouth, "I'm sure you two have a great deal to discuss. I certainly don't want to interrupt."

"Would you care to join us?" Tim asked, unaware of the situation.

"No!" Shea almost shrieked. Both men looked at her—one with curiosity, the other with increasing amusement.

"Thanks, Tim," Alec said, and Shea's heart all but stopped. "But I think Shea wants to speak privately with you. Maybe another time?"

He knows. He knows exactly why I'm having lunch with Tim Schultz. And apparently, he found the situation extremely amusing. That infamous smirk was firmly in place.

"You knew I was here, didn't you?" It was no coincidence Alec Morreston just happened to show up at the exact time she was meeting with Tim, even if it was the lunch hour and this was the only decent restaurant in town. When he didn't immediately respond, she added, "How?"

"I believe his name is Hank. Your ranch foreman? He said you might be having lunch here today."

Alec moved away from their table, giving her a quick wink as if to seal the private joke between them. She immediately turned away, biting back the angry retort that sprang to her lips. *Ignore him*, she told herself. *Just be thankful to be rid of him.*

But before she could enjoy a second of relief, to her utter dismay, Morreston pulled out a chair at a table next to them. In that location he'd be able to hear every word they said. Something akin to panic formed in her stomach.

"So," Tim began as he took the seat Alec had occupied. "How are you, Shea? Haven't seen you in what—three years? I was surprised to get your call. What's going on?"

She forced a smile and reached for the glass of ice water, needing something to steady her nerves. Her hand shook slightly, and a small amount of water spilled onto the table. As she fought to find the right words, her gaze wavered, and she found herself looking directly into the mocking face of Alec Morreston.

"Shea?"

She heard Tim's voice, but her gaze was captured by amber eyes.

"Shea? Is something wrong?"

She couldn't suppress the overwhelming desire to slam something as she stomped out of the restaurant. She was furious. No, she mentally corrected herself. She was beyond furious. She wanted to kill something. She wanted to kill Alec Morreston.

Each time she'd broached the subject of her meeting with Tim, Morreston had cleared his throat or apologetically interrupted to ask Tim a question or made some asinine comment. Between his little interruptions, he'd sat back in his chair and stared, never taking his eyes off her, exactly as he'd done that first day in Ben's office. That knowing smirk had remained etched on his lips, his tawny eyes alert to every movement she'd made, every breath she'd taken. For almost an hour, he'd made her feel like a bug under a microscope.

About the time she'd started to ask Tim if he would walk her to the truck, Morreston had folded his napkin, placed it on the table and leaned toward her lunch date to strike up a conversation. If they'd tried to leave, she'd known Morreston would have followed. Pleading a headache, she'd excused herself and asked Tim if she could call him later.

Now apprehension increased with each step as she made her way to her vehicle. Her time was almost up. It was down to a few short hours before she would lose the home she loved forever. She'd almost been tempted to stand in the center of the restaurant, loudly declare her problem and ask if there were any takers. If she didn't come up with a plan very soon, it just might come to that.

As she drove toward the parking lot exit, the front doors of the restaurant swung open and out walked Morreston— with Tim at his side. Seemingly engaged in light banter, only Morreston noticed her as she passed. He tipped his head to her in silent acknowledgment. She clutched the steering wheel in a death grip. Her hands itched to slap that arrogant smirk from his face once and for all. In the rearview mirror, she saw him turn to Tim, nod and laugh.

In that moment, she knew she never would have a second chance to speak with Tim. Morreston would see to it. That was why he was here. He knew what she was attempting to do, and he was determined to see her fail. The devil had just sprouted horns.

In the same instant, she also knew she'd reached the limit of her patience with the man and this bizarre situation. She slammed on the brakes and, without pausing to give her actions a second consideration, threw the truck into Reverse. It quickly roared backward before grinding to a halt directly in front of the two men. Their conversation immediately stopped and they both peered at her with curiosity.

She rolled down the window, a phony smile pasted to her lips. Alec watched her with guarded interest.

"Sorry to interrupt you gentlemen. But, *Alec—*?" She used his given name, implying a familiarity that was not there and never would be if she had anything to say about it. She gave him a look of pure innocence.

"You know, I've had a chance to think about our meeting earlier in the week. About the little problem we discussed?"

She had his attention.

"And, well, I think your attorney was right when he pointed out your family's unwavering concern that a single, unmarried woman can't possibly run a ranch…all by herself." The sarcasm dripped from her voice. Her tone was venomous.

Tim looked from one of them to the other, as if struggling to understand any part of their conversation.

"Since Mr. Long was so kind as to explain my alternatives and well…since you've gone to all the trouble to stay here in case I needed you, and in light of all the care and understanding you've shown, I think you're absolutely right." She looked directly into the golden depths of his eyes, an effort that challenged her sanity. "I will marry you, Alec. Under the circumstances, how can I possibly refuse?"

Only Alec comprehended the true meaning of her words. His head drew back, his eyes narrowed and her phony smile almost became genuine as she saw the flare of annoyance in those chiseled features.

"If you'll meet me at Ben Rucker's office in, oh, about an hour? I'm sure he can help us sort out any little details we need to address prior to the ceremony."

Before she switched her attention to Tim, she noted with satisfaction that the smirk was finally, effectively wiped from Morreston's face.

"Tim, I'm sorry I didn't have a chance to discuss this with you inside," she apologized. "But my reason for asking you here was to solicit your help in convincing your father to perform the ceremony on such short notice. Would you mind speaking to him for me?" She surprised herself at how quickly and convincingly the lie rolled off her tongue.

"No," Tim shrugged. If he believed this conversation to be as bizarre as it sounded, he managed to hide it well. "I'll see him this afternoon. When is the wedding? And where?"

"This evening. At my house." Her eyes returned to Alec's face and she noted, with immense gratification, he clearly showed signs of irritation. His jaw worked convulsively as he made a futile attempt to remain calm.

"Will eight o'clock be all right?" she asked.

For a long moment, Alec didn't answer. His eyes searched her face as if attempting to discern what she was up to, as though he couldn't believe what she had just said.

"Eight will be fine," he said finally.

If he'd refused, she'd have been surprised. She knew

instinctively that Morreston was not the type of person to back down after the first stone was cast.

She put the truck in Drive and smiled at Alec. His amber eyes narrowed in a silent declaration of war. While she suspected her triumph would be short lived, it would certainly feel good while it lasted.

"I can't let you do this," Ben Rucker stated for the third time. "Suppose the man doesn't refuse to marry you? What then?"

"Then we'll get married," she said firmly. "At eight this evening. Don't worry, Ben, you're invited."

"This is not a joke!" Ben pulled the glasses off his face and stood up from the desk. "For God's sake, don't do this, Shea. Take the money he's offered and buy land elsewhere. I'll help you. You can—"

"No, Ben. This is my home, my family home, for six generations. I can't just pack up two hundred years of memories and close that door behind me saying, 'Oh well.' If Morreston wants this land, *my* land, he'll have to fight for it."

Ben's eyes, full of concern, silently beseeched her to reconsider. "Is there no way I can talk you out of this?"

"Not unless Alec Morreston will renew my lease."

"Which he is not willing to do." The deep voice responded from the open doorway just behind her. Both Shea and Ben looked around in time to see the subject of their conversation walk casually into the room.

He had shed the sports jacket and tie, leaving his shirt open at the neck but still tucked into the navy slacks. They hugged his slim waist, hinting at muscular thighs beneath the fabric. Somehow, his shoulders seemed broader than they had only an hour ago. The strong line of his jaw was set in determination.

"Don't do this, Morreston," Ben pleaded.

"It's not completely my doing," he answered. His eyes focused on Shea. "Ms. Hardin had a choice, and apparently she decided on this option."

"You gave her no choice at all and you know it," Ben argued. "What kind of man are you to take advantage of her like this?"

Alec pointedly ignored the question. "I'd like to speak with Ms. Hardin in private." His eyes never left her face.

"You can discuss anything that needs saying in front of—"

"No, Ben. It's all right," Shea interrupted. This was her battle now. If she had any hope of making Morreston back down, she couldn't do it hiding behind her attorney. "Shall we step into the next room, Mr. Morreston?"

Alec followed her into the small, adjacent conference room and closed the door behind them with a resounding click. For a few moments they faced each other in silence.

"Are you really serious about this?"

"Yes," Shea replied without hesitation. "I am."

"You would marry a complete stranger in order to keep the land?"

"Yes."

"There is other land."

"Then perhaps you should go and find it."

Alec stared at her. "How much more do you want?" he asked quietly.

Had this man never loved anything in his life that didn't have a price tag attached to it? Could he not understand the legacy she was fighting to save?

"Two million," she said flippantly, and immediately saw a knowing look cross his face. The slight nod of his head indicated his initial acceptance of her outlandish but bogus demand. She was tempted to see how far he would go to buy her off but common sense came rushing forward.

"I don't want your money, Mr. Morreston. This is not

about money. It's about my home. My life. Family values and tradition. Things you, apparently, don't know anything about."

He shoved his hands into the pockets of his slacks and walked past her to stand gazing out the large window on the opposite wall. For long moments, he stood there, saying nothing. From the corner of her eye, she watched as he rubbed the back of his neck. His shirt did little to hide the muscular tone of his arms and back. The silky texture of his dark hair caught the subtle light coming through the window, accentuating deep auburn highlights. As he turned toward her, she quickly looked away.

"It won't work, you know." His voice had a slight raspy quality, which, under different circumstances, she might have found extremely sensual. "Even if I agree to this, no marriage can survive for a year under these circumstances. Eventually you'll concede defeat and the land will revert to me. It's inevitable. Why put yourself through it?"

"That's a very chauvinistic attitude, Mr. Morreston. What makes you so sure *I'll* be the one to call it quits?"

He didn't immediately answer as a look of indulgent amusement crossed his features. Then all traces of humor disappeared. Slowly, he closed in until barely a foot separated them. Without any warning, he reached out and stroked the side of her face.

She inhaled sharply and adjusted her stance at the unexpected contact but determinedly held her ground. His hand slid from her face to cup the back of her neck and, applying the slightest pressure, drew her even closer to him. She watched his gaze roam over each detail of her face before coming to rest on her mouth. She noted the faint shadow that darkened his face as he bent his head toward her. His lips, wide and defined, parted slightly as if intending to kiss her, but stopped a mere breath away, and only his thumb touched her mouth, tracing the curving fullness in an incredibly intimate gesture.

Time stood still. The close physical contact brought her challenge into clear focus. The pulse hammered in her throat. She swallowed back the overwhelming sensation of panic that rose within her and tried to look away.

Alec gently tilted her chin upward, forcing her to look into the golden depths of his eyes. The bittersweet fragrance of his cologne teased her senses. She could sense the disciplined power and virility of his body as he stood mere inches away from her. There was no doubt he was all male. Her stomach muscles involuntarily contracted as a shaft of sexual awareness shot through her. An intense heat seemed to envelop her as her breath became shallow, almost nonexistent. A little voice inside screamed to run while she could.

Three

"All right, Ms. Hardin." His throaty voice penetrated the silence of the room. "We'll play this one your way and see what happens. I'll honor the conditions as set forth by our ancestors and we will be married. And there will be no development on any of the land as long as the marriage continues or if this…union…should exceed one year."

He paused, tilting his head slightly as though studying her reaction. "But know this—" the tone of his voice reflected the seriousness of his words "—you *will* be my wife as stipulated in the original lease. Legally and spiritually, body and soul. You'll share my life, as well as my bed, for the duration. Do you understand what I'm saying?"

It was time to bail out. She knew it but couldn't seem to move. He was telling her exactly what she would have to agree to, up front. He was giving her every opportunity to walk away. She took a deep breath and hoped her strength was as unfailing as her stubbornness.

"I understand." Her voice was firm although barely above a whisper.

"Do you?" A sparkle glistened in Alec Morreston's amber eyes. "I guess we'll find out tonight, won't we?"

He released her and stepped toward the door but hesitated before pulling it open. "One more thing. I'll require a prenuptial agreement. Thomas should have time to fax one to your attorney's office before—"

"No."

His eyes narrowed, pinning her to the spot. "Excuse me?"

"You heard me. I said no."

"Ms. Hardin, do you really expect me to marry a woman I don't know and risk losing half of everything I have?"

"I'd say, after your earlier statement, you expect me to give up more than that. No prenup, Mr. Morreston. I want no part of anything you own, other than my ranch. You can trust me on that—" Shea eyed him coolly "—or you can book your flight home."

She could see the muscles in his jaw working overtime as he apparently strove to keep his temper from exploding.

"My personal holdings have nothing to do with this land issue. If, as you say, you want nothing but the land, then signing a prenup should not be asking too much."

"Neither is wanting to keep my home," she countered. "Nothing in the contract said anything about a prenuptial agreement. I refuse to sign one. If you refuse to marry me because of that, then I guess the land is mine. Your call."

Her heart beat so solidly against the wall of her chest she felt sure he could hear it from three feet away. She hoped she looked calmer on the outside than she felt on the inside.

Silence dominated the room. A barely perceivable change in his stance, from tense to an almost exaggerated casualness, conveyed the control he maintained on his emotions. His tawny eyes drifted over her as if trying to discover how much determination lay underneath. The burning strength of his gaze wandered insolently from her face to her breasts, down to her belly, to her hands—held tightly clenched at her sides—then down the legs of her jeans all the way to her feet. Shea could feel the blush spread across her face as he rudely inspected and silently weighed the feminine merchandise standing in front of him.

"All right, Ms. Hardin," he said finally, his tone suddenly menacing. "We'll play hardball if that's what you want. You just upped the stakes and I'd be a fool not to call your bluff. Be ready tonight, honey. Be ready for me."

He stepped back and opened the door. Shea shakily, but resolutely, walked through it. While temporarily disconcerted by his unexpected and candid proclamation, she knew the marriage would never be consummated. He was trying to intimidate her. That's all it was. He would do well to remember that two could play this game.

She had no intention of letting herself become physically ensnared and used by an egotistical maniac. She may have been forced into making a pact with the devil, but he would quickly find she was anything but a sacrificial lamb. Alec Morreston was city bred and raised. He had no concept of the sometimes harsh realities of ranch life, and she'd bet he wouldn't last a month.

In fact, she had just bet the ranch on it.

"Alec…" The heavy concern in Thomas's voice was clearly evident through the telephone line. Alec could picture him gripping the receiver so tightly his knuckles were turning white. He was almost sorry he couldn't be there in person to deliver the news of the pending wedding. "Are you certain you know what you're doing?"

Because their client-attorney relationship had grown into a solid friendship over the years, Alec wasn't insulted when Thomas questioned his sanity. Hell, in the past five hours, he'd begun to question it himself.

"I mean, what do we really know about this woman?"

"I think she's okay, Thomas."

"But what if she's not? What if this is all a setup? Do you have to *marry* her, for God's sake?" His tone was incredulous. "Maybe if you offered her more money?"

"She wouldn't take two million."

"She—" Alec heard Thomas Long swallow hard on that one. "My God! How much more does she want?"

"She says she doesn't want money. She wants the land.
I believe, in her mind, she's telling the truth. She honestly
thinks she can pull this off and make me back down. Un-
fortunately for her, I've committed to building this entertainment complex. The investors are already on board. I'm
down several million and we haven't yet poured the first
foundation. There is no turning back at this point."

"How about we try to find other land alternatives. I could
put out some feelers…"

"A friend who specializes in real estate spent almost a
year doing just that. I originally wanted to build in the East.
He checked land possibilities within a hundred-mile radius
of every major city near a natural waterway from New York
to Florida. We encountered zoning restrictions, municipal
politics, arbitrary city codes, small town gluttony. He found
a two-thousand-acre tract just outside Cincinnati, but the
deed was in probate. There was a five-thousand-acre tract
in Virginia, but it was so far removed from civilization I
didn't want to take the chance it might be *too* far.

"This location is perfect. A little farther west than I initially wanted, but it's actually working out even better than
the original plan. It's centrally located in the US, only fifty
miles from the Dallas-Ft. Worth International Airport and
it borders the Red River."

Alec had already purchased land directly across the state
line in Oklahoma and had most of the permits for that side
of the river. "I've spent weeks restructuring blueprints to
meet local building codes, obtaining land surveys for two
states and finally have received a clearance from the EPA
over some near-extinct bird they thought nested nearby.
I refuse to spend any more time or money trying to find
equivalent land just so Ms. Hardin can continue to raise
her cows. Give me a few days, a couple of weeks at best,
and I'll have her out of here."

"Okay." There was a moment of silence while Thomas,

no doubt, regrouped. "What about a prenup? You're potentially handing this woman a key to a very large door. Your
bank accounts alone…" Thomas paused. "I'll have a basic
agreement drawn up and sent to you in—"

"No thanks, Thomas."

"*No?* Alec—"

"We've already had this discussion. She refused."

Another stunned silence. "Then don't marry her. Let her
have the damn land. Even considering how much you've
sunk into the project, it isn't worth a fraction of your other
holdings. Alec—"

"Thomas, look, I appreciate your concern. But I honestly
feel if it should come down to a divorce petition for any of
my current assets, the bizarre reason for the marriage—my
being forced to take this route in order to regain the use of
my own land—would supersede any claim."

"But we can't know that for sure."

How could he explain to Thomas his gut instinct said
this would not be a problem? There was something about
Shea Hardin, some glimmer of truth deep in those blue
eyes. Nothing he'd seen gave him any reason to suspect
she wanted any more than *her* ranch.

"I don't intend to remain married for one millisecond
longer than absolutely necessary. In less time than it would
take to battle this out, I intend to have her bags packed
and be helping little Miss Tradition out the door. Then a
simple annulment, give her something for her trouble, and
it's done."

He'd been challenged by opponents a lot tougher than
Shea Hardin and had come out on top. He grimaced at his
own expression. Hell, in truth, on top of her was exactly
where he wanted to be. He sensed the blood congregate in
his loins at the mental picture and cursed his weakness. He
had to keep his focus on the reason he was here and stop
letting his imagination run wild.

Alec intentionally changed the subject. "I need you to call Valturego. See if he's ready to sign the contract for the construction of his casino. I'll contact him when I get back in the office."

"I'll call as soon as we're finished," Thomas promised. "But, Alec, back to the prenup thing—"

"Did Rolston sign the revised contract?"

Thomas grudgingly took the hint and began explaining the outcome of his meeting with the banker.

When their business concluded, Alec tossed his cell on the bed in the small motel room and glanced at the digital clock on the nightstand. After six. He probably should start getting ready.

The last time he'd taken vows, there had been more than fifteen hundred invited guests—some he'd known, most he hadn't. The planning had gone on for months. The fragrance from thousands of flowers had permeated the air, almost overwhelming the guests who'd gathered in the enormous church. He could remember the aura of hushed excitement that had filled the large sanctuary in anticipation of the spectacle to come.

Sondra had wanted it all and she had been relentless in making her desires come true. In hindsight, he should have seen what was coming. He should have picked up on the clues. She'd loved to party and her actions had made him suspect she'd crossed the line as far as using drugs. But he hadn't been able to prove it, had never found any evidence, and he'd never known about the other man until the day he came home and found the note. No excuses. No apologies. A strange woman waiting outside his door handed him a baby and said it was his. Suddenly he was alone with an infant son. A month later, Alec learned she'd died of an overdose. The man she'd left him to be with supposedly had provided the pills.

In the years since, the anger over her betrayal had diminished, but the lesson she'd taught him about trust had reshaped his character and would always be foremost in his mind. He'd sworn he would never again make the mistake of marrying. Anyone. For any reason. For almost five years, he'd kept that resolution. But in less than an hour, he would once again stand in front of a minister and make a pledge to love, honor and obey, and this time to a woman he knew nothing about.

Shea Hardin was a total perplexity. She didn't fit into any mold he'd ever come across. At first, he'd believed she was one of the members of Gold Diggers Anonymous he frequently encountered. But if those initial suspicions were correct, she was better than average at setting a trap, because he'd certainly taken the bait. She came across as completely sincere, candid and unwavering in her determination to keep the land.

She was a walking contradiction—intelligent yet naive, beautiful but unsophisticated, sexy as hell yet seemingly innocent. She looked fragile, sensitive, as though her poise and conviction could easily be shattered. But after today, he had the solid impression she was about as fragile as an oak tree, her temper as controlled as a glass vile of nitroglycerin.

She challenged him. She fascinated him.

And she had the most amazing blue eyes he'd ever seen.

Then there was her mouth—full lips that could give a man all kinds of grief, all kinds of pleasure. He'd almost kissed her in the attorney's office, drawing back at the last minute as he realized he wouldn't have wanted to stop with a single kiss.

No, his problem would not be intimidating Shea Hardin. It would be keeping himself from taking her while he did so.

Shea stood in front of her closet later that afternoon, staring at the few dresses hanging inside. Rarely was there any need for her to wear anything other than casual ranch attire and therefore her options were severely limited. She removed a simple paisley dress from the closet and held it in front of her as she viewed her reflection in the full-length mirror. Somehow, it didn't seem right.

She replaced it and reached for another. Wrong style. She bit her lip as she removed a dark green suit from the closet. Not right either. Red? Nope. Black? An impish grin crossed her face at the picture that would create. Quelling the urge, she hung the dress back in the closet and shook her head in frustration. There was no time to go shopping. Under the circumstances she should probably just pull on a clean pair of jeans and be done with it.

Thinking back on her day, she couldn't believe how fast everything had fallen into place for this wedding. Old Doc Hardy had done the blood work on the spot and Jane Simmons at the courthouse had gotten Judge Lamb to push the license through without the three-day wait. It was as unbelievable as her reason for being there.

Suddenly the mirror's reflection caught the motion of a large ball of orange fur as Pumpkin, the old tomcat, jumped onto the cedar chest that sat at the foot of her bed. She spun around and looked at the chest in speculation. Instantly memories of her childhood came rushing back. Memories of her as a little girl standing on top of the chest, trying to be tall enough so she could wear the long silky white dress her mother kept inside. It had been years since she'd reflected on the chest and its contents. On a whim, she set a disgruntled Pumpkin on the floor and then moved the miscellaneous items on top of the chest. A mild scent of cedar permeated the air around her as she raised the lid.

On top were pillowcases, handkerchiefs and small hand towels, their borders bearing floral designs embroidered by her mother. With a regretful smile, Shea set the linens aside. Underneath were two handmade quilts, their colors still amazingly crisp. She noted a date sewn into the corner of one: "A.H.—1812". Her great-grandmother must have made them. Maybe even her grandmother before that. She placed them on the floor next to the linens.

Kneeling over the now half-empty chest, she removed several more layers of tissue paper. Suddenly, there it was, and just as she remembered. Her mother's wedding gown. She rose to her feet as she lifted it out of the chest.

The material was an off-white satin. The years had slightly darkened the creamy color, but time couldn't diminish its simple elegance. The high, Victorian-style neckline, enhanced by delicate lace, covered the bodice and shoulders. Tiny pearl buttons ran down the full length of the gown with a matching row of buttons on each sleeve from the wrist to the elbow.

Tears stung her eyes as she was suddenly overcome with longing for the mother she'd never really known. She gently touched the delicate lace. Should she dare risk tarnishing the memory of her mother's wedding day by wearing it to the marital atrocity about to take place? But the thought of putting it back in the trunk and closing the lid didn't feel right. Something urged her to try it on.

Some ten minutes later, she stepped in front of the mirror and almost didn't recognize her reflection. The gown fit perfectly. Its simple style subtly created an aura of poise and sophistication as it gracefully cascaded to the floor.

She caught her lower lip between her teeth. Sadly, she wished hers would be a genuine marriage, one based on love and respect with hopes for a future. Not a contractual stipulation with an arrogant stranger.

Alec Morreston would no doubt have a good laugh if she appeared in a wedding gown. He'd be convinced she was every kind of crazy. She chewed her bottom lip. When she walked into the room for the ceremony would she feel like a total and complete fool? Circumstances being what they were, it probably was an idiotic idea. Still, a woman got married for the first time only once in her life. Right or wrong, this was it.

There was also the chance Morreston might think she was trying to play him and raise his guard, which could make getting rid of him more difficult. She let out a frustrated sigh. Wearing her mother's gown was fulfilling a dream she'd carried since childhood. If he laughed, why should she care? Let him scoff all he wanted, the hateful man.

"You know what, Pumpkin? Bizarre or not, this *is* my wedding day. I'm going to do it." As soon as she uttered the words, she knew she was making the right decision. There would be just enough time to freshen the dress before Morreston and the Reverend Shultz arrived.

But first, she needed to have a talk with Hank Minton, the ranch foreman. Quickly, she undressed, placed the gown on the bed and then pulled on a pair of jeans before heading for the main barn.

Four

"Do you, William Alec Morreston, take this woman as your lawfully wedded wife, to have and to hold from this day forward, for better or worse, for richer or poorer, in sickness and in health?"

Shea's head swam. This couldn't be happening. Perhaps if she blinked her eyes fast enough she would awaken from the nightmare.

Standing next to her in the old-fashioned parlor, Alec responded to the Reverend Schultz's questions with the reverence and sincerity of a man who was marrying the woman of his dreams. Raising her hand to his lips, he briefly kissed her fingers after slipping the diamond-encrusted wedding ring he'd purchased that afternoon onto the third finger of her left hand.

After the license had been issued at City Hall, Alec had insisted she accompany him to the town jewelry store to pick out rings. He'd ignored her suggestion that they use Band-Aids. In the shop she'd refused to voice any opinion whatsoever, seeing the sparkling gold-and-diamond jewelry as miniature handcuffs intended only as a psychological reminder that she would be shackled to the obstinate man for a year. Less, if she had her way about it, but even one day would be too much.

To the few well-wishers Leona had invited, his gesture probably appeared to be genuine. What would her friends say if they knew the truth? That this man planned not only to destroy her ranch land, but possibly bring about such catastrophic change it would send a tidal wave well beyond her borders and affect the lives of everyone standing in this room. She felt like a traitor hiding it from them. But Leona had agreed that to tell anyone the truth would only create unnecessary worry and add pressure on Shea she didn't need. Her sole focus had to be on the war against this man. And *when* she won, no one would ever be the wiser.

Consequently, Alec Morreston had been introduced as the long lost love she'd met while at college. Family concerns had taken him away but now he was back in her life and neither wanted to wait a second longer to marry. Shea could tell Alec had fought not to laugh when she'd told him the plan, but he'd agreed to it. And why not? He wouldn't be around to explain if this whole thing blew up in her face. She hoped she'd make it through this night without being sick.

"Do you, Shea Elizabeth Hardin, take this man to be your lawfully wedded husband…?"

As she reluctantly, obligingly recited her promise to love, honor and obey the irritating man, she glanced once in his direction and couldn't mistake the pursing of his lips as he fought to suppress a wicked smile from spreading across his face. She gritted her teeth as she shoved the gold wedding band onto his finger, not daring to look at him again. She wasn't near the actress she needed to be to pull off a convincing smile.

"By the authority vested in me, I now pronounce you husband and wife." The Reverend Schultz smiled at her before turning to Alec. "You may kiss your bride."

Reality became surreal as she looked at Alec, this stranger, who was now legally her husband. She had only seconds to comprehend the full impact of what she'd done before he pulled her into his arms and raised her face to meet his.

"Too late for any regrets, Mrs. Morreston," he whispered, as if reading her mind. He lowered his head and his mouth covered hers.

Like a bolt of electric current, something exploded within, causing her senses to whirl and the room to spin. She grabbed the lapels of his suit in an effort to steady herself.

With practiced skill, he parted her lips and his tongue entered the deeper recesses of her mouth. His hand cupped the back of her head, holding her to him, as he filled her mouth with his raw, male flavor. Despite her resolve to remain impervious to this man and unaffected by his touch, she found herself responding to the sensuous temptations he offered.

Her hand left his shoulder to touch the texture of his face, letting her fingertips glide along the strong line of his jaw until finally coming to rest at the point where his mouth joined with hers.

Then he withdrew from her and she couldn't deny a slight feeling of disappointment. With his thumb, he gently wiped the moisture from her lips as he studied her expression. A frown drew his dark brows together and he searched her face as if seeking an answer to a silent question. Had he been as affected by the kiss as she had?

Then a slow, sexy grin spread across his features and a knowing gleam flashed in the golden depths of his eyes before he stepped to her side to receive the offers of congratulations from the small group of people who stood smiling around them. She inhaled deeply, frustrated at her own momentary weakness.

Somehow, she managed to be pleasant as she introduced her new husband to her closest friends and neighbors, all the while praying they would never find out what was at stake beneath the façade of this marriage. The last thing she needed was concerned neighbors who feared for their own livelihood distracting her from her primary objective of getting rid of the man.

The photographer Leona had arranged through the local newspaper began to position them for their wedding photos. Someone made an off-color comment about the wedding night. Everyone joined in the banter and laughter abounded, but it only served to drive home the depravity of her situation.

A chill settled over her. What kind of man was Alec Morreston? Would he be understanding of her feelings or completely insensitive? She couldn't stop her eyes from straying to this man who potentially held the future of the ranch, as well as her own well-being, in his hands.

Alec glanced at his new bride. Immediately he noted the anxiety that was obvious in every delicate feature of her face, and he didn't have to be hit over the head to know the cause. His laughter faded as he recognized the depth of her apprehension. She was frightened.

Of him.

The fact should have made him happy. It was the first step toward making her leave. Such quick success should be sweet. So why did he feel sickened by her fear?

Their eyes met. The glistening blue of hers held him transfixed. Somewhere a light flashed, the brilliance challenging the intensity of the moment, capturing it forever.

Then, she seemed to gather her reserves and in a barely perceived movement, she straightened her shoulders and raised her chin. The near panic and vulnerability he'd caught a glimpse of moments before were now replaced with a look of pride and stubborn determination. With sudden insight, Alec knew that while he'd often admired beauty in other women, never had he appreciated their character or inner strength.

"Good one," he heard someone say. "Now if you'll both turn this way…and let's see some smiles!"

With the speed and brilliance of the camera's flash, Alec knew he was in trouble. He swallowed hard. While admittedly attracted to her, he'd previously ignored the sparks that ignited between them whenever their eyes found each other. He'd told himself he looked at all women the way he looked at Shea Harden. He'd just never noticed before.

He'd lied to himself.

He'd never been smitten by any woman. Whatever he'd felt for Sondra in the beginning was not even close to this. And the soft blush on Shea's face when she'd caught him staring told him the attraction was not one-sided.

There was definitely something between them. Like a force field of pure energy, it surrounded them. The air crackled every time they got close to each other. Where this put him in the overall scheme of things, he wasn't sure. He knew an affair would only complicate matters, but the temptation to throw caution to the wind was overwhelming.

As Shea closed the front door behind the last of the departing guests, she realized that for a few crazy minutes she'd actually forgotten about Alec. Reaching over to pick up a wineglass left on a nearby table, she took several steps toward the kitchen before she noticed him.

Leaning against the newel post at the foot of the stairs with his arms crossed casually in front of him, he had discarded his tie and unbuttoned his white dress shirt at the neck. The long sleeves were rolled up midarm and Shea noticed a gold watch nestled amid the sprinkling of dark hair on his tanned wrist. She also caught the dull gleam of the gold wedding band. The color drained from her face.

She clenched and unclenched her hands around the stemware as something close to panic settled into every inch of her body. She raised her chin in an effort to appear nonchalant as she crossed the room and entered the kitchen. Alec followed. Stepping up behind her, he reached around and removed the wineglass from the death grip she had on it, placing it on the counter next to the sink. The shrill ring of the telephone was a welcome intrusion. She hurried across the room and grabbed it on the second ring.

"I hear you've been looking for me," said a male voice. "It's about time!"

"David?" No. No. No. This could not be happening. Not now.

"Who else?" His voice was as jovial as she remembered. "How the hell are you, Shea?"

"I…I'm good. It's so good to hear your voice." *Understatement. Exclamation mark.*

"Right back at ya, Doc." The nickname he'd always used while she studied to be a veterinarian caused her heart to swell. She could sense him grinning. "So, I got a call from Marcy Allen. She said you've been trying to reach me. What can I do?"

Marry me, she wanted to scream. She closed her eyes as the irony washed over her. Why couldn't he have called yesterday? Or even this morning.

"Ah. Well…actually it's nothing. I mean, the problem has been resolved."

"Are you sure?"

Shea chanced a look in Alec's direction. Was that a smirk on his face?

"Yeah. I'm sure." At least as far as David was concerned. It was just after midnight and the bizarre marriage to Alec Morreston was in full swing. *Her* problem was just beginning.

They spoke for a few more minutes, then with a promise to keep in touch, they said goodbye. And just like that, the positive energy holding the tension at bay seemed to evaporate from the room.

"Old boyfriend?" Alec asked quietly.

She nodded.

"Gee. That's too bad. One day too late." He didn't sound a bit sorry as she crossed the room, returning to the sink, not certain what her next move should be. Alec followed and slowly slid his arms around her waist. His face rubbed against her hair, the heat from his body warm against her back.

"I like your friends that were here tonight," he murmured near her ear. His breath was hot against her neck. In such close proximity, his deep voice caused tingling sensations to dance over her skin. Shea clung to the edge of the counter for support.

She tried to remain calm. "They are good people."

"It was nice of them to come on such short notice."

"Yes. Leona...called most of them."

He stepped away and she heard the clink of ice. Glancing over her shoulder, she watched as Alec pulled a partially consumed bottle of champagne from its silver canister. Holding two crystal flutes easily in one hand, he poured the champagne with the other.

"To what shall we toast?" he asked as he handed her one of the glasses. "A long and satisfying marriage?"

She eyed him coolly. "How about to integrity?"

He pursed his lips as if to contain a devilish grin, then tipped his head and touched his fluted glass to hers. She downed the full contents, desperately needing the champagne's calming effect. She rarely drank alcohol, never champagne, and she wasn't prepared for the sensation. Her eyes clouded with tears and she couldn't stop the choking cough.

Still, the night that lay ahead made her hold the empty glass out to Alec. She ignored the knowing smile tugging at the corners of his mouth as he obligingly refilled it to the brim.

If it were within her power to disappear in a puff of smoke, she'd have done it. For one fleeting second the land didn't seem *that* important. Then the moment passed and she knew she'd see this thing through.

Somehow.

"It's been a long day," he said when she set her empty glass on the table.

"Yes." She readily agreed, some hope suddenly flaring in her chest.

"I suggest you show me our room."

Alec ignored any traces of panic that must have been apparent in her face and, without waiting for an answer, reached for her hand. His was large and warm, his grip firm and solid as he led her out of the kitchen and toward the stairs, turning off the lights as he went.

Lifting the long skirt of the gown with her free hand to ensure she didn't step on the hem, she followed him up the stairs. At the top of the staircase, he paused, silently indicating she should precede him into a bedroom. She walked down the hall, her head held high.

At the door to her room, she stopped. *I can't do this.* She felt light-headed. She could almost hear the chaotic beating of her heart as it pounded against her ribs.

Reaching around her, Alec turned the knob and effortlessly pushed open the door. She hesitated, swallowing back the vile taste of fear that rose in her throat. She could feel the warmth of his body against her back and the soft caress of his breath on her ear seconds before he kissed the sensitive area just below. Wild sensations tore through her. She spun around to face him, her hands braced against the muscled wall of his chest as she tried to keep him at arm's length.

"What's the matter?" he asked, tilting his head in mock innocence. "Wedding night jitters?"

"No." She shook her head. "No. It's just that…well, we…

we don't know each other. I mean…" She took a step back from him, placing her just inside the bedroom.

"I think I know a way we can remedy that problem." He began to unbutton his shirt. With his other hand, he reached out and flipped off the bedroom light leaving only the soft beams of moonlight that streamed through the window to challenge the darkness that now surrounded them. In the dim glow, he watched her, his gaze focused on her lips.

Shea slowly backed away but Alec advanced toward her, matching her step for step. With the last button released, his shirt fell open to reveal the muscular wall of his chest. She hadn't realized he was so powerfully built; so solid. Definitely not the body of a man who sat behind a desk every day.

"You surprise me, Mrs. Morreston. I had expected you to come down the stairs wearing boots and jeans. Instead, you walked into the room in that gown." The deep, velvety texture of his voice made her shiver. "If that was for my benefit, to ensure I knew what a beautiful and desirable woman I was about to marry, you can rest assured, it worked."

"It…it was my mother's."

"It's very nice. Very elegant." He continued to advance toward her. "But now it's time to take it off."

"No."

"No?" He mocked her. "Why, Mrs. Morreston, are you saying you intend to deny your husband on our wedding night?"

"I…I just think we need time to—"

"Don't worry, sweetheart," he cut in. "We have all night, and I certainly intend to take my time."

"No!"

"No? Might I remind you, Mrs. Morreston, you're now a very wealthy woman. You played a good hand and put me in a position of having to marry you in order to keep my own

land. Almost diabolical when you think about it. But all
the benefits don't swing in one direction. It's now my turn
to see what I get in exchange for giving up my freedom."

"No."

"There's that word again." Alec didn't bother concealing
his devious smile. "Are you saying you want to have our
marriage annulled and give up so soon? I honestly believed
your resolve to keep this place, no matter what, would last
longer than the wedding night."

"And I hoped, as a gentleman, you would afford me an
opportunity to get to know you before...before..."

"Who ever said I was a gentleman?" Shea could see the
faint white of his teeth as he smiled in the darkness. "I've
held up my end of this bargain, Mrs. Morreston. Now, I
believe, it's your turn."

"Stop calling me that!" she snapped through gritted teeth
as her inner turmoil exploded to the surface. This only succeeded in causing a bigger grin to spread across his face.

"But that's who you are, *Mrs. Morreston*." His fingers
reached out and touched the tiny pearl buttons at the neckline of her dress. "It was your decision, remember?"

"Only to prevent you from taking my ranch."

"It was your decision."

Shea swallowed back the alarm that threatened to en-
gulf her. He was right. He had warned her. And she had
agreed freely.

Reaching for one of her hands, he began to unbutton the
seam that ran from her wrist to her elbow, letting the satiny
material fall away from her arm. Then, without a word, he
moved to the other sleeve.

That completed, in a gentle but firm action, he turned
her around and began to unfasten the back of the satin-and-
lace gown. His hands moved slowly, methodically down
the dress, releasing button after tiny button.

She caught their reflection in the mirror on the closet

door. The moonlight highlighted the silver-blond strands of her hair and softened the panicked features of her face. Alec's large, dark silhouette loomed behind her, his head bowed as he worked at his task. All traces of his earlier amusement were gone, replaced by a look of serious intent.

Standing practically nude before a strange man was not an experience she'd ever anticipated. The gown provided a frail armor, a subtle safeguard. In a few precious minutes, her lace panties and the white hosiery would be the only pieces of armor that remained.

Their eyes met in the mirror for countless seconds before he bent his head and placed his lips against the sensitive area beneath her ear. Her heart kicked into double time as Alec emitted a low growl, which sent electric sensations racing down her spine.

She spun around in an effort to break the contact. Rather than reach for her again, he removed his shirt, tossed it aside and began unbuckling his belt. The muscles of his shoulders and arms rippled in the moon's glow, the significant pectorals making him seem even bigger than he'd looked with his clothes on.

Taking another step back from him, her legs bumped against the bed. Her pulse tripled. Frantically her eyes searched the room, hoping to detect any means of escape from this reprehensible situation.

Before she could voice any more objections or seize on a reason to try to postpone the inevitable, Alec reached out to her. His hands cupped her face, compelling her to meet his gaze as he took the final step, closing the short distance between them.

Shea clenched her hands into tight fists at her sides, determined to resist this forceful male. In the pale light, she saw his eyes focus on her lips seconds before his mouth came down over hers hard, masterfully firm in its possession. His hands left her face as his heavy arms encircled her body like bands of steel. His sheer strength and size, coupled with the passion of the embrace, rocked her senses and snatched the very breath from her lungs. She was way out of her depth. A feeling of near hysteria enveloped her mind. With a small cry, she tore her mouth from his. He allowed her to pull back but kept her close, his large hands resting on her shoulders.

"I can't...I can't do this." Her fingers gripped his. "I know you said...I know I agreed that...but I...please... don't—"

"Shh." A frown drew his dark brows together. He had to see the frantic, almost terrified expression that must be on her face, mirroring the fear churning inside. "It's all right, Shea. I'm not going to hurt you," he murmured as his thumbs caressed the side of her face. "Just kiss me. That's all you have to do."

Shea scarcely had time to nod her agreement before his mouth once again claimed hers. This time he moved slowly, sensuously, with an easy gentleness that immediately began to tear down the walls of her resistance. His tongue licked and teased her lips, moistening them, as if readying her for a more intense joining.

With consummate skill, he encouraged her lips to open. His tongue slid deep into the cavern of her mouth, sending her heart plummeting all the way to her knees. The kiss was frankly intimate, shamefully enticing and custom designed to evoke a matching response from her. He tasted of champagne and his own uniquely delicious male flavor. It mingled with the bittersweet essence of his cologne, which silently affirmed the raw masculinity of the man who wore it.

His hands rubbed her back, working down her spine, slowly massaging away the last remnants of her inner turmoil. Sensual warmth began to spread though her, intensifying the heat pooling between her legs while a thread of confusion wove its way into her mind.

What am I doing? But the question was too fleeting to receive an answer.

Slowly but steadily, her fear began to change form, turning instead into a fundamental need that refused to be ignored. A fragment of her mind insisted this wasn't right. Her body screamed that it was.

Alec pushed the creamy fabric of the gown from her shoulders. It fell to the floor with a quiet rustle. She should have been shocked, but the realization weighed no heavier than the soft evening breeze entering the room through the open windows. For a few moments in time, she forgot the reality of her situation, of her pledged hatred of this man. Of their own accord, her arms slid up over his muscled chest to rest on his broad, powerful shoulders, letting her fingers play in the thick, silky texture of his hair. Alec's hands moved lower in their rotation until, reaching the fullness of her hips, he pulled her firmly up and against him. The hard, male ridge of his arousal pressed against the sensitive juncture between her legs and a jolt of pure sexual hunger shot through her. Her body jerked forward, uncontrollably, bringing a deep growl from Alec.

He began to alternately kiss and nibble the delicate contours of her neck and shoulder and, eyes closed, she tilted her head to allow him greater access. His hands moved to her breasts, kneading the firmness, making them swell under his touch. Then his mouth returned to hers in a deep, drugging kiss that brought a small whimper, an automatic response conveying the end of her struggle against the inevitable.

Five

Experience told Alec that sound signified her acceptance of what was to come. He knew, at this moment in time she was his, completely and totally. Raising his head, he looked at Shea's face, radiant in the moonlight. Her eyes were closed, her lips parted as if waiting for his mouth to return. As if beckoning his lips to return.

Heat coursed through his body, centering in his loins, making him throb against the restricting barrier of his slacks. A slight tremor reminded him he was about to cross the line. This was not the plan. Seducing her wouldn't accomplish anything except add to the problems he already faced and enormously complicate the entire situation.

He gritted his teeth, closed his eyes and fought for restraint. But even when he couldn't see, her fragrance assailed him, called to him and tempted him almost beyond his control. He knew her body craved fulfillment and her need only served to bring him closer to that moment of ultimate possession, a moment that should never happen. He ached with wanting. His libido screamed, *Take her*!

Suddenly, it was too much.

Damn the land. Damn that contract. Damn this situation. With a groan of defeat, he scooped her into his arms, laid her gently on the bed and followed her down, his mouth again finding hers.

Then, almost unnoticeable at first, a persistent sound of drumming broke into the moment. The sound, hesitant but determined, brought with it a cold reality that refused to leave.

Frowning, Alec raised his head, reluctantly separating his lips from hers. He inhaled deeply, fighting to regain cognizant thought. It sounded as if someone was knocking on a door. Silence. Then it started again. Another hard series of raps caused him to look questioningly at Shea while he fought to latch onto some thread of reality.

"Are you expecting anyone?" His voice sounded rough, even to his own ears.

She mutely looked into his face. Alec drew a deep breath and blew it out, pausing to regain what little mind he had left. Finally, he rolled off the bed and stood up. Taking another deep breath, he walked out into the hallway and down the stairs as the persistent knocking continued. He knew a sudden surge of fury as he reached the kitchen door.

Hank Minton, the ranch foreman, stood on the doorstep. He had his hat in his hands, and a worried look pinched the strained features of his face. He wouldn't look Alec in the eye. Instead he watched the bugs fluttering around the porch light, studied the doorbell and finally appeared to give significant attention to his old, worn boots.

"Hank." Suspicion set off a flashing red light in Alec's still-muddled brain.

"I'm sorry to bother you all with this," the old cowboy said. "Real sorry. Specially knowing it's your weddin' night and all. But we got a horse down and I think Shea's gonna need to take a look at him."

"I see," Alec replied. And he did.

There was no question in his mind that Shea had solicited Hank's help for this perfectly timed interruption. Alec was torn between a desire to toss the old man off the step or hug his neck and thank him for doing what Alec apparently lacked the strength to do himself.

Hank had just provided a plausible excuse for Alec to

stop, which was exactly what *he* should have done in the first place. Annoyance surged through him for his weakness and for letting his desire overcome his common sense.

He definitely should be grateful to Hank. Why, then, did he have the urge to break the old man's neck?

"Come in. I'll get her."

The old cowboy nodded and stepped just inside the kitchen, glancing at the sink, the overhead light, the chairs and finally back to his boots.

Shea sat on the edge of the bed in the darkened room as reality came slamming back. Willing her pulse to steady, she took a deep breath in a desperate attempt to clear her head. Her hand trembled as she ran her fingers through her hair. It had been close. Too close. His touch left the lower parts of her body swollen, unfulfilled and badly in need of something more.

He hadn't made love to her. Technically. Hadn't penetrated her body with his. She should be monumentally happy. Why, then, did she feel ridiculously disappointed?

She stood and felt her way to the closet, not bothering to turn on a light. Her legs were strangely weak. She quickly shucked her hosiery, pulled on a pair of jeans and a shirt and then descended the stairs. She couldn't help but grimace as the full impact of the situation settled over her.

She'd almost had sex with Alec Morreston.

Even worse, he hadn't forced her. He hadn't held her down or tied her to the bedposts. He'd kissed her. That was all. Apparently, that had been enough. She knew it. And worse, so did he. Alec was here to take away her ranch, her home, everything she held dear. She would do well to remember that. He was, inarguably, a very potent package with obvious experience to back that up. She had to be strong.

Alec pivoted from the open doorway as she entered the

kitchen. He didn't appear surprised to see her there. "It seems your presence is needed in the barn." His tone clearly said he was suspicious of Hank's timing.

"It's Crusty, Shea." Hank's voice carried to her from the doorway. "He's down. Me and Jason, we've been working with him almost an hour, but we can't keep him on his feet. I think it's colic." The old cowboy threaded the brim of his hat through his hands in a nervous gesture as he stared at his boots. "I'm real sorry about this. Real sorry."

"That's okay, Hank." Shea glanced at Alec. "I'm sure Mr. Morreston understands." The look Alec gave her clearly said he understood far more than just the claimed need for Shea's presence in the barn. "Give me a second to put on some shoes. Is he in the main barn?"

"Yes, ma'am. I'll go on back out there." He put his hat firmly on his head and turned toward the door. "I'm real sorry 'bout this. Real sorry." Hank closed the door behind him.

Shea ran up the stairs and into the bedroom, wasting no time as she pulled on socks and boots. Just as she stood and reached for her jacket, Alec walked into the room.

"Need any help?"

"No. Thanks anyway."

As she walked past him, he gently touched her shoulder, stopping her in midstride.

"Consider this…a wedding gift. We wouldn't want all of Hank's efforts to be for nothing. But, take fair warning, next time there will be no interruptions. You can accept that or you can prepare to leave here." There was a gleam of promise in his eyes.

His insolence was like a splash of cold water. A scant few minutes ago, she'd been on the verge of giving herself to this man. Now her only inclination was to put her fist firmly against his nose with the highest velocity she could muster. The combined emotions of frustration and humiliation propelled her anger to the surface.

Pushing past him, she almost ran down the stairs.

When she pulled open the heavy barn door, she found Hank holding the lead shank attached to a halter placed on one of the older geldings.

"Figured he might come with you," Hank explained. "Ole Crusty here looks like he just might keel over any minute. A city feller wouldn't know the difference." Shea smiled and nodded. "Was I convincin'? Did I do okay?"

"Yeah." She nodded her approval as she walked toward the old horse. "You did good, Hank."

Her plan had worked. The timing could have been a little better, but even so, good enough. So why wasn't she bouncing-off-the-walls deliriously happy? Why did she feel so incomplete? In all honesty, she had to admit deep down a part of her regretted the interruption.

Alec knew a woman's body. He knew exactly where to touch, precisely how to kiss and just what to do to make a female respond to him. To make *her* respond to him. From the beginning, she'd sensed he would be highly skilled in bed, but she'd never envisioned finding out firsthand. She could still taste him, could feel his hard body against hers. His masculine scent was heavy on her skin. The fire he'd lit still burned, refusing to die out. Taking a deep, shaky breath, she sat down on a bale of hay and rubbed her forehead in an attempt to clear her mind. But the remembrance of what had happened—of what had almost happened—stubbornly wouldn't go away.

"Missy, are you sure you know what you're doing?" Hank removed his hat and scratched his head, which left his thinning gray hair in a tousled mess on top of his head, then replaced his timeworn hat.

"Absolutely." She smiled bravely, confidently at the old cowboy. But she knew she was lying through her teeth.

* * *

Alec watched as Shea almost ran down the stairs. He raked his hand through his hair and took a deep breath. It had been too close. Three minutes, maybe less, and their bodies would have been locked in the most intimate act that could happen between two people and nothing on this earth would have made him let her go. He wasn't exactly sure how he'd allowed the situation to escalate as far as it had and he wasn't certain how to prevent it in the future.

The plan had been to frighten her with an overload of sexual intimidation, come on so hard and heavy that she'd run like a scared rabbit. But instead of running, instead of saying, *Okay, you win, I'll leave*, she had looked up at him with those damned amazing blue eyes and silently begged him not to hurt her, pleaded with him to give her time. And in that instant, with her enticing lips a mere breath away, and those eyes imploring him to understand, he'd made a choice. And that choice had almost irrevocably changed everything.

He couldn't remember ever losing control or being blindsided by the aura of a sexy woman. But this time his strength of will had flown out the window and he'd almost sacrificed everything for a young woman from the back woods of Texas with big blue eyes and one hell of a game plan. So much for his ironclad resolve.

He had to get out of here, at least for a while. Let things cool down and give himself time to regain his perspective, to reformulate his plan. With a grimace, he turned and walked toward the bathroom and a cold shower.

The sun was just peeking over the distant hills when Shea quietly made her way back to the house. The romantics of the world could say all they wanted about sleeping on a soft bed of hay. In truth, it was prickly and itchy and its stiff, needlelike projections could poke through even the thickest blanket right into your skin. She hadn't had a good night. But the few hours of restless sleep had been enough to restore her sanity. In the light of day, she knew the outcome of the previous night could have been much worse.

She could have made love to Alec.

She could be lying in that bed right now with his big, muscled arms securely around her, drowsy in the aftermath of their lovemaking. Feeling— *Stop*! With a muttered oath, Shea pulled open the back door.

When she entered the kitchen, to her surprise, Alec was already there dressed in dark slacks, a clean white dress shirt and tie. He looked disgustingly well-rested.

"Looks like you had a good night," he said, reaching out to pull some straw from her tangled hair. "You give an entirely new meaning to a roll in the hay. Sleep well, did you?" His mouth twitched in amusement as he gestured to the pot of fresh coffee.

Shea ignored his jibes, opened the cabinet and selected a mug. If he expected her to make any comment about what happened last night—or what *hadn't* happened—he could hold his breath until he turned blue.

She couldn't help noticing the way his shirt did little to hide the muscles of his arm as he lifted his cup to his mouth, or the way his full lips opened against the rounded edge of the mug as he sipped the steaming coffee. She quickly turned away as unsettling sensations began to send surges of heat through her veins.

"I need to return home for a few days," Alec said as she reached for the coffee. "I understand this might be viewed as deserting my wife on our honeymoon, but I'm afraid it can't be helped. As far as the contract, I don't recall any stipulation that I never leave the boundaries of the land, only that I ensure your protection from *any and all perils*. If you think you'll be *safe* for a few days—" his sarcasm was apparent "—I need clothes. And I need to make some

LAUREN CANAN 65

arrangements. Do our attorneys need to become involved with this?"

In spite of the temptation to try to deny Alec the time he needed, she knew it wouldn't be right. And there was nothing in the contract to prevent him from leaving the property.

"No. But I wouldn't bother packing a lot of clothes. You won't be here long enough to need them."

At least his trip would give her the time she needed to form a better plan to make him leave permanently. With any luck, he wouldn't come back at all.

He watched her guardedly. "Want to come with me?"

"No, thank you," she quickly responded. "I've got things I need to see to here."

"I'm sure you do," he replied, tongue in cheek. "How's the horse?"

"The horse?" she frowned. It took a few seconds before she remembered the "sick" horse in the barn. "Oh. Fine. Good." She looked down at her mug and away from the scrutiny of those amber eyes, knowing she was incapable of telling a convincing lie. "I expect he'll make a full recovery."

"Oh, I have no doubt."

Alec walked to the counter where she stood and reached around her to place his cup in the sink. "Call a local furniture store and have them send out a larger bed. Get an entire suite if you like."

The surprise must have shown on her face.

"Is money a problem?"

"No." She shook her head. "But a larger bed won't fit into that room."

"Then have it put in a larger room." He cocked his head. "There *is* a larger bedroom, isn't there?"

"Yes, but…"

Alec watched her reaction. "But what?"

There were in fact three bedrooms upstairs. But moving

into the master indicated a permanency she did not want. She just wished he would stay wherever it was he was going and let her life return to normal.

"Nothing." She shook her head. "How long will you be away?" She didn't want to ask. To do so might imply she cared. But she had to prepare for his return.

"A few days. Possibly a week. I can't be sure. Why? Will you miss me?"

She snorted and took a sip of her coffee.

"I'll take that as a yes."

He tucked a loose strand of hair behind her ear before his head dipped toward her and his lips found hers. It was instinct rather than conscious thought that made her open to him. He deepened the embrace, kissing her thoroughly but briefly. Then, raising his head, he broke the contact but remained close.

"You're going to lose," Alec whispered. "But this challenge is becoming more interesting by the minute. I look forward to the next round."

Her expression strengthened into a cold glare. But before she could respond in kind, he turned and walked out the door.

The large private jet sliced through the white clouds en route back to Dallas from New York LaGuardia. After a week of reflection, Alec was no closer to finding a concrete plan that would ensure he maintained control of the bizarre situation.

So far, the only thing guaranteed to work was avoiding her altogether. But not only would that not serve his objective, it was not something he was willing to do.

He glanced at the child, asleep on the small bed across the aisle. This morning, when he'd picked up his bag and prepared to leave for the airport, he'd seen Scotty peeking around the corner of the kitchen doorway. He'd walked over to his son, lifted the four-year-old into his arms and given in to the overwhelming need to hold him close.

"Are you gonna be gone a long time?"

Alec had given him a regretful smile. "Maybe not too long this time."

"Good. Where are you going?"

"Actually, I'll be staying on a ranch."

"A ranch?"

"Yep."

"Do they have horsees?"

"I believe they do."

"And cowboys?" Scotty's eyes had been wide with excitement.

"And cowboys," he'd confirmed as an idea had formed in his mind.

It had been a spur-of-the-moment decision to bring him along, but even now, some three hours later, Alec still felt it was the right one. Scott's preschool was over for the summer. Alec spent far too much time away from his son because of the requirements of his work. This wacky situation actually might provide some time to spend with his son, an experience both he and Scotty would remember.

The only negative he could see was the possibility Shea and Scott might bond, which could be tough on the boy when it was time to leave. It was because of this concern Alec elected to not mention the marriage. To tell Scotty he had a mother only to take him away from her a couple of weeks later was just wrong. He wouldn't do that to Scott.

Alec's mouth quirked as he thought of Shea and the days ahead. As far as he knew, Shea had no children and possibly no experience with a four-year-old. This unexpected twist could prove very interesting.

He rose from his seat and entered the area of the plane set up as his office. They were still an hour out from DFW. He might as well get some work done while he could. He had a feeling his time away from the ranch had provided Shea with ample opportunity to put some plans in motion to try to make him give up and leave.

Good luck with that.

"Okay, that should do her," Shea said, removing the rubber surgical gloves and giving the mare's shoulder a pat. "Take her back to the stall and keep an eye on her."

"Sure thing, boss." Hank picked up his hat and slapped it against his leg to dislodge some of the dirt before fitting it firmly onto his head.

The mare carried one of the best bloodlines in a five-state region. It was the boost this ranch needed. That was the only reason Shea tolerated Bonnie Blue's ridiculous temperament every time the mare needed medical care. Thankfully, it didn't happen often.

With three cowboys holding the high-strung horse, Shea had still been thrown hard against the side of the barn when she'd attempted to inject a tranquilizer. Her shoulder had absorbed most of the impact, providing a painful souvenir she would no doubt carry for a few days. Once the tranquilizer had begun to take effect, it took no time to stitch the mare's cut, apply a topical dressing and give Bonnie Blue the added safety of a tetanus booster.

Shea bent to pick up the discarded cotton, linens and syringes, not bothering to watch the three lanky cowboys lead the now docile mare out of the paddock. When she again looked up, the breath died in her throat as she found herself staring directly into Alec's scowling face.

He'd gone from being like a character from a foggy, half-forgotten dream to suddenly materializing right in front of her as a crystal clear vision. And he was as disturbingly handsome as ever. His tall stature, the broad width of his shoulders and the sheer male essence of him seemed even more pronounced than she remembered.

As she approached the paddock gate, Alec swung it open and then closed it behind her.

"You want to tell me just what in the hell you were doing?"

"What do you mean?" She frowned, clueless as to what he could be talking about.

"You. That horse. You were almost killed."

Rolling her eyes, she moved to walk past him but the distinctive voice of a child abruptly shattered the tension of the moment, halting her in midstride.

"Boy, oh boy! That was *cool*!"

Shea's head snapped around in surprise. She focused on a small boy clinging precariously to the centerboard of the paddock fence, allowing the crown of his head and two large round eyes to peek over the top.

The child jumped from his perch and ran toward the gate to stand directly in front of Shea.

"Are you all right?" His small face held a look of genuine concern. "Did the horse hurt your arm?"

"No, I'm…fine." She sent a questioning glance at Alec.

"This is Scotty." He watched her face as if ready to gauge her reaction. "My son."

Shea blinked. More than twice. Alec had a child? Good Lord! Devils didn't normally produce such angelic-looking offspring, did they?

"Scotty, this is Shea."

She knew a look of disbelief covered her features as she leaned over, bringing her closer to eye-level with the boy.

"Hi, Scotty." She forced a smile and held out her hand. The boy placed his small hand in hers and produced a wide grin. Then, mysteriously struck with a bout of shyness, he stepped back to stand closer to his father, his arm around Alec's leg.

"You never told me you had a son."

Alec flexed his shoulders. "So now you know. As I was

about to leave I mentioned I would be staying on a ranch."
Alec looked down at his son before returning those tawny
eyes to her. "He wanted to come and see the horses and
cowboys."

Are you freaking kidding me? She could only gasp as
her blood pressure shot up to dangerous heights. Momentarily at a total loss for words, she forced herself to breathe
deep and stared at the man standing four feet in front of
her. He was insane. This child had no business on a working ranch. Not only had this conceited lunatic returned, but
he'd brought an innocent child along as his backup. And
she'd thought the situation couldn't possibly get any worse.

"Are you ready for the next one, Shea?" Hank asked
from the side door of the main barn.

"Take a break, Hank." Her voice was unnaturally high
even to her own ears.

"We need to talk." She shot an if-looks-could-kill glance
at Alec and headed to the house, muttering under her breath.

Her shoulder throbbed. She longed for a nice hot soak in
the tub and something to eat, but until she finished checking
and treating the remaining horses, she knew she couldn't
stop. The preliminary work for the annual fall roundup and
branding would begin in earnest in just a few weeks. There
was a great deal of preparation between now and then, and
most of it rested on her shoulders. Alec couldn't have picked
a worse time to return. Let alone with a child in tow.

Entering the kitchen, she tossed the dirty gauze into the
trash bin before washing her hands. To give herself time
to calm down she took a pitcher of tea from the refrigera-
tor and set three glasses on the counter. Adding ice to two
before filling them with tea, she then poured fresh milk
into the third.

"Have a seat," she told Alec, indicating the kitchen chairs
when he and Scotty followed her inside. Her eyes were
drawn to the child. She guessed his age to be four or five.

He was a miniature of his father except his hair was several shades lighter than Alec's dark mahogany brown.

"If you look in the big jar on the cabinet, I think you'll find some cookies."

Scotty wasted no time in pulling a chair over to the counter and climbing up to reach the cookie jar.

"Can I have two?" He flashed a smile that would melt the coldest heart. She'd bet he'd learned that from his father.

"Sure." She tried to return his smile but wasn't fully convinced she'd pulled it off. "There are some paper towels next to the sink. Grab one and your cookies and follow me. You can watch cartoons while I talk with your dad."

"I like cartoons."

With Scotty contentedly watching TV and munching on the homemade cookies in the next room, Shea returned to the kitchen and joined Alec at the table.

He'd shed his usual business suit; snug-fitting jeans now hugged his muscled thighs and a tan sports shirt hung casually from his broad shoulders. Ostrich-skin boots completed the ensemble and to her surprise, they weren't new. His tawny eyes were as compelling and enigmatic as ever.

"You said you wanted to talk?" Alec sat back in the chair looking completely at ease.

"Yeah." She set the glasses of tea on the table and dropped into a chair opposite Alec. Where to begin? What to say to a complete schmuck? "This is a working ranch. What you saw out there today happens all the time. It's what we do. This is not a pony club or a dude ranch. We don't cater to novices who don't know the nose from the back end of a horse. A child could get hurt, especially a little one who has never been around livestock. I cannot halt the operations of this ranch to play nursemaid to either one of you."

He merely looked at her, his eyes sliding from her mouth

to her breasts and back to her eyes. It was unnerving. *He* was unnerving.

"Every year we usually find at least two poisonous snakes near the main barn or around the house," she continued, determined to ignore the pulsing sensation in the pit of her stomach. "Go into the forested sections and you're likely to find cougars or bear. There are wild boars that can take a man's leg off. This is no place for a child."

"Sorry. Maybe I misunderstood. Didn't you grow up here?"

She could only glare. What could she honestly say to that?

"I will not be held responsible if an innocent little boy gets hurt."

He shrugged. "I'll have a talk with Scott. Tell me his boundaries and I'll see he stays within them."

"Then tell him to stay inside this house."

"Don't be ridiculous."

"*Me* ridiculous?"

"I have a son I love very much. I do not intend to leave him back in New York or make him stay in the house for however long it takes you to pack your bags."

Her annoyance shot across the line to pure fury at his insolence. The wooden chair made a screeching sound as she bounded to her feet. Her hands rested on the table as she leaned toward Alec. "I can't believe you'd stoop so low as to bring an innocent child into this...insanity."

Alec met her angry glare and rose slowly from his chair like a mountain lion ready to pounce. His hands rested on his side of the table as he leaned toward her. "*I* didn't cause this. *I* was not the one who refused to relinquish possession of land that didn't belong to me!"

"Oh, yes," she hissed, her voice coated with vehemence. "Just try and convince me you're the innocent victim! Do you make a habit of throwing people out of their homes?

Do you get your kicks from watching them scurry around trying to find another place to live?"

"I offered you a sizeable sum of money to leave. Not exactly the same as throwing you out on the street."

"Money. All you seem to care about is money! I feel sorry for you, Alec. I pity your son that he must live the kind of life you deem appropriate when you don't even know what family or tradition is all about."

"Leave Scotty out of this."

"*I'm* not the one who brought him into it!"

"And you've made your feelings quite clear."

"Apparently not. You're still here."

A movement out of the corner of her eye told her they had an audience. Turning toward Scotty, she pasted a smile on her face.

"The cookies were good," he said, his gaze going back and forth from his father to Shea.

"Oh. Great." *Down shift.* "I'm glad you like them. Is the cartoon over?"

"Are you and Daddy always gonna fight at each other?" He tilted his head in a manner she'd seen his father do. Guilt quickly dissolved the anger as she realized this little boy had heard their heated exchange.

"I...I don't know, sweetie," she hedged and then decided to be honest. If she and Alec didn't kill each other before this was over, it would be nothing short of a miracle. "Your dad and I, well, we have a lot of things to work out between us. There's a lot *he* doesn't understand."

The child seemed to take the answer in stride.

"Freddy Correnski said his mommy and daddy used to fight all the time. Then Freddy and his mommy moved to another house. Are Daddy and me gonna live in your house with you?"

"Uh. Well. Yes. I guess you are," she answered, trying

to force happiness into her tone. Her eyes cut to Alec as she added, "For a while."

"Cool." He walked over to stand in front of Shea. "Sometimes Daddy gets sad and I ask him why and he says he's not sad, but I know he is 'cause he just sits there in his chair and looks real tired, but he says he's not tired but he won't get up." He took a deep breath and looked at Shea. "Will you make Daddy not be sad?"

For the life of her, Shea couldn't think of an appropriate reply. Alec, apparently, had no such difficulty.

"She is going to do her best, Scott," he said as a wide grin spread across his face. The mischievous twinkle was back in his eyes.

"Good. Can I have another cookie?"

Her voice seemed to have abandoned her, so Shea merely nodded her head.

As the youngster scrambled for the cookie jar, she whispered to Alec, "You can bring a hundred kids out here. A thousand. I'm still not going to let you have this ranch."

His eyes roamed over her face. "Why don't you show us where we'll be sleeping?" he suggested, choosing to ignore her blatant declaration. "It's been a long day. I have a feeling we're going to have an early night."

Six

Shea turned and marched toward the stairs. She didn't pause until she stood just inside the doorway to a second-floor bedroom overlooking the barn and paddock area. She crossed to the window and opened the blinds, letting the sunshine in.

"I think Scotty will be comfortable in here. If you had bothered to call and let me know he was coming, I could have had the room prepared. Yolanda, the wife of one of our ranch hands, comes in twice a week and helps with the laundry and general cleaning. She should be here soon to start dinner. I'll have her change the bedding and air the room."

"This is gonna be my room?" Scotty asked in delight, oblivious to the tension still hanging heavy between the adults. "Cool!" He ran to the bed and joyfully bounced on the springy mattress before bounding to the floor and running to the large double window. "Wow! Daddy! Look at this! Is that where you keep the horsees?" He pointed a finger at the barn.

"Some of them." Shea smiled down at Alec's son.

"Can I ride one?" He looked up at her, his bright, eager eyes hopeful.

She reached out and tousled his hair. "You'll have to ask your dad."

"He'll say okay. Won't you, Daddy?" Not waiting for an answer he added, "I like it here." He turned and surveyed the room, then nodded his head as if he'd made a great decision. "Yep. This is gonna be all right."

"I assume you brought extra clothes and personal items?" Alec nodded. "I'll get Jason to help you with your suitcases. Just tell him if you want to change anything around, move the bed, whatever."

"This will be fine."

"Hey, Daddy, where is your bed?"

Shea had started out of the room. This question, however, made her pause. Clearly, Alec hadn't shared the fact he'd gotten married with his son. She couldn't pass up the chance to see how he was going to handle this one. She turned toward him, eyebrows raised, her head tilted as she waited for the answer along with Scotty.

Alec stood staring down at the small child in front of him. He rubbed a hand over his mouth, sighed, then rested his hands on his hips. "Actually, I'm going to be sleeping… in another room."

"Where?"

"I'll be bedding down with Shea."

"How come?"

Get him, Scotty!

Alec put his large hands together, cracking his knuckles as he fought to answer that one. Then his head shot up, he glanced at Shea and back to his son. "She's afraid of the dark."

"Oh."

He did not just say that. She couldn't withhold a snort of laughter, which earned her a glare of warning from Alec.

"Okaaaaay." *Your son. Your bad.* "Well, I've still got a lot of work to do this afternoon. Yolanda will start supper about six." She again looked at Scotty. "What do you like to eat?"

"Hot dogs! With ketchup."

Her lips slid into a full, easy grin and Alec had to wonder if it had the same effect on his son as it did him. Damn, she was beautiful.

"I'll see what we can do."

As she disappeared around the corner, Scotty's voice rang out. "I *like* her, Daddy."

Alec nodded. His son had just answered his unspoken question and he wasn't surprised. He'd carried the far-fetched hope that returning to the ranch would dispel his initial attraction to Shea and he could chalk up the whole thing to stress.

No such luck.

He looked around the room. The wallpaper was faded, its edges peeling away from the walls in a couple of places. Slightly discolored stains on the ceiling indicated water had entered uninvited at some time in the past and left its murky calling card. The light fixture, a remnant from a bygone era, dangled precariously from the twelve-foot-high ceiling. The faint scents of mothballs and lemon touched his senses. But in spite of its worn appearance, this room, in fact the entire house, brought to mind childhood memories of home-baked bread and leftover meatloaf sandwiches. Of the big tree that had been outside his window, perfect for sneaking out of the house to go night fishing with Grandpa Jacob and old man Muldoon.

Alec moved to stand beside his son at the large window. Shea came into view directly below, walking toward the barn.

"Hey, Dad? Do you think she likes us?"

"Oh, I'm sure she does, son," he lied.

Shea was standing next to a big Appaloosa and a portable medic unit writing something on a form attached to a clipboard when Alec and Scotty walked into the paddock area near the main barn. The tension in her carriage was obvious. He was tempted to step over and give her shoulders a quick massage, but immediately decided against it. The last thing he needed was to get so close to temptation.

"What are you gonna do?" Scotty asked her, his eyes wide and curious.

"I gave him a shot that'll help keep him healthy," she explained simply. She patted the horse's shoulder. "Okay, Jason, take him away."

After making some additional notations she turned her attention back to Scotty. "Have you ever seen a horse get shoes?"

Scotty shook his head.

"No? Then, come with me."

Alec followed as they walked to the north end of the barn where a blacksmith had set up his rig for shoeing horses. The clang of his hammer rang out through the late afternoon calm. Alec stood slightly to the side, content to watch the interaction between Shea and his son. It appeared they already were bonding, a fact that both surprised and intrigued him.

"This is Charlie." She nodded toward the burly man dressed in a sleeveless shirt and jeans. A faded red bandana tied around his forehead kept the sweat from his eyes.

"What's he doing?"

"He's making a shoe for one of the horses." Smiling at Scotty, she selected a metal horseshoe from the trailer, handed it to him. Scotty held it as though it were made of gold.

"Each horse has different size feet, just like people do. Charlie selects a shoe close to the size of a horse's hoof, then heats the metal so when he beats it with the hammer it will change the shape a little bit until it fits. Then he cools it and nails it on."

"Doesn't it hurt?"

"Nope. He uses special nails. The horse can't feel a thing."

Scotty looked again at the metal shoe, then held it out to Shea.

"Keep it," she said. "Hang it on a wall in your room. Like this." She turned the metal shoe around so that it formed the shape of a cup. "It will catch good luck." Fascinated, Scotty smiled up at her. He took a few steps in Charlie's direction before stopping and looking back at Shea and his father.

"It's okay, son." Alec assured him. "You can go over and talk to Charlie. Just don't get too close to the horses."

He hesitated only a few seconds before walking over, proudly holding his horseshoe with both hands.

Alec was moved by the gentleness and attention she'd shown Scotty. It was something he hadn't anticipated. There was no hidden agenda he could see. Unlike some women, she certainly wasn't doing it to impress him. She seemed genuine, as though she not only enjoyed teaching Scott about the things in her world, but she honestly liked Scotty, as well. And his son seemed equally fond of her.

She glanced at Alec as she walked past to return to the medic unit.

"Thanks," he felt obliged to say.

She frowned. "For what?"

"For taking the time for Scotty."

She shrugged it off. "I like kids. He's a sweetie. There's no point in making him feel unwelcome. But you brought him. He's your son. Your responsibility. If he gets hurt, it's on you."

With that, she picked up the clipboard and began to check her data.

"How many cattle do you have?" Alec asked, glancing beyond the barn at the distant hills.

"On average the Bar H runs about three thousand head." She turned to him, her captivating eyes moving over his face. "The number, of course, drops after we ship in the fall, but is reestablished the first of the year when the calving begins."

"Shea?" Hank called from the doorway. "Where do you want Shonie?" He led a large painted gelding into the area.

"Bring him over here," Shea instructed, setting the clipboard aside.

"Is there something I can do to help?" Alec wanted something to keep his mind occupied, his hands busy. In the short time he'd been back, his body already had begun responding to her.

His question appeared to take Shea by surprise. "Have you ever been around horses?"

"Some."

"I've got eight more to check." She looked down the hallway. "The stalls are numbered. I'll need to see the ones in eight, twelve and fifteen next. Their halters, with leads attached, are hanging on the doors."

Finding the correct stall, Alec slipped the halter over the head of a docile mare and led her out of the barn.

Shea took the lead from his hands. "She's no problem. I can handle her by myself. While I check her out, go ahead and get Ransom. Number twelve."

She was just finishing with the mare when Alec arrived with the spirited bay gelding. The feisty animal nickered playfully and attempted to rub his head against Alec's shoulder.

"You seem to have made a friend."

"You sound surprised," he noted, turning to rub the neck of the striking animal. He appreciated quality and this big gelding reeked of good breeding, as did most of the horses he'd seen here.

"I am. Hold him here while I take Essie to Charlie. Her shoes need replacing."

* * *

On the horizon, fiery remnants of red and gold accented the darkening sky as Shea checked the last of the horses. When she brought the final one around the corner of the barn, she was surprised to see Scotty perched on top of one of the trail horses tied securely to the fence. Frowning, she looked at Alec, who stood next to the child.

"He's fine." Alec assured her, as though reading her mind. "Having the time of his life." His booted foot was propped on the lower rail of the fence, his jeans hugging his muscular legs and hips. His arms rested easily on the top rail. He looked lean and strong. She swallowed hard, fighting back the insane desire to walk over and step into his arms.

"I'm beat." She could hear the tiredness in her own voice, no doubt the cause of her temporary insanity. "I'll see you back at the house."

Alec nodded before she turned and headed toward the house. She refused to let her mind dwell on the night ahead and the possibilities it could hold. Entering through the kitchen door, she walked to the stairs and made it as far as the second-floor landing when she saw the open door at the end of the hall.

The master bedroom.

She stopped in her tracks.

The new furniture had been delivered, the bed prepared with clean linens and the door closed. It had remained closed—until today. Until Alec returned and opened it. Now it taunted her, dared her to enter and face the moment of truth.

She clenched her hands at her sides, fighting her growing panic. She turned and almost flew down the stairs.

Alec and Scotty were just coming in the door when Shea reached the kitchen. She grabbed her car keys and

a manila folder containing information Leona had asked
for a month ago.

"I'll be back," she muttered.

"Mind if I ask where you're going?"

"Um...I've got to take some records over to Leona."

Without waiting for any further comment, she quickly
walked out the door.

The house was quiet when Shea stepped into the kitchen
much later. Closing the door behind her, she dropped the
car keys onto the counter and walked toward the stairs.

"Have a good visit?"

"Oh!" She spun around in the direction of Alec's voice.
"You startled me." She clutched the neckline of her shirt.

"Sorry." He stepped out of the shadows. "I came down
to get some water and heard you drive up. What are you
doing back here?"

"I live here?"

He shrugged. "I just didn't think you'd come back tonight."

He didn't know how close he was to the truth.

Or maybe he did.

He was clad only in jeans, the ripple of hard muscle
in his arms and chest apparent even in the semidarkness.
She could sense the pure male aura that always seemed to
surround him.

"Did Scotty settle in all right?"

"It took a while, but he's asleep."

Shea gave him a strained smile, nodded and together
they climbed the stairs. When she stopped in front of the
door to the bathroom, he proceeded down the hall without
another word.

Stripping off her dirty clothes, she turned on the shower,
stepped under the fine spray and let the hot water massage
away the stress running rampant through her body. But she

knew it would take more than hot water to make her relax. Alec had to go. Finding a way to make him leave was imperative and she had to do it quickly. She turned off the water and stepped out of the shower.

Her arm was tender from the bashing she'd taken from Bonnie Blue earlier. A large, reddish-purple bruise had begun to appear over much of her shoulder and upper arm. She carefully donned a worn-but-comfortable cotton T-shirt. After drying her hair, she applied moisturizer and brushed her teeth. With nothing more to keep her in the bathroom, she swallowed her trepidation and opened the door.

Two steps down the hall in the direction of the master bedroom, her feet suddenly reversed direction. Vivid in her mind's eye was the picture of lying in the bed, Alec's hands and mouth caressing her body, preparing her, priming her for the sex to follow. While she couldn't argue he oozed sex appeal, he was still a stranger: a cold man whose sole reason for being here was to take away her home.

Quickly, she made her way to her old bedroom, and quietly closed the door. With any luck, Alec would be asleep and never notice her absence. She pulled back the covers and climbed into bed.

She lay still, hopeful, watching the shadows from the leaves on the tree outside her window dance on the ceiling. She was so tired. Slowly, the tension began to leave, her muscles relaxed, and she closed her eyes and let sleep overtake her.

She was floating. Yet she could feel an iron brace holding her firmly against tremendous warmth. Groggily, she blinked open her eyes. She was being carried. Instantly she was awake, and just as quickly, she knew who was carrying her and where they were going.

Seconds later, Alec placed her on the large new bed. Before she could scramble away, he leaned over and placed his hands on either side of her, effectively preventing her escape.

"I told you in the beginning, you *will* sleep in my bed." She could hear the annoyance in his voice. "Unless you want to start packing right now, you'd better learn to deal with it."

Slowly he stood over her and Shea scurried to the far edge of the mattress, eyeing him with apprehension. He frowned, resting his hands on his hips.

"Where's your ring?"

The question threw her. "What ring?"

His mouth quirked. "Your *wedding* ring. Remember the little ceremony when you promised to love, honor and *obey*?"

"It's over there—" she nodded toward the dresser, deciding to ignore his taunt "—in that little box. I…didn't want to wear it while I worked in the barn."

He walked to the dresser and took the ring out of the case and then came back to the bed.

"Give me your hand."

With a grimace, she extended her left hand and he slipped the sparkling wedding band onto her third finger.

"Leave it on."

Without another word, he unzipped his jeans. Shea turned away, hugging the far side of the bed as close to the edge as she could get. He turned off the light and she felt the mattress shifting to accommodate his large frame. Then his heavy arm slid around her waist as he settled next to her.

"I missed you, Mrs. Morreston." His breath was warm against her ear, his voice deep and sexy. "I missed kissing you."

"Leave me alone."

"Remind me of what I missed."

"No." She tried to push his arm away, but her efforts were futile.

Alec's hand settled gently on her shoulder to turn her onto her back. She couldn't hold back a cry of pain when he touched the bruised area. He immediately released her. There was a faint movement and then light shattered the darkness.

"Let me see your shoulder. Take off your T-shirt."

She sat up. "It's nothing. Just a bruise."

"Now."

"No."

"Either you take it off or I will."

The hard lines of his face contained no sympathy, only determination. But she faced him with equal strength of purpose. "You have no right to make that demand. Nothing in the contract gives you the right. If I want to cut off my nose it's none of your concern."

"Does everything have to be a battle with you?"

She clamped her mouth shut and glared. He was about the most demanding man she'd ever met. Nothing in those rich golden eyes and handsome features showed the tiniest indication he would relent.

"I want to look at your shoulder," he stated evenly. "If you don't want me to see, then get dressed and I'll take you to the emergency room and have a doctor check it out. But I'm not going to ignore the fact that you're injured."

She searched his face, looking for any way to pierce the armor of his resolve. Finding none, she turned away from him and eased the injured arm out of the sleeve. Raising the tail of the shirt over her shoulder, she refused to meet his eyes.

Alec inspected her arm with a muttered curse. "You damn near broke your arm. You could have a fracture. I think you need to have it x-rayed. Why the hell didn't you say something?"

"I... It's not that bad." She shrugged. "It's not any more painful than being forced to live with you."

She heard him sigh. "What are you afraid of, Shea?" His raspy voice was compelling, tuning her senses to his every word. "I can feel you respond to me. I know my touch doesn't repulse you. Surely you've had sex before?"

Her head shot up, and she spun around on the bed to face him, pushing her arm back through the sleeve while glaring at him for his audacity. "I've *made love* before. To someone I knew and cared for very much." He watched her intently, his golden eyes again reminding her of a predator amusing himself with his prey while deciding if he was hungry. She turned away from his scrutiny. "I don't know you. And I certainly don't care for you."

He reached out, his fingers grasping her chin, turning her to him. His eyes held her there. "I have no intention of remaining celibate during our marriage. It'll be easier if you try to accept that. Accept me. The sooner you come to terms with it, the better off you'll be. Or you always have the option of leaving and bringing this craziness to an end."

Wrenching her chin from his grasp, she tried to swallow the feeling of doom welling in her throat. "I'm not going anywhere. Why don't you go visit one of your lady friends? I'm sure there must be *one* out there somewhere who isn't completely repulsed. Hell, you supposedly have money. Go buy one."

"Why would I do that when I already have a beautiful, desirable woman in my bed?"

He reached out to switch off the small table lamp, and she noted again his wide shoulders and large biceps. His bronzed skin gleamed in startling contrast to the white linens that barely covered his hips. She swallowed hard.

The light went out and the mattress shifted as he lay back.

"How long has it been, Shea?"

She jerked her head around to stare at him, even though now all she saw was a silhouette in the darkened room.

"How long has it been since a man held you in his arms, touched you…took you to the edge…made you crazy with wanting…then gave you release?"

His deep, throaty voice sent shivers down her spine.

"That's none of your business!" she snapped, her voice sounding hoarse to her own ears. His words planted images in her mind she didn't want to see.

"On the contrary, as your husband I think it's expressly my business."

"Think what you want." She was not about to discuss her sex life—or the lack of one—with him; she refused to give him any more ammunition. She lay down, facing away from him and adjusted her pillow.

"Why are you afraid of me?"

"I'm not."

He was still for so long, she found herself holding her breath in expectation of what he might do. But he made no further attempt to touch her or harass her. Shea lay very still, staring out into the darkness.

A man with Alec's experience would recognize the battle that raged within her every time he came close. She was painfully aware of her limited ability to withstand his sexual magnetism. She'd only ever been with one man and that experience was nothing close to what Alec's words described. His voice, his devastating good looks topped with his apparent expertise in bed made her traitorous body crave his touch. But common sense told her he would use her to his own end. Moreover, his tactics would be as low and cutthroat as he deemed necessary to prevail in this war of wills. She had to hold on.

The sounds of the night closed in around her. A distant rumble of thunder echoed the turbulence in her mind. Sleep, when it finally came, was uneasy. Visions swirled around in her head. The ranch, encased in a fog, began to disappear while the thunder rumbled overhead. Powerless to stop it, she cried out. Then she sensed comforting warmth surrounding her, holding her close and protected. The dream faded, and she knew peace.

Alec held the innocent warmth of her body against the ache of his own. The last time he'd held a woman—just held her—had been too long ago to remember. With other women, there was no reason to stay after their needs had been satisfied, and certainly no desire to hold them as they slept.

After Sondra's infidelities, he made certain his relationships stayed free of emotional entanglements. The women he chose knew the score. It was sex, mutually enjoyable, nothing more. With Shea, her claims to hate him one minute then passionately respond to his kiss the next affected him in ways he neither liked nor knew how to deal with. She was pretending. Acting. She had to be. She couldn't possibly be as naive as she was letting on.

A glimmer of speculation made him question if she could be for real. He hated that glimmer. He hated not knowing. But most of all, he hated the idea that he cared either way.

Sondra had acted completely innocent when she'd just come from the bed of another man. She'd shown him what she'd wanted him to see until the end when she'd displayed her true colors. He knew what women were capable of when they wanted something badly enough. Shea wanted this land. And, like Sondra, there were no rules as far as she was concerned. Nothing was out of bounds. Nothing off-limits. No holds barred until she got her way.

And he'd be every kind of fool if he didn't keep that at the forefront of his mind.

Seven

When Shea awoke in the predawn hours, the birds sang outside the window and for the first time in her life she scoffed at the sound.

Raising her head, she was shocked to realize she'd used Alec for a pillow. Immediately rolling away from him, she eased over to her side of the bed. Holding her breath in the hope her actions wouldn't wake him, she lifted the covers and swung her legs to the floor. His light snoring continued as she made her way to the door. Unable to resist she spared a quick glance at Alec. Even relaxed in sleep, he was an intimidating presence. She had to be strong. There was too much to lose if she didn't find a way to send him packing.

Entering her old room, she grabbed a clean shirt and a pair of jeans and made her way to the bathroom. Her right shoulder screamed as she pushed her arm through the sleeve of the fresh T-shirt. Her head felt as muddled as it had the night she'd tried to sleep in the barn. This was going to be a very long day.

She trudged to the kitchen, needing a strong cup of coffee. When she opened the pantry door to grab the coffee tin, she saw the jar of Yolanda's homemade hot sauce sitting on the same shelf. A smile kicked up the corners of her mouth as she grabbed both the coffee and the jar of liquid fire.

An hour later she sat sipping her coffee while the biscuits finished baking. Scotty had joined her and was busy eating his stack of pancakes. Her mind had finally cleared and was focused on any strategy that would get rid of her unwanted houseguest. She'd just stood to refill her cup when the subject of her thoughts walked into the room.

"Hi, Daddy!"

"G'morning, son. Shea. How'd you sleep?" Alec looked directly at his son.

"Good!"

Alec had anticipated Scotty waking him at least once due to the new and unfamiliar surroundings, but apparently he'd slept through the night. The tantalizing aroma of bacon and freshly brewed coffee stirred his appetite. He poured a cup and let his gaze settle on Shea, who was busy pulling a tray of golden-brown biscuits from the antique oven in the corner. Did she believe the old saying about the way to a man's heart being through his stomach? He smiled. If that's what she believed, who was he to correct her?

"Smells good. I never pictured you as Little Miss Homemaker." He smiled. "I think I could get used to this."

"Have a seat."

Pulling out the chair next to Scotty, Alec sat down. Within minutes, Shea set a plate of eggs and bacon on the table in front of him, followed by a basket of the biscuits.

"Aren't you going to eat?"

"Already have." She nodded to his plate. "You go ahead. Enjoy your breakfast."

With a brief nod of thanks, he dug in with relish. Shea stood to the side.

The first mouthful tasted as good as it looked. She was a damned fine cook. He shoveled a second helping of the spicy eggs into his mouth, but just as he swallowed, an odd sensation brought his chewing to a halt.

It wasn't the taste that gave him the first hint he'd been had. It was the pure liquid lava that scorched his mouth and throat and continued to burn all the way down to his toes that gave him his first clue.

His vision clouded with tears as he reached for his glass. An instant of surprised horror raced through his mind at the realization the glass was empty.

"Oops," Shea said in a bored tone. "I forgot to give you any juice. So sorry."

Grabbing one of the biscuits, still warm from the oven, he quickly bit down and almost broke a tooth in the process. One slam of the biscuit on the table told him he'd have done better biting into a rock.

And his mouth continued to burn.

"Are the biscuits hard?" She leaned over and lifted one out of the basket. "Huh. Guess I had the oven temperature too low."

He glowered at Shea, who still stood, a picture of innocence beside the table, before he ran for the sink.

Turning on the faucet, Alec leaned over and gulped at the cool tap. But instead of relieving the scalding sensation, the water actually increased the burning.

"Are you finished with your plate?" she asked from behind him, her tone indicating she saw nothing odd about her husband gulping water from the kitchen faucet while smoke had to be billowing out of his ears. "You didn't eat much of your eggs. I guess you weren't very hungry."

He could only glare at her, his tongue singed to numbness. She picked up the plate and dumped the remains into the sink. "I've got some errands to run. Jason needs some help with a couple of chores. I told him you'd meet him behind the main barn right after breakfast."

"Chores?" he asked, looking at her suspiciously, before reaching for a napkin to wipe his watery eyes and running nose. "Like what?"

"Some fences need mending. Stalls have to be cleaned. A couple of old trees, downed during the last storm, are blocking the north gate. They'll need to be chopped, split for firewood, hauled to the house and stacked."

"Anything else?"

She smiled. "Jason has a list."

The sound of steady clicking challenged the silence in the old house as Shea stepped into the kitchen. She'd intended to start supper as soon as she got home, but curiosity made her set the sack of green beans and new potatoes—a gift from Leona—on the table. A frown crossed her face as she followed the sound out of the kitchen and down the hall. Pushing open the door to her office, she was dumbstruck at the sight of Alec sitting behind the old desk typing on a laptop, his files and papers strewn all over, her ledgers and ranch records pushed to one side. Immediately her temper flared.

"What do you think you're doing?"

He spared her a quick glance. "Working."

"You're in *my* office."

"There wasn't another one."

"You can't just barge in here and—"

"I have my own work to do. I'm not here solely to be your hired hand." He glanced at his palm and she couldn't miss seeing the multitude of blisters. He grimaced and then pulled open the drawer with his fingers. "I need a ruler."

She crossed her arms in a defensive gesture and refused to respond.

Alec shut the drawer. "Look. My own work can't come to a crashing halt simply because I've changed my address."

"Well, neither can mine! I can't work around you. You've buried my ledger underneath your junk!"

With a barely concealed sigh of frustration, he nodded his head. "All right, *dear*," he said sarcastically. "If you're going to work in your ledger, may I *please* set you up at the kitchen table long enough for me to send some emails?"

Emails? She relaxed her stance. His sarcasm was about

to change into something much more enthralling and she had a front row seat.

"Emails?" She saw him nod as he stood and began to gather her books. "How are you going to send emails?"

"What do you mean, how am I going to send…?" he began, his words dying in his mouth as realization settled in. "Tell me you have an internet connection."

Smiling, she shook her head. "Sorry."

"Well, this is just great." He sat back, rubbed his neck and then flinched from the blisters on his palms. "My cell is useless out here. I can't get through to my office on your landline until some talker named Ms. Hoover finishes the call to her sister."

"That would be Gladys."

"And now no internet."

He tossed the pencil onto the desk and stood up. "This is the twenty-first century and you people are still using stone knives and bear skins. It's amazing old Gladys doesn't break out the drums."

"Hey, if you don't like it…"

Muttering under his breath, Alec stomped past her and limped out of the room, the soreness in his body apparent. Score two points for her side.

The next few days were a repeat of the same routine. After Alec carefully tested the food before eating his breakfast, he and Jason would leave to complete the multitude of tasks needing to be done around the ranch. Because Shea had so much to do to prepare for the roundup—decisions only she could make—Hank had slowly transitioned to the role of part-time babysitter, a job both he and little Scotty seemed to enjoy.

Alec had taken time out to arrange for a wireless internet service. She'd seen the work trucks go up and down the main road indicating the installation of a new communications tower. She didn't even want to guess how he'd pulled that off. Or how much it had cost. He'd commandeered one of the unused bedrooms upstairs for his office. A new desk and chair had been delivered. After a long day of physical labor with Jason, he would often spend hours in his new office, sometimes working well into the night. Phone calls came in at all hours to his cell phone. If Alec wasn't there, the call would transfer to an answering service somewhere. Shea often went to sleep listening to him speak in various languages and wondered if he worked with people all over the world. She had to admit, having him at the Bar H was not turning out to be the total nightmare she'd feared. At least not yet.

A couple of weeks after Alec began working with Jason, Shea spotted the younger ranch hand as he walked toward his truck to go home at the end of the day. She'd been curious if Alec had been making an honest effort to lend a hand. She ran to catch up with Jason before he pulled out of the driveway.

"He's awesome," Jason replied to her question, grinning. "Alec works as hard as I do. No breaks. No hesitation to take on any job that needs doing. He's a great guy. You should have married him a long time ago."

"Thanks." She tried to keep the sarcasm out of her tone. "See you tomorrow."

As Jason backed his truck out of the gravel parking area, Shea wondered what Alec was up to. Why would he work so hard to make repairs on a ranch he wanted to level?

She rounded the corner and walked in through the back door of the old farmhouse. She found the subject of her thoughts standing in the kitchen, a bunch of wildflowers clutched in his fist. Her eyebrows shot up at the sight of the big, powerful man clutching a handful of wilting flowers.

"I picked these just before we headed back to the barn." He held the bouquet out to her. "I thought…well, maybe they might look nice on the table." She heard a touch of awkwardness in his voice, which was completely out of character for Alec. That surprised her as much as the offering of flowers. "The west pasture was full of them," he added. "Like a multicolored blanket almost as far as the eye could see. It was amazing. Anyway…"

Stunned, she accepted the offering. She looked from the blooms to Alec and couldn't stop the smile that widened her lips. It was a thoughtful gesture and one she never would have expected from him.

"Thank you," she said earnestly. "And you're right—the flowers are remarkable this time of year. You might want to stay clear of the blue ones. They're the state flower and I don't think we're supposed to pick them."

"Ah," Alec nodded his head, indicating message received. "Okay. Well, I need a shower."

As he left the room, Shea looked at the colorful bouquet. The mixed colors of yellow, orange, pink and blue would indeed make a pretty table setting. She selected a crystal glass from the cabinet, added water and arranged the blooms before placing the small arrangement in the center of the table.

Alec Morreston had brought her flowers.

He probably had a hidden agenda in there somewhere, but that thought couldn't diminish the delight she felt receiving the small gift. She'd be wise to keep up her guard and watch him like a starving hawk would a mouse. He had to be up to something. But for now, she would enjoy the flowers and consider this nothing more than a thoughtful gesture.

Later, when they all sat down for dinner, Alec spoke with enthusiasm about what they'd accomplished that day, asking her questions about the ranch setup or the livestock, but stopping just short of making any suggestions. Why try to improve something that, if he had his way, wouldn't be here in a year? But it let her see more of the man he was beneath the business suit. Locked away inside her where no one could see, a seed of respect for him had begun to take root and grow.

As she gathered the empty plates from the table and placed them in the soapy water, Shea was suddenly overcome with an intense wave of sadness. Between the gestures of kindness, the unspoken treaty between them for Scotty's sake and the camaraderie that had developed among Alec, Hank and the other ranch hands, it gave the illusion of one big happy family. The evening meals were a time of friendly banter, sharing humorous stories of the past and ideas for a future that possibly would never be. Even little Scotty played into the role of her loving son. And she was beginning to love him. She couldn't keep herself from forming a bond with such an adorable, bright child.

Each day seemed to intensify the illusion and it was becoming more difficult to remember that this was not a family. It was not a time for joking. There should be no camaraderie. This was not a game of pretend. It was war. And it was very real. A mandatory sentence forcing two opposing, equally determined individuals into a life-changing competition requiring constant stamina and strength of mind to win the grand prize, all within preposterous directives set up two hundred years ago by individuals unknown and for reasons she couldn't fathom. It was clearly a chapter out of a Stephen King novel.

At times she felt herself slipping into the illusion, letting it envelop her, as though something deep inside wanted it to become real with a desperation that was off the scale. The dangers of this were obvious. She had to remain focused. She had to remember that this illusion of a happy home with a handsome, caring husband and loving child was not reality. And never would be.

* * *

The ledger remained open awaiting a final calculation, but it was just a closing formality. She already knew the profit margin, while small, was clearly there. As long as the beef prices didn't take a sudden plunge before they shipped, the ranch would have a profitable year.

A soft knocking from the open doorway pulled her attention from the columns of figures. She glanced up to see Alec stroll into the room. His gaze rested first on her, then shifted to the collage of framed photographs hanging neatly on the wall to his left.

"Mind if I just look around?"

She shrugged. "Go ahead."

She tried to return her attention to the ledger but his presence presented a distraction she couldn't easily ignore.

"I noticed these right after I arrived." He scanned the wall of framed photographs. "Some of these pictures are really old."

"I think the oldest ones are from the mid-1800s."

Pictures of cowboys with their horses, branding operations, women dressed in styles portraying Western fashion almost two hundred years ago.

"Is this your father?" He pointed to a picture in the upper right corner of the grouping.

"Yes."

"Who are the two men with the longhorn?"

"My grandfather and his brother," she answered, never taking her eyes from the computer screen. She didn't need to. She knew the snapshots by heart. "They were one of seven families credited with bringing the longhorn back from near extinction."

Alec moved farther down the wall. "There's a kid on a horse getting some kind of award," he said, observing another picture. "Is it you?"

"Yeah." She saw no reason to elaborate.

"And what about this one?"

Shea glanced at the wall. He pointed to picture of a child astride a large dapple-gray thoroughbred. "That's me on Sir Raleigh at the hunter-jumper competition at Fair Park in Dallas. I was about twelve." She nodded to the next picture. "You might recognize the person in that one."

Alec leaned toward the picture. "Leona?"

She nodded, unable to restrain a smile. "It was taken several years ago during a Fourth of July party."

"She looks…different."

"She was smashed. Somebody spiked her watermelon punch."

Alec grinned. "These are fascinating pictures. I feel as though I'm looking at a wall in a cowboy history museum."

He glanced at Shea. In surprising contrast to the usual glare she sent in his direction, she was smiling. He walked over to the old leather wing-backed chair that faced the massive oak desk and sat down.

"When I was a teenager, there was a fairly large stable a few miles from our summer house in Saratoga County in upstate New York," he said, leaning back and resting one booted ankle on the other knee. "The Tall Pine Stables." He shook his head. "I haven't thought about it in years. My dad was determined his sons would learn the value of a dollar. I was given the choice of working in his office during the summer—" Alec nodded at the ledger "—which meant sitting behind a desk. Or I could find my own job. Most of my friends got summer work flipping burgers, sacking groceries or caddying at the country club. I was lucky enough to find work mucking out horse stalls."

"You?" Her eyebrows shot up and her eyes grew wide.

Alec chuckled. "Yeah, me. Not fun, as I'm sure you know. But I loved the horses, so I stuck it out. Went back the next two summers and the second year the owner began to supplement my pay with the bonus of exercising a few of the thoroughbreds. It was…amazing. I loved their spirit. I swore I would have one of my own someday."

"And did you?"

"Nah." He shrugged. "Just never worked out."

He envied Shea her life and the way she'd been raised. Close to the land and nature. It had always beckoned him, but he'd never stopped long enough to heed the call.

"That's really too bad." Her voice was soft, as though she was truly sorry he'd never seen that dream realized. "You've still got time. And I think Scott would love it. He seems to have inherited your love of horses."

Alec nodded. "Yeah. So it would appear." He was thoughtful for a moment. "I might never have known if we hadn't come here. Maybe I can work something out." He stood from the chair. "I'll get out of here and let you finish your work. Guess I'd better go and check on Scott." He walked to the door.

"Alec?"

"Yeah." He faced her.

"Thanks for sharing that with me."

She smiled and while it was cautious and hesitant, nonetheless something deep inside him felt very good.

It was almost midnight when Shea stretched and stood up, flexing her tired muscles. After Alec's visit, it had taken quite a while to regain her concentration on the work she'd needed to finish. To say she'd been surprised by his story of working summers at a stable was an understatement. She never would have pictured Alec Morreston mucking stalls. Or riding thoroughbreds. His professed love of horses seemed to contradict his intent to close the ranch. It was yet another layer of the complex man. It would be prudent to watch him even closer. Apparently there was much more to Alec than she'd originally thought and he could use any accrued knowledge against her, which brought back the earlier sadness and added to the growing stress she already was feeling.

At times, she felt as if she was a stranger in her own home. She wasn't used to not trusting people, to always being on guard, having to watch her every action and word, being alert to anything Alec did or saw as potentially giving him leverage to take the ranch. It was like walking a tightrope and even though she would never admit it aloud, it was taking its toll. Her nerves were shot to hell and frustration was building. She had to wonder how much longer this situation would last before it blew sky high.

With a sigh, she turned off the computer, returned the ledger to the bottom drawer of the desk, flipped off the light and left the office. A hot shower sounded wonderful. The few minutes of relaxation it would provide were definitely needed.

In the bathroom, she turned on the water and peeled off her clothes. Soon steam began to cloud the room as hot water jettisoned out of the nozzle.

Stepping into the shower, she reached for the bottle of shampoo. Empty. Muttering to herself, she stepped back out of the shower to grab a new bottle from the cabinet.

She'd not taken more than three steps when a slick spot on the tile floor sent both feet shooting out from under her. She landed in a sprawling, floundering heap, hitting the floor so hard she swore the earth shook from the force of it.

For a few moments, she lay in stunned silence, then slowly clambered to her feet and gingerly made her way to the cabinet. Grabbing the new bottle of shampoo, she limped back to the shower.

As she applied the soap, working up a good lather, she noticed the water didn't seem quite as hot as it had been just seconds before. With her eyes tightly closed, she fumbled with the taps, trying to adjust the temperature. It wasn't until she had turned off the cold completely that she realized there was no more hot water. At that very moment, the old pipes began to rumble and groan as if building in momentum, and half a heartbeat later, a spray of water from the icy depths of the well hit her squarely in the face.

A squeal of surprise tore from her throat. Sputtering and coughing, she managed to withstand the frigid temperature long enough to rinse out the shampoo, then immediately turned off the tap. Teeth chattering, goose bumps covering her skin, she stepped from the shower, careful to avoid the slick spot this time, and edged her way around the room to the linen cabinet.

She stared in disbelief. The shelves were empty. This morning, there had been at least a dozen bath towels in the linen closet. Now, all that remained were several washcloths and one hand towel.

Dripping wet and shivering, she grabbed the hand towel and began blotting the water from her skin and hair. This was no accident. It had the Morreston name written all over it. Oh, how she hated that damned contract. She wished she could go back in time and do something vile to the ancestor who'd added that insane clause. She combed the tangles from her hair, stepped into her panties, pulled on an oversize T-shirt and slowly counted to ten.

It wasn't long enough.

The bedroom was in darkness but in the soft glow from the yard light outside, Shea could see Alec's silhouette sprawled diagonally across the bed. Still shivering, she walked to the far side. His large frame lay on top of the covers and try as she might, she couldn't dislodge enough of the top sheet and blanket from under his sleeping form to give her even a small amount of warmth.

Suddenly, the urge to whack the horrible man with a blunt object overcame her common sense. A thirst for revenge compelled her to grab the edge of a pillow, yank it from under his head, raise it high and slam it down on top of the sleeping man with all the force she could muster.

"Hey!"

Again the pillow came down on his head.

"What the hell...?"

And again.

"Goddammit, Shea!" He caught her wrist and pulled her down onto the bed, fighting to control her flailing legs and arms. "Stop it! What the hell's the matter with you?"

"*You*. You're what's the matter with me!" she snarled. "Let me go!"

She pushed against him and tried to twist free. He easily controlled her efforts, throwing one leg over hers, catching and holding both her hands above her head and firmly pressing the parts in between against his muscled length.

"I want to know what brought this on."

"Nothing. Just...nothing. Let me go."

"Not happening."

She struggled against him, making one last all-out effort to free her hands before giving up and glaring at him through the darkness. She saw his focus move from her eyes to her mouth seconds before he lowered his head and covered her lips with his own. She tried to turn away, but he effortlessly held her in place. His lips were full and warm and totally enticing. Her mind let go of her earlier frustration and focused on Alec. His slow, lazy kiss made the need to get away from him seem not quite as important as it had seconds ago.

He raised his head and their gazes met through the dim glow from the lights at the barn. It was as though he was offering her a choice. When she didn't move away, he returned to her lips without saying a word, his mouth claiming hers in a deep and passionate kiss. His tongue entered her, filled her, and gone was any want for him to stop. With a sigh, she gave up the struggle. The passion escalated to raw, hungry need.

Her oversize T-shirt was twisted and stretched tightly over her breasts. She felt the warmth of his hand move up her side to gently squeeze the soft flesh. He lowered his head, placing his mouth over one taut nipple, licking and sucking through the thin material. Shea drew air deep into her lungs, her breasts swelling under his touch. His hot mouth moved to the other breast, bringing it to the same throbbing ache, an ache that shot straight to her core.

Taking one of her hands, Alec directed it down between their bodies, placing her fingers against his sex, holding it there when she would have drawn away. "No. Feel me, Shea. Feel what you do to me." His voice was low, gritty, as though the tight rein on his emotions was about to shatter.

She became lost in the sensation. Her hand couldn't fully encompass his girth, but he throbbed under her touch. His lips returned to hers, hungry, wanting. His hand slid down her belly, not pausing until he was cupping her most sensitive flesh. "Open your legs for me, Shea," he instructed, his voice raw. "Do it."

The final remnants of hesitation dissolved as she obeyed, raising one leg, allowing him access to the most private part of her. His skilled hands increased her need for penetration to a level of near desperation. All other motion ceased, her body paralyzed, completely enraptured by what he was doing.

Alec was on fire and close to losing it before he ever got inside of her. He wanted her with desperation he'd never before experienced. The sweet smell of her arousal flooded his senses. Her breath rushed in and out as her hands encircled his neck, holding him to her while her hips pushed against his throbbing erection, leaving no doubt in his mind she needed more.

Seconds, maybe less, before he permanently changed the entire situation, the cell phone he'd put on the nightstand began to ring. Its loud, shrill robotic tone infused the moment with cold reality.

All motion stopped. Breathing hard, he opened his eyes. *What in the hell was he doing?*

With a shuddering regret, Alec rolled to his side, his body protesting painfully, refusing to downshift. He had almost done it again. Making love to Shea was not going to accomplish anything except temporarily easing the pain of arousal. It would open a box full of complications neither one of them needed. He had little doubt that Shea didn't normally partake in one-night flings. This was something they would both regret, albeit for very different reasons, in the light of day.

The ringing stopped. As he lay next to her, willing his breathing to slow, she turned away from him, rolling onto her side. She didn't speak, and damn if he knew what to say. He'd honestly never been in this situation, wanting a woman beyond comprehension but knowing it was absolutely wrong, even as she lay in the bed next to him. He swallowed hard. He had to offer her something. He couldn't ignore her emotions.

"Shea?"

She was quiet for so long, he thought she wasn't going to answer. Then her voice reached him through the darkness.

"I understand, Alec."

Then maybe she could explain it to him.

"It's this whole horrible situation." Her voice sounded strained, as though she was struggling not to cry. He sensed a motion. Was she wiping the tears from her eyes? "I no longer know what's right and what isn't. I lost the map. I don't know how I should feel or what I should do. I want my life back. I want my dad not to have died." She drew a shaky breath. "I want to feel, even for a minute, that I'm not a stranger in my own house. That I'm not alone and fighting against the entire world."

"Hey." Alec gently pulled her into his arms, determined to relieve some of the heartache he had no doubt caused. Her head rested on his shoulder. She offered no resistance. "You're not taking on the world," he responded. "Just me. And from this side of the bed, you're doing a pretty damn good job."

He sensed rather than saw her smile and she sniffed back the tears. Beyond her beauty, she was an honest, caring woman who hadn't asked for any of this. He felt the urge to tell her she could have the ranch. But he couldn't. There was already too much invested, both time and money. There were too many people counting on this project for jobs and investors expecting something for their venture. For the first time since coming here, Alec wished he could just walk away. Let Shea's life return to normal. Hell, let both of them return to doing what made them happy.

That thought brought him up short. When *had* he last been happy? Before coming here, when was the last time he'd slept throughout the night without waking to pace the floor at 3:00 a.m.? How long had he been working such long hours that he didn't know if it was day or night? When had he taken the time to reflect on his childhood and his fishing excursions with Grandpa Jacob? When had he spent as much quality time with Scotty? Everything here seemed to move at a much slower pace. But he felt at home here, like a figurine that had found its way back into the mold. And it all revolved around Shea and this ranch. All the good and positive feelings.

"Shea?" Alec lowered his face to the top of her head. She had fallen asleep in his arms, her head on his shoulder, her arm resting across his stomach. He loved the softness of her hair, how it always smelled like the sweet blooms of the Ligustrum trees that grew in abundance here. He lay back on the pillow, his fingers playing idly in the silky strands of her hair, closed his eyes and drew her intoxicating aroma deep into his lungs. The softness of her breasts pressed against him, her breathing gentle on his skin. It felt so right. While this moment in time was nothing life changing, he knew it was a time he wouldn't soon forget.

For almost a month, he'd lain in this bed night after night, taunted by the temptation of her sleeping next to him. What had happened to his brilliant notion that he would have her gone in a few days? Things had changed. *He* had changed. He wanted her to like him. She stirred him as no woman ever had and they hadn't even been intimate. Although they'd damn sure come close. Too close.

What he wanted from Shea was more than sex—and that was a first for him. And he knew because of the land situation and that damned contract he had little-to-no hope of anything more between them ever coming to pass.

Eight

Shea had just finished drying the breakfast dishes when Scotty ran into the kitchen, eyes wide, excitement pouring out of every pore of his small frame.

"Shea!" He stood next to the table, looking as though he was going to explode. The fingers of his small hands knotted together and then unknotted over and over.

"What is it, sweetie?"

"Hank had to go into town and Daddy doesn't have to work with Jason on account of Jason taking his wife to a doctor and Daddy said he didn't have to work at his other job and we can go fishing and I've never been fishing but he doesn't know where the fishes are." He took a breath. "So...Daddy said to come and ask where you keep 'em."

She couldn't stop the grin from covering her face. Only one place came immediately to mind. Grady's Gulch. About a mile to the north, just past the lake, a ravine wound its way toward the Red River. In one spot near a huge granite bolder, the banks drastically curved, creating a deep cavity that contained some of the best fishing anybody could ever hope to find. Shea knew a moment of hesitation. Few people knew of the spot. Did she really want to share this special spot with Alec? But a second glimpse into Scotty's hopeful eyes made the decision.

"I know just the place," she said, smiling, as his eyes grew even larger. She bent over and grabbed a large empty coffee can from the cabinet under the sink. "Take this to your dad and tell him to dig for some worms in that shady area near the well house. I'll get the fishing poles and meet you guys at the truck."

Scott bolted out of the kitchen and tore down the path to the barn yelling "Daddy!" the whole way.

Within an hour, the three of them were bouncing their way across the meadow. As Shea pulled into a tranquil spot under one of the giant oak trees and killed the engine, Alec immediately heard the sound of rushing water. A small trail led in that direction. Grabbing the poles and can of worms, he nodded for Shea to lead the way.

While she spread the old blanket in a shady spot next to the river, Alec baited the hook. With a cork firmly attached to the line, he swung it out over the water and handed the pole to Scotty.

"Just watch the cork, son. If you see it dip under the water, raise the pole really fast with a quick yank." Scotty nodded his understanding, his eyes not straying from the bobbing red-and-white ball floating toward the opposite bank.

When Alec turned to the blanket, Shea was staring up at him as though he'd grown an extra set of ears. "What?" he asked and looked down at his shirt.

"Nothing."

"Not fair."

She shrugged. "I just find it amazing you know how to bait a hook and can give instructions on how to fish with a cork."

Joining her on the well-used coverlet, he leaned back against the large tree trunk. "You think because I live in a city I've never been fishing?"

"Something like that. At least not without some fancy rigging."

"Well let me set the record straight. When I was just

about Scotty's age, my grandparents lived in a rural area a lot like this. I spent my summers with them. Gramps was big on fishing. He would cut his own cane pole, tie a string to the end, dig some worms and off we would go." Alec couldn't help but chuckle at the thought.

"You talk like those memories are…like they're special to you."

"They are." Alec frowned, not immediately understanding why she would say that.

"Yet you've never taken Scott fishing?"

Alec dropped his head and nodded. "You're right. Kept telling myself I would take him someplace special next week or next month but something always came up and it just never happened." And it was a regret Alec had carried with him for a long time.

"Well, you're doing it now."

He nodded and gave her a smile. "Yeah, I am. Thanks to you."

Shea shrugged as though none of this was her doing. Alec knew different. "How did you know about this place?"

"Because right over there—" she pointed to a granite boulder on the other side of the river "—is where I caught my first fish. Not many know about this place. Dad and his father and uncle guarded it as though the bottom was paved in gold. People tried for years to find out where Dad always managed to catch all the fish he would bring to a fish fry. I don't think they ever did."

Alec tilted his head. "But you were willing to share it with us."

Shea held his gaze, neither speaking nor nodding, and for a few brief seconds in time, the rest of the world ceased to exist. She had placed her trust in him, shared one of the special places in her life and some happy memories she treasured. She'd given Scotty a day of fun and Alec a small measure of relief from the guilt of not spending enough time with his son. He felt a kinship with the rich earth, with the cool water as it splashed against the huge boulders on its way downstream, the towering trees providing shade, their tallest branches catching and swaying in the gentle breeze. In spite of the animosity between them and her fierce determination to keep this ranch, Shea had shared something special with a virtual stranger who would take it all away.

Alec swallowed hard and closed his eyes. He wasn't used to her world and accepting acts of kindness wasn't in the game plan. Her small benevolences knocked him completely off balance. Other than Scotty, his mother and brother, he wasn't used to trusting people. But in that moment, he knew he could trust Shea with anything, including his son. And a shadow of guilt for what he was attempting to do with regard to the ranch seemed to put a dark cloud over the day.

"Daddy! It's gone! The fishies got it!"

Quickly getting to his feet, Alec hurried over to assist his son with the pole. In a matter of seconds, Scotty had landed his first fish. When he held it up, the fish still thrashed about on the end of the line and the boy wasn't certain exactly what to do with it. They should have brought a camera...

"Alec, do you have your cell phone?"

"Yeah, why?"

"Does it take pictures?"

Alec grinned. Of course. Why hadn't he thought of it? "It most certainly does."

Reaching into his pocket, he pulled out the small black phone, changed the settings and handed it to Shea.

She snapped away as father and son posed for a "first fish" picture, then continued to take shots as Alec patiently removed the hook and held the prize catch for Scott to touch.

"How about we let it go today?" Alec suggested. "Then

you can come back and catch it again sometime when we want to have fish for supper."

Without a word, Scotty vigorously nodded his head, clearly still amazed at the entire process.

They lingered next to the small river until the sun dropped low in the sky. It was as though they'd formed a truce and had silently declared this a place of neutrality where legal contracts and land development had no admittance. While Scotty waited for his next fish to grab the hook, Shea and Alec exchanged stories of their youth. The more she told him about special places and times on the ranch, the tighter the knot in his belly grew.

His planned development wouldn't reach this far out from the Red River. Maybe there was something he could do to let her keep at least part of her home. For months, the investors had been maneuvering about where they wanted this or that and adding more and more to the overall size of the project. It was his project and he maintained control, but his professional integrity insisted he consult with them on any major changes. For the first time he seriously considered reducing the overall scope of the project. It was certainly worth looking into.

The telephone rang as Shea entered the kitchen the next morning. She grabbed it on the second ring.

"Morning!" Leona's familiar voice hailed her from the other end of the line.

"I guess," she replied.

"Everything all right?"

"I suppose. So far. I haven't seen Alec or Scotty this morning."

"Well, I called to tell you they're both over here. Rode over with Hank. Alec is getting a tour of the spread, and the boy is with my grandson, Cody. They're playing with the new puppies."

"Oh, that's right. Maggie had her pups, didn't she?"

"Yep," Leona confirmed. "Did you remember tonight is the party to celebrate Ms. Annie's birthday?"

Annie Philpot was considered the matriarch of the Calico Springs ranching community. She'd married and lost two fine husbands, and then, by herself, had raised her nine children and carried on the tradition of producing fine horses and prime beef cattle. Through it all, she'd still found time to care for the friends and neighbors she loved. In times of sickness or when a new baby was about to make its presence known, Miss Annie had been there. In recent years, she'd reached out more via telephone than personal visits, but nonetheless her heart remained with her extended family.

"Oh, Leona, I'd completely forgotten."

"Figured you might have, what with the way your life has been here lately. It's been a while since you've seen everyone. Most of 'em are about to bust open with curiosity about Alec. Try and make it over here, if you can."

"Absolutely." She would have plenty of time to make a pie. Everyone always brought a dish or dessert to these gatherings. But something else tugged at her mind.

"Leona, does anyone know?" If rumors were flying about Alec taking her ranch and his plans for the land, she needed to know before they walked into the party.

A numbing pause followed the question.

"You mean about Alec?"

"Yeah."

"No. At least nothing's been said to me. Whatever he's planning, he's kept to himself. There has been some talk of a big entertainment complex gonna be built across the river in Oklahoma. People are generally either excited about the idea or don't much believe it. Is that what he's doing?"

"I honestly don't know." Alec had never told her and she hadn't asked. Shea wasn't sure she wanted to know. Whatever he had in mind was not going to happen and that was as far as her mind had gone on the subject. Let him build his magical kingdom in the adjacent state if he wanted. Just keep it off her ranch land and out of the community. "Thanks, Leona. We'll see you about eight."

By six o'clock Alec had returned and by seven thirty they were on their way to Leona's house. At least fifty adults and maybe a dozen kids were already enjoying the festivities when they arrived. The aroma of hickory smoke from a huge grill invited all new arrivals to bring their appetites around to the back of the house. Several long tables were set up, complete with red-checkered tablecloths. Shea placed her pie on the table with the other desserts.

One hello led to another and another until most of the party guests had met Shea's new husband. Alec dutifully shook hands and repeatedly answered the questions of the evening: "Where are you from?" and "How did you meet?" He surprised her by responding to their inquiries in a manner both believable and flattering to her.

In essence, he lied.

They paid their respects to the guest of honor, wishing Miss Annie a most happy eighty-ninth birthday. Then they joined Hank and Leona in the chow line and came away with their plates heavily laden with home-cooked fare. Scotty wanted to eat with Leona's grandson and several other kids his age. A table had been set up just for them.

When darkness fell, candles and lanterns cast their soft glow over the crowd. Several strands of white twinkle lights strung in the lower tree branches gave a strange, almost mystical, ambience to the festivities. With an area under the lights cleared for dancing, couples filled the space as the soft melody of a country ballad drifted through the cooling night air.

At the edge of the sphere of soft light, some of the children, including Scott, held sparklers, running back and forth, waving their arms, making circles and glowing formations against the darkness. Their laughter blended with the music and the cheerful mood of the adults, most of them lifelong friends, who'd gathered to celebrate another year of life of one of their own.

Shea knew total relaxation for the first time in a very long time. She sat quietly, eyes closed, listening to the music. Unexpectedly, a warm hand touched her shoulder. She looked up to find Alec standing beside her.

"Dance with me."

Without waiting for an answer, he took her hand and led her to the edge of the dancing couples, drawing her into his arms.

The music flowed in a soft, slow tempo. His arms encircled her, holding her close while they moved together to the rhythm of the song. It seemed the most natural thing in the world to rest her head against his shoulder. She closed her eyes, intoxicated by the musky scent of his cologne, warmed by the sheer strength of the arms around her.

This is so wrong. She shouldn't be dancing with this man—shouldn't be taking pleasure in his arms. By getting to know Alec, by seeing him as something other than the enemy, it was becoming more and more difficult to ignore her growing attraction to him. She liked him. A lot, in fact. Amazingly, the realization wasn't so painful.

As they danced, his thigh intermittently rubbed against her lower belly. She found herself holding her breath when he moved away until another shift in their movements again caused the hard contours of his body to press against her.

His fingers threaded through her hair, cupping the back of her head as he gently encouraged her gaze to meet his. She saw the flames of controlled passion in his darkening eyes before he lowered his head and settled his mouth on hers.

The kiss was pure seduction. A ball of searing heat shot

straight to the juncture between her legs while the world around them ceased to exist.

Alec made a slight adjustment and his swollen shaft pressed solidly against her belly. For a moment, instinct took over and she succumbed to the blinding need to forget everything but the urge to satisfy the ache his touch created. She gave in to her body's natural reaction and pushed against him. She heard his sharp intake of breath followed by a low growl. He lowered his hands to her hips, pulling her solidly against him, and wanton desire scorched the skin beneath her jeans.

The loud snapping of firecrackers close by made her jump. She tore her lips from his as reality came crashing back with ferocity. It was as if someone had suddenly turned up the volume to the music and the voices around them. Her eyes lingered on his mouth. The temptation to return and seek the pleasures it offered was overwhelming.

Blinking, she stepped back and looked around her, feeling as if she'd just come back from another time and place. Desperately she willed her mind to reengage.

They were in the midst of some twenty dancing couples. Glancing around, she was thankful to see that no one appeared aware of the sensual drama unfolding in their midst. She chanced another look at Alec's face, and in the depths of his eyes she saw awareness of her internal battle. He knew how close she was to losing.

"I should go...and help Leona."

"Leona has all the help she needs." He gently smoothed a stray lock of hair back from her face. "Let's go home."

His deep, husky invitation was almost her undoing. "I..." Her eyes roamed over his face while he waited patiently for her decision. He wanted her. He wasn't using coercion or bribery. There were no threats. He was putting it out on the table and she could say yes or she could say no.

She couldn't make love to Alec. Could she? He was still

her enemy. Wasn't he? She didn't believe in casual sex. For Shea, intimacy had to be between two people who honestly cared for each other. And even if she felt that way toward Alec, could she justify one night of ecstasy with a man who was bent on destroying everything she had?

"I...I've got to go." She pushed out of his arms, walked in the direction of Leona's house and didn't look back.

Shea wasn't sure what was happening between them, but at the very least, she knew she already had broken her number one directive: hating Alec Morreston.

"It looks like you two are having a good time," Leona remarked as she entered the kitchen. She handed Shea a dishtowel.

Shea nodded and picked up a plate, unable to meet Leona's eyes. "I guess."

"Things going any better?"

She shrugged. Alec wasn't the adversary she'd initially expected. Either his tactics weren't as cutthroat as she'd first feared, or the man was tremendously subtle and highly skilled at manipulation. Probably both. But since his return from New York with his son, she'd glimpsed another side of the man. Even Scotty was a revelation, providing insight into the complexities of Alec's character. It was as if he were two different people. One was the enemy, a cold and ruthless man bent on destroying everything. The other was a caring and loving father who had gained her respect and was well on his way to becoming someone she cared about.

In spite of what he'd threatened that day in Ben's office, in spite of his determination to force her from the land, he'd given her time. Conversely, the more time he gave her, the more she contemplated what it would be like to love such a man. Lovers with no future, engaged in an affair that was sure to end badly. Who did that? Was she so foolish to fall in love with the very man who would take away everything she'd ever loved?

She picked up another plate and began to rub it with the towel. Leona snatched it from her hand.

"You're drying a dirty plate," she said, her eyes narrowing. "You haven't heard a word I've said for the last five minutes. Do I get to guess where your mind is?"

Blushing, Shea shook her head.

"Just be careful," Leona cautioned.

Shea nodded and reached for a clean plate.

With the few nondisposable dishes washed and dried, and the remaining food covered and put away, Shea stepped outside. She spotted Hank and Alec and walked in that direction. Detecting her presence next to him, Alec reached out to her, his arm settling around her shoulders. "Scott and Cody are going to sleep in their fort tonight. Steve Laughton said he'd stay out here with them and make sure they got inside the house if it starts to rain. Are you ready to go?"

"I guess. Good night, Hank."

The old cowboy nodded and touched his finger to his hat. Alec's hand remained at the back of her neck as they walked to his car. He seated her inside the luxury sedan, then took his place behind the wheel. She sat back in the plush leather seat, her head on the cushioned rest while the car easily ate up the miles to the Bar H. She glanced at the multitude of lights on the front console, then let her eyes move to the large man behind the wheel. He caught her glance and returned it.

"You have some nice neighbors," he said. "I enjoyed meeting them."

"They liked you, too." She turned her head to stare out into the seemingly endless shadows of the night. "It's too bad…"

"It's too bad…what?" he prompted.

"Well, I can't help but wonder what their reaction will be when they discover your plans for my ranch and ultimately this area. Most of these folks are third- and fourth-generation farmers and ranchers. They won't take kindly to some out-of-towner plopping a housing development in the center of their grazing land or paving their neighbor's pasture for a parking lot."

Shea chanced a quick glance in his direction. Alec continued to look straight ahead, seemingly without emotion, but in the dim light from the driver's panel, she noted a brief grimace cross his features.

"For your information, I have no intention of building a housing development here or anywhere else. That's not what I do."

"Maybe not, but you're a commercial developer," she stated, daring him to deny it. "That means destruction. If it's not a housing development, it'll be something else equally as bad."

"Not all change is a bad thing," Alec reminded her. "Sometimes it's for a good reason. It fulfills a need."

Shea swallowed uncomfortably. "And what about people who like things as they are?"

"Change is part of life. Most people are willing to accept it if they understand the reasoning behind it, especially if it benefits them in some way. You're painting me as the bad guy before you even know what my intentions are for this place."

"Oh, I see." She looked at Alec. "I should let you take over my ranch and trust you to develop it in a manner you think is—"

"Shea, it's not *your* ranch!"

"The hell it's not!" she muttered.

"Then show me your name on a deed."

"How can you be so…two-faced? How could you talk and laugh with the people there tonight, sit at their table, share their food, all the while knowing what you plan to do to their community if given the chance?"

"You make it sound like I intend to rob them!" Alec responded, his tone incredulous.

"Stab them in the back would be more accurate."

"For God's sake. You've got to be the most narrow-minded, bullheaded woman I've ever come across in my life!"

"Well, as my grandfather used to say, that's the pot calling the kettle black."

He turned off the main road onto the winding driveway leading to the old farmhouse. As Alec swung into the parking space, Shea grabbed for the door handle and was out of the car before he could turn off the ignition. She walked through the kitchen, up the stairs and into the bedroom, slamming the door behind her.

Angrily, she paced the floor until, finally realizing the futility of the situation she changed her clothes, brushed her teeth, switched off the lights and climbed into bed. A few minutes later, Alec joined her, arranging his pillows but making no attempt to acknowledge her presence. He lay on his side facing away from her. Instead of being relieved, she was irritated, and that was crazy. She should be glad. But she wasn't and she refused to dwell on why.

The distant rumble of thunder shattered the serene silence, waking Alec from his sleep. The sky was still dark even though the clock on the nightstand said it was almost five in the morning. Faint flashes of lightning intermittently lit the room for a few brief seconds as the increasing winds surged around the corner of the old house. He immediately thought of Scotty. Steve would have both boys inside Leona's house by now. It was a new and comforting realization that he could leave his only child in the care of near strangers and trust, without any hesitation, that his son would be well taken care of. Such trust was almost unheard of in his world.

Alec started to turn over, but immediately felt a soft, warm body snuggled against him. The aura of innocence and trust as Shea slept was alien to him. Hell, everything about her, about this place, was so different than what he was used to. Yet, at the same time, it often felt as though he'd come home.

With his sexual frustration at its peak, his body ached with desire every time she came close and now was no exception. He didn't know how much strength remained before his good intentions would go out the window. He'd never have believed he could become this damned infatuated with anyone, especially after Sondra. With a groan of frustration, he eased Shea onto a pillow and got out of bed.

The few days he'd originally anticipated being here had rolled into weeks. He'd surprised himself by actually finding a way to continue his own work and still enjoy the physical labor the ranch required. Ironically, it was in that labor he found an inner peace. A fresh breeze on his face, sweet scents in the air and the sun on his back. Beat the hell out of any gym.

He pulled on some jeans and grabbed a shirt and his boots. He needed to put some space between himself and Shea. A lot of space. One last glance at the bed where she slept was all it took to confirm in his mind what his body had been telling him. He wanted her. Desperately. And the frazzled strength of the single thread of determination that held him at bay was about to snap.

Nine

By six o'clock the rainstorm was over and the morning dawned clear. The eastern sky lit up in glorious color, heralding the sun's imminent appearance. Alec threw the last of the coffee down his throat and turned away from the kitchen window, stepped outside and meandered toward the barn. As he got close, the scents of alfalfa and pine shavings permeated the air. Soft nickers greeted his approach, bringing a smile of contentment to his face.

Entering the barn, he followed the bank of stalls until he came to number twelve. The big bay gelding was licking the last remnants of breakfast from his feed trough.

"You're up mighty early."

He turned to see Hank amble in his direction.

Alec nodded.

"You want me to throw a saddle on him for you?" Hank asked.

He hadn't thought about going for a ride, but the idea immediately took hold and it was too perfect to pass up.

"I'll do it," Alec replied. "Where's the tack?"

A few minutes later, Alec rode the big horse out the main gate and headed north. Ransom was excited about the outing, dancing against the firm hold Alec kept on the reins. Hank had mentioned the old homestead and provided general directions. It sounded like the perfect place to think.

The rutted path eventually grew less and less visible as the big bay continued to carry him through the trees and over the rolling hills. After an hour, Alec began to relax. The serenity of the countryside, the wind blowing softly through the leaves of the trees, helped clear his head. He honestly loved it here. He again experienced a twinge of regret over the changes that would soon come. For the first time in his life, the jubilance of building something great was overshadowed by the nagging uneasiness over the fact that he was about to destroy something very special.

Not surprising, his thoughts turned to Shea. Her determination to keep this spread should be an obstacle to overcome, not something to admire. But that was before their wedding night when she'd been so gut-wrenchingly beautiful and so damn sensual. It was before he'd seen her laugh, before she'd received hugs from his usually standoffish son. Before she'd shared her concerns about the ranch and had begun to trust him enough to open up and talk to him about things that troubled her. Before he'd seen her schoolgirl-like grin over a bunch of silly wildflowers.

It was before she'd become someone special in his life. Hell, they hadn't even had sex. But the longer he was around her, the more he had to remind himself their marriage was based on a very bizarre two-hundred-year-old contract. Becoming involved with Shea wasn't something that should happen. But his gut instinct told him it was too late. He'd already crossed that line.

Shea sat alone in the kitchen watching the morning unfold. She fixed a piece of dry toast, poured a cup of the not-too-old coffee and decided she could afford to take the time to enjoy part of the day. It was only five weeks until fall roundup but all of the preparations had been made, the equipment checked and ready to be taken to the site.

After clearing away the few dishes, she set off in the direction of the barn. Finding it empty, she walked down the main hall toward Hank's house. As soon as she rounded the corner, she saw him sitting on the wooden porch, leaning against a post with a wide-eyed little boy hanging on his every word. Apparently Hank had picked up the boy from his overnight stay at Leona's and from the lingering smell, they'd already enjoyed a breakfast of bacon and eggs.

"...So he lays real quiet-like and crawls on his belly—*real* slow—over to the fallen log. But just as he reaches fer his gun, this old owl comes screeching out of the trees and swoops down right at him."

"Wow..." Scotty's voice held the excitement of the moment. "What did he do?"

"Well, Roy reckons that old owl done give away his hiding place, don't ya see, so he pulls his gun from the holster, counts to three, then jumps out from behind the log with his gun a blazin'. Old Treach figured that owl was after a mouse so he never knew what hit him."

"Boom! Bang! He shot him! Didn't he, Hank?"

"He did fer a fact. Got the reward of all that gold and built him a little cabin right there on the bank of that river. Some people say his ghost still walks along the riverbank to this very day, protecting his gold."

"I wouldn't never go there 'cause he might think I was gonna steal it and I sure wouldn't want him to shoot at *me*!" Scotty shook his head, speaking in whispered excitement. Then he noticed Shea for the first time. "Did you ever see him? Old Roy?"

"Once. When I was about your age." She smiled and winked at Hank.

"Man..."

"How was your campout?"

"It was good!" Scotty answered, his eyes full of excitement. "We got hot dogs and cooked marshmallows on a stick. Mine got on fire."

"You had a campfire?"

"Uh-huh. And we heard the owl way deep in the woods.

Then we hadda go in the house cause of the rain. But it was *cool*."

Smiling, Shea turned her attention to Hank. "Where's Alec?"

"Said he was going to ride out to the north and see if he could find the old original homestead. Left here a couple of hours ago."

"Ride out...on what? You mean on a horse?"

"He saddled Ransom."

"Ransom!" He'd never make it back in one piece. Shea was incredulous. "And you let him? That horse could—"

"He's a big boy, Shea." Hank squinted up at her. "I watched him saddle the gelding and swing up like he'd been doing it all his life. Didn't seem to have any problem with him." He shrugged and bent his head, his attention focused on the small stick he'd been whittling.

Alec told her it had been a long time since he'd been on a horse. To handle Ransom as proficiently as Hank described, he would have to be a skillful horseman. A feeling of unease ran down her spine. She turned and quickly made her way back into the barn.

The stalls were empty. Hank must have moved the horses to the other barn in preparation for the drive. She marched straight down the main hall and back toward the house. Her truck was missing. She supposed Jason or one of the other hands had borrowed it, which wasn't unusual. She didn't see Alec's car either, which *was* unusual. Maybe Alec had let one of the hands use it to run into town. It wouldn't be the first time. She climbed into the only remaining vehicle in sight, the old white Jeep.

She wouldn't sit around and wait for Alec to come back. Something could happen. It was of equal concern that he was nosing around the old home site. It was a sacred place to her. She put the Jeep into gear and headed toward the big gate that opened to the northern pastures.

It was a bright, sunny day with not a cloud in the sky. All indications of the thunderstorms that had blanketed the area in the predawn hours were gone. Thanks to all the rain they'd had this spring, the grass was a deep, rich green. Shea should have enjoyed the outing. The old home site was her favorite place where the world couldn't come crashing in. It was a special place. A private place. Why had Alec headed there? With a grimace, she punched the pedal, and the Jeep bounced along the dwindling path into the deepening timber.

The trail cut through the forested area for several miles, skirting the vast grasslands to the west. It wound its way through the trees, over a rise and down into a small valley. The cooling waters of a small lake glistened in the sun as a gentle breeze sent small waves to lap against the shore. It was just past this tranquil setting that one would find traces of the original home site.

Shea shifted to a lower gear as the vehicle climbed the rise past the lake. As she topped the hill, she spotted Ransom, his front feet tethered, contentedly munching the tender, knee-high grass.

Pulling up a short distance away from the remains of the old foundation, she killed the motor and stood up in the seat. Immediately, she became aware of the silence. Somewhere in the distance, a meadowlark sang. The trees, touched by the gentle breeze, danced to its song.

Leaving the Jeep, she walked purposefully in the direction of the old home. There was very little left of the original structure. Not surprising since fire had raged through the timbers, followed by the ravages of the elements for two hundred years. The giant cinder blocks supporting the foot-thick oak timbers and roughly hewn floorboards were still intact. Three walls, log and mortar, and a corner of the original lower roof remained, their edges bearing traces of the fire that had claimed the house. The tall, sturdy chimney rose impressively as if daring anyone to challenge its right to be there.

"It's incredible." Alec's deep voice beckoned from behind her. Shea spun around, watching him casually walk toward her.

"Yes," she replied warily. "Is this where you're going to build your shopping mall?"

Alec ignored her taunt. He looked at the ancient dwelling. "Tell me about the house. Did they bring in the logs or were there trees this size on the land?" He looked up at the remaining roof.

"The logs for the house were all cut from here. The stones used in both the chimney and for some of the floor support were gathered from the creek bed." Shea pointed to the east. "Down there." Alec nodded, silently encouraging her to continue.

"The house had only two rooms and a loft. The kitchen was separate, over there." She nodded in the direction of the far side of the structure. "It used to have a covered breezeway linking it to the house. You can still see some of its foundation."

"What happened?"

She shrugged. "I'm not sure exactly what caused the fire. Dad tried to find out once, but there were no records. He believed lightning struck the roof. I think he said that someone died. There wasn't a lot anyone could do to save the structure. The remains you see here are probably thanks to a few buckets of water from the well."

"So, after the fire, your family rebuilt in the present location?"

"Yeah." Shea pushed away a strand of hair the wind had blown in her face as she looked at him with curiosity. "Why are you so interested? I mean, what does any of this matter to you?"

Alec turned away, looking out over the surrounding area.

"If you'll remember, it was my ancestors' land. They lived here, too."

She couldn't argue with that. He had as much a right to seek his heritage as she did.

"Behind the house—" she pointed west "—on top of the far rise is the old family cemetery. I think one of your relatives might be there, as well."

"I'd like to see."

Together they walked to the small burial ground. The names and dates on the long-standing headstones were partially obscured, some more than others. The men and women who had come to this land, driven by a desire to build a future and the courage to tame the raw wilderness, now rested in peace on this small patch of earth. At the edge of the area, two headstones stood slightly apart from the others.

Alec read one of them. "'William Alec Morreston. Born 1780. Died 1848.' My great-great-grandfather."

Shea reached out and gently touched William's stone. "Odd he was buried here. He was originally from the north, wasn't he?"

"Yeah." Alec nodded. "My grandmother used to tell me stories of how her grandfather loved the West. He came out here as a young man and fell in love with this part of the country. There was a young woman he met here. Alyssa, I think. He wrote that they were to be married, but she died before it could happen. Eventually, he returned to the family home in New York but I guess this is where he wanted to be laid to rest."

"At least someone in your family had some sense," Shea couldn't resist saying. She glanced at Alec in time to see a grin pull at the corners of his mouth.

"I have some old letters indicating he was a trapper. He used the river for his transportation and supposedly built a cabin, probably more of a shack, not far from here. Does the property reach as far as the river?"

She nodded. "Yeah. About a mile in that direction."

"You up for a hike?"

"We could take the Jeep."

"Let's go."

It took only a few minutes to reach the river's edge. Together, they walked along the high riverbank looking out over the wide expanse of the Red River. Appropriately named—the red clay, seen in the shallow parts of the riverbed and in the steep canyon walls flanking each side, cast a pinkish glow in the late afternoon sun.

"I don't think I'm going to find anything." He stood, hands resting on his hips, gazing out over the scenic terrain. "I'm sure the river has changed its banks dramatically in the last two hundred years. Erosion probably destroyed any remnants long ago." He sounded regretful.

"You're probably right, but it never hurts to look."

Alec's interest in his heritage surprised her. The questions he'd asked about the Hardin home site and now the interest in his own ancestral home didn't fit the image of the modern builder who wanted to level everything. She couldn't stop from watching him as he continued looking out over the scenic waterway. From his tawny eyes and full lips to the strong, deep set of his jaw, his face was temptation run amuck. Add intelligence sprinkled with a sense of humor, and it all added up to an irresistible combination.

In a moment of clarity, she realized she had come to respect Alec. He was a successful businessman and builder, a great father and a man of his word. But the reason he was here sent a twinge of sadness inching its way to her heart.

At that moment, he turned toward her and she made the mistake of looking into his eyes. The smile faded and his eyes darkened to the color of molten topaz. She knew he saw the awareness in her face. She swallowed hard.

The cry of a hawk circling overhead broke the spell.

"It's getting late. The sun has almost set. We'd better get back," she whispered, turning away.

In silent agreement they climbed into the Jeep and headed back to the home site and the trail leading home.

Ransom was still contentedly munching on the knee-high grass when the Jeep pulled up near the old homestead. Alec approached the big gelding and ran his hand down the glossy neck, then looked at the last rays of the setting sun in the open western sky.

"Is it true a horse can find his way back home on his own?"

Shea pursed her lips to hide a grin, nodding. "They usually know where the food is. Go ahead and unsaddle him and turn him loose. You can ride back in the Jeep. We wouldn't want Scotty to think his dad doesn't know which way is up in the dark."

"Ha. Ha."

With the saddle, bridle and tether removed, Ransom acknowledged his freedom by kicking his heels in the air and running for home, his tail held high above his back. Alec put the tack in the Jeep and climbed into the passenger seat. She slid in behind the wheel and turned the key. The engine caught, but immediately sputtered and died. She tried again, but it refused to start. Pumping the gas pedal did no good either.

"Mind if I have a try?" They switched places, but Alec had no more luck getting it started than she had. He walked to the front and opened the hood. "Everything looks okay," he muttered. "How much gas did you have?"

"I filled up last week and haven't really gone anywhere except over to Leona's. It should have plenty."

"Well, it doesn't." Alec closed the hood.

It was miles back to the ranch house. By the angle of the

sun, it would be dark in less than an hour. A quick glance revealed he was thinking the same thing.

He walked over to a small crevice, kicked at the grass, then looked out over the far hills as if deep in thought. He smiled, shook his head, then he began gathering rocks, placing them in a circle around the indention.

"Are you building a fire?"

"Yeah. It might get cold later tonight." He looked at her. "Unless you know of a better way we can keep warm?"

She ignored his teasing. "Hank will know something's wrong and come after us. You don't really need to do that."

Alec dropped more sticks into the circle. "It might be a while. Are there any matches in the Jeep?"

"Not that I've ever seen but I'll look." She walked to the front of the vehicle. Opening the glove box, she found not one, but two lighters and a small box of matches.

"I don't know how these got there, but here you go," she said, tossing him a lighter.

"How about water?"

"We don't keep water in the Jeep. If we're headed out to a branding or mending a long stretch of fence—something that will take a day or more—we load a couple of big ice chests and some ten-gallon coolers in the supply trailer and pull it to the site."

He nodded. "Would you humor me?"

With a shrug, Shea returned to the back of the vehicle. Moving aside Ransom's saddle and an old tarp, she immediately spotted two jugs of water. Frowning, she looked at Alec.

"And...?"

She pulled out the two gallons of water. "I don't understand—"

"It's just a guess, but I think Hank knew we would need matches and water before you ever left the ranch."

"What? What are you saying?"

"This." He gestured with his hands. "Our being out here alone...stranded. It was a setup. It was planned."

"No." Shea denied his words, but at the same time, her heart increased its rhythm. "Hank...wouldn't do something like that."

"Okay." He squatted next to the small pile of wood, tearing dried grass and shoving it underneath the smaller sticks.

"I've known him all my life. He just isn't the kind of person to...to..."

"Play matchmaker?"

"Exactly."

"Take a look in the back. I'm betting you'll find some blankets. While you're there, you might check and see what we're having for dinner."

Shea opened her mouth to argue but closed it again without a word. She set the containers of water on the ground and turned back to the Jeep. Partially hidden farther under the tarp were a sleeping bag, two pillows, a couple of blankets and a small ice chest. A thermos and a few foam cups completed the stash.

"I don't know of anyone else who would drain the gas tank and load the Jeep with supplies two people would need for a night," Alec said, walking over to where she stood. "Do you?"

She was dumbfounded that Hank Minton, of all people, would do this. But it could be no one else. "No." When she got back to the ranch, he was going to get a piece of her mind.

Shea watched the last of the sun's glow surrender to the multitude of stars in the night sky. The wood in Alec's campfire popped and hissed as the flames danced over the dried branches, releasing the tantalizing aroma of hickory and pecan into the still night air.

They ate in companionable silence. The sandwiches in

the small ice chest went quickly, along with the slices of apple pie and coffee.

Finally, unable to hold any more, she dropped the remains of her meal into the baggie. Leaning back against a big rock, she stretched out her legs and pulled the blanket around her shoulders. The temperature had begun to drop as the sun disappeared.

"Want another cup of coffee?" Alec sat next to her, his arms resting on his knees as he, too, looked up at the night sky.

"No, thanks." She leaned her head back against the boulder. "I still can't believe Hank set us up."

"He's from the old school," Alec replied. "Married people don't live separately. They don't argue all the time—"

"They don't leave their wife the morning after the wedding."

"And the wife damn sure doesn't spend her wedding night in the barn."

"You're right," she murmured. "Hank did it."

"I'll bet he had help."

She turned to look at him. "What do you mean? Who?"

"A couple of nights ago, when I tucked him in, Scotty voiced some concern about having to leave here. I hadn't said anything about him returning to New York, and I didn't understand what would cause him to worry about it. He must have figured if we didn't get along—"

"Then he'd have to leave." Shea finished the thought. "Set up by a four-year-old."

"He's smart, capable of a lot more than you'd expect for his age," Alec replied. "Which is another reason I wanted him here with me." He chuckled. "He's run off two nannies so far and his grandmother is on her last nerve, even though she would never admit it."

"Hank mentioned he's been asking about a horse."

"I know," Alec replied. "He's talked about little else since he got here."

"Alec, I'm hesitant to mention this because I still worry over Scotty's safety, but we have a gelding. Been around here forever," she ventured. "He's a small horse, older than I am, and as gentle as they come. He loves people. If you want Scotty to learn to ride, he couldn't be any safer than on Marty. I think Scotty would like him. He's a paint and kinda flashy."

Alec appeared to consider the suggestion. He glanced toward her, grinned and nodded his approval. "I appreciate your offer. I think that would be great."

For a while they sat back listening to the fire crackle. Somewhere out in the woods a pack of coyotes made its presence known.

"Alec, I...I never asked if there was someone special in your life. I mean, it's a little late now, but—"

"No." Alec shook his head. "No one special."

"But you were married...?" she prompted, hating herself for showing any interest at all, but unable to contain her curiosity.

"Yes. I was married. For just over a year." Alec hesitated, as if debating whether to say anything else. Finally, he said, "It wouldn't have lasted that long if she hadn't gotten pregnant. Scotty was the only good thing to come out of it."

He was quiet for a few minutes. "It didn't take her long after we married to realize the role of wife and mother was not for her. I never knew about the other man until after she'd walked out. For whatever reason, she decided to go through with the pregnancy. For nine months, I lived with the possibility that the baby wasn't mine. Then one day, I came home to find a stranger standing outside my door with a baby in her arms. She handed him to me and said he was my son. My ex didn't even bring Scotty to me herself.

After that I heard she started partying pretty good. A few months later, she was dead of an overdose."

"Oh, my gosh! Alec. How horrible. I'm so sorry."

He shrugged as though it was nothing, but Shea sensed it had affected him deeply. It must be a terrible thing to find out the person you love had betrayed you. Alec deserved respect for raising his son alone, giving the baby all the love he needed. Scotty was proof positive Alec was a great dad.

"What about you?" he asked. "Any broken hearts because of this situation?"

The image of David's face popped into her mind, and she couldn't help but wonder what course his life had taken. It couldn't possibly be as bizarre as the direction hers had gone.

"No."

"I find that hard to believe."

Shea shrugged. "There was a guy in college. He was the one who called the night we were married. Haven't seen him in a long time but he's still a good friend. We talked about getting married but we both knew it wouldn't work. We wanted different things out of life. Then Dad got sick. I left school to take care of him and run the ranch. There was just never any time for…anything else."

"What was your major?"

"Veterinary medicine."

"You're a vet?"

She shook her head. "No. I got as far as my master's. That's when Dad became ill, so I came home. I'd hoped to have a practice someday. But things don't always work out like you plan." She shook herself out of somber thoughts that would serve no purpose and smiled at Alec. "Do you have any other family? I mean, besides Scotty?"

"One brother, Mike. And my mother lives with her sister in St. Petersburg, Florida."

"Do they know you're married?"

"No. I wrestled with the idea, but didn't exactly know how to explain our situation."

Shea nodded her understanding. "What's your mom like?"

Alec appeared to think on that for a while. "My mother. How do I describe my mother?" He shook his head. "She's a character. As hardheaded as you are." He shot her a grin. "In fact, the two of you together could make a guy absolutely crazy. She's smart, good-natured, has a terrific sense of humor, but she also has a strength. After my father died, she kept me in school and had the patience of a saint. I have her to thank for where I am today."

She sounded like someone Shea would love to meet, but sadly that probably would never happen. She now understood where Alec got his dogged determination. It also was obvious he loved his mother very much. Apparently they had a close relationship. Alec was, indeed, like an onion, and with every layer Shea peeled away, the more exceptional he became.

He was not a cold, heartless adversary as she'd initially thought. He was a man who respected family values. And despite the situation over the land, he had a good heart. In fact, she couldn't imagine herself ever finding a man better suited to her and to this life.

And that realization was very unsettling.

"I'm hesitant to bring this up," Alec remarked, absently dragging a small stick over the ground. "I keep waiting for a good time to mention it, but...I doubt if such a time exists."

Shea's heart missed a beat. There was only one thing he would be so hesitant to mention. The future of the Bar H. "Well, you have my curiosity roused. Go ahead." She forced a smile but refused to look at Alec.

"There's a meeting scheduled at the end of the month at a hotel in Dallas. All the investors will be there. Probably some of the local jurisdictions represented, as well. We're building a resort, Shea. Hotels, casinos, a theme park, some restaurants on the Oklahoma side. A water park, golf course and a couple more restaurants in Texas." He was quiet for a moment. "I'd like you to go with me to the meeting."

Shea immediately shook her head and swallowed the huge lump that formed in her throat. "That is not where I want to be."

"Shea, it's going to happen. The change is inevitable. You need to come to terms with the possibility that—" Alec stopped midsentence. "Look, maybe there's a way both of us can get what we want. Compromise might be a possibility. I'm open to trying, but you have to see the plans— with an open mind—then tell me if you think something can be worked out."

She looked above her to the millions of stars in the black velvet sky and shook her head at the hopelessness of her plight.

"So you think my cattle can skip the fall roundup and spend a few days at your resort?" She took in a deep breath. "We both know there is only one way this will end, Alec. One of us has to leave."

"So…you refuse to even try to see if there is an alternative." It was as much a statement as a question.

"I don't see how there could be."

"And you won't unless you attend the meeting. See for yourself." Alec tossed the small stick into the fire. "If I were in your place, I would want to learn everything I could about the enemy and their intent."

She shot him a look of surprise.

"Maybe," she finally agreed. *And maybe not.*

She heard him sigh. "It's late. We have a long walk in the morning. I suggest we bed down in the corner of the old house." He stood and poured out the last drops of his coffee. "I don't care to wake up in the morning and find one of your country varmints in our bed."

While they'd been sharing a bed for some time there was something about sliding into a sleeping bag with Alec that screamed disaster. And she needed some time to come to grips with what he'd just told her. A large resort would be worse than a shopping mall. But she didn't have a clue what her friends and neighbors would think of such a thing.

"Do what you want. I'm sleeping in the Jeep," she said. "Take the bedroll. I'll be fine with the blanket."

His eyebrows rose in quiet speculation, but he said nothing as she retraced her steps to the Jeep. It took some maneuvering, but she finally managed to shift around enough junk to make a reasonably sized sleeping space. She tossed him the bedroll and a pillow and climbed in.

"I heard rumblings of thunder earlier," Alec said. "There's no top on the Jeep. Are you sure you want to—"

"Yes, I'm sure," she quickly assured him. The whole day had been bright and sunny without a cloud in the sky. How gullible did he think she was?

She settled under the warm folds of the blanket and tried to get comfortable in the tiny space. By the time the first rays of the sun broke over the distant hills, she would be halfway back to the house.

And the first thing on her to-do list when she got there was find Hank Minton.

And maybe start looking for another place to live.

Ten

The uncomfortable sensation of cold water running across her face and down her neck woke her from a sound sleep. Brushing the moisture away with her hand, she blinked her eyes and pushed into a sitting position. It was dark. So incredibly dark she couldn't see her hand in front of her face. And it was raining—gently, but steadily. As she came fully awake, she noted the blanket was drenched, as were her clothes.

Muttering to herself, she climbed out of the Jeep. The wind had picked up, dropping the temperature, and she shivered as she stumbled in the direction of the homestead and what shelter it offered. The dying embers of the camp-fire provided just enough light to see the last few steps.

As she approached the old log structure, the skies opened up in a downburst. Climbing onto the floorboards, she followed the wall of the building to the back of the structure where a section of the roof remained.

"Over here." Alec spoke from the darkness.

Cautiously she followed the direction of his voice until her toes found the edge of the sleeping bag. Squatting down, she felt for the edge of the bedroll.

"Here," Alec said, and suddenly his hand held hers. "Shea, you're soaked. Get out of those clothes. Don't argue."

Teeth chattering, she unbuckled her belt, unzipped the wet denim and struggled to push her jeans down her legs. Finally, Alec grabbed the end of the legs, and with one hard tug, she was free of the soggy pants. She scooted inside the soft fleece lining, still warm from the heat of his body.

"And the shirt," he said, not bothering to wait for an argument. He efficiently pulled it over her head, tossed it away and lay down next to her. His heavy arms wrapped around her and their legs entwined, as he began rubbing her arm and shoulder, the friction bringing much-needed warmth.

"No 'I-told-you-so's?'"

"Not this time."

The rain surged, pelting the wooden roof above them. The moist air carried the heavy scent of pine, and in the distance a lone coyote called out to its kinsmen. Alec's hands eventually stilled and merely held her next to the warmth of his body.

Her mind whirled, preventing the return of sleep. Alec was as complex as a jigsaw puzzle whose pieces were upside down. One minute he came off as hard and unrelenting, but the next minute he lay in the shelter of a centuries-old, burned-out building, holding her in his arms, ready to protect her from whatever might be out there. And he seemed completely comfortable in either role.

In fairness, she had to question her own sanity. Here she lay in the home of her ancestors, the last surviving heir, held warm and protected in the arms of the enemy, the very man who would destroy it all.

The low, rumbling thunder gradually became louder, the flashes of lightning brighter. Alec lay in the black shadows, holding Shea as she slept. Lowering his head, he breathed in the sweet scent of her hair.

A long, increasingly loud rumble of thunder was followed by more flashes of light. Shea turned her face into his neck and covered her ears with her hands.

"Shea?"

"The storm."

"It's all right, hon." He tried to soothe her.

"I hate storms. Please try to start the Jeep again." Her voice was high, frightened, her words partially muffled by his shoulder.

"It doesn't have any gas, remember?" His arms resumed their circular motion on her back. "We'll be all right. This old house has weathered more bad weather than you and I will ever see."

Another loud crack of thunder shook the floor. She raised her head and, through the flashes of light from the storm, he saw the fear in the blue iridescence of her eyes. Her sensuous lips parted slightly and desire charged through his body like a bolt of the lightning from above.

Slowly, she reached out and placed her hand against the side of his face as if making certain he was there. He didn't move, didn't breathe, afraid that doing so would break the spell that held them. She leaned forward, moistening his lips with her tongue before kissing him fully. The blood pounded in his head, surged straight to his groin.

He responded without thinking as passion flared. He didn't know if she actually wanted him or if she was half-asleep and didn't realize what she was doing. But whatever the reason, she didn't pull away. And despite his earlier resolve, neither could he.

With a last surge of willpower, he set her away from him. "Alec?"

"Shea, listen to me." His voice was rough, even to his own ears. "I can't do this anymore. It's no longer a game. All bets are off. If you don't want me to make love to you, then move away. Now."

In the ensuing silence, he assumed she realized how close she'd come to losing her resolve, that there would be no turning back. The bedroll moved as she shifted her body. But instead of turning away, she kissed his chest, her teeth nipping his skin, her tongue tasting his heated flesh.

Like a man driven by forces beyond his control, he pushed her fully onto her back, pressed her down into the thick bedroll. Warm and pliant, her flesh conformed to his like the rain that filled each tiny crevice of the parched earth.

In that moment, he knew it was no longer a bluff to get her to leave. She was his wife, regardless of the circumstances. And he wanted her. Oh, how he wanted her. He needed to feel his hard flesh sheathed inside. She was his. And he'd make damn sure she knew it. His mouth found hers, plunging his tongue inside, loving the taste of her, the feel of her. And this time Shea kissed him back.

With a moan of defeat, Alec kissed her deeply, urgently, with a hunger that threatened to consume him. He heard her whimper, and the blood pounded in his ears. His hand followed the exquisite contours of her body, cupping her perfect breast, his thumb teasing the taut nipple. He left her lips, kissing down her throat to the supple flesh he held in his hand, teasing the small nub. She arched her back, pushing her chest toward him with a soft moan and he gave equal attention to her other perfect breast. With his hand, he traced over her belly, then lower to the silken curls that framed the center of her desire.

"Alec," she whispered, need heavy in her voice as she pushed against his hand.

The pain in his loins became unbearable as raw, primitive instinct took over.

He moved fully on top of her and she opened to him. His hand fisted her hair, drawing her head back, allowing him greater access to her mouth, and like a starving man, he fed.

Alec raised his head and through the flashes of radiant light, he looked into the blue iridescent depths of her eyes and with a hoarse, almost feral growl, he pushed inside.

The thunder rolled, escalating in power, mirroring the intensity of their joining. Shea struggled to accept him, her body stretching as his power filled her. She knew no fear of the storm. Her mind and body were consumed with Alec, all senses tuned to him. She could no longer think. Only feel. And the feeling was incredible. Every movement of his big, powerful body propelled her higher. Her arms slid up and over his broad shoulders to circle his neck, her fingers gripped his thick hair.

Alec's lips returned to hers, his tongue pushing deep. His hands cupped her head, holding her where he wanted her to be and a pressure inside began to build, causing a need that was almost painful in its intensity.

"Alec!" she cried out against his lips.

"I know, babe. Let it happen."

Rotating his hips, he pushed hard and suddenly her desire crested and her mind shattered into a million brilliant pieces. She cried out his name as wave after wave of complete and total fulfillment coursed through her body.

He kissed her again with animal hunger. He began to move with a driving force, bringing her to the edge of mindless release for a second time. She clutched at his broad shoulders as his hands moved to cup her hips, lifting her, filling her, until, with a wild growl, he reached the summit of his own release. He shuddered against her as the spasms of his completion vibrated through him, and pushed her over the top yet again.

Spent, he collapsed on top of her. His heavy weight made it difficult to breathe, but she never would have asked him to move away. Surrounded by his musky scent she could feel the rapid beating of his heart. Wrapped in the warmth and protection of his arms, she floated slowly back to earth. Outside their shelter the rain continued to fall.

It was as though neither of them was inclined to move for fear they would somehow lose this sweet accord, this exquisite joining of their bodies and souls. She wanted this moment to go on, for him to hold her like this forever.

Rising up on his arms, his eyes captured hers, his thumb gently tracing the contours of her lips. In those moments, time stood still.

Finally, he eased from her but held her close.

"Did I hurt you?" he asked, bringing her hand to his lips.

"No." She smiled and gently touched his face.

She knew the pain would come later.

When this situation was over and Alec said goodbye.

"Shea—" Alec's voice called to her, bringing her back from the blissful realm of sleep. "Shea, hon, wake up."

She moaned her disgruntlement and attempted to snuggle back into the heavenly cocoon of their soft makeshift bed.

"Come on, sweetheart." Alec kissed her before pulling the warmth of the bedroll away from her. "I think we're about to have company."

Before she could respond, a piercing light shattered the darkness, followed by the sound of an engine and tires bouncing through the small pools of water in the rain-drenched earth.

Struggling to sit up, she pulled the top of the sleeping bag around her. "What is it?"

"I think we're being rescued."

"Rescued? What time is it?" The rain had slowed to a drizzle, but the sky was still black.

"Just after midnight."

"You both all right in there?" Hank's voice called from the truck as he pulled up in front of the foundation. "Got kinda worried when the storm broke. Figured I'd better come out and check."

Her eyes locked to Alec's, she didn't immediately move.

Then, with a grimace, he rolled onto his side and reached for his jeans.

Shea found the blanket he'd been using, pulled it around her, gathered her wet clothes and stood up. Hank's arrival had effectively melted away the sweet fantasy and slammed her back to reality.

What had she done?

She didn't look in Alec's direction as she walked toward Hank and the truck.

The trip back was made in silence, her earlier intentions to wring Hank's neck now overshadowed by confusion. She must be crazy. How could she have made love with the man who threatened to take away her ranch and everything she cherished?

A slight tremble ran down her spine and she pulled the blanket more tightly around her. Alec reached out and turned up the heater. But it wasn't the temperature in the truck's cab making her feel chilled to the bone.

Entering the house, she went straight upstairs. Maybe, with any luck she could be in bed and feign sleep when he got there. She quickly grabbed a clean T-shirt and panties, entered the bathroom and turned on the shower. Stepping under the spray, she leaned forward, placing her forehead against the shower wall, and let the hot water stream down her back.

Had she been wrong in making love to Alec? She didn't love him. She couldn't. She *wouldn't* fall in love with him. It had been hormones. Or the rain. Or momentary insanity. She gritted her teeth. This would only make everything worse.

Shower finished, she dressed for bed and pulled open the bathroom door. Alec stood in front of her, very tall, very imposing and very male. He was clad only in a towel slung low around his hips. He must have showered in the bathroom downstairs. He watched her with those cat eyes, alert to the emotions she tried to hide.

She forced a smile and moved to step around him. He caught her arm as she passed, gently halting her forward motion.

"Do we need to talk?"

She kept her vision focused on the floor. She didn't want to see the mockery in his eyes or the smirk that would be back on his face. "No."

He placed a finger under her chin, forced her to look into his eyes. Her gaze dropped lower, to his mouth, full, defined and capable of so much passion. There was no mockery. No contempt. No smirk.

"I disagree. I just made love to my wife, and now she doesn't want anything to do with me." He watched her intently, his head tilted in question. "I'd like to know why."

She shrugged. "I… It's awkward, Alec. For me. I mean, I'm not sure—"

"Where we go from here?"

She nodded. "Yeah."

He moved forward, resting his hands against the wall, his well-muscled biceps on either side of her head, and leaned down to her. "I say we take it one day at a time." His raspy voice was deep and wonderfully disturbing. He moved to her neck, nipped at the sensitive skin just below her ear. "I can't tell you I'll call off the project," he murmured, his breath hot against her skin. "There is already too much time and money invested and too many people involved," he murmured before moving to the other side of her neck and repeating the wildly arousing little bites. "But there has to be a way to work this out."

Every nip sent tingles of hot current jolting through her. He was doing it again. He was seducing her with his touch and his voice. Oh, how she wished they'd come together

under different circumstances. But right then, she couldn't
quite remember why it mattered.

"But for now I see no other immediate changes that are
required." The look on his face told her he was serious.

As they stood in the shadows with his face so close she
could touch her lips to his with minimal movement, the
concern over the ranch faded somewhat. Yet she knew the
only thing they'd truly accomplished was admitting their
mutual desire for each other.

Mutely, she nodded, and his mouth came down over
hers. The stubble of his beard scratched her skin, but she
didn't care. God help her, at this moment she didn't care.

With a barely concealed moan, Alec scooped her into
his arms and carried her to their bedroom, kicking the door
closed behind them.

Eleven

The distant rumbling of thunder announced the approach of yet another summer storm. The humidity was high, the air thick. Alec found Shea in Scotty's bedroom, opening a window to allow the gentle breeze to penetrate the room's stuffiness.

"Does it always rain this much in Texas?" he asked from the doorway.

"Summer showers," she replied, turning to smile at him. "By mid-August we'll be wishing for some of this rain."

"Hey, Dad! Look what I won at the fair!" Scotty ran into the room fresh from his bath. Just after breakfast, Hank had taken him and Cody for a day at the county fair, giving Alec and Shea the entire day together without distractions. They hadn't wasted a second.

Scotty proudly grabbed a huge stuffed owl from atop his dresser. The oval face, covered in gray feathers, framed two huge round eyes. "Isn't it cool? Cody just won a stuffed bear. Boy, I was lucky, wasn't I, Daddy?"

"You sure were, son," Alec replied, smiling at Scotty.

"And I got to ride with Hank on his horse in the parade, and we ate hot dogs with ketchup, and we got some of the candy they threw from the...uh...uh..." He looked at Shea.

"Floats," Shea supplied.

"Yeah, from the floats. Then we saw the biggest pig get a ribbon, and Leonard Mabry let me brush his goat." He actually stopped and took a breath. "It was cool, Dad."

Grinning, Alec leaned over and placed a kiss on his son's head, then rustled the soft hair. Shea turned down the covers of the small bed. "Okay, in you go, cowboy."

Scotty ran to the window and carefully placed the owl on the windowsill. "Hank said this old owl will bring me luck. I'm gonna set it here so it will see me when I ride Marty."

The day after they'd been stranded at the old ruins, Hank had introduced Scotty to his first horse. Marty had indeed been a perfect choice, moving slow and gentle as though he knew his young rider was just learning. After only an hour of simple instruction, Scotty had been off and riding, making endless circles around one of the larger corrals.

The boy turned and jumped into the center of the mattress with a squeal and a giggle. Alec smiled and leaned over to tuck in his young son for the night.

Shea slipped out of the room, giving father and son some bonding time. The wind had picked up, and the sheer draperies fluttered gently inside the master bedroom. Suddenly, the rain began to fall, pelting against the top of the house, falling in heavy sheets from the edges of the roof. She walked to the dresser and took out a soft cotton T-shirt in preparation for her shower.

Large hands came to rest on her shoulders, their grip a welcome deterrent against the rain's sudden chill. Alec's arms came around her, pulling her back against his chest. His chin rested on her head.

"Thank you," he said quietly.

"For what?" A quizzical frown covered her face as she turned to her husband.

"For all you do for Scotty. And for me." He grinned. "Or, maybe I should I say *to* me."

"Both are my pleasure." She beamed.

"Come here," Alec whispered, pulling her down onto the bed and settling himself next to her. He began unbuttoning her blouse.

"I would like to know the name of the idiot who invented buttons," he muttered. "And why my wife insists on wearing clothing with them on it."

"What would you have me do? Wear nothing but T-shirts?"

"You've got it partially right. Just leave off the T-shirt."

She laughed, and he leaned over and placed his lips on hers.

She was so focused on Alec at first she ignored the cool, wet sensation on her forehead. As the feeling persisted, it became an irritant, breaking her focus and causing her to push Alec away. She sat up and wiped at her temple, noting the moisture on her hand.

Before she could assimilate her thoughts, another drop of something cold and wet hit her head then trickled down her scalp underneath her hair.

"Shea, what's wrong?"

She swung her legs to the side of the bed as another droplet of water splattered onto her shoulder and ran down her arm. She sprang from the bed. "Oh…Alec, it's—"

At that moment, with a sickening groan, a section of the ceiling above the bed collapsed, sending a downpour of accumulated rainwater squarely onto Alec's head.

With a shriek, she scampered back from the bed as a flash of lightning illuminated the room. Startled, she took in Alec, sitting on the bed, his hands held ineffectively above his head as a river of water cascaded down.

"Cool!" Scotty called out as he opened their bedroom door, no doubt hearing the loud crash as well as her shriek. His eyes were wide at the spectacle in front of him. "Hey, Dad, can I—"

"No!" Alec didn't give him a chance to finish the question. "Go into the bathroom and get a towel," he barked as he rolled off the bed, sending Scotty running down the hall.

Shea stood to the side, staring incredulously at her husband, who appeared to be in shock. He placed his hands on his hips and stared up at the heavily dripping ceiling, a look of amazement on his features.

Shea clenched her fists in a weak effort to contain her amusement but lost the battle as a fit of giggles overpowered her and she gave in to a moment of full-fledged laughter. Scotty returned with the towel, his giggles joining hers at the sight of his father standing drenched beside the bed.

"It's not that damn funny," he growled, which brought an encore of laughter from both of them. Alec snatched the towel from his son's hands and began to blot his head and neck.

"Hey, Daddy, you want some soap?"

Shea clamped her hand over her mouth and turned away from Alec as she fought to restrain the laughter. Suddenly, she was hoisted up into his arms.

"You think it's so funny?"

Before she could answer, she was tossed through the air, landing with a splash on top of the completely soaked mattress. There were matching screams and giggles from Scotty as he came to rest on the bed next to her.

"Why? Why go to the trouble of checking the foundation of a house you only want to tear down?"

Shea watched as Alec checked the flashlights while he waited for Jason to arrive.

"Because I want to know that it's safe. Obviously we won't be moving out as quickly as I'd originally anticipated." He shot her a knowing glance, his lips pursed to subdue the grin. "As old as this place is, it could be a death trap. I'm not about to endanger Scott's life—or yours—by taking that chance."

"Well, I think you're making this bigger than it is. You're going to extremes."

"I don't care. There may not be anything holding this

house together but the paint and even that's beginning to crack. I'm going over every square inch. It obviously needs a new roof."

"Oh yeah? How can you tell?" They'd spent the night in her old room and while it was not as comfortable as their new bed, especially for a man of Alec's size, Shea had slept peacefully. The cold rainwater shower hadn't dampened his sexual appetite, and after they'd managed to get Scotty back to sleep, Alec had wasted no time proving it.

"Yeah, Daddy," Scotty chimed in. "How can you tell?" A quelling look from his father did little to silence his giggles, but he scooted out of his chair. "I'm gonna go see what Hank's doing."

"Breakfast will be ready in an hour," Shea called. "Tell Hank to have you back here by nine."

"Okay," he replied, as the door slammed behind him.

"This is serious, Shea," Alec said as he poured another cup of coffee. "How long has it been since this house was checked?"

"Checked for what?" She put the strips of bacon into the large iron skillet. The sizzle and aroma immediately filled the air.

"Wood rot. Termites. Faulty wiring. Leaking pipes. Any number of things."

She shrugged. "I really don't know."

"How long since the roof was replaced?"

She again shrugged her shoulders. "Dad always said he was going to have it repaired, but I don't think he ever got around to it. We've had some leaks from time to time, and the roof was patched in those areas." She'd hoped that would suffice until there was money for a new roof.

Alec grimaced. "Then you don't know how much water damage there's been?" Shea shook her head. "What about the foundation?"

"What about it?"

"How long since it's been examined?" He looked at Shea's blank expression. "Never mind. I think I can guess. There's been virtually no protective maintenance. In two hundred years. Amazing. I intend to find out exactly what's going on. I'm afraid the incident last night was only a hint of other problems."

Shea turned the bacon over in the pan and mentally crossed her fingers. If Alec found serious damage, she didn't know where she would get the money for the repairs.

When breakfast was over, Alec went to find Jason, impatient to get started. The two men took the soaked mattress downstairs, Alec still muttering about the roof as they went. Then he located a ladder, loaded two flashlights with fresh batteries and they were off. She knew Alec was more than qualified. Inspecting the house would be like child's play to him.

She called a local roofing company to come out and give an estimate on repairs. For the rest of the day, she stayed close to the house, finishing laundry, preparing a brisket and waiting for the arrival of the roofers.

A few minutes before Shea was about to call Alec and Scotty in for supper, Alec came into the kitchen. He was covered in dirt and grime from his head to his feet. A scowl was firmly in place.

"Give me a few minutes to get cleaned up," he said and walked toward the stairs.

A short time later, Alec reentered the kitchen.

"So, how bad is the roof?"

"It's not good."

"It can be repaired where it fell in and—"

"It's not just the roof, Shea," he cut in. "There's major wood rot and termite damage everywhere. I found extensive destruction to most of the load-bearing walls on the first floor, and the foundation is crumbling. The house has already begun to shift. Its ability to remain standing for much longer is highly questionable." He rubbed the back of his neck. "That aside, the wiring is sixty years old. The plumbing needs replacing, the gas line is highly suspect and I'd guess most of your heat during the winter flies out the old single-pane windows. Did you know several are cracked?"

"So, what are you saying?" She wanted him to spell it out. "If…if it's the cost, I could replace one thing at a time over the next few—"

"Shea, the house isn't safe." His words caused a sick feeling in the pit of her stomach. "We shouldn't even be inside right now. It's not safe for you—or any of us—to stay here. I don't know how much clearer I can make it."

She'd known the old house was long past need of repairs, but because the money wasn't there, she'd ignored the problems. Apparently, her father had done the same thing.

"So…what are my options?"

He shook his head. "The *only* option is tear it down and build a new one. But under the circumstances, that would be ridiculous."

Under the circumstances?

Her mind whirled, not wanting to believe what that meant. Was this his way of telling her it was over? She'd thought they had found something special between them. They made love every night. She'd even begun to believe the marriage was real—or had a chance to become so. Had he been plotting all along? Looking for a bona fide reason to make her leave?

Had he only been pretending he cared for her? If she'd been wrong to start trusting him…if he had only been using her while he waited for an opportunity that would allow him to reclaim the land, she didn't know how she would ever deal with that. She felt her heart drop to her knees as that possibility threatened to knock her off her feet.

She'd let herself believe he cared about her as well as the land. She'd let down her guard. Reality and disappointment hit with the force of a sledgehammer. With her pulse slamming through her veins, she removed the rolls from the oven, set the tray on top of the stove and stared at him. Suddenly it was overwhelming. The news about the house was bad enough. Her life was here, her past as well as her envisioned future rested on this small piece of earth. Everything she knew revolved around this ranch. She had nowhere else to go. Tears burned the backs of her eyes; her breath died in her throat.

But to think she would lose Alec as well, that she'd merely been used to relieve his boredom, that she meant nothing to him. How was she ever going to come to terms with that?

"Shea?"

Covering her mouth with her hand to try to muffle a cry of despair, she ran from the room as the tears spilled over.

Curling up on the end of the old bedraggled sofa in the den, she faced the worn recliner that sat in the corner of the room. Her father's chair. She could visualize him kicked back, his feet resting on the stool as he read his afternoon paper. He was gone now. This house was the only connection she had to him and to her mother. Every room, every space under its roof carried precious memories. She could feel the love from the generations of family who had lived here before. Her dad's boots still sat in a corner of the mudroom. Her grandmother's handmade quilts were spread over the beds upstairs. It was as if the house gave her the strength to carry on alone. It was unthinkable that she had failed to protect it.

"Shea?" Alec entered the room. He stood just inside the open doorway, his hands resting on his hips.

She didn't want to talk with him. She couldn't. He might confirm that she was right in suspecting him.

"In the morning, you need to pack some clothes. I'll

make arrangements for us to stay in a hotel in Dallas for a while."

"And then what?" She gazed at her hands clenched tightly in her lap. "What happens next, Alec?"

"That's something we need to talk about. But regardless of what you decide to do going forward, staying here is not an option." He moved farther inside the room. "I'll still keep the promise I made that day in Ben's office. My original offer still stands. I'll buy you out. You can go back to school, get your doctorate and become a veterinarian. Fulfill that dream. You don't have to live here to do it. You need to be reasonable."

"Reasonable? Define reasonable. Is it unreasonable to want to stay in a place you love? A place you've based all your plans for a future around?"

"Maybe it's time for a change. Perhaps you should consider—"

"No." She shook her head defiantly. "No! Alec, you don't understand. I'm telling you I will not let this house be destroyed. Where would I go?"

"Anywhere you wanted."

"*Here* is where I want to be." *With you.*

Alec nodded, then shrugged. "Then you and your world will fall apart together. But I'll have no part of it."

Obviously, she'd been wrong when she'd assumed he cared about his ancestors, those who had so loved this land. The day they'd roamed around the old homestead and he'd asked all the questions. He'd wanted to see where his great-great-grandfather had been laid to rest. He'd commented that the area, the old cabin, were incredible. He'd shown what had appeared to be genuine interest. Had it all been a ploy to make her think he cared?

Had there ever been anything between them other than sex? She'd fallen in love with Alec, but he'd never said he felt the same. She swallowed hard as that realization hit.

Total humiliation washed over her, followed by a heightened sense of anger at herself for being so stupid. So gullible. Alec didn't love her. He never would. How could she have become so delusional as to believe a man like Alec Morreston would want any kind of permanent relationship with her?

She stood to face him. "I will not leave this house. You think you've won, but you haven't."

He reeled back as if she had slapped him. For a moment she thought she saw pain in his eyes, but it was gone so fast she knew she must have imagined it. The devil didn't have feelings.

"Won? Is that what you think this is about? Winning?"

She refused to answer. She knew what it was about and it wasn't their relationship. There was no relationship. There never had been. She'd played into his hands. He knew it and now so did she,

"If that's what you think, there's nothing more to say."

She walked to a nearby table, pulled a couple of tissues from the box. Wiping her eyes, she took a deep breath, struggling to control the pain running rampant through her body. She'd fallen in love with Alec, so much so she would have given him anything. But his only concern was getting her to vacate the property.

Suddenly, he was in front of her, his hands clutching her upper arms. His face was set in stone, his eyes narrowed. She could clearly detect the underlying thread of exasperation bordering on fury. "You're going to listen to me," he told her. "Tomorrow, you are going to start packing your bags because we are leaving this place—all of us."

"I'm not going anywhere—"

"And you're going to face the reality that life as you've known it is over. It's finished."

"No." She struggled, but he easily held her.

"Shea, stop! Listen to yourself. Take off the damn blinders and look at the truth that's right in front of you."

All she saw standing in front of her was the man she'd fallen in love with. A man who didn't love her, didn't care about anything but making more money. A man who'd done whatever was required to regain the land. Her first impressions had been correct. He was ruthless. She'd just never imagined how truly merciless he could be.

He turned and walked toward the door. "I had hoped that…" He shoved his hands into his jeans pockets and clenched his teeth. "I'm going to contact a building inspector. If you won't believe me, you can hear it from him. And I'm going to call the county. This house needs to be condemned."

She winced.

He paused at the door, his tawny eyes narrow and forbidding. "I'll have my jet readied for takeoff by tomorrow. I'm taking Scott back to New York. I'd like you to come with us, but that's your choice."

What would I do in New York?

The man who stood before her was ruthless and determined, powerful and unyielding, with the money and the resources to back him up. How could she ever have been so foolish as to think she could challenge him and win? What had she been thinking to let down her guard and start caring for him? It was no longer an either-or situation; the goal of winning Alec and the land had become one in the same. With the old house condemned, Alec would be gone, as well.

"I hate you for this." Her voice was low and broken. She gripped the back of the sofa to remain standing. It was a poor attempt to place armor around her heart. The words, like a boomerang, came right back at her, cutting deeply.

The hands of time stopped as they silently faced each other. Then Alec turned and walked out the door. She heard his footsteps going up the stairs and toward Scotty's bedroom, leaving Shea in the center of a room spinning wildly out of control. The searing pain in her chest made her gasp for breath. But it hurt to breathe. This impossible situation had escalated into a nightmare of epic proportions and she was drowning, being pulled down into the center of a black hole from which she might never emerge. Alec was free to return to his own world. Old house condemned. Mission accomplished.

Early the next morning Alec left as he'd said he would, taking Scotty with him. Hearing the child's cries of "but why, Daddy?" and his tearful pleading to please let him stay had almost been Shea's undoing. She'd finally run out to the barn, unable to bear hearing his cries, unwilling to watch them walk out the door forever.

When she eventually returned, the house was silent, as though it knew its time had come, awaiting annihilation like a condemned man awaiting his execution.

The merriment and laughter of Scotty's voice no longer echoed through the halls. But Alec's absence was the hardest to bear. She didn't cry because she couldn't. The numbness wouldn't let her.

Finally, on the third day, she saddled one of the horses. All her life, she'd found solace in the land. It had been a refuge where she could work through problems that seemed far greater than she could possibly contend with alone. Other than her dad dying, losing her home was the greatest hardship she'd ever faced. And the loss of the man she loved, however convoluted that might have been, was earth shattering.

She swung her leg over the saddle, gathered the reins and urged the mare toward the piney woods and the old homestead beyond. She knew going there would renew the memories of the last time she'd been there—with Alec.

The gentle, even stride of the mare was soothing as she carried Shea through the trees and over the meadows. The call of a red-tailed hawk as it circled overhead seemed to mock the fact she was alone. After dismounting, Shea walked to the sacred ground where five generations of her ancestors lay in eternal sleep. Stopping in front of the grave of William Morreston, she wished she could ask him so many questions.

Eventually, she made her way to the old homestead. As she looked at the burned-out hull, she could visualize Alec's face, hear his laugh and feel his arms around her. As the sun set on the horizon, Shea curled up on the edge of the old floorboards a mere foot from the spot where they had made love, and succumbed to the pain shredding her heart into tiny pieces. Unable to hold back her misery any longer, the heartache broke through any lingering restraints and sobs of loss ran rampant through her body.

Twelve

It had been almost a week since Alec had left the Bar H to take Scotty back to New York. Now, en route back to Dallas, he still didn't know what he could say to make Shea understand her safety was his primary concern.

He'd known he needed to get Scotty to a neutral setting. The child didn't need to witness the argument that was sure to take place when Alec went back to the ranch and her hardheaded resistance collided with his single-minded determination that she leave there before she was injured. Or worse.

The onboard office was furnished with the latest computers and advanced communication technology, enabling him to conduct business from anywhere in the world. Anything and everything needed to handle virtually any crisis was at his fingertips.

Except the one named Shea Hardin-Morreston.

His fingers drummed impatiently on the desktop as he gazed out the small window at the darkening sky. He was used to long flights, usually working his way from destination to destination, continent to continent. It helped to pass the time. But on this flight, he was incapable of concentrating on anything except Shea and that damned old house.

Shea's refusal to accept the reality of the situation and see the futility of what she wanted made no sense. It was not just the issue of the house. This was about the safety of a woman he'd come to care about very much. She'd opened a door to a place he'd long forgotten, reminding him of the things he'd loved as a boy. A feeling of peace had surrounded him at the ranch, encouraging him to set aside the abstract world to which he'd become accustomed. It had been a free fall out of the rat race into a new reality of home and heart; he had taken a step back to the things and the people that mattered. And he wanted Shea to be part of his new reality. He'd not imagined it without her. But if she didn't care enough to trust him…if she wasn't willing to let go of the past and take a chance on a future with him, then both of them would lose.

Suddenly, visions of his first wife clouded Alec's mind. Sondra had also wanted it all. The big house, the expensive cars had never been enough. She'd continued the affairs, the parties, the drugs, even after she'd learned she was pregnant, because that had been what had suited her. She'd pushed aside her own safety and the safety of their innocent child for her own selfish wants. And Shea was doing the same thing.

Shea's drug was the ranch. It was as addictive to her as drugs had been to Sondra. Shea was attempting to make him conform, get him to spend millions to put the house back in working order, and then… He didn't want to speculate on what she would do then.

God, he wanted to be wrong about Shea. His feelings for her ran deep. He'd actually let himself envision a future together and he'd never thought he would feel that way about any woman again.

Surely, by now Shea must have accepted the truth that the house wasn't safe. But still, he had to acknowledge it was her home. It was the only one she'd ever known. As she'd said when he issued the ultimatum to get out of that building, the ranch was her life. It defined who she was. At least in her mind. To Alec, she was so much more.

Hopefully the time he'd been away had given Shea a chance to calm down, to realize that things had to change.

Even so, convincing her to leave her home would take every amount of skill he possessed. She had to understand he wasn't forcing her out because of that damned contract. It was for her safety. It was because he cared. He didn't have a clue how it had happened, but he could no longer deny that truth. He was in love with Shea Hardin.

The issue of the land remained a black cloud over both their heads. It continued to drive a wedge between them and that had to end. If he had to choose between giving up the entire project and losing Shea, the project was history. He'd never thought a woman like Shea existed, let alone that he would find her. She had taken away all the suspicions and internal rage that had burned a hole in his soul for five long years, and opened his heart to the possibility of a future of happiness. She'd made him whole again. He was not about to lose her. Not over this land. Not over anything.

He glanced again at his watch. Ten minutes later than the last time he'd looked. Still half an hour out from Dallas-Fort Worth. He wanted to pace, needed some way to let off the tension churning in his gut. He'd never felt this uneasy, never sensed the need to hurry as he did now.

I never should have left without her. That thought kept churning in his mind. *I never should have left her alone in that house.*

Once the jet landed at the airport, a helicopter was waiting, ready to take him back to Calico Springs. This time he would make her listen to him. At the meeting he'd scheduled to take place in four days, he was calling a halt to the project. It was worth any financial loss if it meant having Shea in his life. He needed her. Scotty needed her. And he believed Shea needed them.

The sound seemed to come from far away. Shea ignored it, not wanting to leave the dark recesses of sleep that had finally given her temporary peace.

Almost every day since Alec and Scotty had left, she'd saddled a horse and had come out to the ruins of the old homestead. She'd reflected on her limited options but unlike the previous times in her life, she'd found no solution. There was no peace. In the end, everything came back to Alec and what she would do without him in her life.

The sound grew louder, now joined by a voice calling her name. Blinking open her eyes, she sat up.

Thunder rolled across the sky as lightning flashed, challenging the darkness. The wind roared around the old structure, bringing the smell of the pending rain.

"Shea!"

It was Hank. As she stood up, she saw the truck about a hundred yards away heading toward her at a high rate of speed. He came to a screeching halt in front of the foundation.

"There's trouble," he told her without preamble. "Get in."

Recognizing the serious tone in his voice, she jumped into the vehicle without a word. He spun around on two wheels and they headed back over the rise.

"What?" She was almost afraid to ask.

"It's the house," Hank said. "It's on fire."

"What!" Shea couldn't immediately grasp the meaning of what he said. "The house…*my* house?"

She saw him nod, his mouth set in a grim line.

"How?" Her mind was reeling.

"Don't know," he yelled over the sound of the racing engine. "My guess is lightning. But as old as the place is, it won't take it long to burn down. That wood's like dry kindling."

Shea sat in stunned silence. Hank bypassed the trail and shot a straight line for the house, tearing through the wooded area a half mile away from it. They bounced over stumps and plunged through shallow ravines, sideswiping trees and boulders.

As soon as they topped the last rise, she could see the flames against the darkened sky. Fire equipment surrounded the house along with police and ambulance. Men were running in all directions, shouting to each other and scrambling to battle the flames shooting out the windows. A black wall of smoke engulfed the old composite roof; the large streams of water the firefighters were spraying onto its burning surface had little effect. Bright red, blue and white lights flashed and cast an eerie ambiance over the horrific scene unfolding around her.

She jumped from the truck before Hank came to a complete stop and ran toward the house. One of the firefighters caught her, bringing her to a stop.

"I'm sorry, ma'am, but you'll need to stay back."

"It's my house," she screamed over the commotion.

"Ma'am, you can't go inside." His tone had changed to one of understanding, but he remained adamant in his refusal to let her near the house.

"But—"

"Please, ma'am, you must stay back. The walls could collapse at any time. Please."

She turned away, unable to stop the flow of tears as they streamed down her face. She'd never felt so powerless in her life. The nightmare was coming true, playing out in full color right in front of her eyes. She stumbled to the far side of the three-story structure and watched helplessly as the flames continued to eat at the roof.

At least Alec and Scotty were gone and in no danger.

Then something caught her attention. It looked like a face in the upstairs window. Scotty's room. She brushed the tears from her eyes and looked again. Was Alec here? Had they come back? Was Scotty trapped inside? Between the darkness and the smoke billowing out of the window, she couldn't be sure. Sheer terror gripped her heart. She anxiously searched around her for any sign of Alec.

"Scotty!" Firefighters were pulling more hoses from the trucks, yelling instructions to each other while the anxious ranch hands and their families looked on. Then in the distance, on the very edge of the illumination from the flashing lights on the emergency vehicles, she spotted a white car. It looked like the sedan Alec had been driving while he was here. He'd come back! Frantically, she took one more look around her but couldn't spot Alec in all the chaos. Time was running out. She ran to the closest firefighter, tugged on his jacket to get his attention and pointed to the upstairs window. "There is a child up there."

She had to yell to be heard over the roar of the fire and the commotion on the ground. The man looked in the direction she indicated. A dark cloud of smoke still plumed out the open window.

"I don't see anyone, ma'am," he said, still looking. "We checked the house before the fire got to this stage. There was no one inside."

"But he's there!" She pointed to the window.

The man turned and hurried back to one of the fire trucks, yelling instructions to the others. She didn't have time to wait. Scotty didn't have time to wait. Without another thought Shea took off at a dead run toward the kitchen door. If she hurried, there was a chance she could reach Scotty in time.

Taking a deep breath, she bounded up the outside steps and pushed her way inside. The wall of heat was overwhelming. A thick blanket of smoke filled the room, whirling around her as the fresh air followed her into the kitchen. She quickly wet some towels, held them against her face, and ran for the stairs, taking them two at a time. The closer she got to the second floor, the more intense the heat became, surrounding her like a giant furnace.

As she reached the top of the stairwell, she heard a loud crackling sound and a cloud of dark gray smoke billowed down from the roof. She coughed violently as she urged herself forward. Just a few steps more.

"Scotty!" No reply. Crouching low to the floor, she crawled down the hall. The towels seemed of little help as the smoke burned her throat and lungs. The loud roaring from the inferno brought renewed terror. *Am I already too late?* The smoke burned her eyes, further restricting her sight. Feeling her way along the wall, she finally reached his room.

She hesitated in the doorway only a fraction of a second before plunging into the smoke and ash, not stopping until she reached the window where she'd seen the small face. Suddenly, the smoke swirled away from the open window. She gasped for a breath of air. It was then she saw it. *The owl.* It hadn't been Scotty she'd seen in the window. It was his stuffed owl. At that instant, a loud crash from another part of the house rocked the floor under her feet.

Turning, she began the arduous journey back down the hall. Approaching the doorway to her old room, she knew a moment of anguish for all the cherished things that would soon be lost forever. The linens, hand-embroidered by her mother, the wedding gown, pictures of her father and the family Bible. The only things left of the Hardin family were in that cedar chest. It sat not more than four feet from where she stood. She couldn't see it because of the smoke, but she knew it was there.

Acting purely on impulse, she lunged for the big chest. Grabbing the handle, she began pulling it from the room.

The smoke was thicker than it had been only a few moments ago and every breath was a horrific struggle. At the top of the stairs, she gave a hard push and the chest began to slide down, bumping over each step. It was almost to the bottom landing when the corner caught in the stair railing, halting its progress.

Climbing over the chest, she tried tugging from the

lower side. Suddenly, the railing gave way and the chest lurched forward. The motion threw her off balance and she fell, tumbling the rest of the way down the stairs, the heavy trunk crashing down on top of her.

As she teetered on the edge of consciousness, she pushed at the trunk, but it had become lodged between the newel post and the wall, effectively pinning her underneath.

Her ears were ringing. With each cough, her lungs filled with more minuscule particles of ash. She pushed frantically at the chest, trying to dislodge it enough so she could scoot out from underneath.

The roar of the fire, which now surrounded her, was almost deafening. It was so hot. For a moment, she gave up her attempts to push the chest away and covered her face with her one free arm, desperately trying to breathe. Unable to move, all she could do was look toward the ceiling as the nightmare continued to unfold.

She knew she was suffocating, dying a horrendously slow death. Her thoughts were of Alec, her mind encapsulating their time together. He was a good person. A good father. And she loved him with all her heart. Even if that love wasn't returned. The times he'd held her in his arms she'd been given a little taste of heaven on earth. She could see his handsome face in her mind's eye. His smile. The glitter of amusement in his golden eyes. She could hear his voice, so strong and deep. She was glad she'd had the opportunity to know him. To know what it was like to totally lose herself in his arms. What she wouldn't give for another chance to be with him without the issue of the land hanging over their heads.

There was so much more to life than history and tradition. Alec had shown her that. The really important things were the people you loved, not man-made structures. Even the land couldn't give you a glimpse of the stars and hold you close and protect when you floated slowly back down to earth. Material things couldn't make you feel safe while a storm of trouble threatened to tear your life apart. They couldn't give you hope for the future. They couldn't love you back. Why hadn't she realized it before it was too late? The way she missed her dad should have told her it was the people you love that mattered.

Tears slipped from the corners of her eyes. She could barely feel the moisture running down her face. It was so hot. If only she had a second chance she would make sure Alec knew he was the only thing that really mattered. Oh, how she wished she could somehow let him know.

"I love you Alec," she whispered as more tears joined the first. "I love you." Another crash pulled her attention to the area behind her. Craning her neck, she watched helplessly as pieces of flaming debris fell all around.

The thick cloud of smoke prevented her from seeing the flames on the burning ceiling above her, but she heard the loud cracking of the fire and the deafening shriek of the timbers as they lost their centuries-old struggle to hold up the roof. She heard her own scream, but it was lost in the loud crashing of falling timber. Then blackness swirled inside her head, dragging her down into the blissful realm of oblivion.

Almost as soon as the helicopter cleared the city lights of Dallas, Alec detected a yellowish glow on the darkening north horizon. It was a fire of some kind. While he prayed the cause was a farmer clearing out a brush pile, a churning in his gut told him it could be the house at the Bar H.

"Chuck, can this thing go any faster?" Alec asked the pilot through the headset.

The pilot nodded as if he sensed the urgency, sending them plunging ahead into the darkness. The closer they got to the yellowish glow, the more the fear churned in Alec's gut. Finally he knew. It was the old house.

I never should have left her in that house.

Before the chopper fully set down in an area near the barn, Alec jumped out. The sight of the old, three-story house ablaze against the blackened sky was surreal. His worst fears were confirmed. The firefighters swarmed around the structure, sending streams of water to the top and sides in a last-ditch effort to save even a portion of the building.

Alec looked everywhere for Shea but she was not to be found. As the sky opened and the rain began to fall in torrents, he spotted Hank. The ranch foreman was standing beside the Jeep, helplessly watching the firefighters' valiant efforts to contain the fire.

He raced to the older man. "Where's Shea?" Placing his hand on Hank's shoulder, he spun him around. "Hank! Where is Shea?"

Frowning, the old cowboy looked around. "She was just here. One of the firemen pushed her back from the house."

A quick glance told Alec she was nowhere in sight. An ungodly fear began to fester in his gut.

"I don't know where she went…"

The scream that pierced the night air was a sound that would haunt Alec for the rest of his life. Above the shouts of the men, the roar of the fire and the rumbling thunder overhead, one shrill scream from inside the burning inferno gave him his answer.

"My God, she's inside!" he whispered almost to himself. "Hank, Shea's inside. Get help!" He ran toward the house.

Before he could reach the porch, one of the firefighters grabbed his arm. "Sir, you can't go inside."

"She's in there. She's inside."

"Sir, no one is in the structure and we can't let you go—"

With one well-placed blow of his fist, Alec halted both the man's words and any further attempt to hold him back.

He sprang for the kitchen door, sensing others close behind who might try to stop him.

At first he didn't see her. The combination of searing heat, black swirling smoke and the demands from the firemen to get out almost made him turn away. Then Alec spied the chest at the bottom of the stairs and the still form lying underneath it. For an instant terror flooded his body and the vile churning of his stomach rendered him incapable of movement.

"There!" he shouted and lunged in that direction.

The men pulled the chest from over Shea's limp form. Alec scooped her body into his arms and ran for the door. A loud crash followed their retreat as the roof tumbled to the ground behind them.

Once he was clear of the building, Alec fell to his knees and laid her gently on the water-soaked earth.

Immediately, paramedics and firefighters surrounded her. One of them pushed him up against a fire truck and shoved an oxygen mask over his face, while the others focused their attention on Shea's still body.

The downpour continued as the lightning pierced the clouds overhead. For what seemed an eternity, Alec could only watch in stunned disbelief while the paramedics worked to bring life back to her fragile body. He ignored the rain, the fire, the shouts of the firefighters, every cell in his body attuned to the woman who was fighting for her life.

Finally, a small cough gave him some hope. She was alive. But she'd been in the smoke a long time. Maybe too long.

Within twenty minutes, EMTs had Shea strapped in and the Care Flight chopper lifted off, heading for the special burn unit at Regency Hospital in Dallas. Alec wasn't allowed to ride with her, but he followed in his own helicopter.

Shea was already being treated when he entered the ER. She was alive, but no one could tell him anything more than that. He called Leona. And he waited.

Two hours later, one of the doctors walked into the hallway.

"Mr. Morreston? I'm Dr. Clements. Your wife is stable, but we're going to keep her a few days just as a precautionary measure. She may have a few bruises, but considering the circumstances that brought her here, I'd have to say she was very lucky. The concern is her lungs. She has some indication of thermal injury to her upper airway and depending on the toxicity of the wood, it may take another forty-eight hours for any chemical injuries to become evident. We want to be sure she's okay before she's released."

With a comforting tap on his arm, the doctor left and Alec was once again alone with nothing but a handful of hope and a gut full of regrets to keep him company. He didn't want to think about what might have happened had he not returned when he had. He revisited that narrow escape in his mind a thousand times before the sun peeked over the far horizon.

Three days later, Shea and Alec made the ride in the limo from the hospital to the large hotel on the Dallas outskirts in silence. He sat beside her as he had in the hospital room. Not pushing her to talk, just silently offering his strength.

Shea was grateful to be alive. The fact that Alec was here with her tugged at her heart. They would have to talk eventually. She had to make sure he knew she would not make any further attempt to keep the land. It was his land, after all, and had been from the beginning. After everything she'd put him through, eating crow seemed the least she could do.

She'd been given the second chance she'd prayed for.

She had to use it carefully. She would not screw up again. Every cell in her body wanted nothing more than to fall into his arms and confess how very much she loved him. But while in the hospital, she hadn't been able to stop thinking about their situation, and it had occurred to her that a full confession of her feelings might not be the best way to go.

Apparently Alec had returned to the Bar H, no doubt intending to make sure she'd packed her bags. He hadn't counted on the house burning down. Rather than simply escorting her to the door, he'd been forced to save her from her own foolishness. It was bad enough that he'd risked his life for her; now her immediate homeless status effectively made her a liability. Again.

She wasn't sure how to approach him. Declaring her love could be awkward for him and cause him to feel responsible for her welfare. This was her last chance, her *only* chance, to get it right. She had to be strong, this time for Alec.

When the bellhop opened the door to the luxury suite, Shea glanced around at the opulent surroundings. Never could she have imagined such luxury. It suddenly washed over her: this was Alec's world. After his time at the ranch, she'd come to think of him not as a billionaire but just a nice, if somewhat stubborn, guy. Being here, seeing a sample of how he must usually live was…surreal.

She walked across the wide living area to the wall of glass that overlooked the vast expanse of Dallas.

"Are you hungry?" Alec inquired from behind her.

She shook her head. "No. But I would dearly love a bath."

"To your left through that door, Mrs. Morreston." A man in a hotel uniform stood just inside the doorway to the suite. "Please, allow me to draw it for you. How do you like the water?"

While Shea groped for an answer, Alec interjected, "Very warm. Thanks." When the man disappeared into the next room, Alec looked at her, his eyes glittering with amusement. "Hopefully you'll have plenty of hot water."

She couldn't help but return his smile. He was referring to the night Scotty had used all the hot water and she'd had to finish her shower in the icy tap from the well. In frustration she'd then gone after a sleeping Alec with a pillow.

"You'll find some clothes in the closet and bureau. I left it up to the salesclerk to send over what you'd need until you can replenish your wardrobe. If she missed something, let me know."

"Thanks."

The master bedroom was as spacious as the vast living area. It had the same wall of glass offering the million-dollar view, only it was dominated by a huge bed draped with silken linens so thick and luxurious it looked as if a person could completely disappear into the softness when she lay down.

The dressing room and bath were just beyond it. Shea was quite certain the oval tub could hold ten people. At least.

She emerged an hour later feeling clean and pampered and smelling of lilacs. Dressed in one of the comfortable new white T-shirts from the bureau, she walked directly to the bed and climbed in.

Exhaustion pulled her into sleep. She had a vague awareness that Alec joined her sometime in the night. His strong arms pulled her close, offering his warmth and security.

The rays of the morning sun filtered softly through the sheer draperies. Shea opened her eyes, remembering immediately where she was and all that had happened. On the far corner of the bed she spotted a deep red rose with a note underneath it. After picking up the beautiful flower, she inhaled the rich perfumed aroma, then grabbed the small piece of paper.

*Knew you needed to rest so I didn't wake you. I'm in
a meeting downstairs.*

   *Coffee and juice on the side table. Back as soon
as I can.*
-Alec

He had no need to hurry. As far as his plans for the
ranch, he would have to wait while she cleared the land of
several employees—some of whom lived on the ranch—
the horses and roughly three thousand head of cattle. It
wouldn't happen overnight. In fact, she didn't quite know
where to begin. But now that this stumbling block over
ownership had been resolved, Alec could get back to his
life and somehow she would have to find a way to get on
with hers. Wherever that would be. Whatever it entailed.

Fanning through the new clothes that hung in the huge
closet, she selected a simple yet elegant dress in robin's
egg blue. There were some pumps with the name Trump
in gold lettering on the insole.

As she sipped a cup of delicious coffee delivered by a
hotel employee, she sat back and looked out over the city
of Dallas, her mind on Alec and what to say to him before
she left. It would be painful to say goodbye. She loved him
so much. But she would not be one of those women who
clung to men who didn't want them. Leaving was the right
thing to do. The only thing to do. Maybe he'd stop by and
say hello if his business ever brought him back to the area.
The tears welled in her eyes but she forced them back. This
time, for Alec, she had to be strong.

By late afternoon she needed a new space. She was not
used to sitting idle. Around two, Alec called to explain he
would be tied up for a while longer. She assured him there
was no hurry and went out to explore the hotel on her own.

With a soft ding, the elevator door opened to the mar-
bled lobby. Stepping out, she immediately noticed a large

flat-screen television mounted on the wall behind the concierge's stand. It listed the various shops and meeting rooms and the locations of each. Beneath the Presidential Suite, one name stood out: Morreston.

A chill ran down her spine. Could this be the meeting Alec had mentioned about the development of the ranch? Without any conscious thought, she began making her way in that direction. After rounding the far corner, she took a small escalator up to the next level.

The royal-blue carpeted reception area was deserted. Her hands clenched into fists as she walked silently to the meeting room entrance and pulled open one of the mahogany doors. Immediately she was assailed with the buzz of conversation. About forty men and women filled the room. Some held flutes of champagne while others sipped coffee. Most stood in smaller groups, nodding or arguing some point they were trying to make. But the mood throughout the entire room was excitement.

Stepping inside, she searched for Alec, finally spotting him in the far corner. Like the other men in the room, he wore a dark suit and tie. From the way it fit, no doubt it was custom tailored and probably cost more than the ranch. Surrounded by eight or nine people, his hands moved as he emphasized the point he was making.

The churning in her stomach made her feel queasy. This was it. The meeting. And these were the people, the investors, who'd put up millions to develop the Bar H, putting their faith in Alec to give them America's grandest entertainment complex for their vested interest.

He was at home in this setting. So confident. So self-assured. These people were accomplished in their own right, yet they held Alec and his capabilities high on a pedestal, clinging to his every word. The more that realization sank in, the smaller she felt.

A white-jacketed waiter appeared next to her, offering

glasses of champagne on a silver tray. She shook her head in polite refusal. What was she doing here? Had she honestly thought something good would come of the affair with Alec? And clearly, that's all it had been. At least to him.

Her eyes fell on a large display table in the center of the room. She knew it was a scale model rendering of the future of the ranch. Strangely, she didn't care to look any closer. It no longer mattered. Alec would probably direct the project from his office in New York. When this meeting ended, Alec would be gone.

Tears stung her eyes as her entire body began to tremble. Her heart pounded in her chest as she tried to swallow back the nausea churning in her stomach. She thought she'd been prepared to accept the eventuality of his leaving and say goodbye with an understanding smile, keeping the agony of regret hidden deep inside. She hadn't foreseen that the pain of losing him would be so horrific. Now she had to wonder how she would ever get through this.

Feeling lost in the din of voices, she took one last glance toward Alec. A man separated himself from the others, placed his hand on Alec's arm and nodded in her direction. For an instant, their eyes met before the world tilted and the room began to spin.

Shea turned, making her way back to the lobby, away from the meeting room before her tears fell and she embarrassed Alec in front of his colleagues.

The elevator doors immediately opened when she pressed the button. As she stumbled inside, she heard Alec's voice calling her name.

"Shea!"

His deep voice exploded into the hotel suite. Despite the emotions running rampant, her heart still responded to the sound of his voice. Hastily she swiped the tears from her face.

"They have it wrong." He spoke to her from the bedroom doorway. "That scale model is not even close to what I intended. A few of the investors have a tendency to push things to the limit. What you saw is not going to happen."

"It's okay." Shea nodded and began folding the few items of clothing Alec had bought for her. There had been too many harsh words between them, too much pain, too many regrets in the few months they'd been together. She hadn't even seen the model. She hadn't wanted to look. Alec had already told her the way of life as she'd known it was over. The old house burning down had underscored his point. Changing the scale model wouldn't change anything. It wouldn't change how she felt about him. It wouldn't make him stay. She just needed it all to stop, needed this insane emotional roller coaster to come to a permanent end.

"It doesn't matter," she replied quietly, calmly. "It's your land. You can do with it whatever you want."

"Shea—"

She shook her head and forced a smile as she placed the remaining personal items in the small designer sack that would serve as a suitcase, holding all she had left in the world. Lifting it from the bed and pasting on a brave smile, she turned to face Alec. "Congratulations on your project. I mean that. I'm sure your venture will be a huge success. Your investors have confidence in you. They know you're the best."

She had to accept Alec would be leaving and never coming back. She knew once this was a done deal, the restraints of the old lease over and forgotten, she would never see him again. Fresh tears threatened to fall but she determinedly held them in check.

"Someday, if you're back in this area for any reason, be sure and stop—" She couldn't finish. She couldn't tell him to stop by and say hello. She had no idea where she would be. "Stop by Leona's. She'll know where to find me."

For a long moment, Alec watched her. He opened his mouth as though he wanted to say something, then apparently thought better of it. For that she was grateful. The only thing left was admitting her love for the man who stood so tall, so handsome in front of her. But she wouldn't do that. She would not push him from one awkward situation into another. She respected him too much to do that.

Then suddenly Alec moved, grabbing her arms and spinning her around so her back was against the wall. His lips were hard, almost cruel when they came down on hers. Hungrily, he took her mouth, consuming hers with a passion that threatened to devour her very soul. There was no gentleness this time, just raw need. And she gloried in the strength of him, the taste of him. She kissed him back with all the pent-up longing that had been tearing her apart for days, silently conveying her need for him. *One last time. One final glimpse of heaven in his arms.*

The thin straps of the dress prevented him from touching her. With little effort he dispensed with them and roughly pushed the dress to the floor. His hands cupped her bare breasts, molding them, kneading them, feeling them expand under his touch while his mouth continued to ravish hers. His mouth left her lips, kissing and nipping a path to her neck, then lower to suck the swollen buds of her breasts. She trembled, her hand fisted in his hair, holding him to her.

His hand slid down across her stomach, then lower, to the sensitive area between her legs. The surge of passion at his touch pushed her hips against his hand, confirming her need. Alec quickly removed the thin scrap of lace and stroked her. She moaned at his touch.

She heard Alec let out a low growl.

"I can't go slow," he rasped against her ear, his voice rough.

"I don't...want you...to."

He unfastened his pants just enough, then lifted her, positioning her to receive him. Without a second's pause, he pushed deep inside.

His hungry mouth swallowed her soft moans as her body strove to accommodate him, to accept and embrace him and the heated force that drove him. It was as though he needed to brand her as his. If only that were true. She wrapped her legs around his hips, holding him to her as he began to move, driving any coherent thought from her mind. His muscles hardened as he pounded into her, taking her hard, filling her.

"Oh, Alec. I'm..." She didn't finish the sentence, but he knew.

Grasping her hips, he pushed even deeper, again and again, until she cried out as her passion exploded. The final waves of her climax caught Alec in the storm of emotion and he followed her, pulsating deep inside her as he growled her name.

As the waves of passion subsided, she cupped the back of his head, smoothed the damp tendrils of his hair, kissed his neck and under his chin while he fought for breath.

"I love you, Alec," she said softly. "Forgive me, but I love you."

He raised his head and his eyes found hers. "Shea," he murmured her name, then kissed her again, passionately, silently sealing the bond between them.

He swung her into his arms. Without a word, he carried her into the bedroom, placing her on the soft mattress. Quickly shedding his clothes, he lay down next to her, pulling her close.

Her head resting on his broad chest, she listened to the strong beat of his heart. She was still reeling from his lovemaking and the fact he was here with her instead of at his meeting.

"What do you remember?"

She closed her eyes. She didn't want to do this. Not now.

She hadn't figured out exactly what to say to him. But she answered truthfully. "Everything."

"Why did you go into the house?" His hand played in the fine strands of her hair.

"I...thought I saw Scotty. Upstairs. In his bedroom window. I thought you'd brought him back." She pulled away and looked at him through the pale city light filtering into the room. "I couldn't find you in all the chaos, but maybe if I hurried, I could save him. When I got to his room, I realized it was his stuffed owl that I'd seen from outside. As I was running back to the stairs, I remembered the chest. I thought I could save it."

She lay back on her pillow, covering her face as the somber weight of total loss returned. "It was all I had...from my mother, the only pictures of my dad. After our wedding, when I folded Mom's gown and put it back in the chest, I thought it would be a safe place." Swallowing hard, she turned her gaze to Alec. "Why did you come back? How did you...? I don't understand."

"I intended to make sure you got out of the house before something happened. My timing could have been better. I was on my way back and saw the flames." A rueful smile touched his lips. "I'd anticipated evicting you would be a major hurdle, but I never anticipated having to carry you out unconscious."

She drew in a sharp but shaky breath. There was her answer. He had just eliminated any lingering hope. When Alec had asked her how much she remembered, it included his demand that she leave. And he'd just confirmed he'd meant it.

It had all, finally, come to an end.

In the slender moments before the light of a new day began to appear in the eastern sky, Shea made her way quietly through the suite and toward the door, glancing one last time at the sleeping man on the bed. He had come into her life so unexpectedly. But in the end, he'd given her so much more than he would take away. Now it was her turn to give him the freedom he needed to go forward with his life. And somehow, maybe, someday she could get on with hers.

Thirteen

The week she spent with Leona provided some time and space for Shea to try to work through all the emotions and grief eating away at her soul. Leona gave her plenty of room and didn't try to encourage her to talk but made sure Shea knew she was there for her if or when she needed her.

Alec had called every day, checking to be sure she was all right. She'd heard Leona assuring him that Shea would be fine. It was good to know somebody thought so.

This morning, Shea felt the time had come. The day dawned bright and beautiful, and she knew she'd avoided returning to the ranch long enough. She had to take the next step in saying goodbye. Had to deal with the memories of when she'd been happy, her heart full of hope.

She thanked Leona for her offer to accompany her, but this was something Shea had to do on her own. With quiet understanding, Leona held out the keys to her truck.

The site where the house had stood for so many years had been cleared, all remains of the old structure removed and the ground leveled. Parts of the small path that at one time had led from the kitchen door through the small back yard and out to the main barn were still visible. All of the various ranch buildings were intact. Only the house was missing.

She slowly followed the path across the yard and into the hallway of the main barn. The familiar scents of freshly cut alfalfa, leather and pine shavings filled the air. She stopped to stroke the silky necks of the horses housed inside. When she got to Ransom's stall, memories flooded her mind and pain gripped her heart anew. The day Alec had ridden the spirited animal to the old homestead. The small campfire where they'd talked and laughed and shared the meal Hank had prepared for them.

The rain.

The night that had followed.

Forcing herself away from the stall, she ambled on toward the tack room. Before she reached it, her eyes fell on an object that looked incredibly familiar. Sitting against the wall on the floor was what appeared to be the old trunk. But that was impossible. It had been destroyed in the fire. Frowning, she reached down and touched the top, almost afraid it would disappear. But it was real. The marks of fire damage were apparent on the top and sides, but overall, it was in remarkably good condition.

Immediately falling to her knees, she pushed open the lid. A faint pine scent touched her senses. Removing the layer of tissue paper she saw the family pictures. *How did they get here?*

Beneath the photographs were her mother's handembroidered linens followed by the two quilts bearing the initials A.H., and, finally, the wedding gown. She swallowed hard as she gently reached in, picked up the dress and held it to her heart. Alec was behind this. Somehow, he'd managed to save it all.

Memories of her holding the dress in front of her, trying to decide if she should wear it to their wedding, flashed through her mind. Tears burned the backs of her eyes. She was glad she'd worn it. With a sad smile, she gently folded the dress, intending to return it to the trunk. Then she noticed a loose board on the bottom. Frowning, she set the gown on the quilts and removed the thin piece of wood.

Beneath it…letters. Dozens of letters. Really old, yellowed with age. *What are these?* Picking up the one on top, she began to read.

April 12, 1814
My Dearest Alyssa, My Beloved...

They all were signed William Morreston. Alec's great-great-grandfather.

Glancing over the words, she quickly saw they were love letters. Another look inside the trunk and Shea saw an old photo among the letters. The tin-plated picture had two images: a young woman standing beside a tall, handsome man.

Suddenly, she knew what these were, the pieces falling together like parts of a puzzle. William Morreston had courted Alyssa Hardin, daughter of the widow, Mary Hardin. He'd courted her, fallen in love with her and they had planned to marry. Photographs were rare and costly back in those days. It had to have been taken for a very special occasion. Such as a wedding. The quilts, the linens...this trunk had been Alyssa's hope chest. And it was Alyssa who had perished in the fire at the old homestead. Before she could become William's wife.

One thought exploded inside her head: it had never been about the land. The contract written two hundred years ago, the clause that forced her and Alec to marry, all of it had been intended to bring two ancestors of William and Alyssa together.

It had been about Alec. All along, it had been about him.

An invisible hand gripped her heart. She couldn't breathe. Her body began to tremble as she tried to blink back the tears. But they fell down her face, dropping onto the letters clutched in her hand. Even though she'd left Alec with the best intentions, she'd walked out nonetheless. And even though he'd called to check on her, he wouldn't be back. That truth slammed into her like an airbag deploying in an unforeseen crash. He was gone. Forever. The pain in her heart was unbearable, the sadness so deep, so piercing she knew she would never recover.

Through eyes blurred with tears, she looked at the sparkling wedding ring on her left hand. It seemed like a lifetime ago, the night Alec had slipped it back on her finger and told her to never take it off. At the time, she'd counted the days until her twelve-month sentence would be over, when she would be free of him and could happily throw the ring in his face. But it had become a part of her, as had the man who'd given it to her. Subconsciously she'd never let go of the hope she and Alec could work things out. Now, she faced the grim truth.

She'd failed to keep the greatest gift that fate could bestow from slipping through her fingers. She'd lost the greatest man—the *only* man she had ever loved and would ever love as long as she lived. A man who but for a ridiculous clause in a two-hundred-year-old contract, never would have entered her life.

The tears streamed unchecked down her face and she had no will to hold them back as another wave of misery overwhelmed her. The tears blurred the image of the beautiful ring as she began to slide it from her hand. If only…

"I told you to leave that ring where it is," said a deep familiar voice from behind her.

With a gasp, Shea whirled around. Alec stood just inside the barn, looking big and rugged and entirely too handsome. Dressed in jeans and a white cotton T-shirt, he stood with one hand resting on a stall door, the other on his hip.

It took her a few seconds to find her voice. "Alec? What… what are you doing here? What do you…?"

"What do I want?" he asked, stepping away from the stall, his arms falling to his side. "I want to go back in time where the past few weeks never happened. I want to hold my wife in my arms every night and see her face when I wake up the next morning. Emphasis on seeing her the next morning."

She knew he was referring to the hotel in Dallas when she'd snuck out to come home.

"And I want to see her belly grow with my son or daughter." She noted a flare in his golden eyes at those words. His mouth then pulled into a serious line. "I've shelved the entire project, Shea. My stipulation to continue is it will be built completely across the river in Oklahoma. I don't intend for one rock, one blade of grass, one single drop of water to be disturbed on this ranch. I've spent the last week making damn sure that doesn't happen. If the investors go for it, good enough. If not—" he shrugged his broad shoulders "—I really don't give a damn. Nothing is worth losing you."

A frown crossed his face, his eyes conveying the seriousness of his words, and for countless moments, neither moved. "Why did you leave the hotel? Have I lost you, Shea?"

Shaking her head, she rose to her feet. "You could never lose me, Alec. I love you too much."

Then she was in his arms—strong, powerful arms that were gentle as he held her tightly against him. She gazed into eyes the color of topaz as he cupped her face and wiped away the tears with his thumbs. His lips, hot and oh so incredible, covered hers and she surrendered to the overwhelming love that had grown for this man in spite of all the reasons it shouldn't. The warmth and the feel and the taste of him filled her. The wonderful musky male scent of his skin surrounded her as his hard body pressed against hers. She kissed him back with all the love she had, the tears of misery changing to those of pure joy.

Finally, Alec raised his head, but stayed a mere breath away. She touched his face, amazed that she had a chance to love and be loved by such a man.

"Just so we're clear this time, I've been in love with you since the day you walked into Ben's office," Alec admitted as she looked into his eyes. "I admit I fought it, even after we were married. I told myself I was slitting my own throat, setting myself up for a hell of a fall because someone like you just didn't happen to someone like me. I can handle cutthroat tactics, lying, backstabbing from my adversaries, sometimes even my supporters. My world hasn't left much room for honesty and innocence. Trust is something new to me." His gaze traveled over her face. "But you've shown me I can trust again. I can love. And I love you, *Mrs. Morreston*, with everything I have inside me."

A glint of amusement flickered in his eyes, making Shea smile.

"You know, I think I might get used to that name."

"You'd better," Alec said, in a teasingly threatening tone. "Because you're stuck with it for the rest of your life."

She knew he was telling the truth. This man, this incredible man, truly loved her. He was her husband. Scotty was her son. And it didn't matter whether they lived in New York or Texas or someplace in between as long as they were together. That realization was sealed when Alec's lips again came down over hers in a deep, passionate embrace that left no doubts whatsoever.

His lips left hers, kissing his way to her ear. "Mmm." He growled and nuzzled her neck. "We need to be on our way back to Dallas."

"Back to Dallas?"

"Mmm. To the hotel. To the bedroom…"

Shea grinned, caught her bottom lip, and shook her head as she backed him through the open door of the tack room and toward the stack of blankets in the corner.

"That hotel is much too far away."

Alec's eyebrows rose, then a smile turned up the corners of his lips as he realized her intent and kicked the door closed behind them.

And there was no further talking for a very long time.

* * * * *

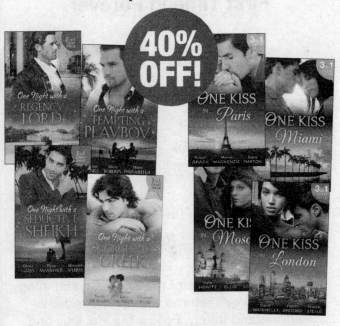

MILLS & BOON®

Desire™

PASSIONATE AND DRAMATIC LOVE STORIES

0215/51